TIME
TRAVELER
1491

ROBERT D. OBERST

First Print Edition
November 2021

For information contact
Global Future Press
Solon, Ohio
RobOberst@sbcglobal.net

This book is dedicated to our nephew, Tom Clausing. While on a rescue mission to save a firefighter near the Grand Canyon, his helicopter crashed and all perished. Tom wrote the book on wilderness rescue, instituted a wilderness rescue school and led Grand Canyon rescue services. Thanks for all the lives you saved and all the EMTs and paramedics you trained to save lives.

TABLE OF CONTENTS

About the Author

In addition to numerous articles on a variety of technical and non-technical topics, Rob Oberst has published four books:

1. ***2020 Web Vision: How the Internet Will Revolutionize Future Homes, Business, and Society***, which appeared in a dozen countries and colleges on five continents around the world. This book accurately predicted how virtual technology would transform our world and empower us during the pandemic—with more of to come.

2. ***The Financial Time Machine: Predicting Our Economic Future***—based on large generations such as the baby boomer's economic behavior, generational economics correctly forecast the Great Recession and the stagnant course of the U.S. and major world economies for over a decade. This book analyzes the generational cycle that has impacted our economy since the Civil War, which will continue to play its role into the future.

3. ***Olympian, All American & National Football Champion—Gene 'Kentuck' Oberst: Rockne Protégé***—Gene Oberst grew up crippled in a Twain-like Ohio River town, then overcame his handicap to become a national championship Notre Dame football player and an All-American who won the first medal for the U.S. in the *Chariots of Fire* Olympics—the only American javelin medal in the Olympic's first fifty years.

4. *Renaissance Olympian: Mentored by Rockne, Gene Oberst becomes a Renowned Coach, Professor & Artist*—The story picks up after Oberst wins the first U.S. medal in the javelin at the Paris Olympics, the first time the American flag flew, and travels to Louisiana for his first coaching position as St. Johns College's founding coach, athletic director, trainer, janitor etc. As portrayed in fifty letters between Gene and Rockne, Gene faces numerous challenges, but Knute is always there to help. Indeed, he may not have married Catherine if not for Rock.

Rob possesses a BS in Systems and Operations Research from Miami University along with an MBA in Policy and Organizational Behavior from Case Western Reserve University and has been a guest columnist for the Cleveland Plain Dealer.

Rob has presented to scores of universities and management groups on a variety of topics. As a management consultant, he served as the regional practice manager for Towers Watson, where he founded its successful hundred-million-dollar HR systems consulting practice. He designed and implemented numerous human resource, hospital, and financial systems and has consulted on behalf of dozens of *S&P 500* companies, including Kraft, Sherwin Williams, Verizon, GE, Toyota, Goodyear, BP, Bank America, Chase, Callaway, Qualcomm, Northrop Grumman, Scripps Clinic and the Cleveland Clinic.

SECTION ONE

1:   THE CANYON

Waking to a deafening roar, in those first few moments while stumbling towards consciousness, I assume I'm safely at home enveloped in my sheets, but, instead, I find myself lying on a crunchy, blue plastic tarp. Lounging there for a few moments, filling my lungs with cool, fresh air, I relish the freedom from ever-present schedules. Gazing up at the crystal blue sky with strokes of wispy, powder-blue clouds, down towards the bright, multicolored walls kissed by the brilliant, diffuse, early morning light, I notice its vivid demarcation line slowly descending down the canyon walls, like a spot light illuminating the dark, grey shadows transforming these into brilliant reds, tans, and burnt umbers.

While stretching, directly across the river peering down, I see a steep granite wall resembling a medieval castle prepared for battle. Turning onto my side and tilting my head, behind I see two, black, foreboding granite pillars guarding the entrance—our only exit out of these perilous depths, beyond which, by mid-day the temperature will soar to a tortuous 120-degrees.

Following the unmaintained, highly restricted trail, our shins aching from the persistent downward trek, it had taken hours to reach the bottom of the mile-deep gorge. The worst part was the desolate, dry desert plateau just above us where Jenny, her eyes flickering in the back of her head, her speech slurred, suffered a perilous stroke. With no cell coverage for miles, hours away from rescue, we were desperate, but thanks to Betty's skillful care, Jenny's OK now. We all know we will have to transverse that stretch again—a much more challenging trial going forever upwards.

We lie by the creek on a narrow strip of sand, below which the turbulent rapids thunder. Down here where there is life-restoring water, little grows other than prickly cacti, and spotty, green grasses clinging for their lives to the steep slopes lining the fast-flowing river.

Peering downriver, I see the variant layers on the canyon walls that tell a fascinating story of what had lain above us— once a vast sea, once a steamy jungle, and once a parched desert. In other eras, it had been part of a mighty mountain range, beneath a deep, salty ocean, and a coastal plain—each period lasting millions of years, each painting their unique signature upon the colorful walls. In my mind, I visualize images of these picturesque scenes, like paintings on glass stacked one on top of another trying to fathom how one location could have been so diverse.

Uncovering a strange, prehistoric world, the bottom of the canyon, where we lie now, had been formed two-billion years ago. Then, long before the first dinosaurs roamed the globe, when the moon was much closer to an adolescent earth, the first continents had just formed. Then, water covered 90% of the planet, inhabited only by blue-green algae, expelling the oxygen that would eventually sustain us other life forms. Somehow, perhaps due to this mysterious prehistoric setting, I feel a powerful force at work here, for it is unlike any other place in the world--deeper, darker, more magnificent.

My four friends lying on the tarp in parallel lines next to me are still snoozing. They share my appreciation of nature and the great outdoors, greatly enjoying our backpacking excursions throughout the U.S. and indeed, throughout the world. We all savor exiting the virtual world of our devices to enter the real world once again, where our senses are reactivated and our fluid relationships, unrestricted by those all-consuming screens, reemerge. Sure, I made my living designing such screens, but I treasure escaping these, too.

I wonder if being down here so far away from civilization, with all you need to sustain life carried on your back, had powered that bizarre dream I just woke from. In it, I had been transported back in time to an era long before digital media—an ideal time—a time when life was so much simpler.

I recall walking along an unfamiliar beach, the sound of rhythmic ocean waves kissing the shore, breathing in fresh, salty, sea air, feeling the moist, rich sea breeze upon my face—amazed at how real it all felt. In the next instant, I found myself above the ocean walking along a dirt road in a medieval village, where the houses had thick thatched roofs dripping towards the ground. There were neither cars nor trucks, just horses and carts passing by. Dressed in ancient garb, the people I saw were friendly and oddly seemed to know me, especially a stunning, strawberry blonde, who as she passed by, looked back over her shoulder and smiled knowingly. Then, when I stared upwards atop a green hill, I saw a Disney-like castle and further in the distance, what seemed to be a monastery capped by a cross.

I found myself walking into a darkened candlelit pub, where, oddly, everyone seemed to know my name. When I walked outside into the blinding light, a fearsome knight in shining armor, holding a raised, sunlit sword, astride a massive, frightful, black warhorse galloped towards me.

No doubt being in nature fueled that dream, or perhaps it was that mysterious force I somehow feel at the bottom of this ancient land formed so long ago. Still, I wish I lived back in that simpler time and fantasized that I would have been able to somehow defeat that fearsome knight and save the fair maiden.

———

After arriving at this oasis, we spent a delightful, solitary couple of days skinny dipping in the muddy river and laying on the scenic beach, until the seven-member, rafting party arrived and literally caught us guys with our shorts off.

Luka, the rafting guide, had already lit their large camp stove and brewed the coffee that smells enticing. I had gotten to know most of her seven-member rafting crew last night, including the delightful teenage daughter, Ann, but had not spent time with Luka, and thought I would like to know her better too.

Standing next to her as she crouches over the propane-powered camp stove, slurping my first heavenly sip, I comment, "This is delicious! Maybe the best I've ever tasted. Where did you acquire such an excellent brew?"

"It comes from Seattle, the home of Starbucks," she replies. "It's not Starbucks, though, but a special blend we grind from rare Peruvian beans. Because it rains so often in Seattle, people appreciate their coffee that much more. It combats the pervasive dreariness and brightens us up a bit."

With a deep tan and short, brown, sun-tinged hair, a body fit and strong, and a brilliant, broad smile, Luka is an extremely impressive woman—strong yet feminine, natural yet attractive, pleasant yet in command. As the leader of her rafting party, she serves as their captain, travel guide, paramedic, and gourmet chef.

I ask, "How is the trip going?"

As she pours another cup for herself and tops mine off, she replies, "Well, we had an unusually wet winter and a deluge earlier this spring, so the previously low reservoir at Lake Powell rose substantially. Therefore, they are releasing more water down the Colorado and the current is stronger than normal, so we floated faster. Plus, I have a well-coordinated crew—one of my best."

"Where do you live?"

"We live in Leavenworth, east of Seattle, on the side of a mountain in a modern house filled with windows. The town is surrounded by picturesque mountains and resembles a German village, with um-pa-pa bands in lederhosen, German restaurants, and rathskellers. It's a bit touristy, but we love our outdoor friends and living in the woods up in the mountains. The skiing is wonderful and so is the mountain climbing. I met my husband while we were on ski patrol. He was already a good rock climber, so that was something we shared. I taught him to guide rafts, and we have had natural adventures around the world: guiding raft trips in Costa Rica and circling Iceland on our bikes during the summer solstice, when the sun never sets."

"The Cascades are spectacular—so tall and angular. They remind me of the Alps. Have you climbed any mountains outside of Washington?"

"We had planned to climb the seven tallest peaks on each of the continents with my parents, who taught me to climb as a teen, and had completed four—North America, South America, Europe and Africa. While we were practicing on Mount Rainier, training for our ascent of Mount Everest, my mom lost her grip and slipped off the side of the mountain. I was attached to her, and as I tried to pull her up, one by one my pitons pulled out, and I too fell off the mountain. She knew my dad could not hold onto both of us much longer, so she cut her rope to save my life, fell into a gorge 300 feet below and perished. I haven't been able to climb since."

With my mouth open, shocked, awkwardly I uttered, "So sorry to hear about your loss!"

Looking affected from the painful memory, changing the subject, she says, "Where do you live?"

"I live in San Francisco in a small studio apartment with a gorgeous view of the Bay that even though it's small, I may not be able to afford much longer."

She pours another cup of coffee for both of us and skillfully flips a dozen eggs, then asks, "What do you do? What brings you all the way down to the bottom of Hermit's Creek, where I know they only allow the most experienced backpackers?

While observing her adroitly flip the ham and crisping home fries, I respond, "For three years, I had been working night and day to develop a revolutionary app that we thought would change the world, which once we launched it in just a couple of weeks had garnered millions of downloads. Our CEO promised us all stock, but sold it for a fortune and laid us off without our shares."

"That sounds terrible. What are you going to do now?"

"After that, losing track of time I was severely burned out, which is why I came here. Nature restores me and I hope she will help me to figure out where to go next. I don't think I can stand tech any longer. Stuck out in the digital lottery, but don't know what else I can do. Maybe I'll become a seaman and travel around the world, or work as a bartender in some exotic port like Bali and learn French. That was Paul's favorite destination— sounded exotic."

By the time the other rafters wake, I've heated up some water and eaten my instant oatmeal. Luka has finished preparing their ham and egg breakfast.

My friends are still groggy, and even Paul, the early riser, isn't stirring. Luka wants to have her rafters, who are lining up, plates in hand, on the river before we begin our long trek.

2:   IN THE RAPIDS

I enjoy being with the larger group, but this is not the remote, natural experience I yearned for. After all, without a soul for miles, there are only thirteen of us, but it still seems crowded. Feeling antsy and wanting some solitude, I decide to go exploring.

Seeing a yawning Jenny, I greet her with one of the few German phrases I know, "Guten Morgen mein freund."

"Guten Morgen."

"It's a gorgeous day. I'm going to take a hike. See ya later."

Extending her arms above her head, she blinks several times, stretches, yawns, grabs her coke-bottle glasses and says, "Be careful." Then she slumps back onto the crackling tarp like a sack of potatoes.

Not wanting them to make breakfast for me, I add, "Oh yea, I've eaten," to which she waves a sleepy hand to indicate she heard me, and flicking her fingers, signals for me not to bother her anymore.

I walk down the beach along the churning river and balancing myself as I go, leap from rock to multi-angled rock as far as I can go, then climb up a small cut in the cliff, bracing myself with both legs on one wall, my back arched against the other while I cantilever to the top. There I find a dusty, relatively flat section, where dew still kisses some of the scrubby green bushes and hike further down river before the sun, about to pop out of the steep canyon walls, ratchets up its intense heat. After perhaps a delightful, solitary half-hour, I hear another rapid and venture to the edge of the gorge, drawn to its thunder as a moth to a flame.

As I gaze over the rim, I am mesmerized by the white, foaming rapids carving through the ancient, multicolored rocks. The awesome power of the thrashing current composed of ribbons of velvety, dark, glistening water slamming into steadfast boulders, propels chunks of brownish-green liquid skyward, that splash back down in slow motion to rejoin the relentless marching torrent, the spray creating a tiny, semitransparent cloud rising out of the morning's coolness. I stand there unable to move, entranced by its irresistible force and majesty. Even though I am 100 feet above, the rapids assault my senses—their deafening roar, the constantly changing, yet consistent vision of it, its earthy, fresh smell, the moisture caressing my face, the rhythmic thumping like fireworks exploding against my chest. This is certainly a mandala that has captured me—pulled me into it. I am frozen, unable to break its hypnotic grip.

The seemingly sturdy rock I stand on that had likely been there for millions of years, suddenly slips. I jump back onto the ground until the loose soil begins slipping. Honed by sports, my reflexes instantly engage. I fall to my knees and locate a grey rock jutting out of the cliff face to the right that I subconsciously stretch for and grab, as my body sways over the edge. Just as I start to pull myself up, the rock pops out and flies off the cliff crashing below. With my stomach and chest against the steep ground, my feet dangling in the air, after sliding down a couple more feet, I grab a root, which, like a green rope, slowly, inch by desperate inch, pulls out, then snaps, me clawing at the rust-colored dirt with my fingernails to no avail, and soon I'm off the side of the cliff, plunging towards the river below, my legs and arms flailing to stay upright, accelerating at an ever-faster rate towards certain doom. The rocks are coming up towards me. I'm afraid I'm going to hit them and break my legs, or worse. Time passes slowly, strangely with no other choice, I decide to enjoy my first and last solo flight.

Then I see that my momentum or wind or both, might carry me past the deadly rocks to that small black pool of unknown depth, so I try to somehow contort my hurtling body towards it. Mercifully, I barely hit the target and with my momentum plunge below the surface, where I slam into silty ground, my legs barely absorbing the intense shock. With my butt inches from the bottom, like a Jack in the Box, I spring back up, gasping for precious air.

Once above water, I can see I'm heading for the rapids. I try to swim to shore, but despite a mighty effort, the strong current, like a drain, draws me in ever faster. My hopes of reaching the shore extinguished, I turn towards the churning torrent. From canoeing, I remember I should head for the Vs formed between the rocks, marking a safe passage, and to the best of my ability try to steer towards these, as the current sweeps me rapidly downward.

Without a helmet, I try to keep my feet in front of me so I won't bash my head, be knocked out and drowned. With my bobbing head barely above the frothy waters, it's difficult to see where I'm headed as I slide up and down feet first, then buttock, then back, neck and head. After successfully navigating through three Vs, I arrive at a calmer section and grab onto a rock, but the current is too strong and pulls me away. I hit even more turbulent waters, feeling as if I am a rag doll in a washing machine tumbling around and around, thrown from side to side, up and down—totally out of control. With my arms out, I'm slammed to the side, where I am barely able to push off a rock before it bashes my head. I can't believe how much strength that took. I feel so feeble.

Suddenly the irresistible current pulls me under, me trying mightily to swim to the surface, gulping for air, being pulled down again and again, until I'm locked under an under-cut rock. I try mightily to swim out, but the force of the current keeps pushing me back under. Bent at the waist conforming to its contours, I am locked against the huge rock, the force of a dozen fire hoses imprisoning me. I'm running out of air and think this is it—I'm going to die. I feel an irresistible urge to take a breath of water and fight with myself not to do so. I breathe in just a little, but it hurts and I want to gag. With all my strength, I try to push to no avail. Nearly out of air, my lungs crying for relief, resisting the urge to breathe, I tell myself that I'm thankful for having a good life and just when I accept my fate, I am able to force my left side towards the current, and like a sail catching the wind, the over-whelming force buffets me upwards. When it slams me back to the bottom, I push off a rock with all my might and am sloshed up to the surface, where I spit out water and suck in heavenly gulps of wondrous air—air that never tasted so good.

The rapids are foaming so much I can't see where I am heading. I know that I can't survive this much longer, my muscles are like rubber, and my lungs are burning from inhaling so much water. I try mightily to keep my head above water, but am unable to do so, constantly trying to breathe without inhaling more awful tasting muddy water. The horrendous trial leaves me exhausted. When I see flat water ahead, just when I think I might make it out alive, a rock smashes my head and my body goes limp.

When I wake, I find myself in a calmer section of the river, where even though my left arm is searing with pain, I'm able to swim sidewise, with my good arm to the canyon wall, where I grab a rock below the surface, spit up water and breathing heavily suck in precious gulps of air. I know I cannot stay here long, because hypothermia from the freezing water has already set in. My teeth are chattering, and I'm shivering uncontrollably. I have to find a place to escape the water but the canyon walls are too steep.

After resting for a bit, I push off the rock while trying to stay close to the wall, pawing along it, from handhold to handhold. I enter an area where the flow has carved out the overhanging basalt, light refracting off the water illuminating the small cavern with mesmerizing blue-green streaks, my heavy breathing echoing off its walls. It is peaceful in here, but there is still no purchase and I'm shivering even more fervently than before. Floating downstream around a bend, I hear the unmistakable roar of another rapid. In my depleted condition, I know I cannot handle another such encounter, but there's still nowhere out of the chilly water to rest. I am being sucked into the rapids, something I know I cannot survive. Then, just as I wind around another bend, I see a cut in the cliff wall, and I swim with all my might towards it—two strokes forward, one back. Exhausted, I finally reach it.

I pull myself out of the water onto a large rock and just lay there, totally exhausted, still shivering uncontrollably, teeth chattering, my arms and legs blue. Eventually, I take inventory of myself. I have a bloody, two-inch gash on my left arm with another smaller gash and a lump on my forehead. Besides that, I also have several minor cuts and bruises on my arms, legs, shoulders and back, from where the rocks had scratched or hammered me. Fortunately, no bones seem to be broken, but my left index finger is jutting up at a 45° angle. I know I have to pull it out, which will be very painful, something I've never done before. At first, I resist, but I know I have to do it. I quickly pull it forward, the pain so excruciating I cry out, the cry reverberating throughout the canyon. Overall, I feel like a battered piece of hamburger passed through a meat grinder.

I take off my t-shirt, wring it out and tear the bottom off. I try to press the sides of the cut together as much as I can with my fingers, and then wrap it as tightly as I can. It evidently has not cut an artery or vein, so before I lose too much blood, I hope it will cake. I will probably need seven or eight stitches from the emergency kit back at camp. From the sports I've played, I constantly accumulated cuts and scrapes, finding that these dings tended to heal quickly. The cut on my forehead doesn't seem to be as bad, so I take another smaller slice off my long t-shirt and tie it like a headband.

Shivering from the freezing waters, not able to use my injured finger, I wring out the remainder of my t-shirt, underpants and shorts. I begin quivering violently and realize I have to get away from the water to go further up, where it should be warmer. Trembling, I rise to my feet and gingerly explore the narrowing, rock-filled cut, which looks as if it extends ten or twelve feet upwards at a steep grade. Halfway up, around a corner it expands. About twenty steep, rocky feet up, I see a yellow spot where the sun is shining. Slipping on the rocks, I climb up to it and place my t-shirt, cargo shorts and underwear on the already hot rocks smelling of baking clay and cement. Then I sit naked in the sun's restoring rays, thanking God I'm alive.

I move myself and my clothes several times to stay in the light until the great yellow orb vanishes behind the overhanging cliff. I walk down to the water's edge where, with the sun near its zenith, the rock shelf is drenched in its soothing rays. I don't know how long I was knocked out or how far I have traveled but judging by the sun's position in the sky, I estimate that it's around noon. I am now on the opposite shore, on the north side of the canyon. If I try to swim to where my friends are on the south side, I will be swept into the rapids—not something I want to endure again. Besides, the walls are nearly as steep on that side, too.

Within range of all that I can see, there is no purchase and I don't know how far I would have to swim upstream before I would find another place to rest. When I floated downstream, I had already seen there was no such place on the northern cliff face. Even though I am a strong swimmer, I know in my injured, beaten-up state, with a bleeding arm that cannot provide powerful strokes, I wouldn't make it. Plus, the forceful water might further open up the wound.

I see a dark blue object bobbing up and down nearby in the water. As it swirls by, I see that it is my Indians cap. Before it sails away, by stepping into the water with one hand holding onto the rock and a toe anchored in the silt, I grab it and think that this is a good omen. Still exhausted from my ordeal, sitting there naked in the sun, my clothes and now my hat gradually drying, my mind not able to fathom a solution to the predicament I've found myself in, I soon fall asleep on the large, hot, nurturing, blue-grey rock.

————

I wake to the sound of shouts, and look out as a large raft enters the rapids below me. I rise up, waving my arms frantically and shout, "H E L P." But no one in the raft seems to see or hear me. No doubt they are focused on the rapids ahead, following Luka's commands to row, unable to hear anything else above the din of the roaring rapids. I jump up and down, waving for them to come and rescue me, and when the raft jerks sidewise, Ann sees me. In an instant, she smiles before the raft turns and she takes a stroke. Evidently, she thought I was waving goodbye, and didn't realize my desperate situation. In another instant they are further down the rapids, out of sight.

Hoping they might hear me on the other side of the rapids, I yell "H E L P!" again, and again, at the top of my lungs, until I realize my voice cannot rise above the churning, thundering rapids echoing throughout the inner canyon. I am alone!

Discouraged and still recovering from my injuries battling exhaustion, I lay back on the rock, hoping another raft will pass by. I keep my eyes upstream so I might catch them and flag them down before they approach the rapids, but despite trying mightily to keep my head erect, eventually I succumb to my exhaustion and pass out. When I wake, adding a stiff neck and back to my inventory of pains, judging by the sun that is about to disappear behind the cliff wall, the western portions of the canyon already shrouded in shadows, I can tell that it's already dusk. Since they do not allow many rafts into the canyon, I know there will not be another until tomorrow - I will be here for the night.

No doubt my friends have realized that I'm either lost in a side canyon or have fallen into the river, and would thus organize a search for me. After they search themselves, since there is no cell coverage, they will have to go back up the steep, unmaintained Hermit's Trail, or perhaps follow the Tonto to Bright Angel Ranch. I hope they would go to the ranch so that we could continue our planned trip. I did not want my slip-up to curtail our much-anticipated adventure. All of this would be a good story to be told around the campfire. In either case, a search cannot be organized until morning.

Since there is nothing I can do until then, I decide that I'll settle in for the night and try not to worry. I know I can last a long time without food, and there's a trickle of water coming further up the cut that I can drink. The Colorado is too muddy to drink without purification, but since I have unintentionally drunk so much of the river's water and seem to be fine, I'm not very thirsty—at least I've gotten lots of minerals in me.

3: OUT OF THE RAPIDS

Fortunately, my clothes are mostly dried out, but being so close to the river, in the middle of a desert, it's already getting cooler. After my bout with hypothermia, I might need more warmth than my still damp hat, shirt and shorts can provide. About half way up the cut, I see a four-foot, green bush with short, thick, rounded green leaves. I could stuff my shirt with the leaves and twigs off the bush to keep myself warm. Somehow, I still have my multipurpose Swiss Army Knife that I placed in one of the many pockets of my cargo shorts. Taking stock, I realize I also have my butane lighter I used on the fire last night and my cell phone from the other buttoned pockets in its padded, "waterproof" enclosure. I pop out the 3-inch saw blade of the knife and begin sawing off some of the small branches, when I notice a small opening at the back of the bush. I saw away more branches, which reveals a foot-wide opening below.

It might potentially be warmer in the cave, so not knowing whether some kind of critter occupies the tiny cave, I exchange the saw blade for the 3-inch, pointed knife and poke my head in. I shine my lighter inside, where the cave appears to be a little larger. By extending one shoulder and collapsing the other, and then wiggling my hips through the tiny hole, pain screaming from my injuries, I am barely able to pass through. Inside, it is much more spacious than I'd imagined. The lighter reveals that it is indeed unoccupied, substantially warmer than outside and with soft, white sand on the ground remarkably comfortable. I'm relieved.

I shine my lighter around the bedroom-sized cave and notice some markings that resemble hieroglyphs. I wonder whether some ancient tribe might have inhabited the cave eons ago.

It will be dark soon, and although I would like to see those magnificent stars again, I don't want to shimmy out of the cozy cave, especially since my cuts and bruises hurt so much. In case an unwelcome animal intrudes, with the blade out, I stick my trusty knife into the ground beside me, roll my t-shirt into a ball and place it under my head. Oddly, I hear two roars—the muffled roar of the rapids from the river outside and a different, more constant, less splashy roar from within the cave. Maybe there is an underground river deep within the cave, which might soon join the Colorado?

As my eyes adjust to the darkness, it seems there is a faint glow coming from the inner portion of the cave. Perhaps there is another passageway, lit by the sun's last glow or the moon or starlight. I am too tired and banged up to go exploring the unknown passage. Instead, I will wait until dawn, when it may be clearer. Perhaps the passage will lead to an exit below the rapids where I can cross the river. Then I could swim across and not have to burden others or worry my friends further.

I feel surprisingly secure and confident in my abilities in my comfortable little cave, remembering what the explorer Bear Grylls said—you can survive three minutes without air, three days without water, and three weeks without food. I have plenty of water and a good shelter where I can stay at night when it gets cool, and I can't imagine it will take more than a day or two to flag down a raft—far short of the three weeks. With all the excitement and naps, despite my exhaustion, I lie awake. To lull myself to sleep, I think about how I got here—back to the start of this expedition, back to San Francisco.

4:   JENNY

The flight from Germany was ahead of schedule, so to make up time, I wound the Porsche through the traffic on the 101 to SFO—what fun. The lumbering SUVs seemed like a herd of slow-moving water buffalo, me a nimble cheetah in their midst. I loved the sound of the throaty engine as it instantly responded to my commands, nimbly changing lanes with just a flick of the wrist, readily avoiding the water buffalo who did not see me as they changed lanes, seemingly running in slow motion.

In the baggage claim area, as I ran to greet her, Jenny looked fantastic. We hugged and I could not stop looking at her. In preparation for our hike, she had lost some weight from her normally somewhat corpulent frame. Her black coiffed hair framed her brilliant blue eyes, full lips, high cheekbones and white skin with a hint of freckles on her upturned nose. In her glasses, she looked like the pretty professor she was.

The last time I saw Jenny was in Germany when she picked me up at the Frankfurt Airport and we traveled through Germany and France. After passing her CPA exams, she had taken a position teaching accounting to servicemen, for a university in Germany. Being there served as a jumping off point for her to travel throughout Europe, Asia, and even the Middle East and Africa before she goes blind. She has a degenerative eye condition, which is why she wears those thick glasses--can't see a thing without them.

Before I left to pick her up, seeing my place in shambles with discarded pizza boxes and Chinese food cartons spread around, moving like a whirlwind at hyper speed, I had thoroughly cleaned and straightened up the long-unattended apartment. We spent a day and a couple of nights catching up and touring my favorite haunts, parks and restaurants, places I had not been in a long time. We visited Ghirardelli Square, where we watched them create their delicious chocolate, sat out on the patio, and while eating hot fudge sundaes looked out into the waters towards Alcatraz, then had oysters at Scott's on Fisherman's Wharf.

Listening to her talk about her latest adventures around the world soothed my troubled psyche. Jenny was such a positive person, a "positor," just being with her cheered me up. I loved the sound of her lyrical voice that resonated from somewhere between the back of her throat and nose that portrayed her honesty and good-heartedness.

Still suffering from symptoms of burnout, betrayal, depression, and self-imposed cloistering, I was a little shaky and phobic in public places, but in her presence, starting to feel better. It had been difficult to be in a restaurant for more than twenty minutes without feeling anxious, minute by minute the tension growing and needing to leave. In a crowd of people, their noise bothered me more that it should have. But now, talking to Jenny, time passed effortlessly.

———

The night before we were to leave, I had packed my backpack with supplies, most of which I kept either in the pack or in the closet next to it. I would carry all the necessities of life—shelter, food, emergency gear, that I would need to live — kind of like carrying my apartment on my back. Anticipating the adventure, not sure what I might encounter, I did not get much sleep that night.

Wanting to avoid the rush to get out of the city on a Saturday, Paul and Betty picked us up before dawn the next morning.

Still groggy, I hugged them then melted into the back seat of their SUV as the other three chatted excitedly while we commenced our adventure. By the time we picked up Wesley at the last BART station on the East Bay and he threw his pack in the back with the others, I was awake. After drinking some McDonalds coffee, I felt excited to be with these special friends I loved, who I had so many adventures with, and joined in their spirited conversation.

Jokingly, Paul said, "So you decided to join us after all. Thought you would sleep all the way to the Canyon."

In a Valley girl accent I said, "Hey guyees thanks for allowing me to joyinn you even thoughhh I'm not one of you chatty morningg pee-poll."

Few traveled the straight, seemingly endless highway from the San Francisco area to L.A. under eighty. As we zoomed down the central valley, I thought about how we knew each other. We all graduated from the same picturesque college in Southern Ohio, but oddly, I did not know any of them before I graduated. Well, that wasn't quite true. I first met Wes at our graduation picnic.

We chatted incessantly, recounting our various escapades. Although they had heard about each other, Wes had never met Jenny and asked, "How did you guys get to know each other?"

"After backpacking with you in the Rockies, I decided I would go to grad school back in Ohio. You belonged to the Salt Lake outdoors club, so I looked for one at school. That was where I met Paul and Jenny. Every week we did things like hiking, biking, spelunking, hang gliding, and backpacking."

Jenny chimed in, "Yeah, that was when we had our epic backpacking trip up Mount Le Conte in the Smokies over Thanksgiving break. It started out as a beautiful day with temperatures in the 50s. As we climbed up the tree-laden mountain trail, we could see Gatlinburg below us growing ever smaller, glad we were in the natural setting and out of the crowded, commercial tourist trap—not that there is anything wrong with it, just not what we were yearning for. We were all in a festive mood, until those last steep inclines, when we were spent. After a delicious Thanksgiving feast of freeze-dried turkey, dressing, freeze-dried mashed potatoes, canned cranberry sauce and freeze-dried ice cream, thoroughly satiated and exhausted, we settled in for the night."

"Soon afterwards, the mountains welcoming nature changed dramatically. Suddenly, it got very cold, down to perhaps ten degrees. The winds soon soared up to seventy miles-per-hour or more and we were enveloped in a full-blown blizzard that blew down our tents and numerous nearby pines. One fell on Beth and Jeremy's tent, but fortunately they had vacated it by then. The ten of us sought refuge in a stone-sided, tin-roofed lean-to with one side open to the elements, where shivering, we huddled close together on a slanted, six-foot, wooden slatted shelf. In the pitch-black darkness, the wind constantly roaring, snow relentlessly pelting the tinny roof, trees crashing around us—shaking the ground, hearing/feeling that unmistakable thump—so afraid for our lives, none of uttering a word, I could not sleep."

"When we ventured out the next morning, there was a foot of fluffy white snow on the mountain top. Happy to be alive, we looked out over a sea of milky-white clouds, above which mountains popped out as if they were islands in the sky.

On the way down, we passed another college group from Georgia. It was in the fifties. Like us, they were in a festive mood as they greeted us. We couldn't burst their bubble by warning them of what they were in for."

Thoroughly engrossed, Wes said, "Wow, that is quite a story. Glad you guys survived!"

———

During the ride through the central valley, we drove through one of the largest agricultural areas in the world. Periodically we passed the canal that fed water from the Sierra Mountains up north enabling such abundance. The long valley did not feel anything like overcrowded liberal, laidback San Francisco, conservative remote Northern California and certainly not hectic L.A. With its flat open, green spaces, containing huge irrigated industrial farms, presided over by massive robotic tractors, its topography more resembled Nebraska with an added Hispanic flavor. Along Route 99, we flew past Modesto, Merced and Fresno down to Bakersfield, where we turned left.

Not surprisingly, Paul drove the whole way. Overwrought with his grad studies, he once felt an urge to be in nature and drove from Ohio State to Montana and back over a long weekend. What was unusual though was that we did not take any side trips. Normally Paul felt compelled to see every interesting site along the way, and we had to prevail on him not to stop at Fresno—"to soak up some of the Latino culture," as he said.

Knowing her adventurous husband well, in a stern, spousal voice Betty scolded, "We have to be at the Canyon before it's too late and we lose our campsite, so we don't have any time for your side trips, honey!"

I said, "Because you got that degree in wine, unlike the rest of us, you only have to work nine months of the year."

In a simulated huffy voice, Paul replied, "It was a master's in oenology, my friend."

"Yeah, I remember when you, Jenny and I toured Northern California, and you found that first winemaking position. Two years after you began working at each winery, after your first crush had aged, your wines would show up in Ohio. You must be doing something right, my friend. After you guys dropped me off at the San Francisco airport, as I flew out, I sensed this is where I belonged. So, that's when I moved to Silicon Valley."

After we were quiet for some time, Betty says, "So Wes, I'm not sure you heard about this. After managing several major projects for the firm in Europe, I took a leave of absence last year and having accumulated so many miles, we acquired gold tickets, which allowed us to travel around the world for six months for free. When we arrived at a small town, in say Slovakia, we would inquire where the winemaker lived. There we met a delightful, older, little guy, named Sergai, who resembled Geppetto in Pinocchio. After becoming acquainted while tasting his wine and comparing notes, Sergai introduced us to the town and its people. Amazingly, on our epic journey, just about everywhere we traveled, anywhere in the world, had a winemaker, who would introduce us to their village, their people and their unique culture. We were like Anthony Bordain, living in the moment and meeting the people."

——

When we were numbed by the long trip, rather than staying on the Route 40 freeway, Paul surreptitiously turned onto Route 66, where we could still see remnants of the once-famous "Main Street of America."—the "Mother Load"—the "Will Rogers Highway." Along the way, we saw a series of signs announcing an upcoming restaurant.

From a distance, we saw a gigantic, red neon arrow curving into a large blue and green neon sign that boldly announced the location of "**PEGGY SUE's**." where we stopped for lunch. The large parking lot could hold tractor trailers, four of which sprawled there along with cars from states scattered around the country—Pennsylvania, Connecticut, Illinois, Texas, Colorado...

After climbing out of the SUV and stretching in the hot, dry air that enveloped us, we walked through the glass door with its plexiglass handle into the refreshingly air-conditioned diner, flooded in yellow sunlight penetrating the large windows that accompanied each booth, the delightful smell of grilling burgers and caramelizing onions permeating the air.

The counter of Peggy Sue's had red swiveling stools and a white, faux-marble, Formica counter. Between every couple of seats stood a small stainless-steel jukebox with a coin slot and tabs to turn the pages, announcing the ancient songs. A thin, medium-aged waitress with dark, flipped up, permanent-waved hair wiped down the counter as she smiled and welcomed us, telling us, "Sit anywhere you like, honey." The truckers had huddled together in a far corner, an older couple sat at the counter, and two other couples sat at booths along with a family with two kids and another with four. Behind the counter, a window occupied the back wall where a half-bald, stocky, white-aproned man stood ready to fry up orders. We had traveled back to the '50's, long before any of us were born, back to our grandparents' era. I felt like Michael J. Fox in *Back to the Future*.

We all scrambled into a long red vinyl booth with a black Formica tabletop lined in stainless steel. The waitress, chewing gum in a short pink dress, white apron and pink sweater, came to the table. Ignoring the nametag that introduced her as Debbie, Paul said, "You must be Peggy Sue." She flashed a broad smile and pulling the nametag up, tugged it within 4 inches of Paul's nose smiling broadly, after which we all laughed.

A la *Happy Days*, we ordered cheeseburgers and fries. The girls ordered cherry and vanilla cokes, Paul ordered a chocolate shake, Wes a root beer float and I ordered a strawberry phosphate, something I had not had since I was a kid. The waitress announced the order to Fred, "five CBs with," as she clipped the slip of paper to the top of Fred's window.

I walked over to the counter and sat on one of the red stools to see her make the elixirs, an art I had not witnessed since I was a kid. She opened the stainless refrigerator behind the counter and pulled out a large scoop of vanilla then plopped it into the silver can, added milk and chocolate syrup, then placed the container under the spindle of the machine, which automatically turned on as it began spinning, whipping the delicious concoction into shape.

She reached back into the freezer and added a scoop to a tall fluted glass then brought it forward to a spigot hanging above the counter next to where I sat and squirted root beer into the glass, finishing it with a cherry and a long-handled spoon. By then Paul's milkshake had reached its full volume so she pulled it off. For my phosphate, she dipped a long ladle into one of the stainless-steel containers imbedded in the surface under the counter, pulled up a ladle of sugary strawberries, poured it into another fluted glass, and finished it with a long pull of soda from another spigot then added ice. Next to the strawberries, separate containers held the vanilla and cherry syrups she added to the cokes for the girls in those iconic coke glasses. I was thoroughly delighted for it was not like Dairy Queen with all the plastic and paper—it seemed somehow more real, surely more delicious.

She said, "Judging from your accent, did you all come from the Midwest, hun?"

Even though there are ten diverse states with over 60 million people, Californians tend to think of it all as one – the Midwest. At least she didn't say the R word, Rust Belt—as if the whole diverse area was composed of old, rusting, abandoned steel mills and unemployed bums looking for handouts.

"We came down from Sonoma, Stockton and the city," I told her. "I enjoyed seeing how you made all those treats. Seems so much more authentic than Dairy Queen."

She replied, "We use nothing but the best ingredients, none of that artificial stuff. Thanks, honey, you're a doll."

The Jukebox had a vast selection of 50's and 60's hits, so I put a few quarters in and played "Surfing USA" by the Beach Boys, "Rock around the Clock," "Twist and Shout" and "Hey Jude" by the Beatles. We all got up and danced to "Rock around the Clock." Jenny and Betty danced together, so Paul and I twirled each other around and Wes grabbed Debbie.

Next, Paul grabbed Betty and I danced with Jenny. Paul of medium height, had a square handsome face, brown eyes with small features. Betty was nearly as tall as Paul. She wore her hair in a short bobbed professional style, had a slight overbite, a petite nose and high cheekbones below her blue eyes.

After dancing a slow dance, Paul had a hard time keeping up with the acrobatic Betty. She wanted to do some more advanced moves, but Paul refused. I grabbed her, threw her up in the air and onto each hip and then passed her under my legs, turning as she slid underneath and popping her back up. Our friends' faces were aghast. Then the entire restaurant erupted in applause as we bowed.

When the jukebox stopped, announcing each move loudly, as it selected, placed the "45"on the turntable, sat the needle down, and spun "Hey Jude," we all put our arms around each other's shoulders and sang the long version of the epic song in a circle repeating the mantric, bonding verses along with Paul and John.

As it played on, we entered a trance, there together, all as one, five great friends, happy to be with each other, rocking to the rhythm of the song, expressing our unity and joy, on an adventure together, singing the iconic, mesmerizing words over and over, and over and over again.

5:   THE MOJAVE

On the other side of the mountains, we entered the Mojave Dessert. I could not imagine a more sun-bleached, dry, desolate or deserted place in all the world than this. During a flight back from the East to L.A., I remembered flying over the desert and from thirty thousand feet seeing hundreds of miles of severe, uninhabited land stretching out to the horizon with rarely a road, a building or any sign of life, and then as we flew onwards, more of the same.

I was thinking how fortunate we were to have air conditioning on this narrow ribbon of uninhabited space in the vast nothingness that reminded me of the surface of Mars. Then, as if fate read my mind, the engine overheated and Paul had to pull off onto the parched, tan desert on the side of the road. Similar to baking in an oven, the inside of the SUV immediately became hotter than a sauna, so we all climbed out where the temperature on the steaming, tar smelling asphalt must have been 125. Fortunately, by then, since it was later in the afternoon, we were not fried by the sun's direct rays. While Paul and Wes tended to the radiator, Jenny, Betty and I sat down on the shaded side of the SUV.

We began sucking on our water bottles when Wes came over and said, "Hey guys, we need the water to quench the radiator's thirst." From one of the bottles, Paul splashed a small puddle of water on the SUV's hood, which immediately began to boil, eliciting puffs of steam into the light wind. Once back on the road, Paul had to turn off the air, and even with the windows wide open and fans on high, we baked and gasped for air all the way to Needles. There took turns attaching ourselves to the water fountain at the gas station. I downed a quart of orange drink and was still thirsty. The Weather Bureau frequently featured Needles as the hottest spot in the nation. By the time we entered Arizona, the air was cooler, and we felt refreshed.

At Flagstaff, we turned north.

I said, "At a ski area a short distance from here, Joe, Wes's brother, and I hiked to the top of Mount Humphrey, grabbing sturdy branches, jumping from rock to rock, we vaulted down the mountain. At the top of the mountain, it was fifty degrees. The next day we slid down the nearby moss-covered stream in Oak Creek Canyon where it was in the eighties. The spiritual center Sonoma and the massive Meteor Crater are also a short drive from here. I think Flagstaff attracts a special type of laid-back folk who enjoy the area and all of its natural wonders."

Imitating a stoner, Wes says, "Yeh it's a heavy place, man. Unlike anywhere else in the world, mannn."

———

Including the stop for lunch and refueling, we made it to the Grand Canyon in less than twelve hours.

We arrived at the campground before dusk. Handing me the charcoal he brought, Paul asked, "Rand, could you make a fire in the grill. Jenny, please wrap corn and potatoes in foil."

Then he reached into the cooler and brought out five, 12-ounce, thick, juicy filet mignons, saying, "Look at these guys, aren't they beautiful?"

After cooking the splendid meal, we all sat at the picnic table, where Paul brought out his most special reserve wine that he pronounced, "This is my Opus Magnum, it sells for two hundred dollars a bottle."

While swirling the wine in the broad wineglass to release its esters, I stuck my nose into the glass and inhaled deeply. It was then that I realized just how special it was.

After we had consumed two bottles of Paul's truly special wine and felt satiated, Betty brought out a chocolate mousse cake she had prepared. When we sat around the fire, I brought out the Drambuie, which, after rinsing out the wine glasses with hot water from the pot boiling on the grill, I delicately poured. We rotated the glasses, sniffing the delightful sweet elixir, slowly sipping it. I proposed a toast. "Here's to good friends. May we have an enjoyable adventure into the old Canyon, and here's to each of us." We clicked glasses.

We were conscious of the weight in our packs on our challenging hike, that we would be eating freeze-dried food, and that it would be a while before we enjoyed such a meal or any regular cooked meal, which is why Paul and Betty provided such a sumptuous feast. Like marathon runners eating spaghetti and meatballs the night before their long ordeal, we filled our carb and protein tanks for our trial.

We laid our bags out on a grassy patch near the picnic table and settled in for the night. On a clear, rainless night, I preferred sleeping on the ground, being out in the fresh air under the stars versus being confined in a tent. When I looked over the group of experienced backpackers and travelers, I could not think of anyone I felt more comfortable with or trusted more with my life, confident that together we could survive any situation that might occur.

—

I slept like a log until Paul woke me early the next morning. I resisted getting out of my warm down bag into the chilly air and put on my socks, jeans and shirt while still in the cozy bag before greeting the day and donning my down vest. Paul had already fired up the camp stove, and the smell of coffee permeated the cool, crisp, dimly-lit air. We all had groggy, half-awake faces as we poured cups of aromatic coffee and settled in around the picnic table in the dark. As we slowly stumbled around the campsite like half-frozen zombies, it became apparent that Jenny and I were not morning people, whereas Wes, Paul and Betty, fueled by coffee, soon became energetic and buzzed around the camp. I knew this from previous trips with Paul that in the morning, he drove us like cattle, but in this case, I welcomed it, for we needed to hit the trail before the sun rose. Betty fried up some scrambled eggs and bacon. I inhaled the delicious scent of it. Nothing better than the smell of bacon frying in the great outdoors.

We took our packs out of the car and laid the contents out on a tarp on top of the dew-laden ground in front of the headlights. Since it was a mile down to the Colorado and a mile and a quarter up the north rim, walking down from the South Rim and up the North Rim; then down and up again would be the equivalent of walking an arduous 2,600 stories, or scaling twenty Empire State Buildings. Therefore, we wanted to carry a minimal amount of weight.

My ranger friend, Fred, had cautioned us against carrying anything that was not absolutely necessary. As experienced backpackers, each of our packs contained everything one might need: backpacking tents, pads, rope, flashlights, small stoves, water purification tablets, emergency kits, moleskin, cook sets, water bottles, Swiss Army knives, etc. All of these things were small and light, but added up.

We determined that we would not need so many duplicate items, so we only carried one emergency kit, one bottle of water purification tablets, two flashlights, one large cook kit, and one thin, blue tarp that we would all sleep on. Since it would be so hot down there, we would not need extra layers of clothes, and since it rarely rained at the bottom, we would not need the backpacking tents.

We figured that we would not need our jackets. Rather, we would unzip our lightweight sleeping blankets and wrap those around us for warmth at night, for on the north rim it typically dipped into the forties, even in June. From the laid-out gear, we each deposited a roughly equal amount in our packs, with us guys carrying more. I took the plastic tarp. The major weight would be our freeze-dried food and water. The group agreed to take the Drambuie, so I poured it into a light plastic water bottle, stowed it in my roomy pack, and after rinsing it in the camp faucet, threw the heavy glass bottle into the recyclables.

With everyone in the campground fast asleep in their tents or RVs, as the first dim light of dawn illuminated the sparkling, waving tips of evergreens above the campground, we drove the Suburban to the ranger's office, where we met Fred.

"Sorry guys, I really had planned to join you last night, but we had a serious incident where a gun was fired. The guy had been drinking and threatened to shoot his wife. I calmed him down, read him his rights and locked him up in the canyon jail. The wife said he was not serious, just blowing off steam, and had him released."

Fred, a handsome sandy-haired, strong, lean, friendly guy, who resembled Robert Redford with the clean-shaven, close-cropped hair and the straightforward manner of a cop that appreciated nature, had prearranged our permit for Hermit's trail and had opened the office early for us.

Paul said, "Hey Fred, take these two filets I reserved for you and your girlfriend."

"Sorry I can't accept it. It could be construed as a bribe."

"We will not be able to carry the steak down with us. It would just spoil in the car."

Fred accepted it, saying, "That would be wasteful, and we try to discourage waste in the canyon."

Paul gave him a bottle of his prized wine to go with the steak, saying, "This is something special. Make sure you share it with that special lady."

We all shook Fred's hand and gave him hugs—something Jenny and Betty seemed to enthusiastically enjoy, while we guys merely had manly hugs. He wished us well, cautioning us about the rigors of the Hermit's Trail, urging us to be careful and carry a gallon of water per person. "It's really dangerous down there guys. Be sure to drink plenty of water, and if you feel lightheaded, stop immediately and rest in some shade if possible. We don't want anyone else falling into the Canyon. Had three die and a hundred and twenty trips to the ER already this month."

We were lucky we knew Fred. Even though thousands visited the canyon every day, only a handful are allowed on the primitive, unmaintained, Hermit's Trail. Fred told us of four L.A. lifeguards, who had just returned from their hike yesterday. "They spent the summer on the beach, under the hot sun beating down on their red caps every day. They left late morning, and despite being highly adapted to the heat, two of them passed out along the way. The bottom of the desert-like Canyon was 120 degrees yesterday guys. Be careful! We won't be able to help you down there. You are on your own!"

6:   THE RAFTERS

Fresh off the helicopter, seven weary-eyed adventurers appear at the dock on the river at six thirty in the morning. Three are executives from a mega-size company back east. The other four constitute a family with two children. Luka, the guide, introduces herself to the group and asks them questions regarding experience level, their physical stamina and capabilities. She is most concerned about the children. Even though he is only twelve, barely meeting the age requirement, Roger, the young boy, plays a variety of sports and seems in good shape. Ann, the incessantly yawning, thin fourteen-year-old girl with fading, long blonde hair, is, as are many girls at that age, all legs. She runs track and cross-country, so Luka thinks she should be able to handle the rigors the river will present. The three implacable executives of various sizes and builds have been specifically conditioned for the trip by their trainers, so they should pan out. All, thankfully, have had some rafting experience.

Luka, having guided trips in Washington State, Costa Rica and the Canyon, has over a decade of experience. In the winter, she and her husband, Tom, run a school to train EMTs for wilderness rescues. During the peak season, Tom directs the rescue service throughout the canyon, where every day people, despite all the warnings, unaccustomed to the rigors of the canyon, experience serious emergencies.

Their large raft has been pre-loaded with supplies for the weeklong journey securely tied to the middle of the raft. After selecting their paddles of the right length for each one's height and loading their bags into the waterproof container, to balance the load, Luka tells each member of the party where to sit. The right side has an executive followed by the wife and another executive. The left side has an executive followed by the daughter, the son and Doctor Thompson, who rowed for Harvard's ten-man sculling team, had competed in the Olympics and is someone that Luka should be able to count on in the inevitable critical situations they will encounter. Luka sits at the back-right side with a long tiller-like oar she will use to steer and propel the raft laden with supplies for the week.

Cheryl, the wife, is a lean, pretty, perky, well-coiffed brunette, who works out at Rumba classes at their country club three times a week and practices yoga. She was a physical therapist before she married her husband, Don, while working at the hospital. Now she is a housewife who takes care of the mansion, ferries the kids to all of their activities and belongs to a myriad of organizations, some of which she has been the president of. Resembling Ryan Reynolds, tall and handsome, doctor Don spends most of his time at his neurological practice.

Living in a six-thousand square foot mansion with six bedrooms and eight baths, game room, theatre, pool, workout room and wine cellar, under the constant influence of social media, induced by their iPhones and relentless activities, the family feels like strangers. The parents live in a large suite on the first floor, whereas the children live in large bedrooms with their own full-size luxurious bathrooms at opposite ends of the long hallway on the second floor. Living separate lives in such a large space, they are often surprised when they encounter each other.

One day, after her track practice, as they were driving back home in their Lexus SUV, Ann had asked her mother if her father still lived with them. With his busy practice and speaking engagements at conferences out of town, she had hardly seen him in weeks. Tears welling up in her eyes, Cheryl had been greatly affected. Earlier in the year she had tried to have the family sit down to dinner every other night, but with their busy schedules, that just didn't work.

She spoke to Don about it and he predictably became upset. To reconnect as a family, they determined that they would take a vacation or a long weekend once a quarter. Ann was thrilled—Roger not so much, since this meant he would have to miss a week of baseball. This trip would be their first such effort to mend frayed familial ties. Ann, a thoughtful, kind teenager who normally would want nothing to do with her parents, wanted desperately to reconnect with them and hoped the excursion might prevent a divorce as had happened to most of her friends.

Before they push off, Roger tries to send a selfie to his buds. Luka tells him that there will be no reception in the canyon and unless he wants it lost or destroyed, he had better pack the phone in his waterproof bag. Cheryl tells him that they really want to get away from their smart phones. He smirks, shakes his head, then reluctantly complies.

With the apprehension that accompanies any unknown passage, the adventurers, obscured by their bright orange life vests and helmets, shove off and enter the flat waters of the mighty Colorado. Soon Luka runs through the safety measures, cautioning them to stay in the boat, row when told to, and if they should be swept into a rapid, how best to survive the tumbling, overpowering water. "You can't fight it. You have to go with the flow and try to keep your feet in front of you."

The initially placid water provides the opportunity to practice their strokes and timing to become a reasonably coordinated crew. It also grants them time to marvel at the immense multicolored walls above, while Luka tells them a bit of the history of the canyon and its first explorers.

The solitude of the mighty canyon is powerful. Even the adults, normally immune to such trivial emotions, sense it.

When they approach the first clamorous rapid, each member of the party is alone with their thoughts. The executives feign false bravado, but their stomachs are churning. As if commencing a roller coaster ride, Roger can't wait for the excitement to commence. Not sure what awaits her, Ann is quietly anxious. Cheryl and Don, having taken on class six rapids, are confident, while Luka positions the raft for what will be an easy test for her crew.

After flying up and down and through the swift current's Vs that signal where there are rocks, jerking left then right, bouncing on the rubbery raft, they exit the rapid, letting out cheers of joy and relief. The bonding process has begun—a process that will bind this group of semi-strangers together, alone in the depths of the great chasm, with everything they need contained in the large raft—their home for a week.

Weeklong trips through the heart of the canyon can span 190 miles on large pontoon boats powered by outboard motors where participants are merely passive passengers. This group has elected a shorter cruise, one that will allow them more time to relax and explore, while participating in the rafting experience. Still, it is a luxurious adventure with gourmet meals prepared by Luka, a practiced chef, with the help of her crew. For lunch on the first day, they have Caesar salads and garlic bread, and for dinner they dine on beef filets with bearnaise sauce and fine French wine, preceded by shrimp cocktails, after which Luka serves chocolate mousse. Since they burn so many calories, they eat well without guilt and sleep like logs in their tents.

———

On the third day, after a hearty breakfast of pancakes and omelets with any imaginable ingredient, the now experienced, synchronized crew enters the raft. With a mighty push, skidding along the sand, Luka and Dr. Thompson push the rubber raft off the bank. As it slides gently into the river, they jump onboard flopping over the balloon-like sides and they're off.

During the mild initial section, Roger complains, "Being back here, I can't see anything. The front of the raft is too high.

Captain Luka, could you please let me go to the front. I want to see where we're going, please?"

Luka considers his request. He has shown himself to be remarkably able, and she was surprised at how strong Cheryl is on that side, so she says, "OK Roger, switch with Fred up front." Of the three executives, Fred was the least able and not much better than Roger, which made it a balanced trade.

As they wind their way through three relatively easy rapids, the crew becomes progressively more confident. But Luka knows one of the worst rapids on the entire river is just around the next bend.

With Roger, Ann and Cheryl screaming as if they were on a roller-coaster, the first portions of the seemingly endless rapids are easily conquered and exhilarating. Standing in the back, Cheryl can see the perilous Devil's Gate rapidly approaching. More akin to a waterfall, it suddenly drops ten feet, but she has lined up the raft perfectly. Slamming to the bottom, they all row fiercely to extract themselves from the hole, but when it hits a rock, Fred suddenly loses his paddle and without water to push off, he is falling out of the boat. Just in the nick of time, Doc Thompson grabs him by his belt and pulls him back into the boat.

Without the two men rowing on a left side, the raft suddenly kicks to the left, pitches at a 45° angle, slams into a rock, and like a seesaw the right front side bounces upwards sending Roger flying into the air. Just then the boat lurches forward and Roger is left behind in the rapids.

Aghast, seeing her boy in the churning water Cheryl stands up and is about to dive in to rescue him until Charlie pulls her down with Luka screaming, "Stay in the raft!"

Coolly, Luka appraises the situation. They are rapidly heading towards a deep churning whirlpool, where Roger will be trapped and sucked down. As they hit the whirlpool, summoning all her leg, back and arm strength, she mightily pushes her tiller to the left, sending the raft to right, where there is a rare, calm tidal pool. She commands the crew, "Row backwards with all your might!"

Roger enters the whirlpool and spins around, then spins around faster the second time, closing in on the downspout. The raft backs up and Luka skillfully steers it around so that Dr. Thompson, with adrenalin flowing, grabs the guard rope with his right hand and leans far out of the boat. Just as Rodger spins around again and vanishes in the drain-like vortex, his father grasps the top of his life vest, but it is pulling him out of the boat, until Charlie grabs him with both arms and with all his might pulls them up and out of the whirlpool onto the sidewall, where Rodger lies like a flopping fish coughing up water.

Luka artfully swings the boat forward out of danger.

Cheryl and Ann's pained expressions turn into relieved smiles, and after they exit the frightful rapid, into placid waters, the entire crew sighs in relief, the executives patting Doc and Charlie on the back, congratulating them for saving Roger. Roger says, "That was fun! Let's do it again!"

7:   INTO THE CANYON

After saying our farewells to Fred, we drive to the end of the Hermit's Road to the trailhead, where like an immense reddish-orange egg yolk, the sun pokes above the horizon illuminating a few high, elongated striations of clouds in iridescent violets, purples and reds. Representing the end of civilization, Hermit's Rest, a small, rustic log structure that serves as a rest stop and gift shop and snack bar had been erected in 1914 and contains the last scenic overlook on the South Rim. Since it was so early, it had not yet opened, but we are able to fill our gallon water jugs at its overturned faucet attached to an iron pipe extending out of the ground, the water gurgling into the jugs, its pitch rising till it overflows.

Since these were the heaviest items we would carry, rather than tie the jugs off our packs, we center them in the lightly filled packs, so they will not slosh around and their momentum pull us off the deadly trail. We also fill the small bottles we keep handy, which we will sip along the way and periodically refill during rest stops. Paul, the consummate backpacker, has a special container with a long plastic straw poking out of the bottom of his pack that he attaches to his neck so he can suck on it as he hikes. According to Fred, we could not expect there would be any other potable water until the Colorado River, a mile down and many miles along the unmaintained path.

We change out of our jeans and sweatshirt, into our shorts and t-shirts, leaving the former in the car. We are cold but know, as we begin hiking, we will quickly warm up and soon miss that cold feeling. We heft the now heavier packs onto our backs, center them above our waists and attach the belt, then walk along the rim, marveling at the spectacular canyon painted by that refracted, golden early-morning glow that makes the canyon pop like a 3-D movie. Paul sets up his camera on a timer on a rock, then slides into the picture, all of us smiling, with goosebumps in our sweatshirts and shorts, standing next to our packs with the brilliantly lit canyon as a backdrop. We post the Gif on social media—our last chance to do so.

As we hike to the bottom of the canyon, we will be passing through two-billion years of the earth's geological history, which we see on the multi-colored layers of the walls in whites and tans, reds and browns, grays and blacks, and I wonder what all of it signifies.

Just past the trailhead, Wes says, "With each step, we pass through an average of eighty-thousand years of history." He pokes his foot forward a few inches. "I have already stepped past the time when Columbus discovered America, Christ's birth, the Roman Empire and when the Greeks founded democracy."

He pokes his right foot a few inches in front of his left and while teetering there says, "Here I am beyond when the first civilization in Mesopotamia was founded and about when Asians crossed over the land bridge to the Americas twenty thousand years ago."

Somewhat introverted, as were most tech wizards, with red hair, blue eyes and freckles, Wes was always in excellent shape. Without any preparation or regular exercise, he was always ready to take on the most challenging x-game or physical adventures such as dirt biking, back country skiing, skate boarding, sky diving, hang gliding, or mountain climbing.

As he counts out four more steps he adds, "We are back to the time when our earliest Homo sapiens ancestors roamed the earth, 300-thousand and some years ago." Not something easy to do with a pack on, he skips forward. "From 100-thousand to 750-thousand years ago, volcanos frequently dammed up the Colorado River. But the last volcano occurred a mere one thousand years ago, back where we started."

Knowing how fickle volcanoes could be I add, "I wonder if it is possible for another one to occur. Sometimes they are dormant for thousands of years, then *kablewy*. From our previous trip to Yellowstone with Paul, I remembered that the last time a major eruption occurred there was seventy-five thousand years ago, but the whole area still bubbled, oozed and fumed as if it might blow any minute, becoming a mega-volcano that would wipe out life in North America and beyond. Old Faithful is a constant reminder of what might occur."

Then we descend into the broad, deep gorge. Even near the trailhead, where a few day hikers venture into the canyon, because of the relatively light traffic, the red dirt trail is very narrow. The first section of the trail is steep, and we walk close to the chasm, something that challenges my acrophobia, so I keep my eyes on the ground following Wes, who follows Paul with Betty behind me, and Jenny bringing up the rear.

Wes continues his narration, "Around that curve, we will see when our earliest evolutionary relative, Hominids, lived."

After we round the curve, Paul jumps up on the narrow path above the chasm and says, "That's one small step for man, and a giant leap for man-like kind."

We all laugh at his exaggerated antics as he imitates a monkey, making chimp-like sounds while scratching his underarms. I start humming the theme from *2001 Space Odyssey*, "Dummm… Dummm…Dummm…KaBum..Bam, Bam, Bam, Bam …"

Wes interjects, "Hey guys, if you do not want me to talk about this geology stuff, I won't bore you with it anymore. Just took a geology class at Berkeley. It fascinates me, but I can understand if you don't care for it."

Paul says, "I don't know. Sounds like walking through a dusty, old museum."

I say, "I've been to the canyon before, looked over the rim, admired the colors and even went halfway down the Bright Angel trail, but did not really understand the impact of what I saw. We have a long trip ahead of us. I think your being a guide will make our journey more interesting." To myself, I thought—*besides, it takes my mind off my acrophobia.*

"I agree," Jenny adds.

"Come on Paul, when we travelled around the world, you were always trying to understand more about where we were, and you liked those old dusty museums." Betty interjected.

"You're right Bett, sorry Wes. Please accept my gratitude for your excellent, portrayal, please continue."

Shaking his head, Wes smiles.

The other trails are much broader. Compared to Hermit's, the Bright Angel trail resembles a well-paved freeway, broad enough for two people to walk alongside each other as another hiker passes them in the opposite direction. The unmaintained Hermit's trail is barely wide enough for one person, therefore, you're constantly close to the perilous edge.

The first five minutes or so, as I adjust to the weight of the pack and my body warms up, are the most difficult. After that, as I tune into the Zen-like rhythm of footfalls on the path, the trek becomes automatic. Eventually, the pack will become part of you.

Similar to geese following their mother, we follow each other, zigzagging through the rocks, stepping over large boulders, as we play follow the leader, periodically changing leaders. The going is rough and perilous. Jenny trips on the loose rock. Before she falls over the edge, I grab her elbow and pull her back.

"Thanks, Rand, almost fell into the gorge. Would have become buzzard food."

"We would have carried you out, Jen, but please watch your step, these rocks are treacherous—not like a walk in the park."

When I was still warming up, Wes points to where the dinosaurs vanished due to a collision with a huge meteor in the Yucatan. "I think this is the extinction layer when most of the species on earth, not just the dinos, vanished. It shows up throughout the world. Took tens of thousands of years for plants and animals to rebuild themselves, which you can see here above the layer. This is one of the things I most looked forward to seeing." We all touch it marveling at its significance, for if it weren't for Wes, we would have just passed it by and not even noticed the change in the wall.

As Betty touches it, she says, "So if we were here back then, we'd be walking through a Jurassic jungle looking out for dinosaurs. Sorry to see you go Brontosaurus, Triceratops, TRex. Well maybe not so sorry about you T-Rex."

Paul sneaks up behind Jenny, and roars, which startles her. "You'd be a tasty morsel my dear," as he smiles and grabs her waist.

Jenny adds, "You wouldn't have to worry, Betty. You could outrun those ghastly beasts. They'd go for me first, cause you're so skinny—no meat on your bones."

Further down, I ask, "Hey Wes, what kind of rock is this cream-colored stuff."

"This is the Kaibab Limestone. It was deposited in an ocean that lay here around 250-million years ago. We've been cutting through what was an ancient seabed up until now. Look here, you can see fossils of seashells."

"I see them, cool!

Betty says, "With all these dinos and time travelling layers, I'm starting to feel like we are in one of those Jumanji movies.

Yea, Wes says. I love those. Which one of us do you think would play the different parts: the Rock, Karen Gillam, Jeff Black, Kevin Hart?

"That's simple," says Jen. "Since everyone plays their opposite, I'd be Karen the drop-dead, gorgeous goddess, and Betty would be Jeff Black, the intellectual professor."

Betty says, "You guys probably wouldn't expect this, but I'd love to be Jeff Black for a change. So since Wes is kind of nerdy, my guess is he would be the powerful Rock"

"Rand, since you're more the Rock type," Wes adds. "You would be sarcastic Kevin Hart and by process of elimination. Paul, since you can't sing a lick, you'd be Nick Jonas."

We all laugh, pleased with our roles. As we hike further along the trail, Jenny walks as if she were a model on a runway, Wes puffs up and walks large, flexing his muscles like the Rock. Betty starts spouting off bogus facts about various rocks, "Um, let me see here, ya, this here definitely is genius rock from the crust-us period one-million, seven-hundred and fifty-five-thousand, four-hundred and twenty-two years ago when it was, oh yes, at the, the north pole, ya."

———

Further down the canyon, Betty stops, looks at the side of a lighter colored steep cliff wall, feels it with her fingers and says, "I think this is sandstone, Wes. It has that feel and looks like what we saw on all those magnificently, architected buildings in cities around the world.

Wes, who is a few steps ahead, turns, "Excellent, Bett, It is indeed sandstone from a Sahara-like desert of giant sand dunes that covered the region around 300-million years ago—think Saudi Arabia. We are essentially walking down through thirty-five stories of compressed sand. Imagine we are walking down seventy flights of stairs surrounded by sand and torturous heat. "

Paul becomes fascinated with Wes's portrayal and keeps his eyes on the ground, looking for fossils, pointing out some ancient lizard tracks and mollusk impressions.

Our first rest stop is at the Santa Maria Spring, consisting of a small, worn wooden shed where a rusty pipe emits nasty-looking water. Other than a little green algae-filled fluid, there is little water to drink. Paul reasons, "Since the spring rains ended some time ago, it has gone dry. Good that we are following Fred's advice and filled our jugs at the top. Even with purification tablets, who would want to drink that muck?"

Out of range of most day hikers, the gray, dusty trail strewn with even more rocks and pitfalls becomes rougher. Following the contours of the gorge, we sometimes go up but mostly go ever downwards. As we distance ourselves from civilization, I feel the magic of backpacking. Similar to walking through an unfamiliar door where you do not know what lay behind, it's an adjustment to leave all that civilization provides—a roof over our head, food in the fridge, water at the touch of a handle, plenty of clothes in a closet, a comfortable bed, a hot shower, lights at night, a car to transport you anywhere.

But you receive much more in return. Here, amazingly, we carry everything we need on our backs. We live as our ancient ancestors, who roamed the earth thousands of years before the dawn of civilization—in a state of nature.

As if she read my mind, Jenny observes "Just being in nature provides benefits,". "The Japanese believe in forest bathing. —walking through a forest where there are supposedly numerous beneficial compounds."

Curious, Betty asks, I've never heard of that before—Forest Bathing?"

"Yeah, there's been studies done that show it's linked to lower blood pressure, stress hormones and anxiety levels, along with decreased depression and fatigue. Scientists showed that walking in the forest also increased cancer-fighting cells. Kaiser even did a study that revealed a 45-minute nature walk improved performance on cognitive tests."

"That sounds interesting Jen. So, how much time do you need to spend doing this? Is it like exercising, where you have to do it for an hour a day?"

"No, not at all. The benefits start accruing after just 120 minutes a week. We are already away from the forests of the

North Rim in desert conditions with little more than scrub brush on the side of the cliffs, but I imagine there are benefits to us even in this parched environment, too. Maybe we are being purified of all those toxins we build up."

After another mile, Wes says, "We are passing through seven climatic zones spanning the climates from Canada all the way to Mexico. At over six-thousand feet, the forests on the North Rim, where we are headed, resemble those of Canada.

As I became more aware of my surroundings, instincts from a million years of evolution, obscured by a few thousand years of civilization, begin to emerge. I become aware of not only what is ahead and on the side of me, but what is behind me too, subconsciously poised to react. Finally, my pack becomes an integral body part. Before when I slipped on a loose stone, with my pack pulling me down, falling to my knees, I struggled mightily to maintain my balance. Now when I slip on an angular stone, I instantly recover.

About halfway down, Paul picks up a rock on the side of the path and shows us the fossil of a fern. Wanting to join the game, Betty notices an odd geometrical design on an exposed rock she was about to step on. "It looks like the fossil of a sponge."

Wes says, "Yes, Bett, these existed about three-hundred-million years ago."

Wes continues, "The Canyon was part of a broad tropical ocean then. Imagine that we are all fish swimming in the ocean." Extending his lips, puckering, and sucking in his cheeks, while fluttering his hands at his side, Paul walks around imitating a fish, wiggling his butt. We all laugh hysterically at his antics and then, as if we were a school of fish, imitate him.

8:   TROUBLE AHEAD

When we finally reach the Tonto Plateau, Wes says, "What we are walking on now was once at the equator."

I ask, "Wow that's hard to imagine that all of this was once way down there. Is that when the Pangea Continent appeared? I remember that from some science show on PBS."

"Good question Rand, but actually that is above us, when all of the continents were glued together as one." He continues, "Here, after the canyon was an ocean, it closed up and had been part of a huge inland sea that stretched from Montana up to Canada over to Lake Superior and all the way down to here in Arizona. Amazingly, this sea was as large as the Mediterranean and we would be at the equivalent of say Marrakesh."

———

Walking along the plateau, we are above the ancient inner gorge where it is extremely hot. Feeling as though it is a hundred and ten degrees, sweating profusely, we all struggle with every step—our legs ache and our shins feel splintered by the long downward trek. In addition, our lungs strain to breathe in the hot, dry air.

Sounding winded, Jenny says, "I can't believe it was in the forties when we started." Her water bottle is empty and we all feel as if we are struggling to push through a brutal desert.

The bottom of the Canyon resembles the weather, flora and fauna of Southern Mexico. That morning I saw the kind of big, fat, reddish-brownish squirrels we all grew up with in Northern Ohio. Now, when we reach the bottom, I spot a thin, scrawny squirrel adapted to frugal desert conditions. Unlike the rich pine forests at the rim, here we see greenish-yellow cacti. In the open on the plateau, the heat beats down on us like steaks on a grill. Sweating profusely, we find it progressively more difficult to breathe in the hot, dry air. Our initially joyous hike slows to a crawl, none of us talking any longer, just plodding along, step after hot, dazed step.

Just in front of me, I see Jenny having a hard time keeping up. She gives me a weary half-smile. "Rand, why don't you go ahead?"

I look at her shaking hands with concern. "That's okay, Jen. Take your time. No rush."

She looks faint but evidently does not want to make the group stop. Jenny labors to take shuffling half-steps. Suddenly, she stumbles, and her body goes limp. I reach out, hands snatching air, unable to catch her as, twisting under the weight of her pack, she hits the ground like a rag doll.

I cry out to the others now a hundred feet in front. "Stop! Jenny's fainted."

I drop to my knees, fumble to unbuckle her hip strap and take her pack off. I hear their packs thudding to the ground as Wes, Betty, and Paul cast them aside, running to help.

To shade her from the sun, we all gather around her. With a sense of controlled urgency, Betty tells us, "She is dehydrated and hypothermic. Quickly, give me all of your water." We give her our water bottles and the jugs from our packs, which doesn't amount to much. Jenny's bottles are totally empty.

Betty douses Jenny's T-shirt with water and pats her head with her dampened bandanna. Jenny slowly opens her eyes and blinks several times, but her face still looks flushed as Betty squirts water into her mouth. Paul takes some small packets of salt from his pack and gives them to Betty to administer to Jenny. Our phones have no signal, so we know it would be hours before we could reach emergency personnel. I look at my friends and see the concerned drawn looks on their faces that conveys the desperation of our situation.

Quickly tossing everything out of my lower central pocket, I grab the plastic tarp. Wes immediately senses what I am doing. Placing our packs on the bottom corners, Wes and I lift the tarp above our heads to make an impromptu lean-to to shade Jenny from the hot sun.

Jenny's eyes are raised upwards to her brow, and she can't talk. She looks very flushed and clammy with beads of sweat clinging to her cheeks, her face is drawn and expressionless. "Maybe we can make a litter out of the tarp and pack frames and carry her out, while someone runs ahead for help," Paul suggests. "We can leave the packs here."

She seems to be coming out of it—her eyes, which were towards the back of her head and flickering, seem to be focusing and her flushed face seems to be coming to life. Betty asks, "Jenny, how many fingers do I have up?

"Four," Jenny slowly responds.

"What is your name?"

"Jenny."

"What month is this?"

"June."

"Can you raise your arms above your head?"

Jenny is able to do so.

"Jenny, stick out your tongue."

After she sticks it straight out, Betty says, "If the tongue had gone to one side or another, that is a sign of a stroke." She turns back to Jenny. "Where are we?"

"Why, Betty, we're in the Grand Canyon. Are you lost?" she replies with a smile.

That breaks the tension and we all laugh in relief.

Jenny continues, "I don't know what happened to me, but I feel much better now. Being in the shade is very helpful. Thank you, guys... Sorry, guys!"

After a couple of minutes, sitting up, she says, "I am ready now, let's go."

Betty puts her hands on her hips, shakes her head firmly and speaking in a firm voice says, "Not yet, my dear. You need to rest for a while, until your system hydrates and we can be sure you are okay."

After another twenty minutes, Betty feels Jenny's forehead and wrist. "Her temperature has gone down, and her pulse has stabilized. She seems much better. How do you feel?"

"Much, much better. Thank you, guys. I love you."

I touch her shoulder and gasping in relief say, "We love you too. You gave us quite a scare there."

Paul says, "We are only a few hundred yards from the gorge where there will be more shade and maybe a cooling breeze coming up from the river. Do you think you can walk dear? If not, we can fashion a litter from the pack frames."

"Yes, I am sure I can."

While Wes and I continue to hold up the plastic lean-to, Paul places the contents of Jenny's pack into our packs and ties the pack's frame to his own. Betty squirts the remainder of our water onto Jenny's hair before she puts her cap back on and gently helps her to her feet.

Once in the Inner Gorge, we rest in the shade.

While cooling in the shade our normally boisterous group is awkwardly silent. To take our mind off the traumatic scene, we just experienced, I attempt to change the subject. "Say Wes, where are we now, back to a jungle or atop a mountain or something?"

Wes tells us, "Somewhere around here we will be passing the Great Uncertainty."

Somewhat confused I ask, "The Great Uncertainty, sounds like my life?"

"We are skipping four periods of the earth's geological history, representing about five hundred million years."

"Wow. So it's like we are in Jules Verne's time machine, setting the dial back and instantly traveling half a billion years back in time," I postulated.

"Yeah, something like that, Rand. Continental drift pushed the lower older layers upward above the newer layers. It fooled the geologists for a long time. We are skipping through time. Make sure your seatbelts are tight and your seats are in the upright position," he says with a smile, which causes Jen to smile too.

I suggest, "Paul, you seem to be the freshest of all of us. Why don't you go on ahead? Get some water from the creek and bring it back for her."

Looking relieved to do something positive he replies, "Sure, sounds like a great idea."

The inner gorge is like something from another world, something I have seen nowhere else in this world. It's dark and foreboding and mysterious. There are few multicolored layers anymore, much of it just dark black, impermeable basalt. It's a strange land that seems to have a strange unidentified force I have never felt before.

As we wait patiently, sitting with little to do but relive the recent horror, to break the tension once again, I say, "By now Paul has followed the trail that led to Hermit's Creek, where he will lay his pack down and pull out his gallon jug, fill it with water and add some purification tablets. Leaving his pack behind, he will quickly retrace his steps and be here any minute now."

When Paul returns, we sit down and have Jenny drink a third of the jug. Our mouths dry from the long hot ordeal, we share the rest, water never tasting any better. Jenny seems much better too.

As we walk on, I can hear the roar of the mighty river growing louder, so I know we are approaching the end. Sweating profusely, we all feel the effects of the heat, but are relieved Jenny is okay. Finally, we reach the river where it is perhaps twenty degrees cooler. Still in the nineties but it feels cool by comparison. When I take my pack off, I feel so light it is as if I am bouncing on the moon. After catching our breath, where the waters of the hot creek merge with the cooling waters of the river, we all go skinny dipping in the refreshing stream. Just before hot creek joins the fast-moving river, there is a little whirlpool. I position myself to massage the tense muscles on my neck shoulders, and the bottom of my soles, relieving my aching feet. Sighing deeply, it feels heavenly. Afterwards, we lay on the tarp on the thin strand of sandy beach feeling proud of our accomplishment.

9:   BOTTOM OF THE CANYON

Feeling restored from our challenging hike, I gather driftwood, Betty makes a fire, and Paul uses his device to purify more water. Over a roaring fire Jenny boils that first batch of water in our big pan, then adds a large packet of freeze-dried stew and stirring constantly, watches it inflate, the wonderful smell permeating the air. As night envelopes us, I stand transfixed gazing at the fire, the boiling stew and breathing in the delicious smell, when I realize I am famished. Even though it is not as good as the previous night's feast, we all greatly enjoy our meal, slurping the last drops of gravy into our hard rolls. Afterwards, Betty washes the aluminum pans and dishes from our mess kits, then we settle in around the fire, proud of what we accomplished that day.

Satiated, looking out towards the river, Paul exclaims, "That magnificent river must go on for a thousand miles."

Wes says, "I believe it's more like twelve-hundred miles. I think it starts up in Utah, but I'm not sure."

As if to relieve myself, I step away from the fire.

After returning highlighted by the fire's glow, I proclaim, "Actually, the Colorado is 1,450 miles long. It originates at La Poudre Pass, which is in Colorado." Then with my hands expanding outwards, I add, "Here's something interesting, did you know that above us, Lake Powell has 1,960 miles of coastline—more than the entire West Coast, including California, Oregon and Washington?"

Jenny squints at me suspiciously. "How do you know all that stuff?"

In a similar tone, with a smile, Betty adds, "Do you have a pamphlet or something?"

"No, I Do NOT!" I respond demonstrably, as if I am offended.

"Okay. Mr. Einstein, how deep is the lake then?"

Sounding like a learned professor, I proclaim, "Well, depending on rainfall or snowmelt and time of year, that varies quite a bit. The Glen Canyon dam itself is 710 feet high with ten billion gallons flowing through it. In 2005, it reached its lowest level at 33% of capacity or 236 feet."

With them all looking a little puzzled, Jenny asks, "Okay Mr. Trivial Pursuit, what's the capitol of, ah, ah... Kazakhstan?"

Still standing above them, I turn to the side where I had my phone hidden to block their view as I typed awkwardly with my right thumb.

"Why Betty, that's Nursultan, of course."

Wes, who was to my right, saw the dim light reflecting off the side of my face, says, "I know there's no cell coverage down here, Rand, you have a SAT phone, don't you?"

"No, I do not. But is there anything else you'd like to know?"

Paul is enjoying this. Wes has a smirk on his face too because he has figured it out. Betty and Jenny look perturbed. Realizing the joke has gone about as far as it can go, I tell them, "It's not a SAT phone. I have a hard copy of Wikipedia on my iPhone."

"All of Wikipedia, that's got to be huge." Paul queries, "I know you are a computer whiz, but how did you do that?"

"Adding the compressed XML version took up less than thirty gig—a fraction of my total storage."

"Cool!"

Looking upset, Jenny says, "Over dinner back in San Francisco you told me you were looking forward to getting away from all your devices, and for you that was a major goal of this trip. And here you are accessing your phone. What's going on, mister?"

"Yeah, and you texted us the same thing," Betty added.

Seeing the girls were upset and the guys seeming to enjoy my precarious predicament, I replied, "I thought I would amaze you all with my superior knowledge throughout our trip, but you caught me right away. Sorry guys, you're right, I won't touch my phone again. I desperately wanted to get away from it. Guess it's an addiction, and it's cold turkey from now on." Then I held it up and showed it to everybody, turned it off, placed it in my waterproof case, and zipped it up.

Betty says, "You know, I think I might be addicted too. When I saw your phone, I started salivating. I probably have a major addiction problem too, because I was concerned about coming on this trip and not having any access to my phone and social media. It was really bugging me."

"I mean, it's everywhere—at work, at home, in the car, at a restaurant, everywhere. I travel a lot, but I never see where I am. Never even look out the window. While waiting in the TSA line, I'm attached, in the waiting area I'm attached, and on the plane I'm attached. Then once I arrive, even in the Uber, I'm attached there too—don't even see the scenery in a country I've never been to before. Imagine being in Paris for the first time and not even looking up at the Eiffel tower. Realizing I might never be there again, in the back of my mind, I know I should look around and take it all in, but despite wanting to, I can't tear myself away. It's like its light casts a spell over me. Did you know that the average American adult spends eleven-and-a-half hours on media every day—nearly half their lives—eighty-percent of their waking lives."

"But it's even more insidious than an addiction because they know everything about you—probably more than you know about yourself. They know where we are all the time, who we communicate with, how old we are, what we look like, who our friends are, where we live, what our politics are, what our vitals are, our DNA, what we do for fun, what we watch for entertainment, what games we play and what we buy."

Betty pauses to catch her breath.   "They even know what we're likely to look at and where we will likely click on our screen. And they all know everything about us, all of them—Facebook, Google, Microsoft, Amazon, Yahoo—because they are constantly talking to each other about us, sharing our information, because our most intimate data has become a valuable commodity to them. And since they have been hacking our systems, our government and our companies, the Russians and Chinese know about us too."

"With artificial intelligence, who knows where this will all lead. We are surrounded by personalized, targeted ads—more and more each day. We are like rats in a Skinner box, conditioned to push buttons on our screens to buy ever more."

Paul says, "Geez, Bett, I didn't know it bothered you that much. I thought you loved your phone, whenever it becomes available, you always get the newest iPhone, and Apple is, after all, more secure than the rest. You are, after all, a techy too."

"It's kind of a love/hate relationship—maybe a type of codependency. I guess being here away from it gives me perspective as to how much it has invaded my life. I'm venting, sorry guys."

Wes chimes in, "As our technologist, I have been researching AI and writing a white paper as to where it is and where it is heading. You would not believe where it's going guys. Much scarier than you could imagine, even for us systems types like you, Betty, and Rand.

"For a regular Facebook user, they collect hundreds of pages of digital data about you and then mix that with all of your other online activity. With all of that information, possibly including videos from your home security systems, voice queries from your online assistants such as Siri and Alexa, including your voice patterns and facial recognition, AI knows more about you than your family or even your BFF."

"They will know what your mood is, your biorhythms, and are able to predict what you will be doing on a given day, and since they will know what food you have in your fridge, what you are likely to eat. China's using AI to classify and rank its citizens. The ranking will determine their opportunities in life and whether they can buy a home or not. Imagine how controlled those people are. Say something wrong on Facebook, or jaywalk and your home loan request is denied, or you can't get a job. It's like 1984 over there, man."

Paul joins the conversation, "Okay, so why do you need this AI, this artificial intelligence stuff? Can you explain it to me without all that mumbo jumbo you geeks speak?"

Wes Says, "Well, it's not all bad. AI will be able to do all kinds of neat stuff like helping the environment, driving trucks, driving your car, fetching your groceries, delivering your fast food, cutting your grass, etc. Much of this we can already do, but it's rapidly evolving, getting better all the time."

"So, think of it this way. There are trillions of bits of information out there about each of us stored on the iconic cloud that for the heck of it, let's call the stratosphere—a collection of a bunch of clouds. It never goes away. And there are billions of us who have all our data in the stratosphere. It's like digital gold, but it's embedded in a bunch of useless stuff. So, the problem becomes how do you mine all that—to make some sense of it, so you can sell it to the highest bidder."

"But isn't it all just gibberish?" Jenny chimes in. "Hard to imagine all that garbage would be worth much."

"At its essence, it is just zeros and ones. That's where AI comes in, making sense of it all. AI has been around for decades, but like most transformational technologies, it can take that long to be fully realized. As a kid, I remember playing around with an AI translator called Intellect developed by Harvard. It was similar to Alexa or Siri way back before them in the early nineties. When we were just toddlers.

"What AI does, it takes all of your bits of information and uses that to build a profile of you. Then entities such as businesses, governments or, say, political parties can use that approximation of you to motivate you to do something they want you to do, because they know what motivates you."

"I'm not interested in politics much, but probably the best example was how Russia and Cambridge Analytica used such a profile to motivate voters to vote for a particular candidate. Diabolically, some of the ads they fed to people were based on fake news and it went both ways, conservative and liberal, to further divide us. It was pure genius and relatively cheap, much cheaper than missiles, tanks and subs and unless there is an all-out war much more effective. Emphasizing the value of such data, Facebook was fined five-billion dollars for what was done on its platform. Five-billion can you imagine that and another $640-million to the UK —over five times what both campaigns spent together. That kind of emphasizes how expensive these golden bits are."

"Underscoring how valuable this information has become, the largest five companies ever in the history of the world, each of whose valuation are approaching one or even two-trillion dollars, are the ones collecting and mining this data to their advantage. That gives you an idea of how valuable it is. Why, it's the gold of the new millennium.

"These companies are even larger than the industrial monopolies of a hundred years ago, such as Standard oil, U.S. Steel, GE, AT&T or Ford. But whereas those companies made real tangible things, these guys sell data—the new commodity. It's more valuable than real stuff guys!"

Jenny, looking a little overwhelmed, responds, "I'm just glad I am here with you guys, a mile under the earth's surface far away from all of that. Wish we could stay here forever. Let's declare this a no tech zone and not talk about it anymore."

I say, "I really love all that, but part of me wishes we were born before the digital revolution. Oh, even before the industrial revolution. And before Dickens time in the 1800s too, when people were moving to the cities and young kids worked in factories. That sounded bad too, so before then."

Paul says, "Hey, near where we used to live in Ohio there were a lot of Amish communities. You could join one of those, Rand. Or if you wanted a limited amount of automation, join the Mennonites. They are allowed to have some mechanical devices for business purposes."

I say, "That doesn't sound so bad, but I would like an intellectual life too, like they had in the Renaissance. Back then they had a rich life of good friends, good food, art, literature, and stimulating intellectual pursuits without all the complications of our modern digital era. Back then they had time to enjoy life and people and their family."

—

After the stimulating discussion, I find myself staring at the burning wood for long intervals, transfixed, thinking about absolutely nothing.

Paul, seeing me so absorbed, says, "The fire is a mandala— something that draws your attention, but gives you much in return—a type of energy transfer."

I cannot understand exactly what he means, but I think it might be something like the Buddhist or Hindu meditation I read about and really didn't understand. I do feel extremely mellow though, relaxed and deeply peaceful thinking we humans have stared into fires for hundreds of thousands of years—something, somehow basic and reinforcing to our instincts.

Growing up in the city, the only fires I remember were the leaves we burned on our street. I loved the smell of burning leaves and remember, after raking them onto the street and setting them on fire on cool October eves, staring transfixed into the orange, red, purple, blue heart of those fires, where the crackling leaves burned brightly. Finding it hard to extract myself, I felt as though I could stare into those sweet-smelling, maple leaf, fires forever, but I did not know it was a mandala. The fire, the rushing river, the smells of the river and campfire, the mellow group, and the canyon were having a powerful effect on me. Toward what end, I do not know, or care.

As the fire sputters out, I throw out the thin plastic tarp for us to lie on. We camp near the river with the water's temperature in the fifties. Thus, the air is substantially cooler, but still warm. Sleeping out in the open on merely a thin plastic drop cloth with no blanket, I look up at the sky whitewashed with millions of stars. Since there are no lights in the Canyon, the sky and the Milky Way are brilliant, more brilliant than anywhere I have ever been. Arcing through the sky, I count four planets shining like diamonds and the outlines of constellations that other than the kite-like Big and Small Dippers, I do not know the names of. It could rain on the Canyon rim without a drop falling on the bone-dry desert far below. Other than the flowing river, there are no sounds and it is supremely quiet. As the fire sputters out, we lay there a mile below the surface alone with no light other than that from the stars.

—

The next morning, we all wake with stiff muscles and Betty leads us in yoga to loosen them up. After adapting to the enjoyable, desolate, hot solitude at the bottom, I find a natural contoured beach chair the current carved into a bolder adjacent to the wild, turbulent, frothy Colorado, where I relax in its cool spray, mesmerized by its constant roaring thunder, thinking perhaps it is a mandala too.

I think to myself that all of this expanse and magnificent solitude was mine alone to enjoy, when all of a sudden, a raft full of people flies by, yelling and waving as they bounce up and down through the turbulent rapids. I had thought I was nowhere near civilization, nowhere near people, then bam, there they were, and as fast as they appeared, they vanish down the swift river. I wave back and smile at the surprise and think I too would like to run the river someday.

Our plans call for us to stay here for another night, then walk on the plateau alongside the river for about a dozen miles, where we will intersect the Bright Angel Trail and cross over the river. There, where the Bright Angel joins the Kaibab Trail, we will stay at the primitive Bright Angel camp site, where a year ago I made reservations, then we will climb up to the north rim.

10: RAFTERS PROGRESS

Along their journey, as the rafting party descends deeper into the mighty gorge, they hike up intriguing canyons and see the remnants of Hopi dwellings. On the third day, they view a picturesque waterfall cascading into a warm pool where they swim, and even the executives away from civilization and the rigors of their responsibilities, letting down their guard, frolic in the delightful, cooling turquoise waters. Initially, they seemed rigid. Sure, they were friendly, but even among themselves, they seemed guarded, as if they could not let their hair down. Rather than letting their beards grow, as Dr. Don did, they shaved and quaffed their hair every day. Unlike the others who wore t-shirts and casual shorts, they wore designer clothes and expensive sun glasses.

That night in their tent, Cheryl and Don speak about how well the trip is proceeding for them, how much they are learning about their wonderful children, how surprisingly well they are all getting along, and how neglectful they have been as parents by not doing this years earlier. That evening, for the first time, Don and Roger played catch with the mitts and ball Roger brought, Don showing him how to throw a curveball and a slider from when he was an all-star high school pitcher, something Roger never knew. Ann tells her mother about the boy she likes at school.

Over halfway through the adventure, the group performs as a well-oiled machine, setting up camp each night and tearing it down in the morning. The lonely canyon has captivated them and cuddled them in her arms. That evening they round a bend and steer for another camp before the next rapids. Unlike their previous unoccupied stops, in the distance they see a group of backpackers laying on the beach. Cheryl, blinking several times, cannot believe her eyes when she realizes the guys are naked, commanding her children to divert their eyes, as the guys, who finally realize a raft is approaching, hastily don their shorts.

11:   TOGETHER

After a leisurely morning spent in my rocking chair lounge and a tasty lunch of pastrami wraps with swiss and mustard, I join the group skinny-dipping in the river. Conscious of the weight of our backpacks, we did not bring swimsuits and did not want to get our shorts wet, because it would take hours for them to dry. Besides, we are in the middle of nowhere, where we might not see a soul for days.

Betty and Jenny put their shorts and tops back on, but as they lay on top of our plastic tarp on the beach, Paul and Wes refuse to do so. Paul grabs my shorts and throws them to Wes, so I have to lay there sans clothes too, which I am not comfortable with but just accept. After all, there is no one nearby and I can't imagine a more private beach. Resting from the previous day's exertion, throughout the afternoon we talk about various topics, just enjoying the river, the peace, and each other's company. We are in the middle of what amounts to a desperately dry desert. But we are next to a roaring river filled with life-bestowing water—an oasis. In each direction, we see spectacular views of multicolored walls in various hues of greens, reds and oranges, browns and tans. This is the most relaxed and peaceful I have been in months, maybe years. As I take a deep breath, breathing it all in, I can feel the tension evaporating from my shoulders.

Betty, who is sitting up on her elbows talking to Wes, notices a raft heading our way and commands us to immediately don our shorts. Initially shocked by the unwelcome intrusion, we guys come to attention. Like Polynesian natives welcoming Captain Cook's crew to Hawaii, smiling broadly, Jenny and Betty run to greet them, after which us guys pull the raft in. One by one the group jumps off the raft, and ignoring our previous state, we introduce ourselves.

Evidently, the three middle-aged older men with short, expensive haircuts and impressive cultivated presences are together, as is the family with two teenage kids. The young girl greets us with a Mona Lisa-like smile, as if she had seen us before we put our shorts on, something that did not bother Paul or Wes in the least but did concern me.

Jokingly, Paul says, "Hey, this is our beach, what are you doing here?" Smirking, used to having their way, the executives look displeased with Paul. Paul is incorrigible and a bit of a showoff, who really does not care much about what people think. We all accept his faults, but others sometimes find him objectionable, particularly when they first meet him.

The well-organized group immediately proceeds to unload and set up their camp—their tents, camp stove, and kitchenette—as we look on, something we find highly entertaining. Now our primitive campsite resembles a little town. Since the number of people permitted at the site is severely limited, we are surprised to see such a large group, but all together there were still only thirteen of us—according to the Website, still below the limit. Since it is getting late, we decide to cook our freeze-dried Swedish meatballs.

Betty asks Luka if we could use their large, propane stove when they are done.

Luka replies, "We are ahead of schedule, and have more than ample supplies, you are welcome to join us for dinner."

Betty cooks our freeze-dried Swedish meatballs as an appetizer—something the Richards are interested in trying. The executives did not touch it, but the Richards seemed to enjoy our plebian cuisine. Paul says, "I guess you guys aren't used to regular food." With judgmental looks, the executives still seem put-off by Paul and his usual antics. That night we had a sumptuous feast of tapas, chicken fettuccine, salad, and key lime pie. We start off dinner with a Chardonnay and then switch to a blended red wine, something Charlie, who is evidently the chief executive, is obviously proud of and had shipped directly from his large wine cellar in his mansion back home.

Paul swirls his glass wildly, spilling a little in the sand and continuously sniffing before taking a sip, finally says, "This is very interesting—I would say 20% Cabernet, 30% Cab Frank, 40% Merlot and (he hesitates) yes 10% Syrah. I like the Syrah, something definitely different, but it works, although I would not add any more than that."

Charlie, a handsome, well-groomed, middle-aged man with speckled, black short hair and a deep tan replies sternly, "How could you possibly know that?" Without looking, Paul picks up the bottle and gives it to him. The bottle did not reveal the percents but agreed with Paul's assessment of the varietals, "This wine was produced by my friend Doug Jones at Sonoma Callers." It is a wonderful 92-pointer.

Then he proceeds to the insulated case, laying it on the beach, picks up each bottle, and pulls out another red, asking, "May I open this one?" to which Charlie reluctantly responds, "Go ahead." Paul readily uncorks the bottle, rinses out Charlie's glass, pours a taste, swishes it around violently, and then hands it to him.

Charlie swirls it around some more, smells it, sips it then brings the glass to his lips and slurping replies, "Oh that's very nice, very nice indeed."

Paul says, "Do you taste the chestnuts, black currants, and charcoal?"

"Why yes I do, this is delicious, perhaps the best Pinot I have ever tasted."

"I made it five years ago. It should be at its peak four years from now."

Paul and Charlie become locked in a conversation about wines. That's how Paul is. He can be a little off-putting at first, but once they get to know him, most people greatly enjoy his intelligence and his company.

After dinner, Luka puts the refuse into a plastic bag to be taken out of the canyon. She says, "Since our stocks have been depleted and we have plenty of room on the raft, we will take your refuse out too, thereby lightening the load in your packs," which we thank her for.

I thought it was my turn to wash our dishes, so I gather them up and proceed to the creek. While washing our aluminum plates and pans, Ann joins me with their dishes, saying, "You on KP too?"

I simply respond, "Yeah. Say... is that really china? I can't believe it would last through the banging you guys must be taking in the rapids."

"It sure looks like china, doesn't it? But it's actually some kind of special polymer thingy made to look like china. We still have to pack it away in a special container because it can break under extreme conditions though."

"My parents wanted us to take more responsibility on the trip. Since our live-in maid, Mary, does all of this stuff at home, they wanted us to do it here. They think we are spoiled, and my dad constantly tells us about how rough he had it growing up in a bungalow and all. We save a little bit of money by doing it but that was not their reason. The parents also help with the chores."

I ask, "Do you mind doing it?"

"No, not all. I kind of enjoy it."

"As a kid I had to do the dishes too. At first, I did not like it. Then after I got used to it, I kind of liked it. Plus, I felt I was contributing to the family. So, are you enjoying your adventure?"

With a bright smile, she replies, "Oh yes, very much so, it's the highlight of my life."

"You are not very old; you probably have many more great adventures ahead of you."

"But not like this. You see, after we moved into the mansion, we hardly ever saw each other. When my dad was a resident and we lived in a small apartment near the hospital, we saw each other every day and had so much fun. Now, my mom will be at one of her meetings, Dad will be at work or on the computer in his home office with the door closed, my brother will be in the game room playing video games, and I will be in my room either studying, reading, or on social media with my friends. We are not even on the same floors. This trip has meant so much because it has brought us together. I would gladly wash dishes after every meal to be here."

"You seem like an impressive young lady. How old are you?"

"I'm fourteen, but I will be fifteen next month."

"So, let me see, does that mean that you were in ninth grade? So, you will be a sophomore, right?"

"Well, actually I will be a junior because, eh, I skipped a grade."

"You must be pretty smart."

"It's the genes. My parents are smart, so I guess I am too."

"Where do you go to school?"

"I go to Saint Anselm's, it's a private school out in the burbs. It's OK but it's very competitive, and I would like to know other types of kids. Everybody there seems to be the same—clones. But my parents want me to go there and get good grades so I can go to an Ivy League college. It's like if I don't get into Yale or Princeton, my life will be over. We will start traveling to colleges in the fall."

"What kind of activities do you do there?"

"I play the clarinet in the orchestra and I'm on the cross country and track teams."

"What events do you participate in?"

"The 400-meter, 800-meter, mile, and high jump."

"That's a lot. When I was your age, I did the 200 and the high jump. I did not like all of the tension at the start of a race so

I switched to the field events. But my favorite was the high jump—to me even though you only leave the ground for an instant, it was like flying."

"That's why I like it too. It's like you take off, fly over the bar, and then there's that moment that I love when you are weightless before you come back down to earth and land in the foam. It only lasts a split second but it's heavenly."

"I thought the 400 was the toughest race and I never wanted to do that. It's like an all-out sprint. Our best guy threw up after every race. Did you ever see Eric Liddell in the *Chariots of Fire* movie, when he won the 400 at the Paris Olympics?"

"Oh yes, I loved him and I love that movie! (she laughs) With his arms flailing like a windmill, he had the worst form imaginable but the best heart. That movie is what inspired me to run."

"So, do the executives help with the chores too?"

"No, they paid extra, but they do help set up the camp, mostly because they can't wait to sit and have their wine. The tall, thin one, Jim, is a nice guy. I like him. He is evidently the Human Resources executive for this, like, really big company. The short stocky bald one, Fred, is not that nice. He is evidently what they call the CFO, whatever that is. I must admit that he has loosened up a little though. Maybe he will be like a regular person by the end of the trip. Charlie is OK, but he seems somehow troubled. He needs to relax more."

"So, I don't know what it's like in high school anymore. Do you have a boyfriend?"

"No, I mostly hang out with my friends—guys and girls. I am so busy with school and activities outside of school that I don't have much free time. There is a boy I like though, Jimmy. He's on the cross-country team and does not seem to be as full of himself or as entitled as the other boys. He is on a scholarship and does not live in mansion-ville, but lives somewhere on the other side of town. We are friends, but he does not seem to think of me as more than that."

"Most boys are kind of stupid. I know I was. Most are not as emotionally mature as you girls. I can tell you are an attractive, intelligent, and caring young lady. You are still very young, but it won't be long until they realize who you are. You may have the opportunity to meet many boys before you find the right one."

"Thank you. You're nice!

12:   THE EXECUTIVES

We finished washing the remainder of the pots and returned to the group, who were gathered around the fire. As so often happens, the men and women were separated. Cheryl, Luka, Betty, and Jenny sat on one log gabbing away. Now that the trip was nearing its completion, it looked as if Luka greatly enjoyed being with other women and being able to relax. Paul and Charlie were sitting on rocks by the river still talking wine. Don, Fred, Jim, and Wes were standing near the fire, their lit faces glowing out of the darkness, conversing and periodically poking, rearranging, and tending to the fire--something, over the eons, guys seem instinctually drawn to do. After stowing our lightweight aluminum dishes away, I join them.

During a lull in the conversation, as we all were staring blankly at the fire, wanting to keep the conversation going, I ask Jim if he was an HR executive. He says, "Indeed I am."

I ask, "For what company?"

He replies, "SPV Enterprises."

"That's a pretty huge multinational, isn't it?"

Fred brashly interjects, "Yeah, we are at the 50-billion mark and still growing. Revenues are a little down this year, but after the reorg they will be up again and our stock options will be worth a fortune."

Jim looks disturbed. Evidently, he was not onboard with the layoffs. Endeavoring to change the subject, Jim asks me what I do.

"I was an app developer, but our company got sold to a mega, mega-sized corporation, so I'm unemployed and not a big fan of big business right now."

Charlie and Paul join us and we sit on logs perpendicular to each other facing the fire. Evidently in deference to Charlie's instructions, having tried to avoid the topic, for the first time on their trip, Jim and Fred start a heated debate about the upcoming cutbacks, Jim relating how much it cost to recruit and train the skilled engineers, who will be laid off. Fred is all about reducing costs, regardless of what it means to the future of the company. Looking intently, Charlie seems to enjoy getting the perspective on the matter from his two top execs and lets them go at it.

Wes, whose wife is an econ prof well-schooled in the topic interjects, "Seems like a shame that you guys shut down plants and lay people off, then send the jobs overseas, to China and the others. Do you ever think about the consequential damage done to those small communities, those loyal workers, and their families, to say nothing of the damage done to the economy? Many of those factory workers are now working at Walmart or other establishments for half of their previous wage with few if any benefits."

Charlie responds, "That weighs heavily on us."

"Yes, it does," Jim adds. "I have spent many a sleepless night thinking about those who have lost their livelihoods and their families too."

Fred adds, "That's what capitalism is all about though—the cream rising to the top, survival of the fittest and all. Here we are at the bottom of the Grand Canyon. Luka explained how all those colors on the walls signify changes in the earth's evolution. That's what happens in business. Why we're a force of evolution. Buy their company, before they buy yours—big fish that eats the smaller fish becomes bigger. It's what makes us stronger. Sure, some people have to adjust, but that's the way it's always been."

"But," Paul interjects, "Do you account for the societal costs of your decisions?"

"OK, so you are a wine maker up in Napa and therefore, you have to be a liberal, but what does your lovely wife do?"

Paul tells Fred that "Betty is one of you. She is a highly paid IT executive for a large firm, which is why we are concerned. She sees the big picture."

Upon hearing her name Betty enters the circle of light surrounding the fire and adds, "I have risen to the top because I have a good education, work hard and work a lot of hours, so I think I deserve more than an average salary."

"I agree whole heartedly with you Betty, you deserve more," Fred interjects. "Again, that's what the free market and the global market is all about. You earn more because you deserve more. Some schmo who wasn't bright enough to go to college and doesn't work hard earns much less."

"But the people at, say, McDonald's work hard too, and I think they deserve more. I can't justify myself making say 25 times more than they do."

"So, Fred, do you like their Big Macs?"

Fred, who was looking down to avoid the smoke temporarily blowing his way, lights up at the thought of the tasty burger, "I love Big Macs. I have to have at least one a week or I go into withdrawal. But if they raise their wages, they will lose jobs to automation. We need to cut back on all of this government interference and all that welfare stuff too, or the country is going to go broke. After all, free enterprise is what has made this country so great."

"I agree with you," Betty, her face radiantly lit by the fire, replies, catching Fred off guard and looking confused. "Even though it's not close to where we live, I have to stop at the Sonoma McDonald's a couple of times a week. I'm addicted too. I've gotten to know one of the servers there named George, who used to work at an electronics manufacturer until the plant was closed and the jobs were sent to China. He's a great guy and I really enjoy talking to him—he's always upbeat. George's wife has cancer and they have two kids. They can't afford the cancer treatments and even though they saved up some money, when his wife was working as a registered nurse, they are going broke and won't be able to afford the treatments any longer."

"George can't afford to feed his family on what McDonald's pays him. So, I thought I'd help him and his family apply for the earned income tax credit. At first, George was too proud to accept help, but was desperate to save his wife and feed his kids. So, I helped them with housing supplements, food stamps, and healthcare. It all amounted to an extra $15.00 an hour or $30,000 more a year, much more if you consider the cancer treatments."

After squatting down to turn a log over with a stick, as the flames burst out, Betty continues, "So, you don't have to pay much for that Big Mac, but it comes out of your taxes. In a sense, we are all supplementing McDonald's low wages. With what the government pays him, he now makes the equivalent of fifty-thousand-dollars a year, fifty-five-thousand if you adjust for the taxes he doesn't have to pay. Now they can get by. Without all the pressure, he and his wife can relax a little and his kids can see that they have a future."

"If you add it all up, in a sense McDonald's is receiving billions of dollars of corporate welfare, so they can pay their employees minimal wages and it's not just McDonalds. You maybe pay a quarter less for your Big Mac Meal, but you pay more than that in added taxes, especially in your tax bracket, Fred. Imagine if the tax on your meal was a dollar. You wouldn't like that would you. I sure wouldn't."

Fred responds, "But if they are paid more, McDonald's will automate more and they will lose their jobs."

"Automation is inescapable, but it's been going on for two-hundred years and still unemployment has been as low as 3.5%. During the pandemic, people ordered through their phone apps, but touch screen ordering has been around for three decades. More automation will happen, it's inevitable, but fast-food restaurants will still need people."

"Studies show that raising the wage is a stimulus to the economy and jobs. A Harvard study of a *Fortune 500* company like yours showed that raising factory workers wages by a dollar resulted in a 30% increase in productivity. Think about it, Fred, people like George spend nearly every dime they make, which multiplies throughout the economy and creates more jobs. Pay them more, the GDP goes up, more jobs are created. Instead of taking various governmental benefits, they contribute taxes."

———

Everyone—with the exception of Fred—looked at Betty admiringly. Jim smiles his perfect smile and pats her on the shoulder.

I refrain from joining the discussion, enjoying the spirited debate, but even though I had not favored raising the minimum wage before, Betty's arguments made a lot of sense to me. Having no time or interest in politics, at first, I felt that such a debate was out of place in our natural environment, but by now, since everyone seemed to enjoy it, I feel better about it. I go in to my pack and extract the plastic bottle of Drambuie. Then, I gather a bunch of the wine glasses between my fingers and to diffuse the discussion, pour a glass for everyone with Fred getting the first glass.

Ann, smiling, asks me if she could have some. "You know in Germany kids can drink beer and wine in bars at 14."

Feeling awkward, I respond, "I don't think your parents would allow that."

Cheryl says, "Maybe just a taste, to toast our successful voyage."

Addressing her parents, I say, "The Drambuie is only half the alcohol of whiskey, so I guess a little won't hurt." I pour about an ounce into a wine glass then tell Ann to warm her hands in the fire, then warm her glass with her hands and after it is warm, sniff and sip it slowly. She smells it, then sips it, and with a grin, says, "Oh my, this is really wonderful. Thank you, and thank you, Mom and Dad, for letting me try it. I promise I won't turn into an alcoholic or anything."

As I had hoped, sipping the Drambuie stifled the political discussion and both groups settled in for the night. I feel a little restless, so I pour the remainder of the liquor, shaking out the last drops into my wine glass and stroll as far as I can wander up stream, where the water is calm. There I sit on a boulder, take a sip of the sweet, amber liquid and look up at the whitewashed sky covered in luminous stars and constellations that even though I did not know their names, can make out their contours. Then I look out over the gurgling, peaceful, black river and take in a deep breath thinking that some of the water and the silt it carries may have originated in remote locals throughout Arizona, Colorado, Utah, New Mexico and maybe even Wyoming, imagining all the various terrains that encompassed— snow laden mountains, forested hills, sandy deserts, verdant fields, ranches sporting herds of cattle, creeks winding past picturesque towns or tributaries passing through mighty cities. These diverse elements from throughout the broad river's basin now flow past me. I stoop down, extend my arm and scoop up a handful wondering where all of it had been.

After I return to my peaceful perch, out of the darkness, Jenny suddenly appears and quietly sits next to me looking somewhat forlorn. I ask, "How is your relationship with Ahkam going." Ahkam was a medical student at the Sorbonne I had met in Paris, who should have graduated by now. They had carried on a long-distance relationship for a couple of years with her traveling from Western Germany, where she taught, to Paris on extended weekends, or he joining her on one of her excursions around Europe.

"He asked me to marry him."

"That's great! ...Did you accept?"

"Well not exactly. He planned to start his practice in Algeria and wanted me to meet his family first. So, we flew there for a week over spring break. His mother was lovely and very accepting, as were his sisters. I could tell they liked me and admired my independent lifestyle, but it's still a very male dominated society, where the women are treated as inferiors. Other than at meals, I did not interact with his father, brother, friends or cousins. I was told that, since I was a foreigner, I could walk around the town and bazaar without a burqa, but his sisters strongly recommended I wear one, so that I would not attract attention—it felt so demeaning, but oddly intriguing for it was as if I was invisible. As the week progressed, I came to enjoy the people and their warm hospitality, but thought if we moved there, I would lose myself."

"Rand, as you know I am used to being an independent American woman who has traveled all over the world, sometimes by myself. I love Ahkam dearly, and if we lived in Paris or Germany or any cosmopolitan city, I would have been happy. Still, I did not want to lose him. After we got back, I struggled with my decision—endlessly weighing the pros and cons, changing my mind daily.

Finally, I decided I couldn't go through with it. When I told him, he said he understood and said that is why he had me go with him to Algiers, to see if I could adjust to life there. That was two months ago and I'm still recovering from the break up."

"Oh Jen. I'm so sorry to hear that. I know how much Ahkam meant to you and how well you got along. He seemed so Parisian, so liberal. I would not have thought he would want to go back."

"That was part of his commitment—why his family funded his tuition. But he also felt that it was his calling—to serve his fellow Algerians. They desperately need more doctors there."

I put my arm around her shoulder and pulling her to me gave her a squeeze. As she looked sorrowfully into my eyes, tears streaming down her cheeks, she said, "I needed that. Thanks!"

"Geeze, I feel so badly for you. Have you thought about getting some counseling to help you through this?"

"Actually, I've been seeing a psychologist at the base. She's helping, but I realize it's going to take some time."

After sitting for a while, just being with each other, we walk along the rocks and beach back to the tarp. As it crunches, we lie down, put our down bags under our heads and settle in for the night.

13:   IN THE CAVE

After thinking about our trip to the bottom of the Canyon with Jenny, Pete, Betty and Wes, just as I am finally drifting off to sleep in my surprisingly comfortable sand bed, I hear the distant sounds of a helicopter. Hoping they are looking for me, I poke my head out of the tiny cave entrance and anticipate the pain of squeezing through that tiny hole again, but by then, the previously deafening thwapping sound is fading into the distance. I think It might circle around again, so I keep my ear to the hole, but the sound continues to get softer, until I can hear nothing other than the rushing water. Since darkness has settled into the deep fissure and it is too dangerous to fly, I know the copter will not return until the morning.

I wake in the middle of the night, reaching to press the nightlight on my digital watch but the glass is still too fogged up for me to make out the time. The watch is supposedly waterproof to 100 meters, so I hope it will eventually come back to life. It must be dawn, because I see a dim light in the cave. I poke my head out the hole to check, but it is still black night. Then I notice light emanating from the back of the cave. When I investigate around the wall, I see another opening where the light emanates from. There, I enter a large room where the walls are drenched in streaks of rainbow-colored fluorescence. Mesmerized I force myself to return to the cave's entrance and retrieve my knife.

With a twenty-five-foot ceiling, the room must be thirty-feet in circumference, shaped like a geodesic dome or more aptly a giant quartz geode for the top is covered in some kind of crystals, from which numerous rainbows emanate and I feel as if I am under a giant chandelier. I see hieroglyphics painted on the wall, and while I'm certainly no expert, these don't seem like the southwestern Indian cave drawings I had previously seen in New Mexico. Rather, they look almost Egyptian. Regardless, some mysterious tribe must have occupied the cave a long time ago—maybe a lost tribe.

While channel surfing a while back, I came across a series on the History Channel about ancient aliens that seemed too implausible to believe. Now, I wonder if they could have drawn these mysterious figures depicting large elongated-headed men with tiny bodies and something circular that could have been a spaceship. But I quickly dismiss the thought as being too fantastical. Looking around, I can see no other evidence that anyone had sheltered here—no animal bones, no signs of a fire. Perhaps it had been a religious site, or maybe just some teenagers.

At the opposite end, the room narrows to a passageway that extends downwards at a fairly steep angle. The further I walk, the warmer it becomes and after a while, I have to take off my t-shirt. Perhaps there is some kind of shaft that sucks in hot air from the desert on the Tonto Plateau above? It seems as if I'm heading away from the river now, but I can't be sure. I slip out the tiny compass on my multipurpose knife, so that I can discern the direction of the shaft, but the needle bounces erratically all over the dial, indicating some kind of severe magnetic disturbance.

When I toured the salt mines under Lake Erie, the first couple hundred or so feet were cool but by the time you descended to 2000 feet it was extremely warm. Maybe I was under the North Rim now, 7,000 feet below the surface and that's why it is so hot.

The fluorescence continues to light the way. The tunnel that had previously been very wide—a dozen or so feet—is narrowing and there are places where I have to duck my head or turn sidewise just to squeeze through the gradually narrowing rocks. I think about going back, yet feel compelled to see where this leads. Maybe it will pop out on the other side of the rapids, where I can swim across to the South Rim and reconnect with my companions. At least there are no side tunnels to get lost in. I do not really have claustrophobia, but being so closed in I'm getting anxious and feel a strong pull to just go back and wait for a passing raft. However, I know it is still too early and they probably wouldn't have launched yet.

The fluorescence fades into darkness but I still see a faint glow not far ahead. Proceeding further, crawling through a narrow passage, once on the other side, I unwittingly slide down about twenty feet on my side into a cavern where it flattens out, and then stops abruptly. The walls are lit in a yellowish, orange glow, it is extremely hot and I smell sulfur, so I put my t-shirt back on and lift up the base of it to cover my nose. There is a shaft, which after my previous nearly fatal experience falling off a cliff into the river, I cautiously go down on my knees to peer over the edge. Below, I see a fluorescent, hot golden-colored river flowing at a rapid pace—it must be lava.

I hadn't thought there were any volcanoes nearby, but then I remember that Mount Humphreys is volcanic and that Wes had said there was lava flowing here only a thousand years ago—a microsecond in geographic time. And after all, I am over a mile below the surface now, ensconced in a canyon of indigenous rock formed two billion years ago, when the earth's surface was alive with volcanic activity. This must be a narrow channel to the molten metal below—a plume, that's it, a plume. Feeling that I had solved the mystery and not wanting to smell the sulfur any longer, I carefully begin climbing back up the black cinder-laden chute I had previously slid down and crawl back through the passageway.

I breathe fresh air on the other side, and as I start to head back, I feel oddly off balance, though it seems that this is probably the result of the gas but somehow different. The phosphorescence becomes extremely white and the cave is suddenly as bright as day. I feel like I am being pulled back towards the chute—not by gravity but by some other mysterious force.

The only other time I had felt something similar had been in a forest above Napa Valley, where there was supposed to be some kind of magnetic abnormality caused by the density of metal below the surface. I couldn't believe it, but I actually feel it here, too.

This is a much more powerful magnetic pull, though. I struggle to walk back up the tunnel, but it pulls me more strongly now and I can hear an ever-stronger rushing roar from the lava flowing below. It pulls me down to my knees, and I lie flat on the ground to rest until it passes. I feel a tingling in my feet that moves up my entire body, up my legs, then to my midsection, my back, arms, shoulders, my face to the top of my head, where my hair stands on end. It feels like static electricity but envelopes my entire body, which feels as if I am being stretched with my feet now ten feet away from my head. With every ounce of my being, I try to maintain consciousness, but when I cannot hold on any longer, I pass out.

I have the strangest dream, almost like I'm on acid or some kind of exotic drug. Images start flashing before me. I can see the campfire and the people at Hermit Rest, then what I saw on Hermit Trail, but going backwards, as if on rewind, going ever faster. Then there's the view from the backseat of Paul's SUV, but I can't see anything out the window—it's flying by too fast, just a blur of greens and blues and tans. I see the view from my balcony looking over the bay, the railing, the patio, the bay itself, but none of the boats. They are going by too fast, as if they were just small insects whizzing by.

Instead of one image, now I see two, then three—one from the patio, one from my couch, and one from my office chair of the PC lit up before me, but nothing distinguishable on it. It's what my life has consisted of over the last three years. Other things quickly flicker by, but I can't make them out. Views from my other offices and apartments flash by ever more quickly.

Suddenly, the images begin to slow down, and I'm on the Pacific Coast Highway going backwards, first at 100 mph, then 50, then 20, then 5.

I think that this is what it's like when you die, when they say your life passes before you. It was, however, not similar to what I experienced while caught beneath the undercut rock in the rapids, and I did not feel as if I was dying now, but this was definitely a forbiddingly, unfamiliar state of mind.

14:   THE TRIP

Suddenly, somehow, I find myself on a hike with Dave and John, two younger backpacking buddies I had met and hiked with at Big Sur after graduating from college. We're heading for Big Sur beach. Unlike a dream, this feels real, as if I'm really there, back in time with them. I pinch myself and it hurts. At first, I am enjoying the journey. Cars, motorcycles and trucks wind around the curvaceous Pacific Coast Highway at what seems like 100 mph, but then they begin to slow and appear oddly as if moving in slow motion. That's kind of fun, I think. The two recent high school grads and I talk incessantly and play around as we begin walking down the dusty, dry beach road. I can taste its grit in my teeth. I think this is not bad, and kind of enjoy it.

The road to the beach is obscure, like a driveway hidden by foliage with no sign or indication of what might be found down the mysterious path. At first, we have a grand time. As we progress along the long, vegetation-laden, winding, narrow road, I start to lose control. Like an Impressionist painting, bushes and trees wave in front of my eyes, their colors vivid and blurred. Walking down the winding gravel and sand road, the numerous stones and ruts challenge both my sense of balance and my sense of direction. After a while, I lose all concept of time and space, as well as my awareness.

My sight is the first to leave me. The scene would normally appear weird, as the road constantly curves as it winds down towards the ocean—narrow, too narrow for two vehicles to pass without difficulty. Being inundated by lush hills and gullies, the foliage resembles a tropical jungle, everything covered in a mysterious, gray dust kicked up by the vehicles. The jungle's hills and trees, painted in vibrant colors, start to reel in S-like shapes, as if these are something out of a tropical Gauguin, Polynesian scene. I lose my depth perception so that it all looks as if it existed on one continuous plane, similar to those Gauguin paintings.

While my companions continue to talk to each other, I feel detached from my body and my senses, unable to focus on anything or anyone. I try to rejoin them, but am unable to do so. I can't seem to speak. I have a strange tunnel-like vision of the world, in which peripheral objects vanish, but I see what is in front of me clearer than ever. I have no attachment to my locomotion, rather feeling as if I am, with difficulty, gliding down the path bouncing from side to side, like a pinball hitting posts on a pinball machine that spring me forward. I have never had a dream remotely like this one before.

I think I will lose control of my mind, so I try to grasp onto something, anything. I keep going with no concept of time. I try to figure out where I am, but I'm so out of it that I can't seem to get control over myself. This has to be a nightmare, so I try to wake myself, but for the first time, I cannot.

I see a formidable and scary gate with a foreboding NO TRESPASSING sign. Three large Dobermans angrily bark and lunge at me from behind the gate; then they rush towards us, and I try to hide behind my friends, but in the next instant, the dogs are jumping on me. They are friendly, though. I pet them and we strangely relate on a previously unattained lower level. A remote, unseen voice calls them back, and we trundle onward. I mentally struggle to regain control, but only feel more and more lost.

In a rare open area on the tree-shrouded road where the sun shines hotly, I find myself remembering the twins, Jan and Judy, from college, who periodically tripped with their roommates when disgusted with men. The fact that they survived—their cherub-like faces, blue eyes, ivory white skin, black hair, perfect smiles, and cherry-red lips—gives me much needed hope to make it through this strange, scary unfamiliar ordeal. My sense of time vanishes, as does my sense of balance, sight, hearing, and kinesis. Events, places and time itself mix like a shuffled deck of cards. In one increment of time, I appear at the fearsome gate, and then I'm back at the dusty entrance to the beach road, and then I am further down the road at a place I had never been before. It feels like I'm on drugs, but I didn't take any drugs—*this has to be a nightmare*, I think to myself, *but how do I extricate myself from it? Wake up, wake up, please God, wake up!*

As we descend down the seemingly endless road, a sinister fog closes in, cool and moist on my skin. At first, the fog seems friendly, a welcome relief from the hot, steamy, dusty jungle I had passed through, then it seems fearsome and sinister, obscuring the scene as if it was erased by a giant white eraser.

The self—something still remains there. It walks on, but the rest of me vanishes, detaches, is barely there. I cling to the image of Jan/Judy for hope that somehow, I too might survive and somehow find my way back to reality and wake up.

The beach suddenly appears. There, weird Hindu-like people materialize in yellow robes out of a weird yellow, graffiti laden bus. How could a bus get down that narrow, winding, jungle road? We walk on the beach. There are some people on the beach. They are naked. I walk into a rock and drop my pack onto it. I go to the water, drawn to the crashing waves, conceding myself to whatever will happen there. Then mysteriously, I don't know how, I am out of the water—instantly transported back to the edge of the forest along the beach, as if I was a ball on a rubber band attached to a paddle.

While walking on the beach, I see dozens of insects buzzing by, that I had never seen before. I see hundreds of ants below traveling at high speeds over the stones, over the grains of tiny sand, as on an ant freeway during rush hour—fascinated by ants on their little, bitsy freeway, going somewhere important to ants—to ant-work in downtown, Antville maybe.

Dave and John are moving now, so I put my pack on my back, following them like ducks in a row climbing a hill. In the next instant, we sit on a bluff overlooking the ocean. I sit on grass woven into the sand. My friends sit down. I see a thousand flowing colors on the water. I see through John, see his face with purple veins that are translucent with blood flowing within them. Can't hear, can't see, just glimpses. Depth gone. Sense of place gone. I feel like Tommy in a rock opera—a deaf, dumb and blind kid.

Dave moves to some people. John follows Dave to the people. I not know where we go. I put on coat, put on pack. How I do that—wow? Follow John. Not able to tell if bumping him with pack. Is pack even on? I can't tell.

I am with the people now in a circle around a big fire in a different place. They smile and are friendly. I follow John. John follows Dave. I have no sense of balance, no connection to this world. I trip. I fall. I'm cold. I need a jacket. John shivering. I want to relate, but do not care.

People, fire, sit. John grabs stew, sit. Try look human like there, like a human being is present in me. Try getting it together. Look at ocean way out in the dark. Sit next John, next to Dave—shield self from people around fire. Unattached hand offers a can of beer, cannot take it, then take. Drink, but can't tell how much drank, if any. Think drink some, not sure. Not look at people—embarrassed by my dilapidated condition. Don't want them to see me like this.

Want look together for the people. Want look human. Do I have clothes on? I know I should have clothes on with people. How do I know clothes on?

Pressure of people is too much. Have to get away. Go into the black night. Walking is hard—going up a hill, stumbling.

———

The rest of my life flies by even faster than before with multiple concurrent screens, displaying views of my life during the day, during the evenings and during the weekends. It does not show my nights when I was sleeping—instead, it shows the places where I spent most of my waking time from my viewpoint, what I saw with my own eyes, on an oval screen encased in a golden lava color. I see my various classrooms flying by—my apartments, my summer jobs, my parent's home's rooms, and the playground where I spent much of my time playing ball. As the odd experience plays the images from my childhood, it goes by ever faster, then it all goes blank for what seems like eternity. All I see is a rainbow of colors in ever evolving mesmerizing geometric shapes, composed mostly of greens and blues, browns, then a brilliant white light. Then nothing and I presume I'm dead

15: WHERE'S RAND?

By the time Betty, Paul, and Wes had woken, the rafters had finished their breakfast and were packing up their camp into the raft. With cups of coffee in hand, they were saying goodbye to the group with whom they enjoyed sharing an evening.

Betty approaches Fred and says, "Fred, I'm sorry we got into all of that last night. I hope you didn't feel overwhelmed."

"Actually, Betty, I enjoyed the stimulating debate and even though I don't fully agree, appreciated hearing the other side." They hug.

Wes notices that Rand is not there. Jenny says, "He went off by himself on a hike. Wanted to clear his head."

By late morning, Jenny realizes something is wrong, "It's been two hours since Rand left. I'm worried something may have happened to him. He knew we planned to leave this morning and he would not have been gone this long."

The rest of the group seems worried too, Wes saying, "We should search for him. Which way did he go, Jen?" Jenny points down the beach and the three hikers follow her to where they find long oblong cupped impressions in the sand.

Wes compares the impressions to his own footsteps and seeing that they are larger says, "These look like Rand, the Sasquatch's, footprints all right."

They follow the sandy steps to the end of the narrowing beach where the footsteps suddenly vanish, leaving the group wondering if he might have entered the water, but there are no clothes on the beach and the first ripples of the rapids have already commenced—"not a likely spot to go for a swim," Wes says.

Paul interjects, "I think he must have gone up this cut to the plateau above. Why don't you girls go back to camp, up the trail, and join us above? Wes and I will climb up and see if we can see any signs of him."

Both Wes and Paul are excellent rock climbers, and by pressing their backs up against one wall with their feet against the opposite wall, they quickly ascend. Half way up they find bits of dirt and rocks that had been dislodged, showing fresh, darker earth where Rand had likely been. Paul comments, "These spots will be dried and sun-bleached by tomorrow. He must have come this way."

They meet the girls at the top and the four of them scan the area for signs of their missing friend. Betty tells the group, "Come here! I think I see some fresh tracks in the dirt along this path." Wes compares the dusty tracks to his own and says, "These are the right size and those cleats look like they came from his boots when I followed him. It looks like there have not been any other tracks this way for days"

Paul looks worried and says to Jenny, who seems stressed, "Jenny, why don't you go back to the camp and wait for Rand to return, while the three of us follow his trail?"

Periodically, the trail vanishes over rocks, but they are able to spread out and repeatedly pick it up. Keeping her eyes on the ground, Betty says, "It looks like he is following the river downstream."

"Yes, it does," Paul agrees.

The trail vanishes at a large rock and after quite a while, they are unable to pick it up again.

"We can't find another trace of him," Wes worriedly says. "I wonder what happened."

"It seems as if he has been following the river," speculates Paul. "We can hear rapids ahead. Maybe he went over there." They look repeatedly near the edge but find nothing.

"Here it looks like a rock recently slipped into the canyon," Wes says, "It looks as if there was a recent rock slide, because the dirt is darker than the rest. Maybe he went over the edge."

As she carefully looks over the steep cliff, Betty responds, "That would make sense and it's possible he may have hit that pool below, which looks like it might be deep enough for him to survive. Otherwise, we would see his body below. Couldn't have handled that."

Looking down, Wes says, "Look, here in the dirt that slid off I see half of a boot print. It matches Rand's cleat marks."

Paul picks up a large rock and hefts it over the edge. When it hits the pool with a kerplunk, it causes a large, cannonball splash and descends far below the surface. "It seems he might have survived if he fell over there."

"We can't get down there, but we can't see any signs of him either," says Betty. "If he survived the fall and landed in the pool, he would not have been able to swim to the other side before being swept up in the rapids."

Wes suggests, "Let's go down river until we pass the rapids and see if we can see any signs of him there."

There another creek meanders to the river. Because of its steep canyon walls, they have to proceed perpendicularly to the river for quite a distance, then climb down a wall into the creek and up another wall. There they look down on the river on the other side of the rapids.

Paul yells, "Rand!" At the top of their lungs, they all repeatedly yell, "Rand… Rand… Rand…" The echo bouncing of the inner canyon walls, and as it fades, they listen intently for any meek reply.

After going hoarse, they lose hope.

As their emotions and worry grows, Wes says, "Because of that steep canyon wall ahead, we won't be able to go any further. Let's go back to camp and try to get some help. Maybe he's back there with Jenny by now."

When they return, only Jenny is there, crestfallen that they have not found him, saying, "What are we going to do now?"

Wes suggests, "It seems we have two choices. Either we go back to the trailhead at Hermit Rest or we go on to the Bright Angel Camp to seek help."

Wes, looking at the topo map, chimes in saying, "Both are fairly far, but climbing up out of the canyon during the heat of the day will be difficult—much more difficult than the trip in. I suggest we go on to Bright Angel as we had originally planned. They should have a phone to the rim where they might have information about his whereabouts. If not, they can mount a search."

Jenny, still looking very stressed, says, "There is one other possibility. We could wait here until a raft comes by. Luka had a SAT phone for emergencies. I would think the other boats would have one too."

Clearly concerned, Betty interjects, "But we don't know when a boat might arrive if at all. There was no raft the first night we were here. I think we should go on to Bright Angel."

They broke camp and split up Rand's packs contents between them, with Wes tying the frame to his pack.

As they head out, Betty suggests, "If you guys could handle my pack, I could run up ahead and be there in half the time."

Paul says with encouragement, "Yeah, she's run a marathon. She could do it. It may be the difference between life and death."

They hurriedly split her contents up too. Since they had lightened their packs before they started, even though the consolidated packs were heavy, these were not overwhelmingly so. Wes extracts the topo map from the pocket in his backpack flap, studies it, and then shows Betty the best route to follow. She will start on the Hermit trail and then will follow the Tonto path. There were several places where she will have to navigate around the creeks. Because of the smaller canyons formed by the creeks, she will be running in and out of the mini-canyons, more than doubling the straight-line distance. Most of the terrain follows the flat plateau, but there are also steep switchbacks and climbs along the way.

16:   BETTY TO THE RESCUE

Betty runs off at a controlled pace, with only her frame and Paul's water contraption, from which she can drink from the long plastic straw along the way without having to stop at all.

Feeling like the first marathon runner in Ancient Greece, Betty runs with purpose and fierce determination, always keeping her eyes on the trail, careful not to slip on the gravel or a rock. After an hour in the heat her gut aches, but she continues. Rather than lightweight shoes made for running, she is equipped with sturdy boots. Rather than a paved street or cushy track, she runs on a twisting and, at times, treacherous trail that periodically winds up or down in switchbacks hugging cliff walls. Rather than being able to obtain water from planned periodic rest stops, she carries her own on her back. Rather than running in moderate temperatures, she runs in unbearable heat that is climbing over a tortuous 110°.

Rather than running toward a time or to win a medal, she runs to save a friend's life, thinking that he may lie injured somewhere alongside the river, with broken bones, bleeding out, and that every minute she can save might be the difference between his life or death. Still, she knows she has to pace herself. If she runs too fast, she might fall and break that vital rhythm, something that for a runner is crucial; something that once lost, in terms of internal resources, is expensive to regain.

The sun bakes the tan dirt trail so that she sees its refracted, undulating waves rising off the desert floor. Fortunately, she can take a sip from the water flask on her back through the straw held firmly below her neck. Since it is already past midday, rather than the sun being in her face, at least it is at her back. "I guess that's something to be thankful for," she thinks to herself. She runs with the light pitter-patter steps of a tall, thin, firm female, as if she were a gazelle designed for running.

As she navigates a double twist on a steep switchback, overlooking the steep canyon below with a rocky stream at the bottom, her foot falls on loose, shale rock. When she pushes off with her toe, the rock slides backwards, providing no support to her flailing right leg. She stumbles, tries to regain her balance, but falls hard on her right knee, then her right hip, just before she plunges into the canyon below. She dusts herself off and bounces up. Seeing the gash in her knee bleeding profusely, she takes off the bandana around her neck and wraps the knee, hoping that in this intense heat, it will dry quickly.

She needs to start running again, which at first with the knee stinging and offering little support is difficult, so she trots with a limp. Having lost her momentum, her muscles stiffen, requiring more effort with each step. In pain, she thinks she should stop and walk but knows she cannot—her friend's life depends upon her. She keeps going. After ten minutes or so, her muscles begin to loosen up and her knee begins to operate smoothly again; she has acquired her rhythm once more. In the intense, dry heat she does not really sweat, rather the liquid in her system immediately evaporates leaving a chalky, white residue of salt on her skin.

Not designed for long runs, her firm leather boots began to rub her toes and she can feel newly forming blisters nagging her. She wishes she still had the moleskin in her pack to fix these, but she ignores the pain—she has to. Paul has it and she can apply it later.

After a couple of hours, on the other side of a creek, running slowly up the switchbacks of a steep canyon wall that provides little purchase, sometimes sliding backwards, she hits the wall. Her runner's high has evaporated. Her legs ache. Her lungs ache. Her knee cries out in pain. She sweats profusely. Her water is nearly gone and under the intense afternoon, heat, she feels as if she is about to faint. Instead of drinking the last of the water, she sprays it on the buff from her blood-caked knee. She ties it around her neck to help cool her overheated body.

Now, with each step part of her wants to stop and walk, but she refuses to do so. She has to go on. Similar to a mantra, she continuously tells herself, *Just a little farther! Just a little farther!* Finally, the path widens, and she thinks she must have finally connected with the Bright Angel Trail.

Exhausted, taking smaller steps, going ever slower, she navigates around a corner and, struggling to climb up a rise, she sees the mighty Colorado below and the beautiful, silvery, suspension bridge. With renewed energy she sprints down to the bridge and daintily pings across the broad river.

On the north side of the canyon, she expects to find the longed-for ranger station–her goal, but she soon discovers that it is not there and she must continue her run to reach it—how far she does not know, but she can't stop now.

Continuing her light, rhythmic steps, she runs along the river, along a sandy path surrounded by rocks, then passes through an area ensconced in scrub brush and cacti. She passes through another stretch with small trees that are surprisingly green—a stunning contrast to the desert she just traversed. Then, as the exaltation of reaching the bridge subsides and exhaustion rises again, her lungs struggling to breathe in the hot air, Betty mercifully enters a cooler, narrow passage along the river with taller green trees and a rock-free, well-trodden path to run on.

She finally enters a campground where tall green grasses and trees surround large campsites. To the left, she sees a young man setting up a tent. Sucking in air, she awkwardly asks, "How," puff, puff, "far to," puff, puff, "ranger...station."

In an Aussie accent he replies, "Its only about a quar mile, mum."

With her goal within reach, similar to a runner's final spurt, she sprints across a bridge, crossing the Bright Angel Creek and soon enters a broad valley. Running through a glade of trees on a broad path marked by stones with green grass on either side—an oasis in contrast to the hot, sticky, treacherous, burning desert she had just jogged through. She passes a group of hikers who look calm and refreshed–what a contrast to her bedraggled self. They look at her as if she is crazy for running with a pack on such a hot day–if they only knew how far she had come.

To her right, the ranger station suddenly materializes—a small brown-boarded cabin with numerous cacti at its entrance. Being nearly delirious, she had almost passed it by.

———

Ranger Brad Kirby, a middle-aged, tan man with short dark hair, brown eyes, square face, and square-dimpled jaw sits at his desk working on yet another boring report. He wears a stiffly-starched tan shirt, bearing the green National Park Service's insignia and Army-green shorts. Even in the depths of the inner canyon, it is an unusually hot day and the constantly-running air conditioner unit sticking out of the wall struggles to keep up with the extreme heat. He has a hard time keeping his eyes open, but fortunately, his shift will soon end–if he can just endure the overwhelming boredom a little longer. Hearing the minute hand of the large, governmental clock tick the slow-moving minutes away, fighting the urge to nod off, continuously jerking himself awake, he greatly anticipates when the long hand will reach the top, he will be free and can have that ice cold beer he's been dreaming of.

Nothing even remotely noteworthy had occurred that day. The mule train had arrived from the south rim on schedule a couple of hours earlier, and there were several medium-sized groups that headed for the campground or the cabins above.

A thin girl walks into the office. Most of those who had completed the trek down the trail were exhausted and looked bedraggled, but gasping for breath, sweating profusely she looks as if she will soon faint. The hair under her cap is matted with sweat and stuck to her forehead. Her long shapely legs are dirty and her right shin is covered in dried blood. He immediately comes to attention and offers her a chair.

"May I help you?" he says with a concerned half-grimace, half-smile.

She struggles to get her breath and in the sudden coolness of the air conditioning, struggles to stay conscious, "Our friend," puff, puff, "is lost in the," puff, puff, "canyon!" she exasperates.

Alarmed, he replies, "Where did this happen?"

Still gasping, "Down river from Hermit's Rapids Camp." She continues to sharply inhale between each phrase. "We think he...fell into the river... near the rapids," she struggles to take in air, "and was sucked downstream., ...we searched for him and called for him but could not find him." With an anguished pleading face – "Please, please help!"

"What's his name?"

"Rand."

"What does Rand look like?"

After taking several gulps from the cup, as her breath comes back to her and she becomes steadier, "Thank you. He's about six foot two or three with brown hair and brown eyes and a moustache. He's in his mid-thirties, thin, strong, and a good swimmer."

"Could you give me a better idea of how this happened?"

"Well, he left early this morning on a hike by himself. After a couple of hours, we were worried and went to search for him. We found signs on the beach at Hermits Rapids and above on the Tonto, where we found his footprints in the dirt. We saw a rock that had been recently dislodged and assumed that he might have fallen into the river."

"What was he last seen wearing?"

"Tan cargo shorts with a white t-shirt that has a turquoise Caribbean diving scene on it and probably his Indians hat."

"How did you get here?"

"I ran all the way."

Realizing what a difficult journey that it would be on such a hot day, Brad looked at her in awe. Offering her another cup of water from the gurgling water cooler, he says, "All the way from Hermits Rest! That's not easy to do during the peak heat of such a hot day."

"I had to! He's a good friend of ours. Please help. Please!"

The ranger immediately calls Emergency Rescue at Grand Canyon Village. The dispatcher turns him over to Tom Carling, the director of Canyon Rescue. Like a Nordic Brad Pitt, Tom is tall with short sun-bleached, blond hair, a button nose, dimpled chin, high cheekbones, and piercing blue eyes. An expert in wilderness rescue, Tom had literally written the book on the subject and operates a wilderness rescue school in the mountains of Washington State during the off-season. Ranger Kirby relays all of the salient facts to Tom.

It is getting late in the day and Tom realizes he did not have much time to conduct an operation before the canyon becomes totally dark, and you would not want to risk flying a helicopter in the depths of the canyon in the dark. He calls for a chopper, but both are on rescue missions. After a copter returns from the hospital with a patient who had a broken leg while climbing, it gasses up. Tom jumps on board and they whoosh off to the Hermits camp.

Once there, they circle around the Hermits area in an ever-expanding arc, looking for signs of the lost hiker. Down nearly a mile in the inner gorge, the darkness descends fast. Tom orders the pilot to ascend to where it is lighter, and they search the Tonto along the river from above. He has telescopic, 20/10 vision and years of experience searching for lost survivors, but he cannot see any signs of Rand. It soon becomes too dark to safely continue the operation, so they have to return to the base. Once back, one by one he calls his highly experienced rescue crew that he personally trained, telling them to join him on a conference call, where he recaps what has happened thus far and tells them to collect their equipment and to be ready to go. Tom tells them to be get some sleep and be at their stations by five the next morning, when they will resume the rescue.

17:   RAFTERS TO THE RESCUE

Tom Carling remembered that his wife, Luka, was conducting a rafting expedition and by that time should have been in the Hermit's area by now. The river was fast and if they made good time, she might be passing through that section and may have seen signs of Rand. If they had not yet passed through there, they could look for him tomorrow and possibly pick him up. Luka helped him operate the wilderness rescue school in Washington and was an expert at finding and caring for lost souls. He calls her on the SAT phone.

Luka and her group had set up camp and were in the process of preparing their dinner when the seldom-heard SAT phone rang out. Grabbing the phone and pushing the receive button, she hears Tom's voice, "Hello, honey? We have a lost person report from the gorge. Where are you?"

Luka replies, "We are only one day away from completing the trip. Where was he lost?"

"Down river from Hermits Camp."

"We were just there this morning. Who's lost?"

"His name is Rand Roberts," Tom tells her.

In shock, Luka responds faintly, "Oh no, I met him last night. He's a really nice guy. He ate dinner with us and breakfast this morning. I saw him walk down the beach before we set off."

"Did you see any sign of him after that?"

"I didn't," Luka considers, "but I will ask the crew, just to be sure."

Luka puts down the phone, gathers the group around, and asks if anyone had seen Rand after they shoved off.

They all shake their heads except for Ann, who seems embarrassed and does not want to respond. After a while, as they continue to eat their dinner, she feels she has to say something. Eventually she gathers her courage and stands up boldly to announce, "I saw Rand."

"Where, Ann?" Luka asks with concern.

"I just saw him for a split second. We were in the middle of a rapid and as the boat turned, I saw him waving at us." She starts to cry, "I did not know he was in trouble. I just thought he was saying goodbye—wishing us well. I feel just awful that I did not say anything then or realize he was in trouble."

"What did he look like?" Luka inquired, desperate for every detail that might lead to clues about his whereabouts or situation.

"He was not smiling. I only saw him for a tenth of a second before the boat jerked around and I had to paddle. I smiled at him but felt somehow uneasy. He was yelling and waving his arms, but I could not hear him over the rapids. I'm not sure. It was so fast and I saw him through the spray of the rapids. I just thought he was waving goodbye."

"Do you remember any more? Did he look distressed?"

Through tears, Ann tries to concentrate and conjure an image of him, "He might have had blood on his forehead, but it might have been dirt." She sobs uncontrollably, "I feel horrible... I really liked him. I hope they can find him."

Luka continues her investigation, "Whereabouts was this?"

"Well, it was after we set off and before lunch. Probably the third or fourth rapids we encountered, they all kind of run together."

Luka relays the information to Tom over the SAT phone. She comforts Ann saying, "You have given us great information that just might save his life." Ann sniffles and cracks a half-smile.

Then Luka presents an idea to her party, "We are less than a day away from our pickup point. If you are willing, I would like to go there tonight and participate in the rescue tomorrow. I would not ask this of every group but you are all exceptional, one of my best, who have melded into a well-coordinated crew. We will be going down-river at night, but with the light of the moon, we should have no problems."

Charlie, looking into the faces of each of them, says, "We are with you, my captain."

Fred agrees, "You may not think so, but I liked Rand and would want to participate in it anyway I could. Besides, I don't think any of us will be able to sleep tonight knowing he is in trouble trying to survive somewhere along the river, and that we might be able to help."

With determined faces, the rest nod their approval of the plan. Standing up in a circle, sticking their hands in together, following Luka's prompting, they all shout, "Let's save Rand!" Ann's tears turn in into tears of joy, as both of her parents put their hands on her shoulders and her little brother hugs her—something that would never have happened back home in the mansion. They had spent nearly a week sleeping within feet of each other and their parents, spending nearly every minute of every day in each other's company, eating the same food, rowing together as a team, experiencing the same thrills and solitude. For the first time in years, she felt they were a family again.

Luka calls Tom and tells him their plan, saying, "Tom, I feel I know Rand, like him, and have to help to rescue him. Call the helicopter and have them pick me up first thing tomorrow morning."

He thinks this is too much for her to do, but from her voice can sense how determined she is and knows better than to argue with her. He calls the helicopter pilot and has him promise to be there at dawn. They will copter her to Hermit's, where she will join the rescue crew. There is no one any better than she is on river rescues and he is glad to have her involved.

Working as a team, they quickly wash the pots and dishes and pack up the camp, then enter the raft and push off. Doctor Don offers to take the tiller oar that controls the direction of the raft, "Let me do this so you can rest up for tomorrow." Normally Luka would never let a guest take the tiller, but she rarely had a guest as skilled as Don, and she had let him take the tiller through a rapid earlier that day.

During a slow spell on the river, Doctor Thompson asks his family to move toward the back, gather around, and hold hands. There he tells them, "I feel I have been neglecting you guys. This trip has made me realize that you are the most important part of my life. I promise to spend more time with you and cut back on all the conferences." Ann is elated, and with a broad smile and a trembling lower lip, she begins crying once again.

Charlie had a purpose to fulfill on this trip that was rapidly coming to a close. Back at their spacious, verdant headquarters, Jim and Fred were constantly bickering. He encouraged divergent opinions from his executive staff, but this quarrelling had grown too severe and far too personal and he also needed teamwork. He signed them up for the trip hoping that they would overcome their differences. If not, he was going to replace one of them, likely Fred because he was the most belligerent. During the trip, the two had the opportunity to spend a lot of time talking to each other and understand the dynamics between financial and human capital, realizing that both were equally important to the success of the business.

He tells them, "I am so pleased to see that the two of you have worked out your differences and are rowing together as a team. I appreciate that you have saved me from taking drastic action. Both of you and your departments are critical to our future success. Thank you!"

Jim tells his boss, "Thanks, Chief, I really did not want to go on this trip, but it has been a life changing event for me, one that I will remember for the rest of my life."

"For me too," Fred adds. "I have not had much contact with nature—never really cared much for it. Actually, I avoid it as much as I can. The first two days of this trip were pure torture. But as we flowed down the river, the austere beauty and solitude of it all really got to me. My life has been one surrounded by numbers and screens. As I relentlessly climbed the corporate ladder, my wife and children had become mere accessories to my career."

Smiling at Doctor Thomas and his wife, he continued, "Similar to Doctor Don, I appreciate my family more than ever and miss them terribly. Seeing how the Thompsons interact and how much they enjoy each other's company has made me miss my family more than ever. Unfortunately for you, Chief, in the future I do not plan to work seventy or eighty hours a week and want us to move out of our penthouse and acquire a house in the suburbs with some land, flowers, trees, and even neighbors—something my wife and kids have wanted for a long time, but I resisted. I just hope it's not too late."

Charlie smiles broadly and looks into his eyes, placing his hand on his shoulder and says, "Fred, that's wonderful!"

18:   LOOKING FOR RAND

Drained from the intense heat, Paul, Jenny, and Wes cross over the silvery bridge suspended on thick wire cables over the rushing, tan Colorado. The bridge sways and rattles with a hollow tinny sound upon each step. They arrive three hours after Betty's arduous run. By that time, shadows shade the entire canyon, the sun lighting only the highest pinnacles of the North Rim. Clouds to the west are cast in deepening shades of purples, reds, and brilliant iridescent violets. Tired from their long-forced ordeal, carrying their friends' packs and goods, the three are exhausted but eager to hear if Rand had been found.

Anxious to see them and greatly relieved that they finally are here, Betty, who has been perched on a rock overlooking the bridge, runs and hugs each of them fervently and immediately gives them the news, "They haven't found him yet but have mounted a search. A helicopter is flying through the canyon looking for signs of him right now."

She grabs the two extra empty packs from Paul and Wes, saying, "I checked us into a cabin. Let's go there so you can drop off your packs." They are enchanted by the continuously greening, cool passage along the creek—a welcome relief from the grueling desert conditions they just endured.

Jenny looks as if she is about to cry, so Betty takes her pack and puts it on her back, exchanging it for one of the empty packs. Betty puts her arm around her friend's shoulder saying, "Don't worry Jen, Rand is strong and resourceful. If anyone can survive, it's him."

They had planned to camp out at the campground, but given the circumstances, the sympathetic ranger procured a rare cabin for them. The rustic stone cabin has two small bedrooms, including one with bunk beds, as well as a small living room and a tiny 50's vintage bathroom—not the least bit fancy but luxurious compared to going in the great outdoors. After a brief respite lying down and rehydrating, they feel they have to do something, so they go back to the ranger station to see if there were any new developments. There, the second shift ranger says they had found no signs yet, and that the helicopter was unable to conduct much of a search once it got dark. He informed them of the plan for tomorrow—to mount a full-scale rescue first thing in the morning.

In rapid-fire, Paul asks, "How can we help? What can we do? We want to join the search!"

The considerate ranger replies, "There is nothing you can do yet. The search party will be composed of experienced rescuers and EMT personnel. The helicopter will scan the inner gorge and Tonto for him, while a raft will search along the river."

Unwilling to accept this, Wes tells the ranger, "I really want to join the search. I am an experienced rafter who has taken on class eight rapids. Plus, I may be able to help identify signs of him. I insist that I join the rescue mission!"

The ranger makes a call to Tom at the headquarters and after hanging up says, "I'm surprised, but he will allow it. He has a lot of respect for someone who has done eights. Be here at 5:00 A.M. tomorrow morning. There is nothing more you can do tonight. As soon as I have any news, I will let you know."

Jenny tells the ranger, "We are in cabin five. Please tell us as soon as anything happens. As you can see, we are desperate for news." The dispirited group talks it over and decides to go to the canteen for dinner, informing the ranger of their whereabouts.

They make it to the canteen just before it closes. Sitting at one of the long tables, even after burning through thousands of calories on their journey, they do not have much of an appetite and they have no desire to talk to the others seated at the table. They think they need to eat so they can be ready to help and therefore glumly eat their generous portions of spaghetti, meatballs, Caesar salad and Italian bread.

A nice-looking young man at the table with long blond hair and blue eyes asks in a German accent, "Did you come from the North or South Rim?"

Paul, who is usually the first to start a conversation, replies, "Sorry man, we just lost our friend in the canyon and aren't in much of a mood for conversation."

He and Jenny carry on a subdued conversation in German, which helps her change her focus from worrying about Rand.

While finishing their meal, the ranger comes in and tells them that someone named Ann remembered seeing Rand near one of the rapids, which grants them a measure of relief and hope.

———

Wes and Ranger Brad set off from the Bright Angel trail while it is still dark in a two-man, extended red kayak. Because they speed down the river and are not hiking around the offshoot canyons, they make it to Hermits Rest in a little over an hour, where the search raft brought in by helicopter had deployed. Brad compliments Wes on his kayaking skill.

Wes responds, "You're good too. That was fun. I wish we had done it under better circumstances. I am so worried about my buddy. We have to find him!"

Downriver, Luka's raft arrives at the pickup point before dawn and it is not long until they hear the distinctive sound of helicopter blades slashing through the air. They all hug and shout above the helicopter's roar, thank Luka profusely, saying that she has helped change their lives. As they became verklempt, the copter whisks her away.

As light begins to kiss the top striations of the North Rim, Luka arrives at Hermits Rest where the rescue raft is soon loaded and occupied. As the experienced crew floats down river, according to the assigned target areas, they relentlessly scan the shores on both sides, paying particular attention to the northern shore where Ann had spotted Rand the day before. Wes identifies the spot where the rock had fallen into the water—where Rand's tracks had vanished and they assumed he had fallen in.

Following her instincts, after the third rapids Luka directs them to pull over to a small cut in the canyon's tall wall before a fourth rapid commences. When she jumps off, she sees signs of what could be footprints in the sand. She also sees drops of blood. They all repeatedly scream out, **"Rand!"** but no one answers. Wes sees the distinctive boot prints that he says are Rand's.

They go over the area with a fine-toothed comb, but find no more evidence. Wes sees some branches from a bush on the ground that looks as if it were sawed, knowing that Rand always carried that absurdly large Swiss Army Knife buttoned up in his cargo shorts. He soon discovers the cave.

Luka crawls through the small opening and sees a long flat impression in the sand suggesting someone had slept there overnight. With flashlights, they search to the back of the cave. Upon finding a side tunnel, they traverse it and slide down a chute with an odd sulfur smell but discover no more signs of Rand. Finally, they determine that he must have left the area and entered the water. Thinking he might have swum upstream, gunning the raft's mighty dual outboard motors, they travel upstream carefully searching for signs of the lost soul. Finding no evidence, they continue to search downriver repeatedly calling out his name through an electrified megaphone, as "Rand... Rand...Rand," spookily echoes through the canyon.

In the meantime, Tom, along with Rand's friend, Ranger Fred, circle the gorge in a helicopter. With Tom hanging on one side of the helicopter and Fred on the other, they scan the rocks and muddy waters below looking for any possible signs of him. They go up and down the river for miles, paying particular attention to the first rapids after Hermits Rest, but they find nothing. Over the SAT phone, Luka tells Tom what she had discovered on the beach and in the cave, so they search the river and its banks even more fervently. The working theory is that Rand had reentered the water and tried to swim to the other side, but had been swept up into the rapids. They search the rocks and the small sandy beaches for signs of him or his body. Then they search the trails leading out of the gorge, but to no avail. It seems as if he had vanished into thin air.

——

After seeing Wes off, other than an early breakfast and silent lunch at the canteen, Paul, Betty and Jenny spend the day camped out near the ranger station, pacing the worn, dusty trail and repeatedly entering the airconditioned ranger station, asking if there is any news. The ranger on duty tells them, "Sorry guys they haven't found him yet, but I'm sure they will, just relax. There isn't anything you can do."

After several fraught hours, by midafternoon, Paul, seeing Jenny with a worried look on her face, continuously wringing her hands and praying, suggests, "Why don't we take a walk to get some fresh air." They walk by the old rustic cabins of Phantom Ranch, then along the Kaibab Trail beside gurgling Bright Angel Creek. The familiar rhythm of their steps on the tan pathway encased in white stones eases their psyches—the silence relieves their anxiety—being together in the familiar pattern, one walking behind the other, provides a measure of comfort.

They hike perhaps a mile up until the broad, green valley closes in. As they venture into the unfamiliar box canyon, the ramparts of its high, darkened western wall provide stark contrast to the blindingly, brilliant eastern pinnacles, set against an azure blue canvas.

Finally, Betty breaks the silence saying, "There was nothing like this on our southern trek. In some ways it's even more spectacular. Somehow, I expected it would be a mirror image of Hermit trail, just higher, but it's not like that at all."

Mesmerized by the grandeur, a portion of each of them want to continue onward in their meditative, familiar rhythm: to escape the horror of what lay below, until Jenny says, "Hey guys, it's getting steep up here, let's head back. Thanks for suggesting it though, Paul. I feel better. As Rand said, being in nature makes you feel better. It has a healing quality, doesn't it?"

"Yes, it does Jen, Paul responds."

As the shadows in the canyon grow longer, back at the Ranger's office, they become progressively more desperate, knowing that the rescue party may have to call off the search soon and Rand will have to spend another night alone in the canyon. Finally, they hear a helicopter coming closer, its noise deafening as it sinks to its prescribed landing site, blowing up dust as it plucks down.

With the blades still rotating, Wes and Ranger Kirby jump out and duck down before the copter revs its engine back up and takes off, rumpling their shirts and blowing Wes's cap off.

Wes sees his friends distressed, pleading faces and looking drained and gaunt himself from the long day on the river, running rapids, recaps the rescue operation, "We went a few miles past our camp—three rapids past Hermit's, where we found signs of him in a cave. Looked like he had slept there last night." Jenny's face lights up with hope.

"But he was no longer there," causing her face to resume its downtrodden continence. "They think he tried to swim for it and had gotten swept up by the rapids. We searched and searched, but couldn't see another sign of him."

"Are you sure you didn't miss something Wes?" Paul exclaims.

"We had a special raft with an extremely powerful motor, so we searched for miles downstream. Luka was with us. She's an expert at wilderness rescue and she had several of us scanning every inch of the banks and canyon walls. There were four of us on each side of the raft—one searched the water, the second the banks of the river, the third halfway up, and the fourth up to the rim of the Tonto looking for any sign of him, such as footsteps in the sand, or broken grasses on trails or loosened dirt. The last two guys on each side had binoculars, so they could focus in on any possible clue. We went miles downstream—further than the current would have gone by that time. We found some clothing, goggles, and discarded containers washed up on the beaches, but nothing that was Rand's."

Paul turns toward Ranger Kirby and asks, "Will you be searching tomorrow, Brad?"

With a reassuring smile, Brad answers, "Of course we will. We will search the beaches and sides of the canyons and the trails. We have alerted everyone downstream to keep an eye out for him. Some of the rangers will go down the trails looking for signs, to see if he started hiking out. There will be a couple of helicopters searching from above in a prescribed search pattern. They know the terrain better than anyone."

"Can we help? It's torture just sitting here."

"Sorry guys, but it's in the hands of Tom Carling and his crew. They are professionals with a plan, experienced in wilderness rescue. I don't think there is anyone better than Tom in all of America, maybe the world. As you know, the canyon can be very dangerous, especially in the summer. We wouldn't want anyone else succumbing to the treacherous heat and dangers down here. That would make our job that much more difficult. I'll tell you what you can do though—you can notify his friends, his family and his work. We will let you use one of the lines in the station. Let them know he's lost, but that we are doing all we can to find him."

Betty asks, "We pray you find him tomorrow, but if you don't, how long will the rescue go on?"

"The limit is five days—so four more days."

"As you know, reservations here at Bright Angel are extremely difficult to acquire. It takes a year to get them and even then, it's iffy, but I've pulled some strings and have made arrangements with the powers that be to have you stay in your cabin until that time."

———

At the end of the five days, Paul, Betty, Wes and Jenny are required to leave. To avoid the intense heat at the bottom of the canyon, they leave before dawn, gradually ascending the south rim as the sun rises. As if they were on the Bataan death march, they hike somberly up the broad Bright Angel trail. Even though they have to go back home and back to work, they refuse to give up hope that Rand with his smiling face and up-beat personality will somehow, someday, magically appear--he's just too resilient not to.

When they reach the rim, drained from the persistent climb, perspiring profusely, they walk to the Bright Angel Lodge. It is likely full, but they hope there might be a cancellation.

In the refreshingly cool lobby, they take off their packs and stretch. After straitening her hair with her fingers and mounting a bright smile, stepping up to the front desk, bringing out her American Express gold card, Betty, in a hopeful voice, asks if there are any rooms available.

The thin, male clerk with swept back, blond hair responds, "Sorry ma'am, we have been full for weeks."

"Are you sure there are no cancellations?" Paul queries.

"Sorry sir, we are full."

As they walk away, heads down, shoulders slumping and dejected, the clerk calls out, "Just a minute. What are your names?"

"Paul and Betty Stowe, Wes Ford and Jenny..,"

Before he says Jenny's last name, the clerk chimes in, "Oh yes, Tom Carling called a while ago and told our manager about your friend, asking that we provide you a room. I hope they find him. Will a suite be okay? It has a spectacular view overlooking the canyon."

"Why yes, thank you so much."

In the spacious room, finally within cellphone range, Paul calls the winery. After hanging up, he tells them, "They said there is a blight on the vines, I have to get back."

Disappointedly, Jenny says, "Can't they handle it?"

"Sorry Jen, but I'm the chief winemaker. It's my responsibility and I know what to do. If we don't treat it right away, we could lose most of this year's crop, and it may spread to other nearby wineries."

Wouldn't your owner, that techy multi-billionaire, allow you to stay here? I wouldn't think losing some grapes is much of a deal to him," she replies with attitude.

"He's a good guy and under these circumstances, he probably would, but it's my responsibility Jen. It's what I do."

Wes turns on his phone for the first time in over a week and calls home, but gets no answer. He starts looking at the myriad of texts and learns from his sister-in-law that his wife had been taken to the hospital last night. She had fainted, they did not know the cause, and were running tests. He frantically makes reservations to fly from Phoenix back home.

Paul volunteers to drive him back, but Wes insists on hopping on a tour bus that the desk clerk arranged for him. "I know you guys want to continue looking for Rand. I can't take you away from that. Wish I could stay and help, but I have to get back. The bus leaves in a ½ hour."

They say a mournful goodbye, each hugging Wes deeply. After what they have experienced, the girls and even the guys have tears welling in their eyes—Jenny is crying profusely using gobs of Kleenex to soak up the tears. After he loads his backpack into the bus's lower storage compartment, as he hops on the bus, Wes says, "Even if it's insignificant, let me know everything that happens—text me regularly guys. That's one of the advantages of our technology. Even though I won't be here, I will be with you in spirit and praying for Rand's safe return."

Following restorative showers and brief naps, they head out to the lodge's steak restaurant. Unconcerned about calories after their demanding hike and prolonged stay in extreme temperatures with no appetites, in which now skinny Jenny lost fifteen pounds, they have a delicious four-course meal, where they hatch a plan.

———

When they return from their sumptuous early dinner, Betty goes into the attached bedroom and starts calling helicopter companies she found and researched online. When she reenters the room, she asks Paul to join her in the hallway where he says, "What's up? Did you find someone?"

"I called five different companies. Two were totally booked. From what I learned, the going rate is $1500 an hour. One wanted fifteen-thousand dollars for the day."

"Ouch!" Paul involuntarily responds.

"The fourth wanted $12,000, which I was about to reserve, because he said it could be gone at any minute. So, I tried one more. This time I told him about our plight and pleaded our case. It's a nearby company with, from what I gathered, one helicopter and one pilot. Because he had a cancellation, he said he would only charge us $9,000."

"Only!"

"I know, but we have to do it."

"Yes"

"So, I signed us up."

"That's good, Bett."

Not disclosing how much it cost, when they break the news to Jenny, she insists that she contribute at least a third.

Betty says, "Look, dear I work for a company, who pays me an absurd amount of money, which at times I feel guilty about, but since it's a financial firm that is all about money and my systems are worth so much to them, I accept it. This is a chance to do something worthwhile with it."

"But Rand is my friend,t too. I have to contribute."

"How about you buy a wonderful dinner tomorrow night."

"Done—the sky's the limit, at El Tovar then!"

———

According to plan, they are at the airport before the sun rises, when the sky is still black to the west, sporting strands of dark blue clouds against a gradually lighting grey background in the east. Dew kisses newly cut blades of grass, the fresh smell of pine filling the moist air. The heliport has a dozen helicopters occupying round circles, like sleeping birds resting in their nests, soon to wake and fly off. Their pilot welcomes them onboard, providing each with headphones. Before they take off, he runs through the safety procedures. The seats are very comfortable and each of them has a panoramic, nearly floor to ceiling, view.

Glad that all she had was coffee and a croissant, Jenny's stomach is in her throat. As the noise ratches up and they take off, to her, it doesn't seem that they are flying, but rather that the ground is falling away from them. She tells herself, *Be strong girl, this isn't about you, It's about Rand—have courage!*

The reason they leave so early is to hit a couple of key camps along the river before the rafters or hikers set off for the day. At the first camp, a few miles downstream from Rand's cave, where kayaks are piled up along the shore, the sleeping group is angry at the loud intrusion. When Paul explains their purpose, they sympathize, but say they have not seen any signs of Rand. They promise to keep an eye open for clues along their journey though.

They fly slowly along the river, as close to the flow as possible, constantly scanning the terrain for any signs of Rand, picturing his tan cargo shorts, blue Indian's cap and Caribbean t-shirt in their minds. They set down on another beach just as two large rafts are about to enter the water. There, no one has seen him either, but the guides promise to call on their SAT phone if they see anything.

After a long morning, their eyes blurry from constantly peering out to the muddy reddish-brown water and the varied canyon walls that progressively change color as the sun rises, pilot Sam suggests they stop at the Supai village for lunch. Paul and Betty did not eat anything for breakfast and are famished, so they agree.

After flying over rocky, desert-dry, red-brown, canyonlands, up tributary creeks with walls reminiscent of enclosed Manhattan streets bordered by skyscrapers, and not seeing any sign of civilization for hours, they are surprised to see a verdant village in the middle of nowhere. As they descend into the valley, like scrolling in on Google Earth, they see a few dozen small homes and scores of green trees. A helicopter has already taken the spot, but fortunately there is another pad to the right to land. While the blades wind down, the three, get out and stretch their legs. On the other side of the fence, they see dozens of hikers in shorts with packs—oddly mostly women. The three hand out flyers that Betty had designed and printed at the lodge's business center, to all the packers, who had the same ruffled appearance they had modeled yesterday. The flyer has a handsome picture of Rand, a brief description of what had happened and their contact cell numbers with a giant heading, "LOST IN THE CANYON", and subtitle—"Please Help!"

Sam leads them to the other side of the patchy grass square surrounding the pads into what he calls the Havasupai Café, where Betty passes out more flyers and asks the attendant if she can leave a pile on the counter, which the attendant graciously agrees to. At the counter, Sam orders a burrito, Paul a super burger, Betty a bean burger and Jenny a club sandwich. For the tables, they get a couple of orders of onion rings and fries. Sam leads them outside to an enclosed patio, where there is a spectacular view of red rocks that resemble twenty-story, apartment buildings with chimneys, but are much more grand.

As he sips his refreshing coke that never tasted better, Paul asks Sam, "What is this place?"

"It's the Havasupai village, which has been here for centuries, probably over a thousand years. They are called the blue-green water people."

"Why are there so many backpackers around?"

"There are several magnificent falls down the creek, which is what draws them, like bees to nectar—it's kind of a heavy, spiritual place. Have you noticed that there are no vehicles? Everything has to be packed in on mules or flown in on helicopters. What we are eating came in that way. The helicopters actually drop supplies in like I did in Iraq, dangling huge bags twenty yards below them. Some of the people you see out there are waiting for a helicopter to fly them back to the road. They hike in, then fly out."

"There's also a lodge nearby with decent rooms. I know you have a purpose for being here, but the falls are something you have to see. We will go that way on the way out to the canyon."

As she grabs an onion ring, Jenny exclaims, "This is such an interesting place. Who would have ever thought it existed in the middle of nowhere?"

Sam is a swarthy guy with a slight belly hanging out over his pants, speckled black hair, a robust, full mustache and thick, wrinkled, dark-tan skin from living in the dry climate that makes it difficult to discern his age. With his Western accent, deep voice, swagger, attitude, and intricately decorated leather boots, he seems more like a cowboy than a pilot."

Intrigued, Betty asks him, "With the four stripes on your epaulettes, starched white shirt, and airline cap (that doesn't match his demeanor), I notice you have on a captain's uniform. Is that something most of the helicopter pilots wear?"

Seeming taken by Betty's striking appearance, he replies, "No ma'am. This is my American Airlines uniform. I had to have a bunch of these, so I wear them—why not get some use out o' 'em. I was a pilot for American for fifteen years, until the pandemic hit, when they laid us off. Not that I blame them much, cause nobody was a flyin' then anyway. That's when I started flyin' here bouts."

Thinking about all the challenging flying and landings he performed in the canyon, worried about his qualifications, Paul inquires, "You flew fixed wing jets and then went to copters. Was that difficult to adjust to?"

"Not at all. Let me go back a bit though. My dad was a crop duster and I learned ta fly when I was twelve. I was a dustin' crops over in the Poston and Ripley by the time I was fourteen. That's down the Colorado 'bout 200 miles as the crow flies. At eighteen, I joined the Air Force and wanted to be a fighter pilot, but had to have a college degree, so they had me flyin' C 130s in Afghanistan. Man, compared to my little duster, those were monsters—more like drivin' a battleship. I left after four years, tried a year of college. My grades were okay, but missed flyin', so I signed up as a Marine helicopter pilot In Iraq. After that, I started flyin' commercial jets."

"Thanks for your service, Sam."

"Yes thanks!" Jenny and Betty added simultaneously.

Sam queries, "Let me ask you a question? Ya know the rescue service did a thorough job a searchin', for your friend. Why did you decide to go out on this here mission?

Looking at Betty who has a deferral look, Paul takes on the question, "We realize they did a great job and are grateful to them. But after just sitting for so long, we had to do something. We just couldn't give up. Rand meant too much to us, and we felt so bad. We thought that, knowing him so well, and knowing what he looks like, and what he is capable of, we might somehow luck out and find him."

Jenny adds, "We know it's a million to one shot, but we had to try. We would never forgive ourselves if we didn't." Taking her last bite, "We should get back to it."

"Yes ma'am", Sam adds, "They will get mad if I keep that pad occupied too long anyways. Believe it or not there is quite a bit of traffic here. Let me ask you one last question before we go... What is Rand like? Psychologically speakin', what is he likely to do."

Betty responds, "Excellent question, Sam. Well, he's tall, about six foot three or so. He plays a lot of sports, so he's pretty strong and athletic, capable and resourceful."

Jenny adds, "He's also a pretty bright guy and an experienced wilderness hiker. They concluded that he probably made a swim for it, but even though he is a strong swimmer, if he was injured, which he must have been to be that far downstream and through all those rapids, he's too smart to risk that."

Paul continues, "We figure he would not take unnecessary risks. Without water, he would not risk hiking out or going along the Tonto. We think he would have stayed put until a raft came along, unless he had a better plan, like using a log to float downstream. In either case, we theorize he would be near the river, at the junction of a creek where there is fresh water."

"All right, that gives me a good idea of where to fly. We'll concentrate on the areas near the beaches and the lower parts of the tributary canyons, where there's water. You likely have noticed that the beaches are where the creeks join the river, which is also where rapids start. It's a logical place for him to stop before encountering another rapid. These are like the rest stops on a turnpike back east."

Before they take off, they stop at the ranger's station, talk to the Native American who mans the office. They are aware that Rand has been lost, have heard of no sign of him, but promise to keep an eye out. Betty hands him a stack of flyers and asks him to give it to campers as they register. She also posts a flyer on the bulletin board. Outside she finds a cute Indian boy of about ten and asks him if he will pass them out at the campground. He agrees and she gives him a twenty, which causes the cute little guy to smile broadly.

On the flight down Havasupai Creek back to the Colorado, one by one, Sam circles above each of the falls they pass, hovers up close and explains each one. Initially, they experience Fifty Feet Falls, which has strands of fairy-like water that look like the delicate lace of a wedding train trailing a bride. Little Navajo Falls resembles a smaller version of Niagara Falls.

Over her microphone, Betty articulates, "Look at that gorgeous water. It, it's turquoise—like the Caribbean. That's why they are called the blue green water people isn't it?"

"Yes," Sam replies, "These waters are sacred to 'em—take it as their responsibility to keep it pure—why there's no gas spewing vehic-les allowed."

Havasu Falls has a high, single stream of white water shooting out of the rocks similar to a mega-sized shower that splashes into the transparent, turquoise waters below.

Next, they fly over Tigabo Supai Falls that has a series of short falls cascading downward that resemble layers of icy blue wedding cake with white icing bordered by soapy, golden accents.

Enchanted by the uniquely beautiful sights they've seen, they next encounter the even more amazing, gigantic Mooney Fall—the people below looking like tiny ants frolicking on the pure white sand beach, leading into the iridescent blue-green pool, surrounded by deep rust-red rocks that rise far above, flowing down to the captivating pool. Sam slants the copter and steers towards the mighty vertical torrent, turning abruptly at the last second then ascending to the plateau above—WOW!

Reenergized from the uniquely spectacular views provided by Sam, the group resumes their quest, flying slowly down river searching for any sign of Rand.

After about an hour, Sam notices they are running low on fuel and peels off to Vegas to refuel, promising to resume the search up river. On the way back, they stop at Temple Bar Marina and South Cove Marina on the Eastern portion of Lake Mead, where they hand flyers out to everyone they see and post one on the bulletin board. In the sweltering heat, the summer boating season is in full force with an armada of boats out on the lake, children and adults frolicking in the cooling water, the sounds of joy echoing throughout the broad, long beach. Paul thinks that on such a hot day it would be refreshing to join in the fun, but immediately reminds himself of their mission.

On the way back Jenny comments, "It's a shame Wes isn't with us. He really would love all the various stunning geological formations we've seen. Would have understood what it all means. It's like we are in some kind of surrealistic Dali world, or a scene from some bizarre planet in Star Wars."

Sam exclaims, "We are nearing Supai Havasupai creek, where we went for lunch and the end of our journey guys. Sorry we have not seen any sign of your friend. When I cut off to Supai, there was a section we skipped over. If you like, we can search that section or just head home."

Disappointedly, Paul says, "We've come this far, might as well complete the job. Then we can feel we did all we could."

Sitting on the right side, as they pass one of the myriad of side canyons, Betty exclaims, "I see something down there in the water. Turn back Sam! Turn back!"

Sam explains, "That's Matkatamiba Canyon. It's very narrow. I won't be able to fly in there."

Paul asks, "Can you set down on the beach over there?"

"Sorry Paul, that's too narrow and too slanted."

"How about if you get close to the ground and I jump out."

"I can do that, but you've got to be careful. There isn't another pilot that plies the canyon that would let a passenger do that maneuver. Jenny, behind your seat is a rope ladder, hook one side onto the bar near the door and throw it out. Paul, I'll get low enough so you can jump down, then use the rope ladder to climb back in."

Paul jumps out and walks up stream. What he sees is unbelievable, looking like stacks of rust-red and brown soapy piles ofpaper in the extremely narrow canyon, each sheet two or three inches high—*must be paper for giants'* he thinks. Further up, he sees white, yellow and greyish-blue reams of rock-paper that approach the sky. He catches a glimpse of something, blue and red cascading over a fall, then twisting and turning and swirling as it slowly ventures along the creek. Feeling hopeful, he thinks, *That looks like Rand's Indians cap*.

His heart races in anticipation as he skips along some stones until he meets the approaching cap. He steps into the sparkling, gurgling water and gripping it as it slides by, picks it up—water dripping off the brim. When he examines it, he realizes it has the Chicago Cub's "C", not the Indian's old Wahoo. Walking down the creek disappointed he looks across the river to the tall cliffs above that have gigantic rock formations that resemble huge, sun-whitened faces of Indians with headdresses, a sphinx, and figures that could occupy Mount Rushmore.

When he shows the girls and Sam the hat, they are disheartened. Sam consequently makes a beeline for Grand Canyon Village.

Paul and Betty leave the next morning for Napa, promising to stop at the Las Vegas police department to check on the remote possibility someone might have found him and to file a missing person report. Jenny stays in Flagstaff for as long as she can, calling Tom Carling and Ranger Kirby daily. Paul and Betty and Wes Facetime her multiple times a day. She stays for three more days until she has to return to Germany for the summer term she contracted for.

Before she flies home, she Zooms with them on her stopover in New York's Kennedy Airport. "I will be boarding in a few minutes, but wanted to say goodbye to you guys while I'm still on US soil."

Paul says, "Hey Jen, we have to stay in touch, which we can do even if you are in Germany thanks to today's tech."

"I know. I will. I promise."

"We all feel bad for losing Rand, Jen," Paul adds.

Jenny emotionally replies, "I believe in my heart he is still alive; I feel it as strongly as I feel anything. There's something down there. I felt it. Something that somehow saved him."

Paul had been worried about his dear longtime friend—that she was having a hard time accepting the reality that Rand was dead, and that she would not be able to move on, until Betty says, "I feel the same as Jen. I know he's still alive and will show up sometime with that same irresistible smile. Goodbye Jenny, love you dear."

"Love you too Bett, and you Paul, and you too Wes."

Paul says, "Bye Jen, have a good trip."

Wes says, "Love ya kiddo, lookin' forward to when we get to see you again. I think there is still a chance he is alive too. Maybe he got knocked out, lost his memory and is wondering around Vegas."

As Jenny boards the plane, she feels verklempt—not the adventure she had imagined.

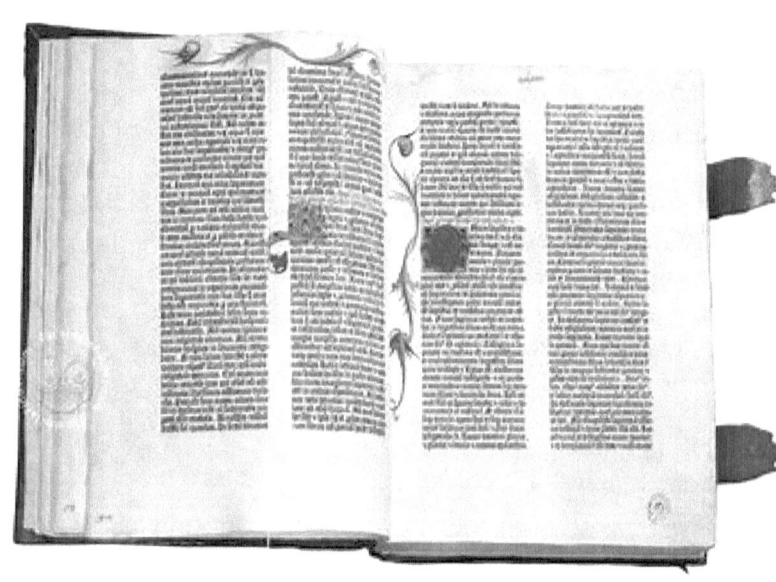

SECTION TWO

19:   WHERE AM I?

When I wake from my strange nightmare, I am no longer at the beach in Big Sur. Regaining consciousness resembles climbing out of a deep all-enveloping grave. I feel as if I am a rock receding into the ground, a rock that is hard to pry out, a rock that over time the earth has reclaimed and grown over—like Rip Van Winkle, who, covered in vines and moss, woke after being asleep for decades. When I am finally able to command my eyes to open, all I see is blackness. I think I am in my apartment but even on the darkest night, the myriad of LEDs from my devices emit their red, or blue, or `green points of light. As if I had been stretched, churned and tumbled in a washer machine, my entire body feels discombobulated. Then, it gradually dawns on me that I am in a cave at the bottom of the canyon. As if I were waiting for my PC to fire up, the operating system that commands my body is slow to respond. Slowly, eventually, I am able to instruct my body to roll over, push up with my good arm, sit, get to my knees, onto all fours and with difficulty, shaking like a leaf in the wind, stand up.

———

In the cool, damp pure blackness, I find my way to an irregular wall and with my left-hand fingering along it, carefully, inch by inch, stumble along an uneven floor. I remember I have my cell phone and find it secured in my right buttoned pocket of my cargo shorts, but it's hot to the touch. Earlier, after surviving the rapids, I discovered the phone, but it would not respond. I had placed it on the sand in the sun to dry. Now, I push the on-button, hoping that it will come to life, but it refuses to do so. Still hot from my ordeal, I take the protective cover off and wave it in the black air to cool it off, then push the button again.

When I hear the familiar jingle and see the welcome screen, I feel a huge sense of relief. I press the flashlight app, Illuminating a broad tunnel in front of me. I do not know which way to go but think I should head upwards. Around a bend, I see a faint light in the distance. In a broad cavern now, I look at the walls and see more hieroglyphics, much more elaborate and denser than I had seen in the other section of the cave. At the other end of the cavern, I see a beam of yellowish light. With difficulty I crawl through a small hole out into the daylight where I can no longer see the mighty river or hear the anticipated rapids and everything looks oddly green and smells totally different. Unlike the dry desert smell of the plateau, or the wet, humid river, it smells clean and fresh with a whiff of flowers or sweet berries and the earthy fragrance of decaying leaves. My body aches all over, even more than the dings I acquired in the rapids--it's a deeper, more all-enveloping pain. Before I can catch myself, my knees buckle and I pass out.

When I wake, I can barely move. Every muscle in my body hurts, and I have a burning thirst. I can hear the faint tinkle of running water. I pull myself forward with my arms, kneeling and continuously falling flat, worming my way towards the sound. I have never been this thirsty, and I know if I cannot reach that water, I will perish. In a half-hour, I have gone no more than forty-feet till I reach the trickle no more than a few inches wide. I check and fortunately, my hat still sits atop my head, which I apply to scoop up water and drink—so good, so good as it coolly passes through my dry lips, down my parched throat into my empty welcoming stomach. Hat-full after hat-full I drink, consuming probably a gallon of the restoring liquid.

The only other time I was this thirsty was when I worked at the grocery store as a teen and the store manager relied on me to burn all of the boxes and crates over the busiest weekend of the year, during July 4th. With fifteen-foot flames leaping out of the huge incinerator, I had to time my throws–jumping forward and tossing a crate into the flaming dragon that instantly consumed it as it spit out its intense flames. With temperatures over 110, sweat dripping through my required white shirt I accumulated a fierce thirst. Afterwards, I attached myself to the drinking fountain in the break room for five minutes consuming perhaps a gallon of liquid. That was the only other time I was this thirsty or drank this much. Whatever happened to me, similar to the intense incinerator, must have drained my system of fluids.

Again, I feel faint. What is this? This is ridiculous. Not again. No, this will not happen! My knees buckle and bam, I'm out.

Previously it had been around high noon. Now it is black and in the middle of the night. I push the button on my now clear watch that reveals that it is 4:00 AM, June 30th, three days later. Have I been passed out that long? How can that be? How long was I dreaming that weird dream? Wow!

When dawn comes, somewhat replenished from the water, every muscle still aching, I rise to my feet and, similar to an arthritic old man, stumble step after step. Ahead I see a long, wide, black stick and stoop down to grab it and I feel faint again. Fighting to stay conscious, I sit and inhale air until I feel more stable. Weakly, I stumble to my feet, grab the stick, and use it as a crutch. As the sky becomes lighter, I notice my legs are dark. It being early in the summer, having spent so much time in my office, I had not spent any time in the sun other than on the sand at Hermit's where I applied copious amounts of the highest UV sunscreen. I wondered how they could be so tan. So are my arms and chest, even beneath my underwear, which has never been tan—all deeply tan, the tannest I have ever been.

My mind becomes a little clearer, and I wonder where I am. It is too green to be on the desert floor at the bottom of the Canyon. I must be on the North Rim? How could I have gotten here? It's hilly? There were no real hills on the South Rim?

Were there hills on the North Rim? I thought it had a conifer forest, but these are all non-indigenous trees—maples, oaks, beeches that I did not think grew in Arizona. Maybe I am still dreaming, but I hurt too much.

I knew from being lost on a previous backpacking experience that water flows downhill into creeks and streams and eventually into rivers that will flow into the Canyon, which can't be that far away. If I follow that trickle, it should lead to a stream and I should be able to eventually find a road that will lead me to the North Rim Village, where hopefully I will reunite with my Jenny, my Paul and Betty, and my Wes. But how did I get up here? Did the plume shoot me up akin to the last scene in "Jules Vern's Journey to the Center of the Earth?" But if I was in the molten lava, I would be dead, wouldn't I? This was all too much for my overly analytical mind to digest, especially in my dilapidated condition.

I feel exhausted, lie on my back and fall asleep. Famished and still very weak when I wake, I have to find something to eat. From watching all of those survivor shows, I remember that grubs are a good source of protein. I turn over a log and there they are, feasting on the wood. I see several white ones that look similar to the ones on those shows, only smaller. I watch it squirming in my fingers, thinking that I could not possibly eat one and get it down. Then I realize it is necessary for me to survive, and since they managed to survive this way on those shows, I grab one, pull its head off, pop it into my mouth, and immediately swallow it without chewing. With a woody, dirty, slimy taste, it's awful. Since I do not immediately throw up or wretch too much, I do the same with a couple more of the little critters, washing them down with a hat-full of water, thanking them for their sacrifice to my survival.

I begin limping, slowly following the trickle of water toward a little creek, where I hear the rhythmic sound of hoofs on a trail maybe a quarter of a mile away. I hobble down a gradual, unobstructed hill covered in tan, red and brown leaves, shaded by old-growth, thick, black-trunked trees. By the time I limp to the trail, I can hear a horse whinny in the distance. My heart is racing. I yell, "HELP! repeatedly" No one comes. Exhausted from the exertion, I lie down and immediately fall asleep.

———

I awake to see the beautiful pale face of a woman with blue eyes and long, reddish-blond hair and rosy cheeks. She seems pleasantly surprised to see me, as if I have risen from the dead or something. With a brilliant smile, she asks me in a deep brogue what my name is.

"Rand," I manage to reply.

"Where da ye come from, Mister Rand?" she asks cheerfully.

When I reply, "From the South Rim," she looks at me suspiciously.

Then she asks me, "No, what shire do ye come from?" But I'm not sure what a shire is.

"I am from San Francisco."

She looks at me strangely and says, "I ner heard of that place afore." Then she feeds me a kind of chicken soup and a hunk of soda bread, which I rapidly devour.

An older man with a square face, dimpled chin and similar features to the woman—including those same piercing blue eyes enters the room. "Good ta see yer awake, laddie. We were afraid you might have left us for heav'ns gate."

Then he speaks to the young lady, asking her if I'd said anything yet, and she repeats my answers, then he looks at me with a puzzled expression and says, "San Francisco, ye say? I don know any San Francisco anywheres near here. Where that be? Spain?"

Growing frustrated with this ruse, I say, "It's in California."

"I think he be still daft," the man continues. "He's na from here bouts, sounds English but not like any Englisher I er heard a fore. His skin is too dark to be from England. That painting on his shirt looks like tis some wheres to the south. It has what I know to be the palm trees that I saw grows in Spain when I be a sailor. He must be from Spain or maybe Portugal, which explains his strange English accent. Maybe Californa is part of Spain, like Castile? I'll fetch the doctor back. You tend to him."

The pretty girl brings another bowl of soup and another big hunk of bread, and then she says, "I see ya have a fine appetite. Tha be a good sign."

"What is your name?"

"I be Gwendolyn. Gwendolyn Marie McCarron. Who be you?"

"Rand, Rand Roberts. Nice to meet you." I extend my hand. She takes it and curtsies with an impish, embarrassed smile.

When my nurse leaves, I realize that I'm in a fluffy feather bed covered in a handmade quilt. There's not much in the room other than a small basic side table with a picture of a woman, a tall armoire, and a crucifix with a scapula with yew branches around it, where there would normally be palms. The low, dark, wood-beamed ceiling has off-white plaster between the beams, as do the walls. There's a small window with glass panes set in a wooden frame—single panes that seem irregularly-shaped and rippled. The dark wooden plank door that I would have to duck under has a latch rather than a door handle, which I find odd. I try to sit up, but cannot, since every muscle still hurts too much, though, thankfully, not as much as before. If I don't move, I don't hurt. I look at my watch and see that another two days have slipped by, something my mind cannot fathom.

I think I must be in some kind of quaint bed and breakfast near the North Rim. There were so many foreign tourists in the Canyon, and evidently these people are from Ireland or Scotland, or maybe some remote part of England. They must have stumbled upon me, rescued me, and taken me to a quaint cabin on the North Rim. I don't really know what I think, because I am a little ditzy still and am having a difficult time making out what is real and what is part of that weird dream. I am still affected by my previous experience, which seems so real and yet so unfamiliar and so depleting. Perhaps the pretty girl is part of the dream, too, and I am still dreaming.

A short man with long mutton-chop sideburns, a white beard but no mustache, a red face, blue eyes, and a pug nose in a tweed jacket enters the room and examines me, asking, "How da ye feel," again in that brogue.

"I feel weak and still a little sore, but other than that, I'm fine. Do my friends know I'm here?"

"Who might they be?"

"Paul and Betty Stowe, Jenny Jacobs, and Wes Ford."

"I ha not seen 'em, lad."

"Has my rescue been reported to the authorities?"

"The constable knows ye be here."

Confused and still muddled, before I can form any other questions in my blurred mind, unable to keep my eyes open any longer, I nod off.

———

Gwendolyn wakes me to feed me again, saying, "Since you look much better, the doctor said ye can have more substantial food." She begins feeding me a delicious stew filled with carrots, onions, celery and lamb.

Eating ravenously with the wooden spoon, I ask for another bowl, to which she smiles and says, "Tis good ta see ye have recovered yer appetite."

When she returns to retrieve the bowl, I ask her "How did I get here?"

"I was a walkin' don the lane when I spies this lump in the bushes. I thought ye be dead, but I stooped down and could feel yer breath on me palm. I ran back and fetched me da and Seamus, who brought the cart and brought ye back 'ere. Ya looked near death's door, and we thought ya would na last the night, but the doc says ye was a strong young lad, and ye might just make it, but not ta get me 'opes up. Fer days, ye was in and out of it, talken like a daft man bout all manner of crazy thins, but mostly just sleepin."

I ask as calmly as possible where exactly I am.

She explains, "You're in me da's house, the house of Michael Mc Carron."

"Where is that?" I ask.

"Why, you're in Bunkillarny, don ye know?"

"Where's Bunkillarny?" "Is it near the Canyon?"

"It be near the Swilly."

"Is that in Arizona?"

"No, you must think yer still in that Californa," becoming more frustrated and red with each question, Gwendolyn continues. "Da thought that were from Spain. Are ye from Spain?" she adds with a quizzical expression.

"No, I'm from America."

"America?"

"What country is this?" I demand.

"Eireann," she says matter-of-factly in a huffy voice.

"Ireland," I repeat slowly, unable to comprehend what she's telling me.

"Yes, Eireann, don ya know, up north near the Swilly. Scotland is just cross the waters."

I freeze, and Gwendolyn, having had enough of our confusing conversation, abruptly leaves the room. Confounded by what I've been saying, she looks back over her shoulder with a scowl that makes me squirm. I can hear her talking to her father outside the door. "He's still daft, da."

"At least he's recovering, though."

I think that I must still be sick, or dreaming, for there's no way I can be in Eireann or Ireland, near the sea, near Scotland.

This must be some kind of joke my friends are playing on me. I can see Paul and Wes perpetrating such a ruse, but, given my beaten-up condition, Betty and Jenny would think it too cruel.

It takes another two days before I can sit up by myself and walk across the creaky oaken floor to the window where I had heard people talking, horses clomping, carts bumping along and wagons passing, but oddly no car engines. Other than the rhythmic sound of some nearby machine, there are no mechanical sounds at all. My goal over that time has been to prove to myself that I am indeed on the North Rim and not in Ireland. *I can't be in Ireland, that's impossible.* Once I make it to the small window, to the left, brightly lit in yellow sunlight, I see a dirt street, a few quaint storefronts, people, horses, and carts passing by. Immediately in front of me is a small cottage with a thatched roof. I can also hear a flowing river that must not be too far away to the right.

I think I must be in some kind of recreation village, such as 18th-century Colonial Williamsburg in Virginia, or late 19th-century Newport, where people dress in period costumes and assume their period-based character's roles, refusing to admit that anything related to modern times exists. Once, when touring the classic late 19th-century Breakers Mansion in Newport with Jenny, I asked one of the period-dressed guests to take a picture of us with my iPhone. He refused to admit that such a device could possibly exist and would not take the shot. They must be playing a part, I think to myself.

When I look to the right, under a bright sun and blue sky with only wispy clouds, I can see farmland rising and green hills in the distance with tiny thatched stone cottages, which could not possibly be part of the Canyon. I think once again that I must still be dreaming, and I hobble back to bed.

Gwendolyn comes in regularly, clearing the chamber pot, feeding me, and talking to me— since there is no TV, a much welcome diversion. Evidently, I occupy her bed, but she says she sleeps in the attic above now, where her sisters had been. Apparently, they were both married to brawny lads and had wee ones. Thin and statuesque, with creamy skin and a turned-up nose sprinkled with freckles, she has a bright, endearing smile that lights up the room. She holds herself very erect with her chin held high and well balanced, as if she were a model or an aspiring actress.

I've formed the vague impression that she thinks of me as an animal, such as a dog, a cat, or a bird that she had rescued and nursed back to health. Although I greatly appreciate all she has done for me, I feel she treats me as her pet, either that or her mental patient. Generally kind, she has an Irish temper that can flare up whenever I say something from modern times that she supposedly can't comprehend. I still think I occupy a cottage in some kind of reenactment village, for she wears long dresses, and her father wears baggy trousers, homemade sweaters his daughters had likely knit and faded white shirts with leather laces rather than buttons.

A thought eventually occurs to me. Maybe these people are like the Amish. Of course, they are not Amish or Mennonites, because they don't have German accents. But maybe they are some kind of Irish Amish or an offshoot of the Irish gypsies that I heard of. But the gypsies don't eschew modern conveniences. Perhaps they are some other religious group originally from Ireland that avoids modern technology. Maybe they still pretend to be in Ireland. They have bought a section of land here in Arizona, near the North Rim, built a town and now live without technology. Before, I had desperately wanted to escape all of my technology—and, well, be careful what you wish for—here I am.

I learn that Gwendolyn's mother had died in childbirth— evidently a lovely woman, who she would never know. A small picture that her artistic sister had painted after she died, for her younger sister to remember her by, sits on the table next to me. As in Newport, I guess if you're avoiding technology, you would not use a camera to take a picture. Gwendolyn periodically looks at the picture longingly. With no TV and little else to occupy my time, I find myself staring at the painting for minutes at a time and realize that Gwendolyn resembles her beautiful, kindly-looking mother. When Gwendolyn stands by the light of the window, her long flowing hair is blond resembling her mother's. In the shadows it becomes red. From what she tells me, when her father worked ten to twelve hours a day, six days a week, her older sisters had largely raised her. Now she cares for him... and for me.

She tells me that her father is a printer, which explains the mysterious, rhythmic mechanical clunking sounds I hear throughout the day and imagine is part of the reenactment—how they printed stuff in olden times before electricity. I had been to a recreation of mid-19th-century America at Hale Farm and Village in Ohio, where various craftsmen made glass works and iron works, as they would before the Civil War. Colonial Williamsburg operated similarly. Evidently, this is a recreation of an Irish Village near the North Rim—how realistic. I think that they have done an incredible job keeping up the ruse and smile knowingly to myself, glad I had finally solved this mysterious puzzle.

The next time Gwendolyn comes into the room to bring me some cheese and bread, I confront her with a smile and smug tone, saying "You guys have done a tremendous job simulating this Irish Village—you all pretending you live and sleep here. Where do you and your father, if he is, indeed, your father, really live?"

Surprised she says in a voice that continuously rises, "What are ye talkin' bout? My father is a kind man. And look at all I ha' done fer ye--tendin' to ya, given ye me bed, feedin' ya and takin' out the chamber pot, an all. And this is the thanks ye say!"

"Oh, you have done an incredible job here, with the horses and carts, and thatched roofs and your accents. You really had me going. For a while, I thought I was in the Twilight Zone. And that doctor. He's a great actor too. I'd like to see my friends now. Where's the camera? Are they looking at me?" I wave my hand, "Hi Pete, Hi Jen, Heh Wally, Heh Betty. Glad I could provide you some entertainment." Then I begin clapping my hands, "I applaud you all, but it's over now. Let's go home. Time for you guys to go back to work anyway."

As I speak, Gwendolyn's pale face is slowly turning deeper shades of red and shouting, she releases a torrent. "What are ye talkin bout? Are ye a seein' ghosts? Actors, why I never! I had me doubts, but now I know you are surely daft."

She raises her hand and is about to slap me, then takes a deep breath and as her voice goes progressively higher, says, "Oh I had such high hopes fer ya. Thought ya were a getting better. Guess I'll get the doctor ta see if he can do fer ya, but I doubt he can. I be done wi' ye."

As she storms out and slams the door behind her, in the hall I hear, "Twilight Zone, surely he be daft. I'll have to say some more prayers for him. Oh my!"

Periodically Gwendolyn brings me old books to read. The next day, she opens the door cautiously, as if she would rather be anywhere than with me, hands me a bowl of mush with a wooden spoon. She quickly turns to leave the room but with a look of disgust, turns and grudgingly gives me a copy of the *Bunkillarny Reader* that they just printed; the smell of ink still fresh. On the *Reader* I notice the date, just below the masthead at the top: **July 8, 1491**.

My mouth wide open, my mind now clearer, I reluctantly realize I have been somehow transported back to late 15th century Ireland, a fact that takes me time to adjust to. I do not know how this happened, but I'm not just a prisoner in a reenactment village, but a prisoner of time. The clothes, the sounds, the smells, the people, the houses, the horses. It all adds up. I have to reluctantly accept it.

"Gwendolyn, I'm truly sorry for what I said yesterday. I must have had a fever. I greatly appreciate all you and your dad have done for me. You are kind people. Please, forgive me."

The nasty expression on her face softens, her lips pierce in a slight smile and she bows her head slightly acknowledging my apology.

I decide to say no more about San Francisco, California, the Grand Canyon, Arizona, my time or my friends, because it just makes me seem crazy and stokes Gwendolyn's Irish temper—a response that in my dilapidated condition is draining to endure. As a result, eventually, they notice that I no longer seem daft, and chalk up my previous manifestations to delusions from being so beaten up and sick, or a spell that some witch had cast upon me.

There in bed with little else to do, I have plenty of time to think about my life—something I had hoped to do on my backpacking trip into the Canyon, for I had found that getting away from my normal life, away from all the tech, and into nature usually provided perspective, healing, and eventually, a sense of direction. The last three years had been a blur, working seventy, eighty and even a hundred hours a week, without a break and with little social life other than occasional breaks or late-night trips to the bar for food and relief with my workmates. While working so hard, I found laugh breaks to be essential. If we had not laughed in some time, I knew the team was stressed to its limit and looked for ways to relieve the tension. After the betrayal by the CEO of our startup, I had been so depressed and so burned out. I felt so deceived, not only for myself, but for my team that had worked so diligently. Well, I think, being in 15th century Ireland should certainly provide some perspective—perspective for when I find my way back. I remembered how it all came apart, back to that fateful day that started out so wonderfully. Oh, how fast things can change. How fast your whole life can change.

20:   BETRAYAL

Enticed by the fragrant aroma of brewing coffee, I had ambled into my kitchen flooded in bright morning light, poured a shot of almond milk into the tall mug, added the aromatic blend, then sauntered to my panoramic window. Beneath the bright blue sky, silvery white clouds shrouded the bay, the twin reddish-orange spires poking out of the milky whiteness still shrouding the distant docks lining Sausalito, obscuring the abodes of Tiburon. I knew it would burn off by noon revealing the placid blue-green, frothy waters below.

Inspired by the stunning day, I pulled up the Murphy Bed into the wall, then spinning the rotating handle, the wall gradually slid along the rails revealing my home office. I fired up my laptop to work on the new app before commuting to work, thereby avoiding the heavy rush hour traffic. In contrast to my normal morning tension to get to work and get things done, I felt supremely relaxed and proud of what I had accomplished. As the state-of-the-art machine came to life, mug in hand, I walked to the balcony, where the remnants of the receding fog left the black cast iron railing dripping in a light layer of dew. The peaceful white cloud below hid the dynamic city churning to life, a muffled cacophony penetrating the peaceful white blanket, the enticing smell of frying sausage wafting upwards from some unknown abode below. I felt as if I were a Tibetan monk on a mountaintop by myself. I inhaled it all in, then breathed out.

Leaning over the balcony, the railing pressed to my stomach, off to the right I saw round, stony Coit Tower poking out of the white sea. This is what my Californian brethren called May gray to be superseded by June gloom, when the coastal fog rolls in in the morning and out by noon—a shroud that does not penetrate just a few miles inland, where it is likely bright, sunny and already hot. When I was recruited from Ohio, I thought there were no seasons—just sunny and warm all the time, after all it never rains in sunny California, right? I soon discovered there is a rainy season, a dry season, a foggy season and a fire season that seems to be getting longer and more devastating each year. Not the same four seasons but four seasons just the same.

Normally, I would have woken at 6:00 and headed for the office by 6:30, but this Monday was special. We had launched the app two weeks ago and already had over a million downloads. Saturday, we celebrated our success with a glorious party at the top of the Hilton on Union Square, where, with a magnificent 360-degree view of the night-lit city below, we reveled in our triumph and danced the night away.

Towards the end, we had been working 80 to 100-hour weeks to complete the brilliant app and meet their absurd deadline. Now, I was able to slow down, work normal hours and catch up on life–a well-earned interregnum —a halcyon period of decompression when I could take a deep breath and not have to worry what critical tasks must be accomplished. After the launch, I could spend my mornings in my home office before leisurely commuting to work.

I also hoped to catch up on my reading, looking forward to that Grisham novel I downloaded months ago—just something frivolous and entertaining versus all those dense, technical documents I had been submerged in. Next, I wanted to read a historical novel about one of the empires I so enjoyed, perhaps on the 18th-century British Empire that spanned the globe, or the 15th-century Spanish Empire fueled by exploration, conversions, conquest and gold. For months now, no years, my life consisted of a series of screens on my work desktop, my laptop, my iPhone, my iPad and occasionally my big screen TV or game console, not to mention my Fitbit and iWatch. At night, I dreamed of the screens I was designing, tweaking the details, moving fields around in my head and thinking in code. Haunting my dreams, one night as the critical deadline approached, as my anxiety ratcheted up, the screens grew to immense proportions, taking on aberrant personalities, laughing at me, while dancing mockingly to a fiendish, sea-shanty jig.

Looking forward to a restful night, for the first time in months, I had turned my phone off. After relishing a night uninterrupted by late-night calls, I turned my iPhone back on, which insistently began beeping. The stinging text from the CEO said I was... *laid off*! In shock, I reread the message, which surely must be a joke, but I was, indeed, *laid off*! They had just sold my app for, no doubt, a sizable fortune and would no longer need me or my team.

I could not believe that Steve would lay us off and by text rather than face-to-face or at least call. Hastily, I threw on a shirt, jeans and my Reeboks. Impatient with the slow-moving elevator, I vaulted down the stairs, where at the building's entrance, I saw a passing cable car climbing the hill. I ran after the bright, red car, grabbed the long, stainless-steel bar and using its momentum to pull me forward, jumped on the side platform. After it descended into Union Square, I caught a BART.

Along the ride to Palo Alto, jerking from side to side, my tension built—my neck and shoulders hard as rocks, my blood pressure surging. To calm myself, I clicked on my relaxation app and tried to take deep breaths in time to the calming voice with crashing waves in the background playing over my ear buds. It didn't work.

From the station, I took a hybrid Uber down the main street onto a side street to a tertiary street to one of the thousands of innocuous, single-story buildings that each held a dozen or so startups like ours, some of which would prosper, while most would fail and vanish without a trace in a year or two. I went to one of the obscure entrances, swiped my keycard but after repeated tries, realized it would not register.

A car swerved and screeched into the spot in front of me. Mike, the tech project leader, opened the door and walked up from his SUV. He continuously ran his thick, stocky fingers through his long, dark red hair and sighed. His normally light, freckled complexion looked white as a ghost's, with an odd gray tinge. Automatically, I said, "How's it going?" after which I immediately realized how stupid that was.

He looked at me with widened blue eyes as if I was an idiot. "Not well, Rand. Not well at all!" He continued, "After I received the text, I was able to reach Steve."

Steve had been a long-term buddy of his from a previous startup. On the trip down, I had tried to call Steve numerous times with no success. Evidently, he was not taking any other calls. While on the BART, all of my people had texted me, but I could not give them any new information.

According to Mike, we would all receive three months' pay. After completing the app, we were all supposed to receive stock options, but the deal happened so fast that it was no longer going to happen. "Steve, George, the CFO, and the VCs (venture capitalists) would pocket all the profits," Mike said. "Steve and George will become eight- and nine-figure multimillionaires. Steve will likely buy that place in Saint Bart's he dreamed of. "I cannot believe the greedy bastards did this to us."

Mike drove me to our favorite Irish pub in his black, extended Suburban, where we met the rest of the gang he had texted to meet there. We dragged several tables together with a great deal of screeching to form one long table, where we drowned our bitterness in pints of Guinness, Harp and rounds of Bushmills.

I had never been to the bar on this side of noon, the darkness seeming an odd contrast to the brightness outside. My heart ached for them. It was not easy to recruit talent in the Valley, and all of them could have found more lucrative positions elsewhere. When I hired them, I sold them on the potential of the app and that they would have a share of its success. During the rough times when we all worked late into the night under intense pressure, I inspired them with that thought.

After buying the first round, I said, "Guys, I feel awful. We were all promised stock by Steve, and he pulled the rug out from under us. You all did an amazing job, working as a team toward a lofty goal that was not easy to obtain. You should all be proud of yourselves—the app is magnificent. I have not given up and will try to extract the promised shares from Steve." I raised my glass. "Here's to you all, each and every one!"

Mike ordered a round of breaded mushrooms and caprice flatbreads and added, "I totally agree with everything Rand said. You guys are totally awesome, and it was a pleasure to work with you. I have not given up either. Just so you know, neither Rand nor I received any extra compensation. We all got the same three months and we all got screwed."

I added, "I will be writing a signed letter of recommendation for each of you that will highlight your skills, diligence, team orientation, and creativity. If you ever need a reference, I promise to give you a glowing one."

Cathy, our tech writer, said, "An actual letter, you mean the kind you mail?"

"Yes Cathy. I will mail it to you both as a signed e-mail and through snail mail."

"Wow! The last time I received an actual letter was when I was accepted to Stanford grad school."

Jose, the young graphics artist I hired, took a handful of napkins from the dispenser, sprinkled some Guinness on them and began forming the darkened clump with his hands. Before we could make out what he was doing, he left for the bathroom. There he evidently dried it with the hand dryer and drew on it with a sharpie. When he reappeared, he held up a paper mâché bust of Steve that looked remarkably similar to him, including his ever-present tan. We all clapped at the amazing likeness and then booed the effigy. He placed Steve's head on the empty nacho platter, brought out a butane lighter, and turning it all the way up, torched him. We all cheered wildly to the consternation of the late lunch crowd.

Somehow, the misery of a group of warriors who had battled mightily towards a shared, worthy goal seemed comforting. But even though we had won the battle, we had lost the war. After the lunch crowd left, we drowned our sorrows in our beer. Wanting to lighten the mood, Cathy played our anthem, "Roar," on the jukebox, which we sometimes played on the PA system to get our blood flowing, and then she pushed us onto the floor. Mike refused to dance until Cathy and Marie Chan literally dragged him up. There, dancing one last time with the group to the Katy Perry selections, to "California Gurls" and "Firework," felt somehow cathartic. While dancing, I looked around at these young guys and gals dancing together, acting out, laughing one last time. I loved them all and knew I would miss them.

When the after-work crowd began to filter in, the time we used to arrive, the group began to leave, hugging each other and promising to stay in touch. As a grizzled old veteran in my 30's, I knew that the relationships we had forged in battle would gradually fade. We might gather for a reunion or two, and some of us might work together at a future startup, but most of us would move on.

Still, after spending so much time together, knowing each other's talents so well and implicitly trusting each other, if an opportunity presented itself years from now, we could call upon each other and renew the relationship.

Marie Chan drove me to the BART station saying, "Rand, I feel terrible about all of this, but we don't blame you. I enjoyed working for you. You take care of yourself and don't take this too hard. We all gained some good experience and learned a lot from you." Then she kissed me on the cheek and drove away. That felt good. Glad I had not driven home, I fell asleep on the BART and almost missed my stop.

21:   MICHAEL

Michael McCarron has his daughter's wistful blue eyes, a cleft chin, pronounced cheekbones and black hair sprinkled with white. A kindly older gentleman, he told me he did not marry until his thirties.

"There was just too much to learn and to see. Most Irishmen could na read, but I had a quest for knowledge, and at the bequest of me parents, studied to be a priest until I realized I couldn't commit to the celibacy, could I."

Gwendolyn said one day when she was nursing me, "While at the seminary, he devoured nearly every book in their library, The reason he left the seminary was he ran out o' books ta read. He fashioned himself a poet and a ladies' man, me da a ladies man, oh be golly. But he finally settled down. Otherwise, I would na be 'ere," after which she produced a instantly enduring laugh.

Michael visits me regularly and responds to my questions, gradually telling me the story of his life. In dramatic contrast to the sedentary life of the seminary, he says, "In a quest for adventure, I went down to the docks, hopped on a ship, and became a sailor for four years, sailing to England, France, Holland, Spain, Germany, and even into the Mediterranean and ta Rome. After me adventures, due to me education, the lord hired me to keep his books and granted me the opportunity ta read from his extensive library, where I becomes fascinated with the new technology of printin."

During another visit, after I was able to get around a bit, I asked, "I heard that the Irish monks preserved early literature."

"Yes lad. Our seminary's books were all hand-copied. In the fifth century, after the Roman Empire dissolved, pagan tribes ruled Europe. During the Dark Ages, when all of Europe fought endless wars and plagues wiped out as much as half the populace, little attention had been paid to classic Greek and Roman literature. Indeed, many books that previously existed had been burned, destroyed, or not being cared for, simply rotted away.

The Germanic tribes who conquered Rome cared little for their philosophy, literature, culture, or even their science—a thin that surprised me, cause it may ha helped 'em make better weapons. The feudal kings did na want their people to waste time on such frivolous pursuits; rather, they wanted them to be engaged in tendin' to the land and fightin' their wars to gain more land, or defend against those who coveted their lands and their wealth.

Whether consciously or unconsciously, they discouraged education and a learnin'"

Since he had been a librarian, who cared deeply for books, I could see this distressed him. I remembered it was a pattern that would be repeated numerous times throughout history, with the burning of books and imprisonment, or outright murder of intellectuals by dictators who threatened them, recalling those such as Mao in China, Hitler in Germany, Stalin in Russia, Mussolini in Italy, Franco in Spain, the Taliban in Afghanistan, and ISIS in Syria. Millions of books were burned and uncounted millions of people, including especially intellectuals, were killed or "reeducated". I could not say that to him since it was yet to happen.

"The early Irish monks, far away from the pandemics and wars that plagued Europe—on the outskirts of the known world—practiced what they called the green monasticism, livin' in nature that is. Through fasting and labors, they endeavored to free themselves from evil. A portion of their labors were spent a copyin' the ancient texts, but this was not just a mindless, repetitive task, for they discussed what they learnt with each other in a collegial manner, thereby preservin' the ancient civilizations and intellectual curiosity. Something I greatly enjoyed doing in the seminary too, I did"

"One of our monasteries existed at the outward most outpost of the known world, seven miles off the southwestern coast of Ireland on Skellig Michael Island, a 7-mile-long, 700-foot-high barely accessible mountain of rocks it were."

"What does that mean?"

"Skellig means "splints of stone" in Gaelic—an apt description, don ya think. Michael refers to Michael the Arch Angel, the saint I be named for. There, on a steep, rocky, barren outcrop, where the Atlantic first kisses land and fierce storms blow, they practiced their monasticism far away from the Viking invaders who plundered Northern Ireland, where we are now. At the end of the known world, there be powerful natural and spiritual forces, there be." I realized that this rocky island would be the furthest frontier of the British Isles—the first to experience fierce Atlantic storms, the closest land to America. As a Star Wars fan, I remembered this as the desolate island, where Luke retreated from the world.

Michael continued, "The monks, on the edge of civilization away from the constant European ferment and wars, had taken it upon themselves to preserve the classic works in Latin and Greek that otherwise wud ha' been lost to civilization forever—works such as thon by famous thinkers such as Cicero, Seneca, Socrates, Plato, Aristotle, Homer, Virgil, Lucretius, Augustus, Horace and Caesar. Some of the works of literature, which survived intact that we hand-copied, includin' the Book of Kells and the Book of Darrow, both of which contain gospels and are brightly illustrated. These books are works of art. Realizing that our books would last for a long time and be seen many times, by many people, we painstakingly wrote each letter in each word, in each sentence, on each page. It were a kind of prayer, something ye could lose yourself a doin'. Some days each monk might only make eight or ten pages, the did.

"Who were these early monks and did they ever travel out of Ireland to spread their precious knowledge, they did?"

"Well this is a subject I had been interested in, and I talked to some of the older brothers bout it. As they told the story, after European culture devolved, monks such as Columbanus and Gallus travelled to Scotland, England, France, and the Germanic regions, establishing monasteries that would preserve and teach theology, mathematics, astronomy, science, and literature. Indeed, by the 9th-century, nearly all of the major European kingdoms employed Irish scholars."

"Naturally influenced by Celtic influences on the outskirts of the know world, Irish Christianity differed somewhat from Roman Catholicism in that it allowed married priests, divorce, and was independent of the Roman hierarchy, not that there was much left of Rome at the time. Why at one time the pope was located in France and later there were three popes at the same time. The monasteries where many young European nobles went to study were more independent, and had higher educational and scholarship standards than thon in Rome. It wasn't till the 12th century, when the Normans conquered Eireann that the monasteries came under the pope's rule, they did."

———

According to Michael, because he has exceptional handwriting and graphic skills, part of his education at the seminary included illustrating manuscripts. "Indeed, the major reason the lord hired me was because of my superior hand writin' and illustratin', so I cud copy manuscripts he borrowed from other nobles throughout Eireann to build up his library. Periodically, I would travel throughout Eireann a visitin' castles and monasteries, searching for the manuscripts on his list. While there, I wud ask if there were any particular works they wanted for their library and when I had no work for the lord, I would copy his works for the other nobles, which became highly lucrative. Good scribes can make a good living."

"Bein' a scribe is an art form in itself, ye ken. First ye ha' to ken how to properly trim ye goose feather quill and to line the pages so the letters align but barely see the lines. Then ye ha' ta be careful to apply just the right pressure at each point of each letter, so that the thick portions and thin portions are just right. Ye ha' ta get each letter of each word right too—many scribes miss whole words, which is why it's important to get an original document if possible or as close to. There aren't many good scribes in all o' Eireann other than what's in the monasteries. Producin' a book isn't just about a copyin' and illustratin' though, it's also about sawin' the board for the cover, binding the pages together and coverin' it all in a fine illustrated leather cover. I was sure to learn all these steps while at the seminary.

Michael continued, "Later the lord had sent me to Germany to collect newly published books. Gutenberg invented the printing press and movable type in about 1440 in Mainz, but as I was amazed to see that by the 1470s, every German town seemed to have a press. In Cologne alone, I discovered that the various print shops were printing thousands of different books a year."

By now, "he tells me, "There are probably printers in over 150 cities throughout Europe that are likely producing over ten million books a year—a number I have difficulty comprehending meself."

With his passion for literature stirring, he felt that before it passed him by, this was a revolution he had to be part of. "Even though I had left the seminary, I felt a sense of guilt, that I was selfish and there was a hole in me soul that all of my travels and readin could not fill. I felt that God wanted me to be a printer—that this was my calling, bringing the classic literature to Ireland. I would facilitate my countrymen's enlightenment by helping them learn to read, and think better."

When he returned with boxes of books for the lord's library, he told him all he had seen— "There were so many books being printed in the Germanic areas on all manner of topics, and I thought it would change the world. "Copying a book could take weeks, whereas hundreds of copies of the same book cud be produced during that time on a printin' press."

"Inspired by my passion, the lord wanted to be part of the revolution too. His family had founded St. Paul's and had stocked its library. Indeed, half the books I acquired in Germany were intended for their library. The lord thought that, considering the cost and availability of the best books in the world, the college could now afford multiple copies of the same book, and that students in their small classes could all read the same book at the same time before returning it to the library. For a key medical book, a well-off families could afford to buy the book for them to reference for the rest of their lives.

"Such books were precious—objects to be cared for and handed down throughout the generations. That is part of what attracted me to the printin'—that what you preserve will last forever—what a legacy eh?"

While working for the lord, Michael eventually saved up enough to buy a press. "Although I had enough for the press itself, I did not have the funds for the type and I wanted more than just the basic typeset. So, with the lord's help, I opened up me shop. Rather than going to the mainland or waiting for someone to hand-copy a book, the lord would now have access to books produced in our town, and he would also have a say as to which ones should be printed. Plus, he might even make a profit. And since I had built relationships with nobles and monasteries throughout the land, I had a built in market for these much less expensive books to build up there libraries, don't ye ken."

22:   THE PRINTER

While still recovering, I ask, "So it sounds like most of the presses were manufactured in Germany. Did you travel back there to get your press?"

"I sailed across the Irish Sea and back up the Rhine to Cologne in order to obtain a press from there. I told the manufacturer that I needed to learn how to use the press though. To attain the sale, he set me up in a nearby shop, where over the next six months, I learned how to set type and handle the ink, the paper and the press. They did not pay me, but provided food, lodging, beer, and since I occasionally spilled ink, some worn clothing. At first, I spilled a lot of ink on meself, I did. I even learned how they manufactured the lead and tin-type. Such an endeavor would usually require a multi-year apprenticeship, but printing evolved so quickly that print shops throughout the town needed all the help they cud get."

"So, could you speak German?"

"During my travels as a sailor, I learned a little of the major languages, including German. My biggest challenge, though, was perfecting me German. To be a parful printer, I had no choice."

Being highly motivated, Michael learned rapidly, becoming fascinated with the various fonts and the process of printing illustrations. Impressed by his rapid learning and developing skills, the Cologne shop desperately wanted to keep him, but Michael wanted to set up his own shop in Ireland. Even though there was a press in England, his press would be the first in all of Ireland—the second in all the British Isles, something he was very proud of.

After completing his printing apprenticeship, Michael stopped by the manufacturer to arrange for delivery to Ireland, but they had misplaced his order, which now understanding German better, he figured was due to a communication error. The order was slated for delivery a year later than he had expected. Due to the high demand and a backlog for presses, after apologizing for their error and expediting the order, it would still take an additional four-months to fulfill. Then he discovered that they could not deliver to Ireland.

"But Hans said you could ship it down the Rhine and across the Atlantic to Ireland."

"Hans no longer verks fer us. You vere not the only one he made such promises to. Ve fired him."

"It does me no good to have a press here. I guess I will have to cancel me order and get one from another shop."

"Vell, ve do have an order going to London. Ve could ship your press to dere."

"Let's do that."

After haggling with them, they arranged to send the printing press to William Caxton's print shop in London along with the press Caxton had ordered. Michael would have to figure out how to ship it to Ireland from London, which as a former sailor familiar with the port of London, he could readily accomplish.

As I recovered, on another visit to my bedside, I asked Michael, "What happened in London? Were you able to arrange for the shipment?"

Being extremely bored, similar to a kid waiting for his bedside story, I greatly looked forward to his stories, which as a born storyteller and an accomplished author, he told with flair. Plus, he often brought a bottle of whiskey, which helped with my pain. He sat in a rickety chair on the right side of my bed facing me, where he would periodically pour a bit o' the whiskey into our glasses, and as we swirled and sipped the golden liquid, he weaved his fascinating stories. I could not drink a lot of whiskey, so I nursed mine, whereas he drank freely, his gestures becoming more animated with each pour.

With nothing else to do, Michael traveled to London and showed up at William Caxton's shop, "I saw they already had two presses clanging and slurping away, and smelled the familiar odor of the oil-based ink drying on the pages hanging on the line, so I felt at home. After introducing meself, I asked for a temporary position."

"William had a backlog of type setting that was limiting the number of books he could produce. With his new press and the increased capacity it implied, the backlog would only grow worse. He was working long hours doing it himself and editing the work of others that was still filled with errors. Understanding that I would only be there for four months, William said, 'I do not want to spend time training someone that would soon leave. I won' hire ye. Be on yer way.'

Never one to take no for an answer, Michael asked William, "Give me a one-week trial, in which I will operate the press and set type with no training. I will work for free and if you do not think my work is up to par, I will leave. You have nothing to lose."

According to Michael, his work was fast and nearly flawless—far better than any of Bill's journeymen. "Mr. Caxton hired me at a premium wage for the four months and paid me for the week. With me, he was able to reduce the backload and finally spend some time at home. By the end of the period, we had become grand friends. After all we had much in common— we both were interested in a broad range of topics, and passionate about books, readin', and the unfoldin' printing revolution. We spent hours over dinner at the nearby pub or at his house sitting down to a wonderful meal his house mistress would prepare, talking about our profession and what we had read."

Bill was fascinated by Michael's travels, especially the tales about pirate encounters, even suggesting that he write a book about these, "I would print it myself, but I think that is something you would like to do on your new press, my friend."

"I learned much more about the business of printing from Bill. I learned there is more than just printing the pages and binding them together. I learned that acquisitions and sales were important too. You have to figure out what people will want ta read. Bill was sponsored by the queen mother of England, something I hoped to continue with King Edward. Without him and his recommending me I would not have been able to build me business."

————

Back in Bunkillarny, once Michael set up his press, he went to the nearby monastery to talk to Abbott Donald—"a rotund man with a round friendly face, a full head of thick, white, bushy hair in a bowl cut and a sturdy chin."

"The Abbott taught me about the history of the monasteries in Ireland. He was the second son of the O'Donald clan that ruled the Northwestern corner of Ireland. Because he would na become king, joining the church was a path for him to still exert power and influence. The church dominated nearly all of Europe. Some of the younger sons of royal families used their clerical positions to accumulate lands and wealth, but Donald was truly a holy man, a good man, someone who even though I had left the seminary, I looked up to as my mentor, someone I relished talking to. He had told me he respected my following my conscience and leaving the seminary before I had taken me vows."

"I walked along the familiar winding dirt road up the green hill overlooking the swilly to the collection of buildings that held the ancient monastery. The seminary with the college occupying an equally picturesque adjacent hill, holding an impressive array of gothic-architecture buildings, with an inspiring view of the sea below, was an ideal peaceful setting for prayer, contemplation and learnin', it tis."

"The monasteries of Ireland occupied sacred land and as such were immune to the periodic wars between the various clans, until the Vikings invaded aound 900 A.D. Since they were pagans, the Vikings perceived no such restrictions and freely pillaged the monasteries throughout the British Isles for their gold and treasures."

"Legend has it that when the Vikings came to Bunkillarny in the 10th century, Abbott August prevailed upon the Viking leader to spare the monastery. They promised to give them all of their gold, except and for one chalice and the cross on the altar. Exhibiting remarkable courage, the abbot explained the significance of the cross and the story of Christ to the Viking king, who although he did not convert to Christianity, acquired respect for the religion and spared the monastery. The monks interpreted this as a miracle—when God interceded and changed the fearsome Vikings' hearts. Abbott Donald still has the legendary chalice and cross in the chapel. Once you are better, you can still see the chalice and crucifix there and the beautiful views from up on the hill."

"I showed Donald one of the Latin books I acquired in Germany, the letters of St. Paul, a book that I had painstakingly copied by hand, while at the seminary. I explained that in the month it took me to copy the book, on my press I could print a thousand copies."

"The priest said, 'The printed book looked nice, but it did no have the same feel of a hand-written page, one that a monk had invested a part of his soul in. Besides, what would the monks and seminarians do with their time?'"

"Well, your eminence, they would have more time to grow more food, more time to repair or expand the ancient abbey, more time to teach at the college or the seminary, more time to pray, and more time to brew that delicious stout you sell in town. Besides it would take half the ink and half the paper."

"As one who constantly worried about the financial aspects of running the monastery, a college and a seminary, Donald began to sway. He was very fond of his brew, and the prospect of making and selling more stout seemed especially appealing, plus there was nothing against the monks still spending a portion of their time copying books—for spiritual enrichment."

"Then I sweetened the deal, I did and said, 'For each book we print, we will give you the first ten copies and a percentage of the profits, which is only fair since your monks have been preserving these priceless texts for centuries and now the whole world will be enlightened by them."

"Abbot Donald smiled and fervently shook me hand then poured two liters of his renowned stout for us to enjoy. Afterwards we spent the rest of the afternoon sittin' on the patio adjacent to the abbot's office with a serene view of the sunlit, sparkling bay rekindling our friendship, discussing my trip to Germany, and discussing Greek philosophy. The abbot was pleased that God had finally shown me my calling, something he had prayed for. I was pleased, because since this was one of the few monasteries that had not been destroyed by the Vikings, they had works that existed nowhere else in the world."

Michael began printing some of the more popular books from the monastery that he sold to religious institutions, churches and intellectuals around Ireland. Through the Middle Ages, much of the world's literature had been lost. Irish monks had meticulously copied and preserved many of the most precious books, which otherwise might have disappeared. Michael felt it was his calling to produce mass copies of the works and began traveling to monasteries throughout the island begging to borrow these manuscripts. In return, he promised them multiple copies and a percentage of the profits, stressing the fact that now the other monasteries, not only in Ireland but throughout Europe, would have access to these precious works, as they, in turn, would have access to the other's treasured books.

At the lordship's urging, he also began printing some more recent popular titles. One of his fellow dropouts from the seminary, Jimmy Brogan, a thin, handsome fellow with a long equine nose, intelligent eyes and glasses, agreed to translate the works from Latin into English. Jimmy, who had seven children, loved the work, which he performed diligently and flawlessly. Through his contacts in London, the lord found an agent to sell the books there and acquire additional titles abroad to print. Michael had successfully mastered the advice Caxton's had given him regarding acquisitions and sales—vital aspects to growing a successful printing and publishing business.

23:   MARY

While gazing at the ever-present picture of Mrs. McCarron on the bedside table, I asked Michael, "How did you meet your beautiful wife?"

"Before me trip to Germany when I acquired me press, Lord Bunkillarny had asked me to gather various texts on Irish heraldry and to write a book on the subject, which I would have had printed on the continent and sold to prominent families in Northern Eireann. He had seen a similar book while visiting Dublin and wanted to capture the history of the prominent families for posterity, plus it would help secure their land rights for their children.   Lord Bunkillarny told me there were no English printers, but since there were numerous such printers in Paris, he wanted it written in French, something I felt I could accomplish.

"After preliminarily researching the book, I visited the domiciles of the various local nobles and landholders to complete me research and interest them in procuring a copy. Along me travels, seeing the nobles' growing libraries, I sensed how printed books were increasing in popularity and that's when I first thought about becoming a printer meself—when God's inspiration came to me. I would not be able to sell many books, but since the book was about the nobles and their families, the lord and I knew we could command a substantial price.

"In the hamlet of Ballyangle, I knocked on the door of a castle belonging to the O'Flannery's—one of the contacts the lord recommended to me. While waiting in the den, where I could not help perusing an impressive books collection, I turned to see what I thought to be an angel dressed in white, dazzlingly illuminated by the sun streaming through a window behind her, her blond hair shining as if it were a halo. She looked at me quizzingly, asking 'Why do ye have that book in yer filthy hands?'

"Still stunned, practically unable to speak, I stammered, 'It is, is, is one of my favorite books,' then bowed and introduced meself."

"She smiled, 'It is one of me favorites too.' Then, in an immediately endearing voice, she announced herself as Mary."

"We began talkin' 'bout the books, me unable to take my eyes off her. Even when her father appeared, as I explained my purpose for being there, I found it difficult to pry my eyes from the fair Mary, who, since she loved books so much and had read all of the library, was intrigued to learn of me occupation as the lord's librarian and his children's tutor. Most of their books had come from France and were written in French or Latin. The newly printed books were so much more affordable than the hand-copied ones, so they were now able to afford more. Her father, though, became concerned about my attention to his beautiful daughter, for he had long planned that she be marryin' one of the lord's sons. Realizing that I worked for the lord and at the insistence of his daughter, he agreed to review what I had on the O'Flannery's and buy a copy once it became available. I could still tell he had doubts about me and said he would only pay for such a book once it had been printed and delivered."

"Without inviting me to enjoy their usual Irish hospitality, Lord O'Flannery abruptly called for the servant to lead me out. Mary said, 'I will show him the door,' and before her father could object, she had taken me arm and led him me out of the room."

"At the doorstep, she asked, 'What other books have ye read?'

"You should stop by the Lordship's library to see his extensive collection of books. I plan to research a biography of St. Patrick next." After leaving, I felt as if I flew on a fluffy, white cloud all the way back to Bunkillarny, a feeling I had never felt before."

"To pique me interest and not seem too interested in me, after waiting two weeks, she appeared at the door of the library dressed in a powder blue frock with white trim, tightly fitting her thin waist, a cross over her exposed bodice, dainty, sheer sleeves and a small, stylish red hat with a red bill and white rim—the latest fashion directly from Paris, she wore—a vision I shall ner forget. She had little doubt that I was interested in her, for after stumbling to the door, I was immediately tongue-tied. The basis of our blossoming relationship, books, dominated our conversations. Over the following weeks she frequently visited the lord's library, and we walked through the royal gardens, discussing religion, philosophy, history, and our travels to London and Paris.

"Already in me 30s, it did not take long for me to consider proposing to the fair Mary. I knew that as I were not a noble, her father would never accept me, so I discussed the matter with his Lordship first, who said, 'My oldest son has already wed, and my second son, John, is in love with an O'Neal, a union I will surely bless, for we would value such an alliance.'"

"Then coming closer to me, he continued, 'You are an outstanding young man of considerable character, knowledge, and kindness, you will make an exceptional husband. Even though you are not a true noble, you possess rare noble qualities of intelligence and courage."

The lord offered to intercede on Michael's behalf to Patrick, Mary's father, 'But first, you must meet with Patrick on your own.'

———

"Before I reached for the knocker, fearing rejection, I walked away. Then, realizing how much I loved Mary, I forced meself to bang the heavy knocker with resounding authority, I did. I would rather fight a raging wolf barehanded than face the fearsome Sir O'Flannery. After I nervously waited for Patrick to appear in the den, I was surprised to see him welcome me warmly, shake me hand, and have a servant bring us brandy."

"Without hesitation, I launched into my oft-rehearsed dissertation of how much I loved Mary, my bright prospects, the future of printing, and what a dedicated husband and father I would be. Patrick just sat smirking, which I took as disdain."

"Afterwards, as I waited for the boom of rejection to fall on my mountain of hope, Sir Patrick reached over and shook me hand, fervently saying, 'I will give ye permission on one condition. I want a copy of each book you print for me library.' Then we drank the remainder of the bottle, as Patrick discussed his joy in reading about St. Francis. He also reminisced 'bout his time as a student at Saint Paul's, where he was one of the first to graduate."

Earlier, the lord had talked to Patrick, stressing Michael's good character and bright prospects, which is why Patrick, realizing the lord's sons were not available, welcomed the union.

"We were soon wed at the O'Flannery's castle in a lavish wedding feast that the lord attended. Our first two daughters arrived within a couple of years. I went to Paris and hired a printer for his book on heraldry, where I became fascinated with printing, and my dream of becoming a printer became more feasible. I researched my book on St. Patrick and convinced the lord he should print it in English on a press we would own together as partners."

———

Building on his experience in Germany, Michael even translated some of the most popular classics (those of Greek and Roman philosophers and playwrights) from German or Latin into English, which, since there was only one other press in the British Isles, found an eager market in London.

As I listened to Michael, I could feel his passion. I knew that Gutenberg had invented the printing press sometime in the mid-15th century, somewhere in what would become Germany centuries later. I also knew that through Martin Luther the printing press would lead to the Protestant Reformation.

Still trying to adjust to my extraordinary situation, I endeavored to relate my experience here to my time in the 21st century. The only invention that seemed comparable in impact to me was the invention of the Internet that occurred in 1969 but did not flourish until after the invention of the World Wide Web some 20 years later. Before then, the Internet was primarily used by universities and the Department of Defense. The World Wide Web made the Internet available to the common man. Similarly, before printing only the clergy and nobles had access to reading. After the invention of the printing press, the common man could have access to the world's evolving knowledge.

I knew that it often took time for pivotal innovations to catch on. After all, I had learned somewhere that the TV was invented in the 1920s, but few families had one before the 1950s—some 25 years later. After the advent of the Web, the Internet spread like wildfire throughout the world. Computer illiterate folks throughout the world felt compelled to learn how to surf the Web. Even poor children in remote African villages had inexpensive, hand-cranked PCs that granted them access to all of the world's news and knowledge. So Michael was evidently an early pioneer of a revolutionary new technology.

Curious about writing and the history of printing, I looked it up on my iPad—on my downloaded copy of Wikipedia. The only other revolutionary communication technology that compared to the invention of the printing press or the Internet was the invention of writing itself around 3200 B.C. by Sumerian scribes in the ancient city-state of Uruk, in present-day Iraq. According to Wikipedia, cuneiform writing was created by using a reed stylus to make wedge-shaped indentations on clay tablets. This innovation was primarily applied as a means of recording business transactions—i.e. farmer Akhmad sold three gur of wheat (78 bushels) for five kug coins.

Similar to the Internet, printing presses spread throughout Europe at a rapid pace. In the late 15th century, a burgeoning middle class of shop owners, tradesmen, and guildsmen could now afford to read. Given the advantages reading bestowed upon them, they were motivated to read not only for themselves, but for their children too. If the opportunity presented itself, even some ambitious serf could learn to read and advance himself. In terms of the advantages it afforded, learning to read in the 15th century was similar to acquiring a college degree in the 21st century.

Before, because people could not afford to buy hand-copied books that might cost months of wages, it made little sense for them to learn to read or even practice reading. Now that books were more affordable, they had an incentive to learn. Before they relied on priests to interpret the Bible, now they could read it for themselves. After all, the first book Gutenberg produced was the 1200-page Bible, which would become the biggest seller of all time.

Before, they had to rely on lawyers and bureaucrats to perform the transactions of daily life, hoping they represented their interests honestly; now they could read such documents themselves. Before, few besides the wealthy had access to knowledge, the world's literature and thinking; now the common man could learn, potentially improve himself and his lot in life. Following the Middle Ages, this burgeoning middle class composed of shop owners, tradesmen, merchants, guildsmen and bureaucrats, for whom reading was vital to their professional interests, became readers. This class could now afford to teach their children how to read and improve upon their parents. This burgeoning middle class would alter the balance of political power throughout Europe, but that would take some time.

As the number of books grew exponentially, knowledge in all fields expanded by leaps and bounds. For generations the masses went about their daily lives with little awareness of anything beyond their immediate environs, and had no access to cultivate an interest in history or culture. Now, there was a thirst for knowledge that stretched back to the Persians, the Greeks, and the Romans—when the known world was under one rule and interconnected by trade, roads, shipping, and common laws. They revitalized those works, leading to the Renaissance in Italy that, aside from Germany, had the most print shops. The Renaissance along with a growing hunger for knowledge took hold and spread like wildfire throughout Europe, as evidenced by the spread of print shops throughout the continent.

It is not always clear what causes these major transformations in civilization. Is there a natural cycle or an unknown force, or God that directs such seismic change? I had to wonder if somehow the force is why I arrived at this time—if there was some kind of parallelism between the two times that deposited me here, now? Similar to Michael, was this my calling?

24:   RECOVERING

As I became more mobile, I noticed a small board in the center of the town square near the stocks, containing announcements, which I asked Michael about.

"As a member of the shire counsel and its secretary, I took control of the proclamations, continuously adding more to my handwritten notes. Since I also operated the press and the messages grew to be more than would fit on one handwritten page, I thought I would print it on me press. Soon, since the type was set, rather than just posting it to the board, I thought I would press multiple copies to pass around town too. Gradually, it grew to contain more than just the typical town happenings, such as pronouncements, rules, births, deaths, marriages, church events, and festivals."

I realized he, in effect, published a weekly one-page newsletter for the area, calling it the *Bunkillarny Reader*—a predecessor of what would, over a century later, become newspapers. For all I knew, this could have been the first newsletter.

The town mayor and the townspeople who walked into the shop provided brief stories and it grew onto the backside and Michael soon charged readers a ha'penny, basically enough to cover the cost of paper and ink. Eventually, Gwendolyn assumed the duties of writing the *Reader*. He figured that people who would be motivated to read the news would soon want to buy books. And, "as human kind tends to be interested in the latest gossip, the *Reader* would be an inducement for them to larn ta read."

Michael published a copy of his Irish poems and his voyages as a seaman, which became popular sellers, especially due to the chapters involving pirates. He had three young apprentices who helped with the printing and bookbinding, but considering the demand and the time it took to print a book, he thought about buying another press and hiring more apprentices. Unlike rapidly evolving computers, this press would be basically the same as his current press. Even though these were ancient times, the process of printing a book was not a simple one, for this was a truly ingenious machine. The Gutenberg press would remain the standard for printing until the 19th century—some 300-plus years later.

Michael and his deceased wife, Mary, were firm believers in education. At the time, there was no formal education system for anyone besides the wealthy. Therefore, Mary spent much of her time teaching her older daughters how to read. Through her and the books they read, they acquired an unusually high level of education for the time. Since Michael had access to the lord's expanding library, and Mary taught them French and Latin, they had an extensive education. They in turn taught Gwendolyn, who, similar to her father, became a voracious reader and soon became involved in the printing operation.

Although he wanted to increase the subscriptions to his newsletter, he realized that most of the area's inhabitants could not read. He felt it was part of God's calling, so Michael set aside an hour a day to teach the children of the village and interested adults in the vicinity how to read and write. Once Gwendolyn took over this duty, she expanded it to three hours a day three days a week, and not only taught reading, but also arithmetic and other subjects she learned from the books and her well-educated sisters. Father Clancy came in once a week to give religion lessons and read Bible stories. The classes became so popular that they added a room in the back with a long table for adults and a smaller one for the children to sit at on benches in an L shape. With Gwendolyn in the center, she taught both groups simultaneously. Gwendolyn, in effect, became the town's first teacher. She was so busy reporting and teaching that the family decided to hire a maid, Daisy Quinn, to care for the house.

His business being more established and finally profitable, Michael did not have to work 70-hour weeks any longer. He wished Mary were still alive so they could enjoy each other's company under their more comfortable circumstances.

———

I learned about the McCarrans and their history over my recovery period listening to Michael's stories. Later in the evening, he would come to my room with the bottle of whiskey and two glasses, regaling me in his brogue of his adventures. He said, "Whiskey is the medicine that will help ye ta heal, me lad." I looked forward to his visits as a relief from the boredom of the bed and my slow recovery.

During one of Gwendolyn's daily visits, I asked about my clothes. Her face contorted in disgust. telling me, "In the woods, I found ye without any trousers and because of your nakedness, it took courage for me to approach ye to see if you were alive. At first, I thought ye was an aimless, disgusting, drunken vagabond, or that highwaymen had robbed ye and taken yer trousers."

In either case, she thought she should not go to me. Instead, she walked away, but realizing it was her Christian duty she came back, fortunately for me. With her Irish temper flaring, she said, "I ha never seen so much of a man before. Twas disgusting, it twas.

"I ha never seen an undergarment with printing on it or a hat with a red-faced, big-nosed, big-eyed scary demon on it," she said of my Cleveland Indian's cap. "Where did ye acquire such items that might be considered anything other than the

Devil's do. Obviously, even the brigands wo no have stolen such shameful things."

Daisy had handwashed my clothes and Gwendolyn presented these to me adding a look of distain, handling my "devil's undergarments" with just two fingers. I remembered that I had my cell phone in my cargo shorts, along with my Swiss Army knife and a lighter, each in different buttoned pockets that survived my near-drowning.

When I had previously pressed the on button of my cell phone, I realized it would not start. Then after drying in the sand, when I was in the cave it miraculously came back to life. I had used it in the cave to light my way. When I pressed it this time, the opening jingle played, the screen lit up, and the home screen apps appeared. Of course, there was no network in the 15th century and would not be for hundreds of years, so I immediately turned it off. Fortunately, Daisy had taken it out before she washed it, otherwise it would be a mangled mess. After hearing the jingle, her face lit up and she asked what the strange object was? Searching for an explanation that might make some sense, I said, "It is a Spanish music box that captures light like a prism.

"Cud I plays it sur?"

Showing her the crack, I said, "Sorry Daisy, it's broken."

In the meantime, Michael had loaned me a pair of his baggy trousers, which Gwendolyn had lengthened. She crocheted a sweater for me and Daisy sewed a couple of shirts. With me sitting in bed for all of those days, they had become used to looking down at me. With the assistance of Gwendolyn and Michael, when they lifted me out of bed for the first time and saw I towered over them, they were shocked at my height. Though I was only 6'3", I was much taller than most men in those days. When Daisy came in and saw me taking slow deliberate steps, she ran out of the room yelling, "He be a giant, he tis!"

Day by day I gained my strength walking around the room, walking into the kitchen for meals, walking around the house, walking out back to the outhouse or into the backyard to sit in the sun, while reading, pushing myself to go just a little further each day.

There was no TV or PC or Tablet, or Xbox. At first, I missed my digital devices terribly. Sure, when I went backpacking for a week, one of the best things about the journey was getting away from these, getting into nature and feeling more alive again. Afterwards, I would feel more in touch with nature, more in touch with my thoughts, more in touch with myself, and more in touch with those around me. But in the back of my mind, I knew I would reunite with them soon. The devices give you so much, but they take something away too.

I remembered a weekend backpacking trip in the Appalachians in southern Ohio. After we drove off the freeway, off a main road, onto a small, narrow dirt road that wound over the creeks and through the hollows, where we rarely saw a house other than a trailer, it felt as if we were withdrawing from civilization into unfamiliar, "Deliverance" country. Similar to discarding your winter coat, hat, and scarf as the earth warms, as we left our car and hiked deeper into the woods, we discarded the layers of modern, digital civilization—activating the decivilizing process. That Monday when I walked outside for lunch in downtown Cleveland, for the first time I smelled the car fumes, noticed all the noise, and felt the grit on my face—things I had built an immunity to that, because of my time in the woods, I noticed and for the first time, it bothered me. Here in the 15th century, I went through severe digital withdrawal with no future prospect of reconnecting to the Web—be careful what you wish for.

25:   BUNKILLARNY

Soon I began walking around town greeted by stares and open mouths, not only because of my unusual height but also, because of my mere appearance in the close-knit community, where everybody seemed to know everyone else.

Michael was in the habit of visiting McNab's pub on Friday evenings. According to him, it was part of his calling to capture local tidbits for the *Bunkillarny Reader*. Even though there was no such thing as a newspaper yet, he had the innate instincts of a journalist and felt that he could knit the community together with their stories.

One Friday, he asked me to join him. Remembering the stares I engendered while walking around town, I thought that would not be a good idea, but he insisted saying, "They needs ta get ta know ye, laddie. Once they do, you won be such a novelty na mo."

Not that I was against going to a pub. After my long recovery, it being a hot summer's day, I actually looked forward to an ice-cold beer, something that despite the long hours every other day, we would do at work back in the twenty-first century. Even if I was going to labor through the weekend, having a cold beer or two with my workmates on a Friday helped demarcate the end of the week—something to look forward to as a release from the normal tensions of the workweek. So, I agreed to go with Michael, but still had an uneasy feeling with regards to those I would encounter there—those who looked at me as an unwelcome stranger in their close-knit community.

There were a couple pubs in the village, and McNab's tended to attract the town's shop owners and guildsmen. The outside of the pub had little to distinguish it other than the sign above the door—Mc'Nabs. Other than the muted light streaming through its two dirty windows, it was dark with a rough hewn, off-kilter, oaken floor that pitched towards the bar, which after a few pints, I thought might be difficult to navigate. The dark, small, simple wooden tables and chairs did little to lighten up the dingy environs. On a hot day, though, its cave-like coolness felt refreshing.

We sat at the small bar, which, unlike the rest of the joint, had ornate black walnut spirals and finials that had been hand-carved by a craftsman. There were only two taps and, unlike my Irish Bar in Palo Alto with dozens of bottles of vodka, rum, scotch, Irish whiskey, and other assorted elixirs, there was only a keg of Irish whiskey on the tiny back-bar that holds two types of glasses—baked clay mugs for ale and small simple tumblers for whiskey—no wine, no mixed drinks, no foo-foo drinks, no ice; there was just warm whiskey and ale.

I appreciated that we had gotten there early. The only other patrons were two middle-aged men sitting at a far table locked in a high-pitched argument. I was introduced to Sean McNab, the owner who stood behind the bar--a scrappy little fellow with a red beard, strong arms (likely from pulling the tap) and carting pints and kegs, and a peculiar off-kilter grin. From his sour expression, it seemed that McNab did not care much for me. Michael began talking to him in Gaelic, which I could not understand, thereby leaving me alone with my thoughts.

Despite the obvious differences, I felt at home sitting at a bar. Funny how a familiar scene can make a stranger feel at home in a strange land. Everything else in this town, in this time, seemed so unfamiliar and disorienting. I thought that it was fortunate that I was backpacking immediately before that strange phenomenon happened to me, because by then I was already away from civilization, carrying everything I needed on my back. I guess the level of civilization here was better than being stranded in a cave or in the woods, where I would have to fend for myself.

The stout was disappointingly warm. It did not taste like any other stout I had consumed, but with its sweet, bitter flavor, it went down easily. For the next pint, I tried a surprisingly familiar warm ale. I wish it would have been cold, but I guess I could not expect it to be cold for there was no such thing as refrigeration. Michael introduced me to each of the men as they sauntered into the pub. After a couple of pints, as I loosened up, they loosened up too. Michael was obviously one of the most respected and most popular men in town. His vouching for me meant a lot. "If Michael vouches fer ye laddie, why yer fine wi me," one of them said.

I did not say much, but mostly listened and laughed at their stories. Although I could not understand all of it, I was starting to understand the brogue, even sounding a little less 21st-century American myself.

When they asked where I was from, I was caught off guard and stumbled, for I knew I could not tell them I was from 21st century California. As I tried to form some plausible answer in my head, fortunately, Michael intercepted the question. Pointing to the scar on my head, where I had been bashed by a rock in the rapids, when they all came closer to gawk at it, he said, "The poor lad had been set upon by brigands, he had. Hitting him and kicking him, they beat him within an inch of his life, they did. Then they stole everything he ad, includin' his 'orse and clothes and left him for the angel of death to collect his soul. Because of the bump, he is still recoverin'. If it weren't for me Gwendolyn finding 'im in the woods and nursing him back to 'ealth, he'd be dead by now." I nodded in recognition and gratitude for her efforts on my behalf. "Doc says he has a kind of amnesia and can no longer speak proper English or remember where he's from. Poor lad!"

They all examined my bump and nodded in agreement and gave me sad, understanding looks, while I nodded with pierced lips looking a little dazed with my eyes pointed up to my forehead to enhance his story. He continued, "Even though 'is speech is still muddled from 'is ordeal, judgin' from 'is breeding and bearin', it is obvious he's from London or thereabouts, he is. Even though he canna remember 'is trade, with 'is intelligence, he's is obviously a tradesman." With that they all patted me on the back and toast me, "To Rand, he's on' o' us."

Earlier I had noticed that a long table to the right attracted older men and another long table to the right attracted younger men. Those at the bar tended to be the middle-aged shop owners. After a couple of pints, though, the men throughout the bar began mixing, the noise level ratcheted up, and as it became more difficult to hear, it seemed everyone knew everyone else in this tight-knit community.

McNab's wife and two twin daughters, Shannon and Sharon, waited on the tables and cooked simple meals—corned beef, cabbage, lamb stew, soda bread, etc. The daughters were both thin, light on their feet with long red hair, petite features, alabaster skin, and sea-blue eyes. Other than a hunk of bread and cheese, those around the bar did not eat anything. If they wanted supper, they sat at a table, something Mrs. McNab insisted on. She did not want them making a mess and insisted upon a modicum of manners from each of them. They were afraid of her, for she had a fierce Irish temper when they stepped out of line and a large broom she used to poke, bat and sweep them out of the bar. McNab, for his part, let her do the enforcing of the rules so he could be the good guy presiding over the bar.

Earlier in the evening, women occupied the tables, eating dinner with their husbands, but as the night wore on they left. As I learned from thick-tongued, slightly tipsy Shamish Mc Neely, who owned the funeral parlor, the McNabs lived above the pub and they constructed three rooms out back for travelers. Evidently, McNab's was an inn too. "One of the rooms is oft used for the drunks, pilin' up to five in the bed, it is."

Later Shannon and Sharon came out dressed in blue-green tartan kilts, one with a fiddle and the other with a wee accordion-like instrument. Those throughout the bar promptly stopped talking, settled into chairs or stepped to the back of the room. As soon as they started singing, the entire pub joined in. I did not recognize the songs as any I had ever heard, especially the Gaelic ones, but soon sang along or rather produced sounds similar to the thick, deep-brogue drunken words I heard, occasionally getting one or two syllables right. It was not really about the words anyway, but more about joining in and being part of the gregarious group. At times, after the pub started a singing, the girls put down their instruments and being light on their feet, similar to ballet dancers, danced a high-stepping jig, while the patrons clapped out the rhythm. The girls were lovely and highly talented and I could see that all the young fellas were in love with them.

When we stumbled home, somewhat "fluthered and knackered," and totally exhausted, I told Michael, "I had a grand time. Thank you for forcing me to go." With eyes barely slit open, he smiled knowingly, then headed to bed.

———

From that night on, I felt more at ease walking through the village. Evidently, word had spread that the poor lad had indeed been beaten and robbed by unscrupulous, dastardly highwaymen and was knocking at heaven's gate, until he was rescued by the noble McCarron's. Michael thought it was such a marvelous story he published an entire paragraph in the next installment of the *Reader*, including an account of my amnesia.

As I began exploring further around town, I came to know it better. There was a main street where the pubs and shops, including Michael's went on for ten blocks, with two to four streets to either side. The houses were very quaint, some built of stone or cobblestones, others of wood, and some with thatched roofs. Over the centuries, many had minor additions, so that there was little space on the main street, and there was no common architecture or city plan. It resembled one of those quaint medieval Christmas villages you might assemble and add to year after year.

Behind the main street where the McCarrons lived, lay the Bunkillarny River, which gradually wound its way down to the bay below their house. I could see the twenty-foot-wide river from the backyard and hear the falls at the east end of town. Sitting in the backyard, looking out at the peaceful river flowing by, listening to the falls and reading, did much to restore my body and spirit and helped me to adjust to my extraordinary situation, which I still could not fathom, but was growing accustomed to. Periodically I would say a little prayer to myself—*God grant me serenity for those things I cannot change.*

Each day as I regained my leg strength, I tried to walk another block further. At the west end of the main street, to the north, I could see the blue bay of the Irish Sea with green hills on the opposite side, set in the shadows of white clouds passing above. Drawn to the sea, after another week, I was able to reach the strip of sandy beach below. I sat there watching the choppy waves crash against the shore, listening to the white gulls high-pitched, fog-piercing squeals as they soared and dived, the smell of sand, seaweed, salt and fish in the air, the bright sun caressing my face, as a caravel sailed by, heading for the docks to the right.

Walking back up the street, my legs straining to make it, I had to sit on a rock wall for a wee bit. There I could see furrowed fields at various angles, patterned farms dotting the hillsides with obscure blue-grayish mountains rising above to the distant horizon. The farmers and shepherds came into town regularly, but I had difficulty understanding their unique mixture of Gaelic and English. They were friendly and greeted me as I greeted them in the little Gaelic I had picked up—"Dia dhuit," which I had come to learn meant God be with you. In addition to English, Michael spoke Gaelic, German, Latin, and Norman French, the language of the Norman overlords, who had ruled much of the British Isles.

As I walked more and built my muscles back up, I discovered that most of the industry centered around the farms and sheep ranches, where they spun the wool, then knitted sweaters, trousers, and blankets. There was a tanner, where they processed the hides and made sheepskin coats; a miller down river who ground wheat, rye, and barley in his mill powered by the flowing river; a baker who turned the flour into bread, cakes and pastries. A grocer sold produce from the farms. A butcher cut up the lamb, chickens, pigs and cattle. A fishmonger sold the fish caught by the fishermen, who plied the bay. And, there was the one brewery that brewed a dark, delicious brownish ale made from the grains.

The town was big enough to support two Catholic churches, one grand nearly-cathedral sized that, with its tall Gothic spires, towered over the town. The Normans had established this church with a Bishop, who ruled the shire. In addition, there was a monastery with a chapel and a seminary that drew candidates from throughout the region. Even though they may not have been headed to the priesthood, well-to-do shopkeepers and tradesmen from throughout the area sent their sons to the seminary or college for an education. Close to the seminary was the small Norman college, St. Paul's, the only other source of higher education in all of Northern Ireland that drew from prominent families throughout Ireland—and some from nearby Scotland too.

When I finally built up enough stamina to walk up the hill to the college, I saw boys who looked to be anywhere from twelve to perhaps twenty, so I was not sure if it was more of a prep school, a college, or perhaps both. I think it was more of a high school, but that concept probably did not exist yet. The views of the bay and picturesque landscape, including small hamlets from this vantage point were spectacular. I had to sit on the side of the towering hill on the thick, cushy, deep-green grass, where I could gaze out over the hills, the farms, the town, the beach and the docks to breathe it all in—a truly spectacular site. In the distance on the blue sea, I could see a large ship headed for the docks, from I had no idea where. A flag flew on its main mast, but I could not make it out. Perhaps it was the French tri-color, but I could not tell. I imagined that being a port town with ships stopping from throughout the region, with their international sailors enriched Bunkillarny both economically and culturally. Michael had told me that he sold his books printed in Latin to the captains, who would take these with them to sell for a substantial profit at other ports. Back in my time, I constantly referenced Google Earth to orient myself to the various cities I travelled to. Having this Google Earth-like view of the city helped ease my troubled psyche.

———

Recalling my western civilization classes, while sitting at the bar on another occasion, I asked Michael about Henry the VIIIth. I knew that he had pulled away from the Catholic Church sometime around the 1500s, because he wanted a divorce, and consequently established the Anglican Church. He said I still must be recovering, because the king was Henry VII. Then he said, "Queen Elizabeth had just given birth to Henry's second son. The first son, Arthur, will succeed him, perhaps as Henry VIIIth, if that's the name he chooses ta take."

The main street was crowded with people, wagons, horses, and handcarts. Due to the frequent rains, it was muddy much of the time. In addition, the village had two blacksmiths, one of whom worked for Michael, a carriage maker, an inn, an undertaker, and a clockmaker/jeweler. All the multicolored, multi-shaped shops carried Irish names: O'Neil's Tavern, Flannigan's Bakery, O'Leary's Butcher Shop, Harrigan's Brewery, Cleary's Clothier, etc.

As I learned, due to its proximity to Scotland and England, Bunkillarny had been an active port for hundreds of years, at least since the Viking invasions going back in the 10th Century. Ships delivered goods from Wales, Scotland, and England in exchange for woolen clothes, produce, pork, whiskey, and lamb. I visited a store in town that carried a wide variety of these goods, including crafts, leather goods, linen, cloth, and manufactured items.

Some of the men would travel to Scotland in the fall to help with harvests and earn extra money. With their common terrain, Celtic heritage, Gaelic language, Catholic religion, and common clan names, the area greatly resembled Scotland.

St. Paul's College had a small medical school; therefore, there were three doctor's offices and an apothecary in town. Overall, it was a prosperous, friendly town where everyone knew everyone and was happy with its growth and peace.

———

At the pub where I learned so much about the town, I also heard stories of wars to the west and to the south, but none near here. To the west, the O'Donnells and O'Neals periodically fought each other over land. From what I overheard, both clans traced their roots back to St. Patrick in the 5th century and were somehow related. To me, they sounded like the Hatfields and McCoys.

Always obsessed with knowing where I was, I learned that Bunkillarny lay on a bay or what they called St. Patrick's Swilly on the northeastern coast of the island. The long, deep, narrow bay cut deeply inland, something that in Norway might be called a fjord. Even though it was the middle of summer, it was somewhat cool on many days and sometimes it rained. One cloudy, foggy day as I explored further, I came across a curious abandoned wall overlooking the sea. Climbing the rocky structure and looking at the outline of other smaller rocky walls, I realized that it must have been a sizable fortress or castle with a picturesque view of the mouth of the bay. Looking so dilapidated and old, I figured that it may have dated back to Roman times.

When I inquired about the structure, Michael said, "It had indeed been a castle, Laddie, that belonged to a Viking King around 1,000 A.D. The Vikings invaded Bunkillarny, ransacked the town, would have ransacked the monastery and enslaved many of its residents except for the Miracle of the Abbot. Over time, the Vikings intermarried and merged into the local populace. I surmise that many of thon in town probably had some Viking blood and some of me best friends had Viking names."

One such friend, Francis Xavier Harold, claimed that his great ancestor was King Harold of England, who ruled for a short time until William the Conqueror defeated him in 1066 at the Battle of Hastings. Afterwards his sons supposedly fled to Ireland and raised families here as they hatched plans to overthrow the Normans, but never successfully executed the plans.

I met Francis at the pub. He was a heavy man with a round face, deep pretentious voice, brownish thinning hair, hearty laugh, and light blue eyes. He seemed to be a bit full of himself, but someone I still enjoyed. Everybody in Bunkillarny seemed to have blue eyes. Since Francis claimed to be the unofficial town historian, I asked him about when the Romans left Ireland.

"They ner invaded Eireann, which is why we are unique in the civilized world. The Romans conquered Britain but stalled out at Hadrian's wall in Scotland, cause the Scotts are so fierce. So, our brothers, the Celtic Scots, be pure too."

Since he claimed to be of Nordic blood, I asked him about what he meant by pure. "Well," he replied, "The Vikings were not conquered by Rome either—not influenced by their trade, culture and commingling were they." I wanted to pursue the matter further, but realizing I would get nowhere, just let it go.

Now that I was becoming stronger, I wanted to run. Similar to a shower, running cleansed my insides—my circulatory system and lungs. Plus, I missed the endorphins. Unlike heavier, sturdy boots, my hiking boots were reasonably light and flexible, so I could run in them. Other than kids, you never saw anyone running around town. These people worked hard and did not really need any additional exercise. I did not want to call any more attention to myself, than my mere presence already engendered, therefore, I did not run in town. Something that would be ubiquitous in modern America would seem very strange here, as if I were being chased by a wild boar or those bandits. When on one of the outlying roads or on pathways through the woods, I would run until I saw someone coming. Then I would stop and walk quickly, with my heart racing. Gradually, over time, I came to run farther, building up my endurance and my resilience.

26: THE FIRST ENGLISH BOOKS

Earlier, I had asked Michael if I could help him. He smiled one of his toothsome grins, as if he had been waiting for me to offer, but since I had been so ill had not wanted to pressure me. "So, Rand, I see that ye can read, how are ya at the writen' then?"

"I've actually done quite a bit, but it was in a different form of English."

"I see. Well let's give ye a try then," he replied seemingly doubtful that I would be able to handle the job, which motivated me to prove myself.

He put me to work helping out with his printing business. Taking a load off from Gwendolyn, who had graciously spent so much of her time taking care of me, I would receive the news items people submitted and rewrite these for the *Bunkillarny Reader*. Although Michael had to fashion the final story to the local vernacular, he soon appreciated my writing capabilities. The *Reader* had become the major inducement for people to learn to read, so that they could obtain the freshest news and the gossip. As a result, more people attended Gwendolyn's classes and those who could read and correspondingly could read the *Reader*, acquired status in the community for they were the ones who knew what was going on and could tell the others with authority.

My first major article concerned adding a side chapel and a new rectory to the Norman church. The two additions on either side of the current, rectangular church would remake it into the shape of a cross and therefore with its high tower, high ceilings, and flying buttresses, after a century of construction, it would finally, officially, qualify as a cathedral.

I talked to the Bishop as well as the architect, masons, and guildsmen who worked on the addition. I enjoyed watching the masons, trimming the stone with their chisels and using ingenious pulleys and levers, on wooden scaffoldings to lift heavy stones into place, at dizzying heights. The construction site was a beehive of activity, the smell of cut stone dust and mortar wafting in the breeze. The bishop brimmed with pride, now that the long project finally neared its completion. Afterwards, I wrote a two-page article, eclipsing anything previously printed in the *Reader*—something I was proud of showing off. When I presented the lengthy article to Michael, he looked at me with a puzzled grin and trimmed it down to a single paragraph. I realized journalism had a way to go and my future articles would be brief and to the point, as close to weird, 15th-century, Gallic, Norman, English vernacular as I could make them.

Evidently, there was no formal concept of spelling. I noticed in the books I read that the same word could be spelled differently on two facing pages. With a mixture of Old English, these words were spelled phonetically. Dictionaries would not exist for a few centuries and there certainly was no spellchecker, which I had desperately relied upon throughout my career. I was never very good at spelling, usually one of the first out in the grade school spelling bees, and found the lack of such restrictions freeing. Even, according to 21st-century norms, when I was sure I had spelled a word correctly, Michael might "correct" it. He did try to be consistent though. Next, he taught me the tedious art of laying type. It certainly was not easy to spell backwards and reverse the letters, so that the mirror image would come out right.

Michael also owned the blacksmith shop next door, where John McCarthy worked along with his two sons, Ryan and Christopher. When we went into the forge, we saw John from the side. I immediately noticed the dirt and sweat on his face, while he was mercilessly hammering away at the glowing, red tip of a black metal bar. A large man, with a barrel chest and massive arms acquired from years of shaping metal to his will, John had dark thinning hair and a large square face and, of course, blue eyes. I could tell that this was someone I would not want to mess with. After he completed his task, Michael introduced us and John smiled broadly. I could see right away that he was a good and kind-hearted Irishman. Afterwards I met his two sons, Christopher and Ryan, who although leaner, resembled him and looked nearly as strong.

In addition to producing the larger iron items the town needed, John also performed the delicate task of creating the movable type we used in the print shop, a process that Michael asked John to show me.

After his time in Germany, as I had learned earlier, Michael had spent four months apprenticing in London under William Caxton, the first English printer. Michael said, "I learned much from William at Westminster, and we became the best of friends. Through him, I not only learned more about printin', but also about the business of printin', I did. It's na just 'bout printin' the page but what you decide ta put on the page and what ye do wi' it after that."

Interested in the first English printer and what books he produced, I asked Michael to tell me more about Mr. Caxton.

"When Bill was in Cologne he had told me he worked on *De Proprietatibus Rerum*. I can tell by the confused look on yer face ye had not read or heard o' it, laddie. It means on the Properties of things, it does. I have the two books over here, which you are welcome ta read. The original was comprised of nineteen hand-written books dating back to the mid-13th century."

I looked over the books and was fascinated by what looked to be the first encyclopedia and after the Gutenberg Bible, one of the first books ever printed. Even though I was still relearning Latin (not that I ever knew it well), as I fingered through the pages, some of the titles fascinated me:

- Book 2 *De proprietatibus angelorum* - On angels, good and bad
- Book 3 *De anima* - On the soul and reason
- Book 5 *De hominis corpore* - On the parts of the body
- Book 6 *De state hominis* - On daily life
- Book 7 *De infirmitatibus* - On diseases and poisons
- Book 10 *De materia et forma* - On matter, form and fire
- Book 11 *De aere* - On the air and weather
- Book 14 *De terra* - On the earth and its surface
- Book 16 *De lapidibus et metallis* - On rocks, gems and minerals
- Book 17 *De herbis et arboribus* - On plants and trees
- Book 18 *De animalibus* - On land animals

Michael continued, "I studied these books, which represented the thinking of the Middle Ages. Many have been distributed throughout Europe, enlightening many souls. Before, only a handful of men could ever read the tediously, hand-copied works. Now thousands have read it. It's like an explosion of learnin', which our printing is facilitating, it is." I could sense his passion as he spoke.

"After Bill Caxton returned from Cologne, he printed the first book ever printed in English - *Recuyell of the Historyes of Troye*, which means a collection of the history of Troy. The book was originally written in Latin, then in French. Caxton was an excellent editor who translated it into English. While in Westminster, I read the book, which I too found fascinating." Michael reached into the shelves and pulled out his copy, handing it to me. Saying, "This is his lordship's sons' favorite book.

As I gently paged through the book, I could see it was in Old English and the spelling of the words was different from our 21st

century standardized, dictionary-governed versions. I read a section, "In the wrytyng of the same my penne is worn/ myn hande wery & not stedfast myn eyen dimed with overmoche lokyng on the whit paper," which at first looked like someone had their fingers on the wrong keys when they typed this—something I was prone to do.

Even though it took time to decipher, I could soon understand it--"In the writing of this book, my pen is worn, my hand weary, but not steadfast, my eye dimmed with too much looking at the white paper."

Having struggled with my writing from time to time, this was a feeling I could identify with. Evidently, this ancient writer felt the same as I did.

I said, "Is this about the Trojan Wars?"

"Yes it tis."

"Homer's Trojan Wars? As in the Illiad?"

"Why, yes."

"Then the subject dates back to around 1,000 BC," I stated.

"Yes, but the *Recuyell of the Historyes of Troye* has even more detail than Homer's original epic poem."

The Odyssey and the Iliad were two of my favorite books in high school English class. Evidently the subject was popular in the 15th century too, but why wouldn't it be?

I remember seeing a segment on the evening news several years ago that said an original copy of this book sold for over 1.8-million-dollars, which was probably nowhere near in as good condition as this mint one. Realizing I was holding something worth millions, I handled it carefully back to Michael, and contritely asked if I could borrow it to read in the backyard overlooking the river.

He replied, "Of course, you are welcome to read any of the books in me library."

"I will handle it with care, because as the first English book, it will be worth a fortune someday."

Michael responded, "I guess I will have to take good care o' it thun."

———

He continued to talk about Caxton, "As you can see in the front of *De Proprietatibus Rerum,* there is no date or indication of who produced the book—who printed it, something Bill later regretted. So, Bill was also the first to print an English book with an imprimatur in *1477--The Dicts and Sayings of the Philosophers.* I think I have it somewheres. Oh, let me see. Yes here tis. That is why all of our books have our imprimatur, which as you have seen consists of a picture of the falls, our name, 'McCarron Printers', and the date. Now, this be the first book ever printed in the British Isles, in London it were. The previous book was printed by Caxton in Belgium in 1475, which I only knows because William told me and I wrote it on the front page."

"This rare book, also one of the first printed in English, was originally written by an Arab of all people. They were the most advanced civilization during the Middle Ages, they were. Then it was translated into Spanish and then into French. When Bill translated it into English, he added some more philosophers. Bill was the most intelligent and wide-read man I ever met, he was."

I found how the path of knowledge travelled over the centuries fascinating. "Most of these philosophers wrote in Greek, so it was translated from Greek to Arabic to Spanish to French and finally to English. "Why was it not translated directly from Arab to French? Why Spanish first?" I asked.

"Well, Rand. You know when you were laid up with all that Californa stuff you be a talkin', and that shirt with palm trees, we thought you be from Spain. When I were a sailor, we sailed to the southern Spanish ports, where I saw palm trees like those and felt its delightful warmth even in March when it be shiverin' up here. The women there seemed exotic and their learnin' superior to ours.

"Spain has been dominated by the Moors for hundreds of years and though I hate ta say it, they ha a much more advanced civilization than the all o' Europe combined in terms of mathematics, science and literature. Our agent, John, is trying to access their ancient texts at Salamanca University, which has the oldest library in the world and prized books that exist nowhere else. We thought that now that the Christian royals, Ferdinand and Isabella, have taken back nearly all of Spain, we could acquire and publish thon priceless works in English. That would be quite a triumph. I can't wait to get me hands on those treasures. If we could acquire them, with the interest it would engender, we could keep our press busy for years. Why, we would have to add another press and hire more apprentices."

"So why did the Moors have such an advanced civilization, more advanced than Europe? I asked"

"It has to do with the paper."

Somewhat confused I said, "Paper, so the Moors invented paper?"

"No, actually, the Chinese invented paper sometime around the first century. During me travels as a seaman sailing through the Mediterranean, this was a subject I was very much interested in. In Rome, I learned that for hundreds of years, due to their papermaking technology, the Chinese were able to produce books more readily than we were. Therefore, they were able to spread knowledge more easily too. Since business and bureaucracy depended upon the recording of transactions and such, they were also able to advance commerce faster. Therefore, they had a more advanced economy and a more advanced civilization."

"Then, in 794 the Moors defeated the Chinese in a critical battle and obtained their papermaking technology. For 500 years, due to this knowledge, they had a much more advanced civilization than we here in Europe, except for Spain, which, of course, was controlled by the Moors."

Still confused, I asked, "Why was paper such a big deal?"

"All we had here and in Europe was parchment or velum, which were made from animal skins and extremely expensive, something only the wealthiest men could afford. Imagine how many sheep or cattle skins ya would need to print a book. Leather is not cheap, Lad. But now we have a major advantage."

Intrigued, I asked, "What's that?"

"Arab characters are very hard to produce, because they overlap, and therefore are not adaptable to printin'. But our Roman characters are easy to set up as we have been doing in our press. Each character takes up the same amount of space." He drew some long lines and some short wavy lines on a sheet of paper and said, "Arabic characters are like this, which we could not make into type. Our interchangeable letters make it easy for us to set up a page, whereas the Arabs have to carve out a page in a block of wood." Because the Chinese have separate characters for each word, we have an advantage over them too. They need tens of thousands of type for all their words, they do."

As he began digging through some stacked paper, he said, "I've got it here somewhere. Oh, here it is, a sample of Chinese characters. I have no idea what this means, if anything. I copied them while in Rome—found them fascinating. Have no idea what they mean though. They just looked interesting."

嘈 嗷 嗆 嚙 嚈

"They do look Interesting, thank you Michael for explaining that to me. So, it seems the path of civilization has followed a trail of paper and printing technology."

"Yes"

I looked through the table of contents and saw many of the philosophers I remembered from my philosophy and mathematics classes: Hermes; Homer; Solon (who founded democracy); Hippocrates of the oath; Pythagoras of the theorem; Diogenes who looked for an honest man; Socrates; Plato; Ptolemy who was the first to think the planets rotated around the sun 1,500 years prior to Galileo; Alexander the world conqueror; and my favorite philosopher—Aristotle, who taught Alexander. It boggled my mind to think that the material I studied in my 21st century philosophy class might have come from the book I held in my hands.

So, this Arab collected the wisdom of the ages dating back to 500 BC and preserved it in the 11th century. Bill translated it into English in the 15th century, and I studied their wisdom in the 21st century—what an amazing arc of knowledge. I wondered what might have happened if that Arab had not done that. Would all of this have been lost to mankind forever? What a tragedy that would have been.

As I recalled, the Middle Ages were a turbulent time of wars and famines that wiped out up to half of the population of Europe more than once, when the vast majority of people could care less about learning the wisdom of the Greeks. They were more concerned about their daily survival. Back then the Arab and Chinese civilizations were much more advanced. If it were not for them, would those kernels of wisdom have been lost for all time? Would 21st-century students learn less about the wisdom of the ages?

Later I checked Caxton out on my downloaded copy of Wikipedia on my iPhone and found an interesting description of him, where I learned that his works included *Aesop's Fables*, that he coined 1,500 English words, and that he wrote the first English romantic novels, translated from French. He died in 1491—this year, oh geez! Something I could not tell Michael about—this being his mentor and good friend.

With the art of printing growing so rapidly, the early printers fiercely guarded their secrets. Since Michael would be setting up the first press in Ireland, I sensed William felt more open and found Michael's passion, intelligence, eagerness to learn and to please, irresistible.

Michael said, "William also printed Geoffrey Chaucer's poem *The Canterbury Tales*. While apprenticing with him, I helped with a revised version of the popular book with corrected text and added illustrations. From William, I learned the importance of editing and precision. While there, I also learned the art of making type. Even though I had seen this done in Germany, in Westminster, William helped me to learn to do it myself."

"Here, I have both the original Canterbury Tales and the revised version I worked on. You can see how the second edition improved on the first."

I wanted to say that I had read this book in high school English class but caught myself. Wow, I held the original, first edition. Because it was difficult to understand, I did not truly appreciate it back then. I finally understood its importance. From a feature on the evening news, I recalled it had sold at Christies for $7.5 million some time ago, eclipsing the previous record for a portion of the Gutenberg Bible at something like $5.5 million. In 2021 dollars those books would be worth 11 or 12 million dollars each. I looked at Michael's shelf and saw the illustrious Bible there too, which he had acquired while apprenticing in Germany. I noted to myself that this was the entire Bible in nearly flawless shape, containing both books, the Old and New Testament, which had to be worth two or three times as much—$20-30 million, maybe more, for a book—WOW!

Holding the Chaucer book and pointing to the Bible, I said, "Michael, someday these original works will be very valuable too.

Because the German type he planned to obtain contained many characters he would not need in English, Michael had bought his first English type from Caxton, "Bill started out using the German type, but later made his own and kept improving on it, creating several new kinds of letters."

As a computer geek who delved into myriad fonts to find the perfect one for the Web pages I designed, it dawned on me that Caxton had created the first English fonts. I wondered if Caxton originated any of the fonts that I had taken for granted in the 21st century—Helvetica, Times Roman, Old English, maybe? The fonts in these books looked familiar.

Michael said, "When I apprenticed in Cologne, them shipping presses throughout Europe, it was the center of the booming printing industry. Most of the classic works dating back to Roman times, and nearly all of the Church's works were reproduced in Latin, representing perhaps 70% of the books printed up until now. Thus far, there have been very few English books, something I intend to remedy."

I could feel his passion and felt inspired by what I had seen and heard, and felt that I was joining a worthwhile enterprise.

27:   MULTI-MILLION-DOLLAR BOOKS

My head reeling from my casual encounter with Michael, I felt as if I was an archaeologist uncovering priceless works of ancient art. Although I was not all that adventurous, I felt I was becoming something along the lines of an Indiana Jones on the hunt for ancient archeological treasures in Egypt. I never thought much about book collecting, or how many people might be interested in such an endeavor, but I imagined they would have been thrilled to experience what I just experienced— holding the first books ever printed in English and being told the story of the first English printer by someone who actually knew and worked closely with him—WOW!

I took Michael's copy of *Recuyell of the Historyes of Troye* to the backyard and overlooking the river sat on the warmed, black, wrought iron bench, which John had fashioned. It was a warm day: the sun shining, the grass a deep Irish green under a blue sky dotted with high-flying white clouds in the shape of swans and sea turtles. As I began reading this book, I could not believe that I held the first book ever printed in English. As I carefully turned the treasured pages, I soon became enmeshed in the story. I had to pause though thinking that what I held would someday be worth millions. After I finished it, I planned to read the book on philosophy and peruse the Bible next, both worth even more—something unfathomable to me.

Sitting there listening to the gurgling brook and the gushing falls, smelling roses on the mild breeze on such a perfect day, reminded me of how much I enjoyed reading on my balcony back in San Francisco, or on the beach, or by the pool on a rare Mexican or Caribbean vacation—a treat I had not been able to relish for several years as my life began slipping away while I slaved away on that darned app.

There is something immensely restorative about being lost in a novel and occasionally gazing out at a beautiful scene, something I would do after each chapter. Perhaps it was the sun, the positive ions, the fresh air, the lack of stress, or all the above. On my balcony, I could look out onto the magnificent San Francisco Bay, onto Fisherman's Wharf, onto the Golden Gate Bridge, onto Alcatraz, out to the docks in Sausalito, and over to the distant, miniature, quant dockside restaurants of Tiburon, where I had dined.

It also provided an opportunity to gain perspective on life. Odd that I was lost here in the 15th Century thinking about such things. I decided that if I ever were to find my way back, I would change my life, seek more balance, and read more on my balcony.

I felt as if I were in the midst of a revolution. Back in the 21st century, I thought of myself as a soldier in the digital revolution—someone who made a minor contribution to what was happening at the dawn of the 3nd millennium, at the dawn of the third wave. But I had wished I worked for Gates and Allen at Microsoft, or Jobs and Wozniak at Apple, or Brin and Page at Google, or Bezos at Amazon. Each of those companies is worth over \$1-trillion and are the largest in the world.

I wished I were one of their first employees when they deployed their revolutionary technologies that changed the world—Apple employee #25. As I understood, before them the world was dominated by multi-million-dollar IBM mainframes. Those pioneers brought the power of the computer into the hands of the common man – "More Power to the People," as one *Fortune* 50 executive said. After Jobs invented the iPhone, we suddenly had more power at our fingertips than one of those old house-sized mainframes—actually much more, since through the Web we had all the world's knowledge literally at our fingertips.

If I had been an early employee at one of those companies, I might be a multimillionaire by now. But it wasn't really about the money, it was more about being in on the ground floor, participating in the revolution, helping to architect a brave new world—making history—advancing civilization.

I had been so immersed in the technology that I had lost perspective of what it all meant—what the digital revolution had done for us. But being here in the 15th century, I was able to gain perspective. Now the steps in that revolution seemed clearer. It all started with Intel and the microchip. As I had done so many times before, I had to write it down, so I went to my composing desk and grabbed a quill pen and the bottle of ink. From the stack of paper about to be printed, I grabbed a couple of pages and went back out to the bench then wrote my thoughts down.

1. *In the '60s, Moore's Law predicted that the number of transistors and consequent power of the processor would double every 18-months, which had held for over fifty years.*

2. *In the mid- 80s Microsoft's Allen and Gates developed Windows for Apple's Macintosh to apply the chip's power and put it into the hands of the common man—more power to the people.*

3. *Numerous people advanced the Internet invented in 1969, but it wasn't until Bernes-Lee established the World Wide Web in 1990 that it took off.*

4. *Brin and Page at Google invented their dominant, powerful search engine that enabled us to make sense of the trillions of pages on the Web, thereby making the world's knowledge potentially available to anyone in the world.*

5. *Jobs at Apple produced the i-phone, which put the power of a mainframe, the Web, the search engine*

in addition to a myriad of applications at our fingertips.

6. *Bezos at Amazon advanced our ability to order and receive goods online at our door.*

7. *Zuckerberg at Facebook and the other social media companies such as Twitter and Zoom connected billions of us, leading to political revolutions.*

I reread the list, let it sink in and marveled at how much our world had changed through these seven steps and how much of that change depended upon a handful of innovative, visionary young men, many of whom didn't even finish college. Perhaps the structure of college would have been an impediment to their genius. Of course, they were supported by armies of professionals who labored to develop these marvels. As a reward, similar to the Rockefellers, Carnegies, Vanderbilts and Chases of the industrial revolution (the second wave) they became the richest men in the world. I wondered if the digital revolution depended upon these particular individuals, or if they did not step up to the plate, that someone else would have taken their place, for progress seems irresistible, inevitable, as if it were dictated by some kind of cosmic force.

Now, here I am in the 15th century, working with one of the pioneers of the previous revolution, the largest technological communications revolution up until the digital age, perhaps even bigger: a revolution that will also provide "more power to the people" and transform the world. I still could not figure how or why I was here, but I promised to make the most out of this unfathomable opportunity.

Sitting there, daydreaming on a delightful, restorative day, I thought that if I could somehow find my way back to my own time, I could take these books back with me and sell them for $30-40 million, or probably much more because they were in mint condition. I could not take Michael's books though, but after I earned enough money, which would take over a year, I could purchase others.   And I could buy other classic, first-edition works too.

Then, I figured, if I could find my way back through that cave, I could take the books with me and sell them for tens-of-millions of dollars. Geeze, the books I could carry in a child's backpack would be worth a fortune—a hundred times their weight in gold. I could hire back Mike and the whole gang and we would finally build that app that I knew would be even more spectacular than the last one—a world changing/revolutionary app itself. We were like a well-oiled machine that, relying on each other and trusting each other implicitly, could perform miracles in record time, for as a team, we had all the skills needed to conquer the world. Since I would fund the company, we would not be hounded by venture capitalists. I would pay a fair wage and not demand unreasonable hours of them to meet ridiculous deadlines. And, of course, I would give them shares in the enterprise up front. We would be like those early digital pioneers—like Michael, William Caxton, Gutenberg and the other 15th century print pioneers, and we would all be multi-millionaires. And maybe we would buy a large place up in the Sierras near a lake, where we could all go with our families, or maybe a large architectural mansion on the beach.

I hadn't thought about the betrayal for some time now. Being here in the 15th century, so far from my time and place, had helped my psyche heal. But the memory of Steve selling our app for hundreds of millions, flooded back to me. Unlike when Mike and I went to Steve's house to seek revenge, I would finally be able to get even with Steve and save my team.   I remembered that after Steve hadn't given us the promised stock, after he had effectively stolen our app we worked so hard to build, he laid us all off. Mike, the burly Irishman and I went to his house to confront him, not only for ourselves, but for our teams too.

28:   FINDING STEVE

Three years ago, when I considered the job, Steve had painted a glowing picture of the venture he had barely gotten off the ground and had secured initial funding for. Even though Steve had decent coding skills, he lacked the people and project management skills to make the app a success. Oddly, he was a great salesman, constantly promising to meet impossible deadlines to the VCs that Mike and I had to somehow deliver on. I repeatedly cautioned him about making such unrealistic promises, and he repeatedly said this was the last time, but it never was. I liked to design realistic project plans with realistic deadlines that would not overwhelm my teams so they could have a semblance of a life. Of course, we always had to work long hours towards the end to make up for unforeseen hurdles, when we battled together as if we were warriors and won the war. That was fun and then we got to celebrate, something I felt was important.

Back then Steve had exclaimed, "With your proven analysis, design and project management skills, you offer the missing puzzle piece that will make this app a sterling success." The salary was half as much as I could obtain from Google or Facebook, both of whom recruited me and had fabulous perks, but with the promised stock on what looked a sure winner, I would be set for life. Besides, I didn't like working for mega-sized companies, as I had earlier in my career where employees got lost. I liked the various hats you got to wear at a smaller enterprise. That was the game in Silicon Valley. "We can't afford to pay you much, but we will give you stock. You will work long hours for a chance at being rich beyond your wildest dreams."

It was similar to playing the lottery, but the odds were actually better. I always looked at all those icons who had made it—kids in their twenties like Zuckerberg, Gates, Brin, Blazos and Jobs. They all became multi-billionaires, the richest men in the world. Just think of all the fun you could have and the good you could do once you too became a billionaire. The Bay and the Valley were filled with people like them, not just the big names but hundreds, maybe thousands of those who worked for them and now lived in multi-million-dollar mansions. That's why it was difficult to find a decent 1,500-square-foot house on a postage-stamp lot for under a million and a half.

Throughout the project, whenever the going got rough, like the proverbial carrot and a stick, Steve kept promising the stock, which I, in turn, promised my team. When pressed on it, he said the lawyers were working on it with the VCs. Then I got too busy to think about anything other than the all-consuming app—the blinders were on, and for nearly all of my waking hours, I was immersed in a virtual world of rectangular, lit screens. I was the one who designed the app, including both what it looked like to the user and also all the interactive programs running behind the scenes. I was the one who met with the VCs to present our technical plans, demo the prototypes and demonstrate our progress, assuaging their fears that we were aimless and burning through their cash too fast. I was the one who obtained that next round of manna-like cash that allowed us to survive another month.

Now that I was in my 30's, I was already geriatric in the Valley. Burned out, I did not think I would be able to do this again. I had just struck out on the digital lottery—my last.

———

I had to find Steve. I had to confront him. Not just for me, but for the people on my team too—for all of us. But I did not know where he lived—something he oddly did not disclose to anyone. While working late one night, after all the others had left, and the cleaning lady had emptied my nearly full wastebasket, my mind numb from trying to design an optimal screen layout, no longer able to make any progress, I ambled into the break room for a diet coke from the fountain. Like a computer with so many billions of instructions per second, I only had so much mental capacity—maybe one instruction per second. When I kept going, searching for that elusive solution, an hour could go by and I would be in a loop going nowhere. It was difficult to pull myself away, continually thinking the solution was just around the corner, but it never was. Eventually, I learned that whenever I reached a seemingly impenetrable roadblock, although it was difficult to pull myself away, the best thing I could do was to take a break. Somehow, my mind would continue to work on the problem subconsciously, and when I returned, the solution would suddenly appear, as if it was resolving itself, waiting for me to come back to it. It was as if someone had magically appeared and written the solution down for me before disappearing.

Gazing out the window towards the empty, black parking lot with a bunch of white lines, dimly lit by a lonely streetlight, wandering by the pool table, taking a couple of shots while my mind cleared, I noticed Steve's office was lit.

I walked in and casually asked him where he lived, to which he replied, "It's not far from here, Rand, in a place with little furniture. Where I live doesn't matter much to me, 'cause I'm so focused on this venture and don't spend much time there anyway. Why spend a lot on a pad you rarely visit?" From his description, I imagined he lived in a typical, nondescript 400- to 600-square-foot barebones studio or one-bedroom apartment similar to mine. He had a large office and I sometimes saw him sleep there on the couch, so I never asked again.

I spent a lot of time working closely with Steve, and although I realized work relationships were tentative, I thought we were good friends, which is probably why the betrayal stung so much—I trusted him to do the right thing and he screwed us over.

I had to find him. He might be moving soon, and then we would have no recourse.

I went online to try to track him down, but all of his accounts had been deleted—Facebook, Twitter, Instagram, LinkedIn, What's App, Snapchat—all gone. Even his phone number was out of service. Frustrated, I slammed my fist on the table causing my keyboard to rattle. I stormed around my apartment then opened the sliding door to the balcony and looking over the scenic bay, I took some deep breaths to calm down. Not surprising, with the talent arraigned against him, Steve had deleted everything. If we could find any trace of his devices, they would be infiltrated and destroyed. Desperately, I tried some hacks but still could not find his address.

I knew that he and Mike were good friends, so I called Mike hoping that he might know where he was. I took my cell phone out of my pocket, touched contacts and tapped Mike's picture.

Mike said in a raging voice, "I know where he had lived. I want to confront the bastard too. We had better go immediately, because I heard through a mutual friend that he will be moving out of the country to Saint Bart's soon."

I mounted my trusty red Porsche and hopped on the 101. I picked Mike up in Mountainview, where he recklessly plopped into the passenger's seat. Without saying anything, I glanced smugly at him, to which he responded, "Sorry dude, I'm used to climbing up, up into my SUV, not sitting six inches off the ground. And where's all the tech, man? You got no screens, no cameras, nothing. Really man. Such a sweet ride but no tech?"

"This is my inner sanctum, Mike. I spend all day and night developing technology, so I special ordered it without any of that stuff. I want to be in contact with the road and the driving experience. All the tech just gets in the way—it's a distraction.

The only things I have are the best stereo I could buy and that holder for my cell phone. Besides, this is where I get my best ideas and penetrate critical obstacles."

A couple of miles down the road, in the far-left lane I was effortlessly passing a myriad of water buffalo/cars, when a Mercedes SUV pulled out. Without thinking, I automatically feathered the brake and steered into the berm, narrowly avoiding her, then tapped the horn, causing her to reenter her own lane, obliviously smiling back.

Being in the passenger seat, inches from the errant monster, Mike stared at me like someone who has just avoided death. "That was amazing man—how you responded so quickly, amazing, dude!"

"It's because I don't have all the tech. I'm linked to the car, and it's linked to me. Otherwise, we would be smashed up on the side of the road with that hapless woman waiting for the cops to show up, looking back at all the looky-loos gawking at our unfortunate accident."

Mike took some getting used to—a gruff, crude, mesomorphic Irishman with a barrel chest who still spoke in a Southern-California-flavored Boston accent. He grew up in Boston where his father labored as a longshoreman before the family moved near the San Pedro docks, where Mike attended middle school. Fueled by a constant stream of Diet Cokes and Red Bulls, Mike, the consummate technician, worked at a frenetic pace, typing faster than I could talk, spitting out line after line of perfect systems code. He worked the same long hours I did, with one exception: Saint Patrick's Day, when he didn't show up until noon the following day blurry-eyed but groggily worked till midnight.

Most people's first impression of Mike was that he was an uncouth, uneducated Irishman, but Mike received his undergrad from USC and his Masters in Systems from MIT. Despite taking some getting used to, Mike was the kind of friend who would always be there for you.

With a throaty roar of the engine, we stormed off to Steve's town, effortlessly winding our way along the picturesque, curvaceous coastal highway. The house resided in one of those gated communities up on a hill overlooking the ocean, where Mike hacked the keypad to open the gate.

All the houses in this rarified municipality had the typical red tile roofs with light, pastel-colored stucco walls, no doubt prescribed by the tawny community. Occupying spacious quarter- to half-acre lots overlooking the peaceful blue Pacific under a velvety blue sky, with a minimum of 3,500 square feet, the homes must cost three million or more. Squadrons of Latinos tended the well-manicured green lawns and lush shrubbery that occupied what was once a mesa. I remembered seeing it before they hatched the development. What they did was to scalp the top of the mesa, flatten the top it so it looks like an overturned mixing bowl, strip off all the sparse natural vegetation, cover it in black plastic tarp and plant multimillion dollar homes accompanied by lush green vegetation, none of which is natural to the area and required constant watering and tending. It was so artificial—like Steve.

Remembering how much Steve had done to remove his digital tracks and how much my red Porsche stood out, we parked a couple houses down. Feeling like rookie detectives, we crouched down behind the bushes beside his house, our knees becoming wet from the recent sprinkling. Parting the dark green branches, we spied a moving van in the drive. I feared he had already departed the premises. I felt ridiculous, but knew I had to go through with this unfamiliar role—after all it was for our people.

We saw a stunning, voluptuous, tan, blue-eyed, Southern California blonde in a short, low-cut tangerine dress step out of the domicile, who took my breath away. Our eyes followed her every rhythmic step as she turned her bare back and faced a thin, short, tan dude with sweptback black hair who just appeared in the doorway. We could barely hear him say, "The

Gulf Stream leaves for the island in a couple of hours. The movers can finish up here. We should head to the airport, babe."

Then she ran up to him and gave him a big, juicy kiss as he pulled her tiny waist close to him. "I can't wait to be on that gorgeous beach, sunning and sipping a long, cool Mai Tai with you, honey," she said.

It was Steve.

Mike turned red. "If I had a gun and knew how to use it, I'd shoot the bastard right here, right now!"

We followed the bushes to the backyard, where we got down on our knees and barely squeezed through an opening between two of the bushes, hoping no one would see our comic skullduggery. We daintily pranced to the side of the house and around the corner, where we saw that the backside was filled with windows overlooking a large infinity pool that, in turn, looked out over the ocean. Obviously, Steve had a lot of money from his previous ventures, and I wondered why I was always sweating to extract more funds from the VCs. Or was he siphoning off our funds to pay for this palace? It was certainly no 400-square-foot studio.

We tried a couple of windows on the side to see if they would open. If we went to the front door and knocked, no doubt he would see us on the security camera and call the cops. I whispered to Mike, "We have to do something, and we have to do it quickly, before they get away."

Then the beautiful *Bay Watch* girl stepped out of a sliding door, walked to the pool, and dipped her meringue-colored toes into the water, then, as if on a catwalk, glided back. When she closed the door behind her with a shimmy, we did not hear a click, so we sneaked over to it, slid the door open and slipped in.

Super-consciously, our skulking around felt stupid. *But we have to do this—we had no choice.* Once inside, we saw a huge kitchen with all the large, premium stainless steel restaurant-grade appliances that looked like they had never been touched.

We tiptoed through a hallway past a couple of large rooms, past an office and a den, searching for him when we heard some cooing and moaning. Tiptoeing, we stealthily made our way through a couple of open rooms, toward the sound. When we located the source, we saw the blonde sitting on Steve's lap, his hand pawing her long, shapely, tan leg, passionately making out.

We exchanged a grimace before we got down on all fours and crawled behind the white couch, where they were totally enmeshed in each other, oblivious to anything else.

We stood up.

I cleared my throat. In a deep voice, said, "Hello, Steve."

Shocked, Steve threw the woman onto the carpet. She rolled over before looking up at the intruders aghast.

Struggling to regain control of himself, Steve nervously asked, "What are you guys doing here?"

"We are here to get what is owed to our teams."

Taking control, acting like the boss, "But I gave you each three months' salary. That's more than generous. I did not have to do that, you know. You all signed the required employment-at-will form, under which you could be fired any time."

My sense of outrage burning, I said, "That would not even be close to paying for our overtime. If you had paid Mike and me twice that much, it would still be less than what we would have made elsewhere over our three years. You promised us stock. We built the app. All you did was come up with a concept—one that was not that unique and not very well thought-out. All the ideas were ours, and we and our teams killed ourselves to make it happen. Without us, you would have nothing."

Mike had been trading glances with the pin-up girl sprawled on the floor, until I hit him in the elbow. She meanwhile sneaked over to the doorway on the opposite side of the immense, sun-drenched room where she fiddled with her cell phone—I guessed ready to take pictures as evidence in case we murdered Steve, because judging by the expression on her face, she obviously saw how disturbed we were. Surprisingly, she smiled sympathetically at me, like she knew he could be a jerk.

After he stood, we came around to the front of the couch to block his escape, when Mike pushed him back down onto the couch, where he bounced a couple of times.

Looking as if he felt empowered, Mike said, "How much did you make off our slave labor, you gutless shyster?"

Steve, shaking, no doubt afraid Mike might pummel him, replied, "After the VCs took their share, it did not amount to that much."

Mike bent over him and stuck his finger at Steve's nose. "From our investigator, I heard you took in over a half-billion. You and that greedy bastard CFO still held forty percent of the stock, thirty-five percent yours. I did the math Steve. If you gave those who designed and built it a mere five percent, you would still run off with $175 million. Isn't that enough for you?"

A minute ago, Mike was about to punch Steve in the mouth. Now, I was afraid, seeing how red and inflamed Mike had become, that he might wring Steve's neck, and I would have to pull him off—something I was not sure I would do.

Steve held his hands out in supplication. "Believe me, I tried many times to get the VCs to give you all stock, but once we gave up control we had no power to do so. If we would have delivered the app sooner, I would not have had to give up the controlling interest and you would have gotten the stock you all deserved."

"You could have still given us some of your shares," I pointed out. "That would have been the decent thing to do."

"The contract and the lawyers would not have let me do that,"

Looking like he might burst, Mike added, "We are going to sue you for every penny, you f—"

"Go ahead and try Mike," Steve growled, his lips open in his typical forced, perfect smile. "You don't have a leg to stand on. The law is on our side, and the VCs with their deep pockets can fight you for years. Besides, I won't even be in the country. So you won't be able to get to me, Mike."

Seeing that Mike might do some serious damage to his pretty-boy face, Steve, who was obviously feeling highly threatened and thinking I would do nothing to stop Mike, continued, "I do feel bad though. You and Rand were there from the start and deserve more. I will give you an extra three months' pay out of my own pocket—that's an extra half year's salary."

"What about the rest of our guys and gals, most of whom were there for two years faithfully working ungodly hours?"

"I can't do anything for them."

There was a loud knock at the door. Two security guards in gray uniforms with silver badges appeared at the door, who the attractive blonde immediately let in, looking relieved that they were there. She must have pressed an icon on her phone calling security to our GPS location—an act she had disguised with her perfect, beguiling, oft-applied smile.

As they walked into the room, Steve stood up and pointed. "Arrest these two! They broke into my house and accosted us."

As the two approached, Mike looked at me as if he was ready to rumble. Looking at the two of them and realizing that Mike was a stocky guy, I realized we could take them before they had a chance to reach for their mace.

In the distance, I heard sirens. The smaller security guard seeing the stressful situation, must have called the police. I had no desire to go to jail, so I said, "Let's go Mike!"

As if he were a deflating balloon, Mike let out a sigh. The tension in the room lowered dramatically with that sigh, until he turned, took a step, then spun around and with all his might, connected with Steve's jaw, sending him flying across the room.

Mike then calmly proceeded to walk out.

The stunned, larger, portly security guard, not really wanting to take us on, meekly responded, "Do you want us to have them arrested, sir?"

Steve got to his knees, looking dizzy, blood dripping from his mouth. In a barely audible, gurgled tone, he said, "We have a plane to catch. Let them go." Holding his mouth, trying to get to his feet and recover what was left of his dignity, he stumbled and fell to his knees again.

Once on the manicured lawn, hearing the siren coming closer, we ran to the Porsche and sped away.

On the way back, Mike group-texted our team a description of what happened. The phone continuously played the first few notes of "Born in the USA" as they enthusiastically responded with messages ensconced in emojis.

"Mike, I don't condone violence, but…" I shook my head and laughed. "That was awesome."

He grinned wickedly. "Would you have helped me with the security guards?"

"I haven't been in a fight since fifth grade, and even then it wasn't much of a fight, but I would have taken them on."

"I could see you were ready to go, buddy, and they looked very pensive. You're a big, athletic guy. They were afraid of us. We could have easily taken them. I grew up in a large Irish family with three brothers. We were always fighting. It was our exercise routine."

"I didn't know about the legal case. How far has it gone?"

Mike sighed. "After spending the three months' salary on legal fees, the lawyers told me that even though what Steve did was despicable, we did not have a case. I talked to my team and we will plaster all their names across the Web so no other developers will ever work for them again, but sadly, I don't think they care much. But it will hopefully hurt the VCs' efforts in the future. Developers who see it spread all over social media will not want to work for them, but even if they have to go to India, they will find developers, or just hide behind the scenes in a fake subsidiary." Mike's expression softened, as if he had some regrets. "Scratch one friend. I can't believe Steve did that to me. What an unethical bas—"

"Yeah, that's a shame. I thought you guys were tight. What a jerk."

We had not won anything, but oddly, I felt as if we had gotten a measure of retribution.

29:   DEPRESSION

For a couple of days after the confrontation, I felt better. I wrote recommendation letters for the team and mailed them to each of them. I thought about pursuing Steve in St. Bart's and harassing him there but realized that would be fruitless.

I spent endless depressed days on the small patio of my studio apartment on top of the precipitous hill, looking down the canyon-like street and out to the Bay—my only consolation. I watched the daily fog gradually roll out in the morning then roll back in in the evening, logging when it cleared and began to reappear on my iPhone. I watched the ships come in, dock and roll out, playing the blues station on Amazon Music over my ear buds and that *Dock of the Bay* song over and over in my head. It fit my dire mood. I watched the sailboats on their weekly regattas sail around the bay like bees circling their hive.

My life transpired like one of those slow-motion videos with the fog rolling in and out and ships and sailboats flying around the bay, the iconic, orange bridge lighting up at dusk, the fog obscuring it in the morning. When my supply of food evaporated, I ordered Chinese, subs or pizza online, and the only people I saw were the delivery boys or girls. Days blended with nights. I had not left the building for I didn't know how many days—or was it weeks? I felt lethargic and lousy. My place was a mess, but I couldn't muster up the energy to clean it up.

After hearing about the layoff, sensing my depression, my friends Paul and Betty, who lived up in Sonoma, invited me to spend some time with them and tour the wineries. Paul, who was the chief winemaker at yet another new winery, said he could use some help trimming the vines, but I was too depressed to go. They still hoped that I would join them for the

Grand Canyon trip, but I did not think I could do that. I texted back, "Sorry guys I'm not going—too bummed." I just could not extinguish the sense of betrayal from my mind.

As the days passed, I couldn't sleep until early in the morning, then slept till noon, nodding off throughout the day, just moping around, watching the slow-motion video of the bay playing out. I felt sluggish and awful. Finally, I couldn't stand it anymore. I had to get out. Before, I had never gone more than a week without running, and my body craved endorphins. I ran along the Bay Trail with a strip of well-maintained grass in between the asphalt path along the choppy waters, a mild, warm breeze blowing in my face. After a couple miles, I sat on a bench, sipping from my water bottle, just staring out towards Alcatraz, transfixed for I didn't know how long.

Running another mile was surprisingly difficult. My legs felt like rubber, I was breathing heavily, my heart pounding out of my chest, I had to stop and lie down on the soft, green grass. I glanced at my Fitbit. My pulse was over 200—amazing how fast I had gotten out of shape.

I had to walk the rest of the way back to the trolley. But after the run, similar to a shower cleansing my inner body, under the influence of delightful endorphins, the effort seemed to cleanse my blood system of toxins while clearing my mind. I suddenly realized I had to join Paul and Betty, Jenny and Wesley on our trip to the Canyon. I did not want to miss this opportunity, or them. Geez, Jenny was coming all the way from Germany for the trip we had planned months ago. How could I not be with her?

I texted Paul, "Hey dude, I'm in for GC."

He texted back, "Cool man. Betty can't wait to see u. Should b a blast!"

I stopped at the trolley turnaround and helped the tourists turn the trolley around, grabbing the Hyde Street trolley back up the steep hill. Maybe it was the endorphins, or maybe it was the wind rushing by as I held on with my right arm and leaned out of the trolley, but this was the best I had felt in weeks, no, months. I knew I had to do something to extract myself from my funk. I knew I had to get away and be with some long-time friends. I knew I was burned out from months of excessive hours and being betrayed. Being in nature, backpacking always seemed to restore my soul.

———

When I first moved out, I lived in Silicon Valley and worked for an ethical startup that granted all of us stock options. As one of the major systems analysts and designers, I had quite a bit of stock, and after they sold out, I used the proceeds to buy the Porsche and fund a failed startup. Given how expensive and difficult finding parking was, it just did not make sense to drive in the city. When traffic was not gridlocked, I would drive to the office, otherwise I would take the BART. Besides, I loved walking in the city or if it was over a couple miles, riding on the trolleys, the busses, the streetcars and the BART. I felt more in contact with the city that way.

I kept the Porsche in a friend's garage, using it to periodically drive to work, Yosemite or Wine Country, or down to Carmel or Big Sur on weekends. Similar to New York, or I suppose any major city, most San Franciscans spent nearly all of their lives in the city, rarely getting away. Because of the high housing costs, many commuted an hour or two away from the city and did not take advantage of all the area offered. Spending so much of their lives encased in a car, the last thing they wanted to do on a weekend was drive somewhere. I guessed the megalopolis somehow absorbed them, and because of the horrific traffic and commutes, on the weekends, they stayed close to home performing their prescribed chores, soaking up their families and their expensive abodes.

I loved driving along the curvaceous Pacific Coast Highway (PCH) with the windows and sunroof wide open, hugging the turns, soaring like a gull above the azure-blue Pacific where the waves crashed into the rocks and propelled spray high into the air, taking in the endorphins, inhaling the salt water, redwoods, mariposa pine and eucalyptus—happily smiling as I flew along. I would stop at the hippy-run Nepenthe restaurant perched far above the ocean on the side of a cliff with breathtaking views of the gentle mountains cascading down to the sea and a peaceful atmosphere for lunch, or backpack in, sometimes with friends and sometimes by myself, where I would always meet some interesting, nature-appreciating folks.

Big Sur was a spiritual place for me. I first came there immediately after graduating from college. After hitching down the coast in a hippy van, following one of the hippy's advice, I hitched further down to Big Sur. As a city kid, I had never heard of backpacking before, but being short on funds, since camping in the woods was free, I ended up venturing deep into the woods, and up into the mountains, where I had some amazing adventures under the kindly giant redwoods and discovered ancient laid-back Indian ruins and a spiritual Buddhist retreat that took me in and taught me how to meditate. There, under the influence of the magnificent redwoods, the peaceful river, the Pacific Coast and Mother Nature, I ascertained my purpose in life. I hoped the trip to the Canyon would similarly help me figure out my future direction. That first trip also addicted me to the bay area, foreshadowing my future there.

———

After the late hours and continuous snacking while building the app, I had put on a dozen extra pounds and was desperately out of shape. Before the layoffs, I had managed to run occasionally, not far, but enough to maintain some semblance of muscle tone and relieve all the built-up stress. I also managed to walk in a park not far from work during the one or two lunches I took a week, when I worked through seemingly unsolvable, tangled obstacles. Now I ran every other day and filled my pack on the off days and walked up and down the steep San Francisco streets. The plan was to complete the Grand Canyon circuit from the South Rim to the North Rim and back—not an easy task. I had to get in shape because I did not want to hold my friends back.

Now, when I looked out over the city and the bay, instead of the random arcs of boats and people and cars, I suddenly saw purpose in the chaos of the seemingly random metropolis. I saw dozens of container ships entering the bay and docking at the myriad of slips on the embarcadero or going on to Oakland. The sailors brought in goods from exotic ports of call for the millions of us in the Bay Area or to be driven to supply the rest of America.

I also saw bums panhandling in the park and on the streets below. They did not contribute to society, which bothered me. But I could not judge them, for I did not know their stories and I usually gave them my change or a buck as I passed them by. Still in a funk, I did not want to end up like them and hoped I would somehow find a way to engage in life again.

With doubts about my chosen profession, I just did not know what I would do. Mine was certainly a high-demand, well-paying career, but I was so done with it. Most of those people below me did real things. I worked on imaginary things—software—not something hard or concrete. Not something real. Maybe I would become a sailor on one of those ships and see the world, experience it. Or maybe I would get a cabin in the woods near Big Sur and commune with nature and the laidback people like Jack Kerouac, Steinbeck and Arthur Miller.

Similar to the '49er's 170-some years ago who struck gold in "them there" hills, I knew several people who had struck it rich in the bay area, building applications similar to mine. I still felt stung but was not totally jealous, for many of them would no longer contribute to society. They may acquire a mansion or two, a Ferrari, an island, a yacht, and eat at expensive restaurants and attend ritzy charity balls, but they would no longer be contributing to society and the purpose-filled economy I saw below me. Similar to Bill and Melissa Gates, many would make amazing contributions to the world through their charitable pursuits. Others would be little more than rich bums.

30: PRINTING

Michael had me work on laying out the type to be printed, so I guess I became a 15th Century typesetter—a profession I could never have imagined for myself, although it was not all that different from my 21st Century job. One fresh, dewy morning John, the burly, friendly Irishman, showed me the process of manufacturing type. On a piece of paper, Michael had drawn out a super-sized letter "$\mathcal{K}$" in a new font, which he presented to John. Using the drawing as a guide, John cast a punchout of the letter on hard metal, saying, "This is a delicate task that requires intense concentration it is, and I oftens have to throw out a couple o' attempts before it looks right ta me, lad." After Michael inspected and approved the punchout, John used it to press into soft copper, which he calls the matrix.

I could not help thinking that this matrix resonated with my understanding of modern computer printing. A matrix printer prints letters using tiny pin pricks of ink according to a square pattern. This is similar to the lights on a high school basketball scoreboard that combine to produce the various digits—0 through 9 to display the score. The advantage of a matrix printer was that you could print multiple copies at the same time on carbonless paper because the pinpricks would push onto the other copies.

The copper impression served as a mold. According to a formula Michael had learned from William Caxton, John poured a mixture of tin, lead, and antimony into the mold. As he extracted the long bar from the mold. he told me, "There are three kinds of type for each letter—a large capital letter, which we don' need many o, a regular-sized capital letter, and a lowercase letter, which we need a lot of, cause we use a lot of thon."

I used the large caps, similar to this 𝔛, for headings as well as at the start of a paragraph, similar to what Michael had done when he transcribed books by hand at the seminary. With the capability to produce any kind of type, Michael expanded his fonts, including some that were truly elegant. Plus, when the old type wore down, he could readily replace these without having to wait for type to arrive from London or Germany.

———

The freshly produced type was placed in wooden trays stored in what John called a type case. I drew letters from the type case to set up a page. Of course, there were more of the frequently used letters such as i and e in their cubby holes than x and q and there were additional cubbies for punctuation marks too. Using a document that Michael handwrote with a quill and ink, the letters needed to be arranged backwards, something that took me a while to adjust to. I had to make sure that letters such as p and q, and d and b weren't errantly inserted for each other—I had to mind my ps and qs. I guess that's where the phase came from.

Since I had designed many computer screens, my coding background provided a good foundation for me to rely on. At one point, I thought this was too complex, but then realized it was easier than laying out a Web page in hypertext and really easier than learning a whole new language, which since technology was always changing, I frequently had to do. As Michael taught me, I put each of the letters onto a composing stick containing one line of the document. After checking the layout twice, I would place each of the composing sticks onto what Michael called a galley, "cause it tis broad and shallow like the ship lad, do ye ken" a term I recognized from 21st-century printing, but didn't know its origin.

My first task was to typeset the *Bunkillarny Reader*, which consisted of two columns on a single piece of paper. To separate the columns, John provided extra-wide blank bars that I used in the middle of each line, thereby saving me laying out six blank type. To construct a page, I placed filler between the lines to firmly wedge the lines in place on the form.

Soon I laid out books that consisted of two pages, each page having two columns of type—four columns in all. We would print at least two pages at a time by placing two galleys into a form—a square tray that held the galleys. By doing this, the boys nearly doubled their output.

Because they had to be folded into a book, the pages were not sequential, so that keeping the pages straight was complicated too. The only way I could picture this was to think of a newspaper. Let's say you're reading an eight-page folded newspaper. When you examine it, page one and page eight are on the same side of the sheet with page two and page seven on the backside. Groupings of eight or sixteen pages would be sewn together during the binding process. After making a few mistakes, when I had to start over, I was starting to feel like a pro.

Next, I would take the form over to the apprentices, who would print a test page for me. Because we would not want to have to throw out, say, 100 pages due to errors, Michael would proof the page before they started printing multiple copies of the final pages. Paper, after all, was expensive.

———

Michael would hand back the corrected pages to me and although he did not openly criticize me, I could tell he was frustrated with my errors, particularly for the Latin books. Many of the works I laid out were in Latin for the church or for others, since practically anyone who read these days—the wealthy, the learned and the ecclesiastical, read Latin. With so many variations and dialects throughout the continent, Latin was the international language of the time that bound Europe together. Even what would become Germany or Italy 400 years from now, had scores of dialects and no standard spelling.

As a high school freshman, I took a class in Latin because it seemed to be the root language for French, Spanish, Italian, and in part, English. I then took a year of Spanish in high school and another year in college, but because of my technical major I was never required to take more. Now, I wished I had. Still, some of the Latin came back.

When I asked Michael for a Latin to English dictionary, he looked at me and smiled. Then, rummaging through a large pile of books and papers on his desk, he pulled out a book he acquired in London and said, "This is the first of what you might call a 'dictionary'—the *Catholicon* written in 1287 by Johannes Balbus. This copy was printed by Gutenberg around 1460. When we were copying the books, the other monks and I frequently referenced it."

Then he gave me the book saying, "After the Bible, this was one of the first books to ever be printed going back to around 1460."

I carefully thumbed through the book, which had 330 leaves.

I told Michael, "I really do not understand what I am laying out, but would like to. I think I could do a better job if I did." Michael recommended I spend some time with Jimmy Brogan, since he translated works from Latin to English. The translation moved slowly at first, but I felt much better when I could understand what I was laying out and despite my lack of talent for languages, Jimmy actually made if fun.

Plus, occasionally I would find an error, which Michael greatly appreciated—considering how many copies we might print, he was a stickler for accuracy. "The lord and gentry would not be pleased paying for a book that was riddled with errors, he said." I could see that few people in the 15th century would have patience for this type of work, but since I had to be a stickler for detail in the systems I developed, the tasks fit me well.

Michael's Gutenberg's Bible, which I perused was printed in Latin with beautiful hand drawings and consisted of two volumes, the old and new testaments, comprising 1,200 pages in all—what an epic work! It is, indeed, the revolutionary book that would soon change civilization forever. Seeing how precise and time-consuming the process was, I thought that Gutenberg must have been inspired by God or, at least, a remarkable Christian to take on such a monumental task—creating the first printed book.

Curious about the origins of printing, I later learned from my iPhone that the Chinese invented movable type in the mid-12th century, but since their language did not have individual letters, they used 50,000 typefaces for each of their words. Therefore, Gutenberg's typeset was much smaller and more manageable.

I also looked up the *Catholicon* and found that one leaf of the book had sold for $6,000. The book I held earlier today had 330 leaves in nearly perfect shape, which if sold separately might be worth two-million dollars or probably more in mint condition. I added this to my list of books to acquire and take back to the 21st century promising to sell it whole, for cutting it up seemed criminal to me. I did not know if it would be worth more separately or together, but didn't care.

31:   THE SHOP

Our little shop resembled a factory assembly line, with Jimmy translating; Michael writing, editing and formatting the pages; John molding the fonts; me doing the typesetting; and Tommy and Seamus running the press and binding the books. Michael had recently hired a third apprentice, Ronan to help with the press and binding. The smell of drying oil-based ink, paper and leather being bound and the rhythmic sound of the press permeated the shop—the smell and sounds of productivity—a smell I loved.

I occupied the composing desk with rows of letters in tiny cupped holes that I placed into the form, while looking at the pages resting on an angled stand Michael fed to me. The desk was slanted and high as was my stool. Behind me in the middle of the shop stood the press manned by the apprentices with its rhythmic sound constantly spitting out finished pages. Behind the press were rows of clothes-lines stacked four high, where they hung the pages. The bottom two rows held the front pages, while the upper two rows held the finished pages. On the opposite side of the lines was a table where Ronan bound the pages together with boards and a leather cover into a book—an art in itself.

Gwendolyn occupied a small table to the left, next to Jimmy and Michael had a small office in the back with a window overlooking the river. Michael had added the single floor shop with a slanted roof to the house along the side facing the street. In front, there was a half-wall, where the finished books were stored, where patrons could peruse and purchase a book. In reality this was not much different than the open offices I had worked in, except that, lit by the few windows and candles, it was much dimmer. Although, since it wasn't the typical antiseptic bright office space, it seemed more like the factories where I had worked my way through college, and where random workers occupied odd crannies dominated by machines and the dictates of production.

The work days were long but we all would stop for lunch and eat at the long wooden kitchen table, where Daisy prepared a filling lunch for us all and we relaxed and talked. Sometimes I would take my plate out to the river and just watch it flow by letting my mind and fingers recover from composing. Sometimes Gwendolyn would join me whose company I enjoyed. There we discussed the books we were working on or had read and I came to appreciate her intelligence and thirst for knowledge. Being careful not to talk about the 21st-century, I taught her about things she had not read about.

It soon became apparent that Seamus did not care for me. Whenever I brought over a form for a test print, he would scowl. At first, I assumed it was because I interrupted their process, which I did feel badly about, because they had such superb rhythm, and they had to take out the production form to slip in my form, then take mine out and reinsert theirs. Of course, if it were near the end of a run, I would wait.

Michael told me that Seamus had expected to be trained in type setting—the next step up the apprenticeship ladder, but because he needed to advance his reading skills, he did not feel he was ready for it yet. And also, Seamus did not yet possess the patience and accuracy required to do the setting—something that despite my initial difficulties and Michael's doubts, I was able to prove myself at doing, but considering my skills laying out Web pages, was not much of a stretch.

While they were inking a new form, I overheard Seamus tell Tommy that after he finished his apprenticeship and became a journeyman printer, he planned to ask Gwendolyn to marry him, but he felt that I interfered with his plans and that I would somehow marry her instead. I thought Gwendolyn was a very pretty, intelligent girl and would make a fine wife, but at 20, I felt she was too young for me.

As I came to know more of the people in town, I realized it is not unusual for a man in his 30s such as I was or even in his 40s or 50s to marry a much younger woman. After all, life is short, and since so many women died in childbirth, it seemed the men in town outlived the women by something like a decade. And since the average woman might have five to ten children, the odds were not in their favor. Of course, when it was wartime, there were fewer men to go around.

As I looked around town and listened to the stories at the pub, it seemed that many families were missing a mother such as Gwendolyn, a father such as Seamus, or both, like Tommy. Even though they tended to have large families, many children were lost shortly after birth or to disease before they reached five. Children were not coddled, but rather seen as assets to help out on the farm, herd sheep, or work in the shop, and since there were few formal schools, they were put to work as early as six or seven. Many children lived with their grandparents, an aunt or uncle, or an older sibling. With death always lurking, families had to pull together.

Still, I saw a large contingent of older people in town. It seemed that if you made it out of childbirth, out of childhood, out of having children, and out of the wars, you could manage to live to a ripe old age. Despite the turmoil of life, although they seemed hardened by these traumas, the people of Bunkillarny were surprisingly cheerful. When walking along the main street, when I passed them, they invariably smiled and nodded. If it was someone I knew, say from the pub, we would stop and chat for a bit. Their religion offered them solace, community, security, and help during challenging times, plus the promise of a glorious afterlife. I imagine that living in this close-knit community resembled living in small-town America. Having grown up in the suburbs and living near an impersonal big city, I appreciated the feeling of togetherness.

—

According to Michael's instructions, I next needed to learn the art of printing. After Michael approved the form, I took it to the press—a seven-foot high, seven-foot long, three-foot wide sturdy, complex machine that must have looked as baffling in 1491 as a mainframe in 1991.

Unfortunately, Seamus was the one who showed me how to operate the press, constantly berating my efforts. Getting the right amount of ink on the form turned out to be tricky. On my first attempt, whole words were missing from the page. On my fourth attempt, many of the letters were blurred with too much ink, whereupon Seamus elicited a Gaelic swear word that I fortunately could not understand.

Knowing he could do it, I challenged him to do better. With a condescending smirk on his face, he ran through the entire process. Seeing his craftsman-like technique, finally provided me with what I needed to know. Even though it took me twice as long, my next attempt finally proved successful – what a relief, for I was starting to believe him that I was, indeed, a boob.

First, I learned to pour the oil-based ink on a wooden platform. Gutenberg invented the ink, which adhered much better to the paper and lasted longer than water-based ink. Then, I grabbed a large mushroom-shaped device lined in goose leather by its stem. I put the mushroom-like top in the ink. Then I grabbed a similar mushroom and, being careful not to have any bubbles or clumps, rolled the two against each other creating a thin layer of ink. Next, pressing hard as Seamus had done, I rolled the mushrooms over the type on the form, being sure every letter had enough ink, but not too much as to blur the raised letters.

Alongside the form was the frisket—a two-part wooden device that held the paper and performed the same function as the paper feeder on a desktop printer. I took a dampened piece of paper and placed it on the frisket that folded over the form. Then I slid the form under the press.

The press resembled a wine press—where Gutenberg evidently got his inspiration. It consisted of a handle and a screw with a flat board at the bottom (the platen) that pressed down flatly on the paper.

Instead of screwing the press down upon grapes to make wine, the press pushed the paper onto the inked type. I pulled the long handle called the Devil's Tail that forces the platen to screw down on top of the frisket causing it to press against the form, thereby depositing the ink on the paper. If all has gone right, there is a delightful little smacking sound indicating the ink has indeed deposited onto the paper—*voila* a printed page! I thought to myself that this is truly a complicated process—one that took me some time and frustration to learn, but I reveled in my minor accomplishment.

The first time I produced a printed page, I was ecstatic. I proudly hung page after page on the lines draped across the shop to dry, the smell of oily, fruity ink wafting through the air just as it had with that old mainframe printer. After the pages dried, using pinholes for alignment, I printed the back pages. I was very slow and deliberate, but it came out right--*Voila*.

Following this process, the guys could produce over 2,500 pages a day, the equivalent of 10 to 30 books per day, as opposed to just a few pages of hand copying. In a year, a monk might copy one book, whereas in a month they could generate over 600 books. Similar to dancers, they worked in concert with each other and this glorious machine. Hour after hour, day after day, I loved seeing the pages and books piling up—no less industrious than a 20th century assembly line.

From Wikipedia I learned that early bestsellers by authors such as Luther or Erasmus were sold by the hundreds of thousands in their lifetime. Even though it was nearly 50-years since Gutenberg invented the printing press, our press, type and ink were the same. Amazing how a genius can accomplish so much by inventing an apparatus that will transform the world, expand knowledge, educate the populace, challenge the powerful, end the dark ages, enable the Renaissance, and eventually lead to revolutions in religion and politics. I had thought that the invention of the Internet was the most transformational communication technology, but now I thought that the invention of the printing press was even more so.

On my first intern job, when my indoctrination included operating a mainframe computer, we had an old 1,200-line per minute printer that resembled this first press. Paper literally flew out of the back of the printer at 1,200-lines a minute. This was not radically faster than this original printer, which could produce about 200 lines per minute.

When all the pages for a book were assembled, the next step was to bind these together to produce a book. Since my work setting the type was done before they got to this point, I offered to print the last pages so they could start the binding process. Running the press built up my arms again and was something the apprentices appreciated. To me, it was similar to working out on an exercise machine. And after sitting in a chair setting type for hours, it was welcome relief.

Publishing a book was remarkably similar to publishing a Web site in terms of the research, design, graphics, editing, and even operations. This, too, was state of the art for the time. Even though it was 500-years earlier, the work did not feel much different—something that soothed my troubled psyche. The act of going to work every day and its subsequent regularity greatly eased my transition to this strange time. Plus, there was no commute. My bedroom was down the hall from the shop and up a small ladder to the attic, since Gwendolyn had reclaimed her bedroom. The Web pages I designed might be seen by hundreds of thousands or hopefully millions. These book pages might be seen by thousands of people. And, it was easier than messing with HTML, JAVA, and servers.

32:   RUSH ORDER

One gloomy day, as I was setting type on a form, Michael tapped me on the shoulder. He had a worried look upon his face when he asked the apprentices to stop the press and asked Megan and Ryan to join us. He held up a sheet of paper and said, "This is an order from our agent in London for 300 copies of my book on Saint Francis." With broad smiles, everyone seemed as excited as I was by this fabulous news, until I looked at Gwendolyn, who had a rare and unexpected sour expression on her face and was shaking her head at me.

"The Archbishop of Canterbury ordered the books over a month ago and as our agent, John, explained, he could not find a ship sailing for Bunkillarny for nearly a month. So, we just received the order yesterday. The archbishop demanded that the books be there in time for Saint Francis' feast day. He plans to distribute these to the royal family, nobles, priests, and bishops throughout England. If we cannot get the books to him in time, he will cancel the order. I talked to the harbormaster, and there is a ship leaving for London in five days, which will not give us enough time, so I'm afraid I'll have to turn down the order. Unfortunately, this will damage our reputation with the archbishop and jeopardize future orders throughout England."

Everyone looked crestfallen.

I said, "Michael, with the improvements to the process we've made recently, I think we can make that order."

As an app designer, a major portion of my job had been to analyze processes and to look for improvement opportunities, which is why our app had been so successful. I applied this to my new role, where I had been working on some ideas. Even though I was amazed at how well this ingenious machine worked, it still seemed somewhat clunky. The most time-consuming step was inking the goose leather "mushrooms." I had thought that maybe a roller would cut down on that time—something like the paint roller I used to paint my apartment.

I had asked John, who also worked with wood, to fashion a device similar to a rolling pin. Then I experimented with various types of felt. I went to Cleary's Clothier down the street and asked for leftover swatches of felt. Cleary tailored the elaborate gowns that the royals and nobles wore to their extravagant balls and felt superior to just about everybody in town, so he looked down his nose at me. But he kept these in a barrel where they would eventually be repurposed as rags, so I was able to buy them for practically nothing.

The first one I had tried would absorb hardly any of the ink—it just smeared it all over the letters leaving large blotches. The second try missed half the letters. By the 10th try, I was thinking this was not a good idea, until the eleventh one laid out the right amount of ink without blotching. Just a week ago, I glued the felt to the roller. Then after all the daily print jobs had been completed, I tried it out on the press. This experimental felt roller worked—a eureka moment! I fashioned a roller long enough to span the entire form. When Seamus first tried the device a couple of days ago, he was sure it would not work. Then he saw the results and despite trying his best not to, he could not help but smile. We had just started using the new roller this morning, something Michael was not aware of. Something, once it was proven, I wanted to surprise him with. I thought it would cut the time for this step by about 70% and reduce the number of errors when a page had missing or blotched letters after which we would throw it away. Not an insignificant expense, considering paper was much more expensive now.

Another cumbersome step in the process was packing the space between the lines with discarded paper and cloth so these would not budge—a very clunky and messy process. If I did not do this right the lines would be wavy, something that drove Michael crazy. John and I had created long metal bars with a nub in the middle. Then he filed a notch into the type so that the type fit tightly against the bar for each line. We would no longer have to spend time packing the lines of type. Instead, we used the bars and notched letters to tightly secure the type in place. I estimated that this innovation would save about 70% of effort for that step too.

With a sense of expediency, the entire shop shifted into high gear. Page by page, Michael completed the final draft of his revised book on Saint Francis. As the pages came to me, I set the type at the composing desk. Gwendolyn proofed the book and reviewed my pages. She was a stickler for accuracy too. She also helped with the type setting. Megan and Ryan worked on the graphics. The apprentices printed and bound books together and after they were done, during the night, John and his three sons took their places. When I had time, I would spell the apprentices and pull the Devil's Tail, something Gwendolyn also did. It was surprising to see how strong this thin young lady was. The sturdy press ran 24-hours a day.

As the deadline approached, it became apparent that we were still not going to make it. Due to our Herculean effort, we were going to be able to print nearly all the pages—but given the amount of time it would take for these to dry and then bind them into books, we would still fall short. We were all drained and disheartened. Then Michael came in and said, "I talked to the captain, paid him off, and he agreed not to sail for two more days. He said he would deliver them to the Archbishop as soon as they dock and we will barely make the deadline. All ten of us gaily worked on the final binding step together.

After the final book was bound and loaded onto the ship, Michael ordered a keg of beer from the brewer and Daisy laid out roast beef, bread, cabbage, and haggis, a special dish from their Scottish cousins and we had a grand feast, toasting each other on our success.

———

One of the skills that Michael learned at the seminary was hand-drawing pictures in the books he manually produced. While in London, he learned the art of block printing from William Caxton. Showing me some graphics in books he printed, he told me, "I picked this up while foraging for books in Germany to add to the lord's library. It's a book on Euclid's geometry produced by Erhard Ratdolt in Augsburg, Bavaria, about ten years ago." As I thumbed through the pages that, other than being in Latin, could have been my 10th grade geometry textbook. He added, "Look at all o those diagrams, there be over 400 of' em. Can you ken that?"

Michael showed me how he printed pictures in the books he produced. First, he drew a picture of a simple tree on paper then carved it out of a wood block. Next, he put the block on the press and inked it. Then while folding the frisket with paper over the form and sliding it into the press, he pulled the Devil's Tail to press the image into the paper. Following the same process, he could produce hundreds of copies. Along with the text, the graphic could be placed anywhere on the page.

The first block-printed books had hand carved letters, but Gutenberg improved upon this process. Further demonstrating the process, Michael placed the graphic of the oak tree on the form. Then he added the letters representing each of the words. He inked the leaves of the tree in green and the trunk in black. The letters were inked in black too. Then he printed the form producing a perfect page with a stunning graphic.

He said, "For some of the illustrations we even use blue or red ink that we mix up ourselves, so we have colored pictures in the books," which he showed me and I marveled at.

Here I was, 500-plus years in the past seeing how books were printed and suddenly it dawned on me that what I witnessed was not that much different than the work I had done laying out pictures in Web pages in my apps. The tools were certainly different, but the required skills, attention to detail, and results were not that dissimilar. This, too, was an artform. Most people do not think of a Web page as art, but then there are so many poor Web pages.

His second oldest daughter, Megan, a petite, pretty, bouncy blond with a perfectly symmetrical face who was around twenty-three, had become an accomplished artist, who, after leaving her children with her sister, would come to the shop for about a half a day and draw the illustrations.

At first, Megan looked upon me suspiciously. After all, I had taken over her sister's bedroom, where I had been for weeks eating their food and her sister tending to me. My questionable origins, accent, amnesia, and mannerisms were very dubious to her. Once I started working at the shop and came up with the improvements, our relationship dramatically improved. She was a delightful young lady who was fun to joke around with and had an infectious laugh, which I enjoyed eliciting.

Sometimes she brought her son Michael, named after his grandfather and her younger daughter, the cute little miss Miriam, who brightened up the shop. Little Michael loved the printing process and wanted to help out by hanging the pages to dry on the lowered line just for him or by sweeping the floor. The usually joyful kid, oddly loved sweeping, periodically riding the broom as if it were a horse. Inquisitively, he constantly asked me questions about the pages I was laying out. One day the little guy saw me cleaning the type. After the boys were done with a form, I would have to disassemble the galleys, clean them and place these back into their cubbies, which was not something I enjoyed doing. When the chiseler, as they called him, meaning young boy, asked to help I immediately showed him how to clean the type. Even though he was only about five, Megan had taught him how to read, so I taught him how to place the cleaned letters into their cubbies, telling him to mind his ps and qs. I felt I might be violating some child labor laws, which would not exist for hundreds of years, but still thought I should not take advantage of the chiseler. He loved doing it so much though, I could not stop him, especially after the rest of the shop heaped praise upon him. It was a game to him

John's second eldest son, Ryan, used a quill pen and ink to trace over Megan's drawings, then pressed the pine block over it, carefully carving it out with a wee, very sharp knife. Megan drew an illustration of the falls in blue ink—Bunkillarny's most iconic landmark. Once added to the *Bunkillarny Reader*, it became the weekly newsletter's masthead. With the tree inked green, we had a three-color newsletter—more color than most 20th-century newspapers. In the fall when the leaves changed, Seamus mixed up some reddish-brown ink for the tree, which delighted the townsfolk.

Even though Ryan was a skilled carver, it took quite a bit of time to carve the graphics onto the wooden blocks, and even though he was very cautious and precise, any error would require him to start over. Considering the time involved, I thought that perhaps etchings might be a better approach, but other than seeing a few etchings here and there, knew nothing about it. So, I went to the back of the shop, fired up my iPhone and on my copy of Wikipedia saw how these were fashioned.

I explained the process to Megan that consisted of etching her artwork onto a piece of copper covered in wax. Afterwards, Ryan carefully applied acid to the sheet of copper, which ate away the unwaxed portions. The plate would then be placed onto the form and inked for printing. The ink filled in the etched portions that, when pressed against paper, left the desired graphic.

The etching process saved an immense amount of time, versus carving out each block. It took Megan several attempts to get the hang of it, but she had little resistance to the concept and soon became a highly skilled etching artist, who continuously improved her artwork. She was able to add much more fine detail to her graphics and found that by pressing harder she could create deeper lines. Now it became easier for us to add more graphics to our books, thereby increasing their desirability. When Michael showed the lord the first book we produced with etchings, he was astonished.

———

Since I walked nearly every day, I accompanied Tommy, the younger round-faced, red haired, red cheeked, freckled, blue-eyed (of course), short apprentice along his weekly delivery route. Afterwards I offered to deliver the newsletter myself. Even if it was raining, which in Northern Ireland it often was, I enjoyed the walks as relief from type setting, plus I could converse with the friendly shop owners. Tommy, who merely handed the broadside to the subscribers, did not care for the task and was glad to offload it on me. I suggested that Michael keep copies of the paper in the office where those who periodically came to town could stop in and purchase a copy for a ha'-penny.

I even wrote up an occasional story I overheard at the pub. The shopkeepers regularly thought up stories about their shops, which, although it was an unfamiliar word to them, was actually a form of advertisement. For instance, fastidious Cleary told me about his new line of tweed tunics that came directly from Glasgow. Flannigan asked me to write up a story about the new pastry he had baked especially for Easter that everybody loved so much and planned to bake again for the harvest festival.

I talked to Michael about adding advertisements to his paper for the merchants—evidently a foreign concept. "We could print the 'ads' on the backside of the paper and charge the merchants a few shillings for each."

At first, he thought the idea to be crass and rejected it, but realizing that the paper might finally make a profit, he told me to give it a try. I walked from shop to shop trying to sell the concept, but it being such a foreign notion, no one bought into it. They thought I had reverted to my previous daft state, and I felt I had lost some of their newly-obtained respect for me.

I walked into the last shop on my list, McNab's Pub. Instead of launching into the ads, I asked Sean about his business, how he was doing, what ideas he had for expanding it, what problems he was having.

Standing behind the bar, me sitting on a stool, the boisterous Irishman enjoyed my queries saying, "I am extremely busy late in the night, but because it is so crowded and boisterous, decent customers turn away. Me wife wishes that more of them comes earlier and eats their supper and brings their wives so it wasn't just all boisterous men. She says she's, "tired of sweeping up the drunks every night," and wishes our place would be more civil. 'Let them go to the other pub if they just want to get drunk!', she says to me. This is a family business where our daughters participate."

"Perhaps you could offer half-priced pints for two hours early in the evening, from say 4:00 to 6:00, to induce people to come at that time," I suggested. "Since that is when they would normally be eating their supper, they might bring their wives."

He loved the idea and signed up for our first ad. The ad drew a crowd and because they not only bought drinks but also ate, it was a huge hit. Sean added to his coffers. And his wife was happy that the pub became more than just a bunch of noisy, boisterous, ill-behaved men. The presence of their wives indeed made it a more civilized establishment. Seeing Sean's success, others signed up for advertisements too. The net effect was a stimulus to the town's commerce and their regard for my daft idea turned into praise, something I greatly appreciated, making me feel that I finally fit in into this unfamiliar time and place.

33:   BACK TO THE CAVE

By now, my body had recovered from the rapids and time traveling and I had become acclimated to life in Bunkillarny. Picking up a bit of the brogue, I was even starting to sound like a Bunkillarnian, but I still felt a strong desire to get back to my own place and time. Early one morning, I ask Gwendolyn to show me where she discovered my limp body, telling her that it might help me recover my memory. She leads me a couple of miles down a dirt road and shows me where she had found me in the bushes of an old growth forest. We walk up the hill alongside of the trickling stream, where we soon see a tall outcropping of rocks. I search for the opening to the cave but cannot find it and sense that she is becoming impatient. Then, I spot the tiny hole behind a pricker bush and say, "I think I spent time in this cave and I want to go in."

"I do na want to crawl through that tiny dirty 'ole." She says in her sweet endearing voice.

Thinking I will soon be transported back and never see her again, I hug the dear girl who saved my life and feel a little choked up. As if she somehow knows she will never see me again, tears glaze over her eyes.

Fearing I will have to go through the same pain as I did before and possibly die, I hesitate before I squeeze through the wee hole. I feel that I do not belong here and must go back. With my lower lip trembling, I look back over my shoulder into her eyes and smile then wiggle through its far-too-small entrance.

On the other side, I use my trusty little flashlight from my Swiss Army Knife, but it's too small beam cannot illuminate much of the broad cavern, just giving me glimpses of wee rock clusters. I need to see more, so I grab my phone, turn it on and hit the flashlight app to see the entire cave, where I am able to discern a passage similar to that in the Grand Canyon's cave. Concerned about burning my way through my phone's battery, I immediately turn it off and use the tiny flashlight to light the way. I go to the back of the cave and explore around several turns until the passage becomes illuminated by the same strange blue-green fluorescence. I gradually make my way back to a point where the slope proceeds downwards at a steep angle, then levels off above a deep chasm. Remembering my previous experience falling down the slope, I slide down on my butt on the volcanic black cinders until I arrive at the chasm, but peering over the edge, I see no hot flowing lava.

I lie down with my arms crossed for some time hoping it will fire up and transport me back to my own time, but nothing happens; it is not hot and I feel no magnetic pull—no tingling, no electricity. Then in the distance, I barely hear Gwendolyn calling, "Rand, Randy, Oh Randy where are ye?" Fearing that without a flashlight she might stumble on a rock and injure herself in the dark, I get up, climb up the slope and quickly step along the path around the now more familiar turns. Somehow, she had managed to walk through the darkness and found the fluorescence. When I reach her, she gives me a relieved hug and says she was afraid I was lost or injured again. With her face glowing like an angel's in pinks, blues and greens, she asks, "What is this strange glow. I ha ner seen anything like this before?"

"I do not know, but isn't it wonderful?"

"Is it from the fairies or elves?"

"Maybe"

Lighting the way ahead, walking behind her, for the first time with each dainty, ballet-like step, I notice how shapely her figure is. Then she trips on a loose rock and falls into my arms, as we both tumble to the ground. She looks into my eyes as if she wants me to kiss her. Although I have strong feelings for her and she is extremely desirable, she seems more like a younger sister or a niece. Someone I care deeply about, but not romantically. Still, after all, we are not actually related, and I am tempted. Before I lose my resolve, I say we should head back before it gets dark (before I took advantage of the situation). She seems disappointed, but after a dissatisfied glance moves onward, as if nothing had happened.

On the way back, as we walk close to each other, I have mixed feelings. She is a very attractive young woman who many men would take advantage of. But she is also the one who saved my life, faithfully nursed me back to health, and I owe my life to her and her father. She is young and pretty and will no doubt soon get over her infatuation with me. Before she seemed aloof, but that was not just with me, it was with all the young men in the village, who periodically tried to woo her.

In an attempt to relieve the uncomfortable situation, I ask her about Seamus, "Do you like Seamus? He seems like a handsome, strong young lad with a bright future. Once he completes his apprenticeship, he will be a good provider."

She replies, "I like Seamus fine. He's a parful worker and a big 'elp in the shop, but he's not that smart. Oh, he's good at workin' wi' his hans and figurin' out thins, but he na much interested in readin'. I want someone who reads and thinks."

———

I sit in the backyard listening to the gurgling brook trying to fathom an explanation for how I got here and why I had not been successful getting back. I had taken all those science courses in school and enjoyed watching the science channel. It seemed like there should be some rational explanation for what happened to me. I remembered there was a powerful magnetic field in the canyon's cave that had caused my compass to gyrate radically. Perhaps the fast-flowing lava created the magnetic field. Water flowing through a dam spins a generator through a magnetic field, which generates electricity. The two billion-year-old dense rocks at the bottom of the deep gorge may have accentuated the anomaly. Maybe that was it?

There were certainly a lot of forces at work there—the intense heat of the lava, its rapid flow, the intense pressure under a mile of ancient rock, the roaring river nearby, that magnetic field, and a strong gravitational pull. Plus, I was at a unique place in the history of the earth—at the bottom of the 2,000,000,000-year-old Grand Canyon. Who knows what types of forces might lay below all of that? What types of mysterious forces might have existed then that I somehow unwittingly tapped into? And then there were those hieroglyphics that indicated others had occupied the cave who might have had mystical powers, or, although it is difficult for me to fathom, been aliens.

Somehow my molecules got scrambled and transported back in time to Ireland. All of this seemed a bit like the telephone line, in which voice waves are converted into electrons transmitted over a wire and then reassembled into voice waves at the other end. Or similarly, how voice waves are transmitted through the air to a cell tower and reassembled into voice waves at a friend's cell phone. The lava flow and the earth's iron core could have somehow transmitted me to Ireland, which all seemed unfathomable... but it happened. Like phones at either end of a line, the two caves were nearly identical. And both caves had the same type of hieroglyphics, which itself was mystifying since the same ancient tribe would not exist in both Arizona and Ireland. An ancient Irish tribe, predating the Celts in Arizona—not likely.

If this were true, then how could I replicate those conditions and get back? My mind racing, I struggle to find the cause. Like a sci-fi novel, it seems I had passed through some kind of time/space portal, the physics of which I reluctantly had to admit were a mystery to me. Perhaps it had something to do with the theory of relativity.

Using the cell phone explanation, the caves would be similar to smart phones and the lava would be similar to radio waves, the earth's core would be like satellites or cell towers. That would explain how I got here, but why this time? Searching for any theory to assuage my growing anxiety, I think about the parallels between this time period and my own time 500 years from now. Then I remembered the 500-year cycle theory I had read about, in which major events occur about every 500 years that drastically change our human condition and civilization.

As I recall the theory, around 500 B.C. the Greeks overthrew the largest empire in the world, Persia, and under Alexander ruled over an even larger empire that extended to India and Egypt and established the first democracy. Then, the Romans conquered the Greeks. The Roman Empire was founded around the year 0 and continued until around 500 A.D., when the Vandals invaded Rome and ended the greatest empire ever, leading to the dark ages and plagues, in which half of the European population perished. When you are struggling to survive and half of everyone you know is dying, you don't think much about advancing civilization.

Around 1,000 AD, Leif Erickson discovered America, and the Normans conquered Britain--what would later become a worldwide empire.

The theory also applies to all the world's great religions—all with billions of adherents founded near the 500-year intervals. Around 1,000 B.C. Solomon built the temple in Jerusalem and Hinduism was founded. Around 500 BC Confucianism and Buddhism were established.

Christ was born around the year 0, instituting Christianity. After Rome was sacked, around 500 A.D., the church relocated to Constantinople and shortly thereafter Muhammad was born.

Around 1,000 A.D., Eastern Orthodoxy broke off from Rome. Or, since the Church was centered in Constantinople, perhaps the Roman Catholic Church broke off from the unified church. I guess that might depend on your perspective.

Around now, 1,500 A.D., now, the invention of the printing press is radically increasing the availability of knowledge throughout all of Europe leading to a renaissance of art, literature, philosophy, and science. The press will soon enable the Protestant Reformation. And next year in 1492, Columbus will discover the new world.

If the theory were true, then the year 2,000, the new millennium, represents the beginning of another cycle. The theory postulates that similar to Columbus discovering the new world and all the opportunity for mankind that represents, man's leaving the earth and landing on the moon for the first time represents another revolutionary event. In addition, man will soon land on another planet—Mars, and we will expand our realm beyond earth.

The other event that is revolutionizing civilization is the digital revolution symbolized by the World Wide Web. Coincidentally, man's walking on the moon and the invention of the Internet both occurred in 1969, within the 50-year band of the 500-year cycle.

Similar to the layers of geologic history exposed in the Grand Canyon, these were all seismic shifts that revolutionized civilization and the way mankind lived from then on—major fault lines. The invention of the printing press in this, the 15th century, was similar to the invention of the Internet—both revolutionary events.

The Renaissance, starting in the 15th century, is similar to the digital revolution in the 20th century in terms of its impact upon the future of human society and mankind—one enabled by the invention of the printing press, the other enabled by the invention of the Internet. During the Global Pandemic, fearing for our lives, we avoided physical contact. Fortunately, by that time the Web, social media and apps like Zoom enabled us to live and work in a virtual world. Students of all ages went to virtual schools. Half of us worked and communicated virtually. Grandparents kept in tough with their grandkids through Zoom. We ordered groceries on-line and other items on Amazon. Worldwide researchers shared information regarding the Covid-19 through the internet and we scheduled vaccinations through the Web. After the pandemic, our existence will never be quite the same. You almost wonder if the Web wasn't predestined to enable us to survive.

Why the seismic shifts in civilization occur every 500 years is not clear? Perhaps it is the nature of civilization or perhaps there is a force behind it--like a 500-year clock. Perhaps it is coded into our DNA establishing an evolutionary rhythm or perhaps it's God's plan. Perhaps this force somehow transmitted me from one 500-year boundary to another... Perhaps?

Getting a headache, I could not handle thinking about it any longer. Thinking that there might be some rational explanation, regardless of what that might be, helps to relieve my stress and accept my current situation.

34:   PLUMBING/STOVE

Following the unsuccessful attempt to return to the 21st-century, I was adjusting to living in 15th century Ireland. Of course, now it seemed I had no choice, but I still had hope that somehow, someday I would find my way back. Even though I had my iPhone, there would be no electricity to recharge it for 300 years and no Internet Service Provider for 500 years. I had to be careful how I used up the remainder of its battery, for the knowledge it contained could be invaluable. I missed my social media, my friends and my family and was still terribly homesick. I missed all the modern conveniences too, and I missed my big screen TV, my laptop, and my quirky, liberal city by the Bay.

I did not miss the kitchen appliances, which other than the microwave and coffee maker, I seldom used. Daisy's homemade meals of lamb stew, Shepherd's pie or corned beef were much more delicious and probably healthier than processed foods and my Lean Cuisines. But the convenience I missed most was a bathroom. During my recovery, as I sat overlooking the gurgling river in the peaceful backyard during those long, warm summer days, periodically my thoughts drifted back to the Bay and to home. It somehow felt like I was back there at that time.

When the wind came from the south, permeated with the rank smell of the outhouse, which tainted my delightful experience, it stimulated thoughts of ways to bring water from the river to the house. While backpacking around Europe with Jenny, I was amazed to see that the Romans had aqueducts and sewer systems. While visiting my favorite Greek Isle of Santorini, which was destroyed by a massive volcano that shook the entire Mediterranean, leaving a beautiful bluesea, filled caldera that preserved the ancient modernistic city of Akrotiri, I saw that they had a sewer system and toilets some 3,500 years ago. Amazing how the dark ages had extinguished these ancient conveniences.

As fall came, on the colder mornings, it became harder to get motivated for the trips to the privy. Plus, even while holding my breath, the two-holer seemed even smellier and nearing its capacity. One sunny warm day I saw Ryan digging a hole in the yard and asked him what he was up to. "I'm digin a new ole for the privy, master Rand." he replied, "Afterwards we be coverin' up in the old un. It were gettin' kind o full and smelling bad, it were."

On my excursions through town, I had walked by the grain mill downstream and spoke with the miller, O'Doul, who gave me a tour of its fascinating operation. Water in the river entered a sluice and turned a wheel with paddles. Inside there were a series of wooden spoked gears that, in turn, turned a heavy millstone that ground the grain for the bread that was the mainstay of the town's diet. O'Doul poured the wheat or barley or oats onto the path of the wheel and when it was ground, collected it and poured it into sacks. Similar to the printing press it was another ingenious machine. I strolled back and studied it again, thinking that I might adapt what I observed to bring water to the outhouse.

With quill and paper, I drew up a plan for an alternative to the outhouse and walked through the diagram with Michael. Fortunately, Michael owned the three properties leading up to the falls—the print shop, the blacksmith shop and the bakery that he rented out, which lay just below the lower falls. My plan called for a wooden sluice to take water from the top of the falls and send it down a channel to a holding tank. Wooden pipes would carry the water from the tank to the house. There it would branch off to an indoor toilet, bathroom sink, and a sink for Daisy to use in the kitchen. From the bathroom, clay pipes would carry the waste-water to a covered cesspool in the back yard.

Michael looked over the plan skeptically, but as an innovator in a burgeoning field, he was not one to immediately dismiss the idea. Plus, my previous ideas for the press had panned out, so he had confidence in me, saying "There are too many obstacles to overcome here, but on the other hand, if it worked it would be bonnie."

"What I propose is not that innovative, since the Romans had built such systems over 2,000 years ago and the Minoans had such systems for entire cities 3,500 years ago"—a fact that astonished him.

I continued, "The concept of a wooden sluice resembled what the miller built downriver," so Michael did not have a problem with that part, but he had several other questions he posed.

"How would you make these wooden pipes?"

"I will ask John to forge a long iron drill bit that we will use to drill holes in logs. The end of the logs will be tapered so they fit securely into each other and will be sealed with tar, so they won't leak."

"How would this 'toilet' thing as you call it work? Sounds French."

"There will be a tank above with a pull chain attached to a valve that will fill the tank with water. You will sit on a seat and after you do your business, you pull a second chain that will release water into the toilet, which will flush it out to the cesspool. I will work with John to fashion the valves. The cesspool will be covered with stone slabs and dirt."

"And these clay pipes?"

"They will be about 6-inches wide with a flange at one side that will fit into the next pipe and be sealed with tar. We will dig a trench and lay the pipes underground from the house to the cesspool. You won't even see anything above ground"

"Hmmm. Where will you acquire these clay pipes from? I have not heard of anything like these."

"I notice a lot of brick houses in town, which means there should be a brick maker nearby?"

"Tis one in Bonneyglenn, but he makes bricks na pipes."

"I'll talk to him."

"You talk to him and if he can make these pipes, I will give ye me blessing and pay for it. Nice thinking, Rand."

I asked Michael how often it froze. If it was below freezing, for a long time, the water in the channel and pipes would freeze. He said, "Water rarely freezes in Bunkillarny and the falls has ner froze. Even during the few days in the year, tis freezing, tis almost always thawed by midday."

Since the water in the channel would be moving it would likely never freeze and the storage tank would be large enough not to freeze as would the wooden pipes, which provided insulation.

———

I had taken some riding lessons but had never become an accomplished rider. Bonneyglenn was too distant to walk to, but the prospect of having to ride a horse that far by myself seemed daunting. Thankfully, I rode the Mc Carrans' gentle horse, Glory May, to Bonneyglenn without incident. Once there, sporting a sore butt, I met Kevin Mc McCarthy. Kevin said that he could not make such a thing but that his brother-in-law, Breardan O'Brian, the potter who used the same clay he dug out of the clay hole, might be able to do the job, "Surely, it be more in line wi wha Breardan be doin."

Following Kevin's directions, leaving my horse behind, I walked bowlegged down a grassy dirt lane shaded by towering poplar trees, beside a peaceful, slow-moving river, to Breardan's shop. There I saw a variety of vases, plates, bowls and pots under a long-roofed patio. Inside, I found him and two men working at potters' wheels and one glazing bowls in a kiln. I asked for Breardan who was in the midst of turning out a tall pitcher on the wheel. He raised his hand to fend me off, until he finished the long spiral movements of an elegant spigot. With one of those fresh, Irish faces that never seems to age, he looked extremely young and handsome.

I introduced myself and offered my hand, which after he wiped his off with a rag, he enthusiastically shook, accompanied by a broad, welcoming smile. When I explained what I proposed for the Mc Carrans, he smiled again, "I would love to do something for them, cause Michael had taught me readin. He is one of the finest gentlemen in the entire shire, he is."

He stood there for a while considering the idea, then flashed another toothsome grin and exuding confidence said, "I'll do it, I will."

I was a bit worried because I was afraid that unlike bricks, the price might be more in the range of vases, but with another one of those engaging smiles, he gave me a very reasonable price per 3-foot long pipe. "I'll set to it, and after it has been dried and fired, I'll bring a sample to ye at Bunkillarny in three days."

When he stopped by, the pipe was exactly what I wanted—hard, straight and perfectly round with no imperfections inside or out. He said, "I built a wooden mold to fit over the clay and mandrel that would speed up the process. I'd like to show the finished product to Michael," who was as ecstatic to see one of his favorite students as he was the transformational pipe.

Michael immediately approved the concept and said he could not wait to try it out.

I asked Breardan, "Can you make curved pipes?"

"That would be easy to mold." Then, I showed him my plans for a rough clay toilet with a bend molded into it. I also asked Ryan to fashion a hinged seat.

I was somewhat worried about interfering with the future invention of the toilet, but my design was still very rudimentary and not much beyond what the Romans used. Besides, many ideas like these that are ahead of their time soon vanish. The television was invented in the 1920s but it was not until the 1950s that most homes had one. The internet was invented in 1969 but it was not until the 1990s that it caught on. Many brilliant inventors who invented extraordinary devices struggled in anonymity, because they were too far ahead of their time.

I went over the plans with John and Ryan who would do most of the work. John thought it was such a grand idea he had me modify the sluice to have his house behind the shop equipped with a toilet, two faucets and a line to the forge where they used water to quench the molten metal. The same channel would feed both and save his youngest son from constantly carrying water from the river.

When the project was completed, it was an unseasonably cold day. Throughout the day, we all tried it out and marveled at how it would make our lives easier and more pleasant. Even though she promised to clean it daily, Daisy could not stop exclaiming her joy over not having to carry water and be able to use the facility in the house – "This wo make me life sooo much easier. I love it! I be makin us a big roast to celebrate."

———

Even though the temperature still climbed into the fifties or sixties in the afternoon, the mornings seemed especially cold. Nobody else seemed to mind, since they just put on their thick Irish woolen sweaters and they were used to it. The living room had a fireplace and was generally warm but other than Michael's bedroom, the other rooms had no fireplace, instead those in the house piled on blankets during the colder weather. The shop, however, had no such fireplace and on cold mornings, with numb fingers, it became very difficult to set type. Michael planned to install a fireplace in the shop, but given its size, it would not be enough to heat it all.

I worked with John to design something similar to a Franklin stove that with a baffle would capture most of the heat before it escaped the metal chimney. It would burn peat. We positioned it and its twin in the room so it would heat the entire shop. Michael, Gwendolyn and the apprentices were happy with the results and were able to work more comfortably and more productively.

SECTION THREE

35:   THE LORD

One damp, dreary, drizzly afternoon Michael looked distressed, so I dropped by his tiny, cluttered, wooden office, where books and manuscripts were piled high. He said that the agent in London, the one who sold their books and acquired new material to print, had suddenly died at the age of forty. Despite being a dear friend whom he would miss, his death would severely impact our business. Instead of adding another press as he had planned, he would probably have to let an apprentice go.

Two days later over Daisy's breakfast of eggs, sausages and mush, Michael told me, "I want you to go to the lordship's castle with me today to discuss what we will do with the shop."

You could see the Bunkillarny castle high on the hill that overlooked the town, but I had never been there for it seemed imposing and somehow threatening. I had never seen his lordship and knew little about him other than what Michael told me, or what I read in his book on Irish heraldry. As I had learned, his lordship remained a mysterious, powerful figure that reigned over everything within a couple of days' ride.

According to Michael's *Northern Irish Heraldry*, his Norman ancestor fought in the battle of Hastings in 1066 when the Normans from France defeated Harold and conquered England. This great ancestor was a senior knight who commanded a regiment of the invaders and distinguished himself during the battle, whose efforts helped win the day.

Afterwards, that ancestor and his offspring occupied high posts in the Norman court that controlled the eastern lands of England and subjugated the Anglo-Saxons, treating them little better than serfs on what had previously been their lands. Another of his great grandfathers helped in the subsequent forays into Eastern Ireland. The current king of England, Henry the VIIth, officially reigned over Ireland, but other than some of the eastern ports such as Dublin, where the Irish regent ruled, he realistically held little sway over most of Ireland.

Over a couple of centuries ago, the King of England gave the lands of Bunkillarny to his lordship's ancestor. At first, they ruled with a stiff hand and clung to their Norman traditions and French language, but over the centuries, they had become assimilated into Irish culture, something that evidently concerned King Henry. Periodically there were rumors, circulated in the pubs, that England would exert more control over Ireland through military force, but these were dispelled by its internal struggles, such as Henry's difficult assumption of the thrown following the War of the Roses. Plus, fierce Scottish nationalism provided a buffer to Ireland. Lord Bunkillarny not only controlled the town but all the villages and hamlets throughout the area—the entire shire or the equivalent of a large county.

Michael had Christopher attached two horses to a two-wheeled cart for the steep ride up to the castle. Even though I was not an accomplished rider, I would have preferred to ride a horse because with no springs, I felt every bump and hole on the ride up. As we rounded the last bend and emerged from the woods, I saw all of Bunkillarny castle—immense compared to any building in town other than the cathedral.

After we crossed over the moat on a lowered bridge, we entered a broad courtyard where there were numerous armed men milling about, practicing their craft, dueling with large broadswords, shooting arrows into distant targets, knights in armor with lances charging targets suspended from wooden posts. Others practiced swinging spiked iron balls attached to chains. The clanging sounds of metal on metal, sword on sword, hoofs on the ground and whizzing arrows filled the air. The spectacle did little to relieve the uneasy feeling in my gut. I guess I knew that it was a time when warring reigned, but I had only occasionally seen soldiers in town. We walked through a large doorway into a massive, dark, cool hall with several long tables and various armaments, flags and coats of arms hanging from the tall walls and the rafters above. At both ends of the hall, stood immense fireplaces one could walk into that elicited the sweet-smelling maple and cherry smoke permeating the air. Other than a few scattered servants, the dimly lit hall was empty, and we could hear the echoes of our steps on the hard-wooden plank floor.

We passed through the hall and down a hallway to another large door guarded by two men of arms holding large axe-like weapons I later learned were called halberds. One of the soldiers opened the door revealing another large room that was about 30-feet high with finely carved dark wood, several crystal chandeliers, and several works of art including pictures of, what I assumed were past Lords of Bunkillarny. His lordship sat at the opposite end on a large throne, where he was speaking with one of his ministers.

Michael introduced me to "Edward Harold Charles Robert, Earl of Essex, Knight of the realm, Lord of Bunkillarny." Mimicking Michael, I bowed low. Looking down his regal nose with disdain, his lordship did not seem the least bit pleased to meet someone as lowly as a printer's assistant—as lowly as me. He sat intimidatingly above us, adorned in a red velvet robe with white and purple trim. He had piercing blue eyes, thick eyebrows, thin lips and an equine nose, with blondish-whitish hair and a neatly trimmed beard and moustache topped by a rich red cap trimmed in gold. His manner, bearing and affectation reeked of breeding, wealth, control, and the exercise of power. His accent sounded nothing like those in town or even Michael's. It sounded regal and a bit French. I had met powerful CEOs in mega-sized corporations and a couple tech multi-billionaires, but none compared to this man. I felt that I had to be careful and watch my step or I might suffer serious consequences.

I did some quick calculations in my head and thought the lord looked much younger than I had imagined, as though he were in his late 40s. The lord had facilitated Michael's marriage to Mary. But, Michael's older daughters were already in their mid-20s and the lord had older sons, so I thought he would have to be in his late sixties. Later I learned that the previous Lord Bunkillarny had died. Afterwards his oldest son had assumed the throne and continued the relationship with Michael. The son, this Lord Bunkillarny, also had a fierce passion for books and printing, inherited from his father.

He smiled at Michael saying that we should proceed to the library. There in the midst of tall shelves holding scores of books, he seemed more relaxed. Considering his immense wealth and responsibilities, I did not think our little printing business was of much concern to him, but I soon realized that books and printing was his passion. The transformation symbolized by going from a room where he reigned and made decisions that would determine people's lives, to a room where he relaxed, surprised me. The two of them discussed some of the recent works he had acquired and read, and the books Michael had printed, along with a couple he presented to the lord. Michael showed him the ledgers and a summary report that Gwendolyn, who also did the accounting, had prepared. Looking at Michael's handwritten copy for the first time, I could see that this was indeed a highly profitable business, the profits of which he shared equally with the Lord. I stood behind them as they went through it line by line.

Half of the sales came from London, which underscored the importance of the lost agent. In addition, Michael said that most of the books they printed were acquired by the agent and without these works their business would suffer, and rather than adding a press, they would have to cut back on their printing.

As they continued to discuss the matter, I looked over the ledgers—what amounted to an income statement and realized which types of books were most profitable. Somewhat reluctantly, I asked permission to speak. Michael looked at the Lord who seemed annoyed by my presence and intrusion but reluctantly replied, "Proceed."

I took a deep breath and then launched into my dissertation, "After a quick analysis, it appears that the most profitable books are those written by English authors, which we print and sell in London. The sales figures are high, as are the prices, whereas the royalties paid to the authors are small." (Evidently, there were no copyright laws yet and the authors sold their works at a fixed price with little or no compensation for the number of books sold.) "Sales in Ireland are growing at a much slower rate and judging by our book production rate, would be enough to keep only one and a half apprentices and not enough to keep me employed, which I understand and can seek other employment. Therefore, considering the upward trend in England, the profitability of the venture and future viability is proportional to English sales."

His lordship inquired in a gruff voice, "Why aren't the sales higher here? This is after all where the shop is located and we don't have to ship our books overseas?"

"It appears that the sales in Ireland are increasing, but since there are fewer readers, the English market offers much more profit potential. Plus, I imagine they educate more readers, who would buy more books. With some of the innovations we have introduced, we have been able to reduce the time and expense to print a book by a quarter. If we can increase sales further, and because of economies of scale, we will be able to substantially increase profits."

The lord interjected, "What do you mean by economies of scale," which brought a concerned look to Michael's face," and made me think I should not have opened my mouth, but plowed onward.

"Well, your lordship, since we will be able to produce more books on our current press, each added book costs less. The press and the shop are the fixed costs that have already been paid. The variable costs are paper, ink and the labor, such as the apprentices and myself."

Michael and his Lordship looked somewhat stunned by my assessment, his lordship seeming more open asked, "What can we do to increase sales here in Northern Ireland and make more profits?"

I continued, "Michael and Gwendolyn have been teaching people to read. If more people read, there would be a larger market for books in Ireland. Judging from the steadily increasing sales in England, evidently more and more people are learning how to read there. With lower costs and growing sales, I would expect our profits to grow by up to 50% over the next four years, provided we can retain the English market and increase education here in Ireland." Realizing I might have said too much and used too much jargon, I added, "Please forgive my intrusion."

His lordship laughed heartily replying, "Well done!" For the first time, I relaxed—my shoulders, previously tied in knots, slumped and for the first time in a minute, took a long breath.

"But," his lordship continued, "Even if we increase reading here in Bunkillarny, Bunkillarny only has a fraction of the population of London, so we would not increase our book sales that much."

"Yes sire, that is true. What if there were more Gwendolyns?"

Looking at me with a puzzled look, Michael asked, "More Gwendolyns? Yet, there be only one Gwendolyn."

"What I mean is, what if there were more people similar to Gwendolyn who taught reading throughout Ireland, by, um… um teaching teachers how to teach reading at the college—at Saint Paul's" Like Gwendolyn, they could also teach arithmetic and writing and other subjects too.

"Interesting idea," the lord responded."

Since he could not place my accent, Lord Edward asked, "Are you from Northwestern England lad?"

Michael ran through his now greatly dramatized story including my amnesia, adding, "He must have had an extensive education in commerce. I was amazed at how quickly he picked up typesetting and had invented improvements for our printing business. Because of his obvious intelligence and broad knowledge of other subjects, he must have had an advanced education, perhaps as a student at Cambridge or Oxford."

Lord Edward exclaimed, "He must be an Oxford man such as myself." Hoping to win favor, I nodded in plausible agreement, since this was not entirely misleading, for I had actually gone to college in Oxford, Ohio.

"Although I did not think it twood be the case, your man seems highly capable, Michael. We should send him to London to sort through the agent's work, patch things up and find another agent as soon as possible." Demonstrating he did not pay the least bit of attention to my name before, he asked Michael, "What's his name?"

As we bowed and began backing out to leave the room, Lord Edward invited us to join him for dinner. Feeling I had escaped with my head still attached, I had been relieved we were leaving, but had no choice. We went into a large living room where we sat in large comfortable chairs and drank claret, discussing various books, philosophy and politics. Picking up his copy of *The Dicts and Sayings of the Philosophers,* Lord Edward commented on how much he enjoyed reading it. Feeling more at ease after a couple of glasses, I said that I was currently reading the book and that my favorite philosopher was Aristotle then explained how his philosophy of life inspired mine.

A beautiful woman, ensconced in a regal blue gown with gold trim and a low bodice entered the room. Michael bowed, took her hand, kissed it and then introduced me to Lady Catherine, the Lord's wife. Similarly, I bowed deeply, kissed her hand as I looked at her alabaster skin and deep purple eyes, bordering a long regal nose, high cheekbones, above red lips, leading to a firm chin, all framed in cascading black hair.

She smiled saying, "Enchanté", to which I replied "Enchanté". She proceeded to speak in French. On my backpacking trips around Europe, I carried a book that included phrases from each country I visited. Unlike those quickie-day-per country trips, I spent four or more days in each city and attempted to speak their language, which amounted to little more than tourist French employed to order food, obtain directions, acquire hotel rooms, etc. I immediately responded with "Non Parlez-vous Français."

She looked at me disappointedly, but graciously began asking questions in regal English. After noting my unusual accent, she asked where I came from, to which I responded with Michael's story of me being beaten, robbed and having amnesia. She seemed intrigued and sympathetic. His lordship surprisingly came to my aid saying that even though they did not know for sure, it was obvious I was an Oxford man, which seemed to impress her.

She told me she was from the royal family in Paris—a cousin of King Charles VII, asking if I had been to Paris. Concerned that I might not be able to relate to 1490s Paris, I honestly said, "I have been there and greatly enjoyed walking along the Seine, the Sorbonne and seeing the magnificent Cathedral of Notre Dame," which I knew were all in place at this time.

She asked, "Have you been to the palace."

Then, in case she asked about other current feature I should know, I responded, "Not that I know of your ladyship. It constantly surprises me that my amnesia allows some memories, whereas it blocks others."

36:   DINNER IS SERVED

Lady Catherine urged us to adjourn to the dining room, which even though it was not the immense hall, was still large and elegantly decorated. Large, dark walnut posts led to a high, broad tray-coffered ceiling offset in off-white plaster squares each depicting intriguing scenes of hunting, along with pictorial settings of the shire, England, France and palatial pastimes. Sitting up to thirty, the regal table held gold gilded charger plates and a variety of glasses. Her ladyship, took me by the arm and walked me around the room introducing me to a couple dozen other dignitaries and their wives, including a related lord from London, a royal cousin newly arrived from France, the bishop of Bunkillarny, and a several lesser lords who ruled areas within the shire. Then she sat me next to her at the end of the table, with Michael fortunately directly across from me, and Lord Edward at the opposite end.

As the endless courses appeared, they discussed a variety of topics. Afraid of being embarrassed, I carefully watched Michael, as to how to eat the various dishes. We started off with a delicious creamed turtle consommé finished with sherry, followed by raw clams in a tangy sauce I could not recognize, then poached trout. These were accompanied by a fine French wine resembling a Sauvignon Blanc, which I attentively swilled around the crystal and sniffed, smiling approvingly to Lady Catherine, to which she responded with a gracious smile.

The next course, lamb shanks came with cucumbers and a new wine that after swilling and smelling, I greatly enjoyed. She asked, "What do you think of et?"

I said, "It seems like a delicious blend of Cabernet, Cabernet Franc and Burgundy."   Then drawing on my periodic trips to

Napa, feeling more relaxed after the claret and Sauvignon Blanc, mimicking Paul, added, "It has hints of currents, honey with a hearty deep oak finish."

I felt I had gone too far until she said, "You are very perceptive, exactly. All wines from France."

Then a mysterious young woman entered the room and sat down, who after the men rose attentively, sat demurely towards the opposite end of the table. In a delightful regal French accent, she apologized to the lord and her ladyship, saying, "My 'orse had fallen with moi on 'im and since I was injured, it took me time to dress appropriately."

To concerned queries and expressions of sympathy, she replied, "I am perfectly fine, merci."

Lady Catherine introduced her as her niece—Lady Marie of Burgundy. As dinner proceeded, I could not help stealing glances at her with her long, soft, light brown hair adorned with natural streaks of blond, no doubt from riding in the sun, brown eyes, high cheek bones, bright reluctant smile, and perfect porcelain features highlighted by the sun. The men near her tried to engage her, but other than smiling coyly, she seemed aloof and unapproachable—their wives seeming annoyed by the attention they paid her.

When a course of filet mignon appeared served with a béarnaise sauce, carrots, peas and an additional wine poured into a third wine glass, the men at the table began talking politics.

Evidently, the O'Donnell and O'Neil clans, who for centuries had controlled the two larger shires to the west, were feuding again over a parcel of land on their borders. Even though they could trace their heritage back to St. Patrick in the 5th Century and were somehow related to each other, they periodically fought, which worked well for Bunkillarny, because as the two mightiest kingdoms in the north they fought against each other, leaving the shire in an extended period of peace.

From a noble to my left, I heard that Lord Edward, an extremely competent general, and when younger, a mighty warrior, kept his army in peak shape thereby discouraging others from attacks. His alliance with the Regent of Ireland and Henry VII further discouraged others from coveting his rich lands. He periodically sent a portion of his well-trained, well-disciplined and well-equipped army to assist embattled Irish kings to the south, or Henry in his periodic battles, where they garnered a reputation as an elite, effective fighting force and were handsomely paid. But he would never send them to assist either the O'Donnells or O'Neals, because the other might look upon him as an enemy. This strategy kept his armed forces in shape and battle ready, which discouraged others from coveting his lands. The extended peace allowed the economy of the Shire to flourish unimpeded by the strife, discord, depleted treasuries, lost young men, and the devastating destruction accompanying war, something all his subjects appreciated and loved him for.

I was somewhat confused by his title. As I interpreted it from the perspective of England, he was a lord, but from the perspective of the other lords at the table, the burgeoning middle class and peasants in the shire, he was their king. From my reading of history, kings could report to kings who in turn reported to kings. Evidently, there were hundreds of kings in Germany most of whom were under other kings.

Through his extensive reading and contacts, he kept up-to-date with the latest weaponry—another passion of his. John, also an accomplished swordsmith, helped to provide some of his weapons and armor, a passion John and Michael shared. As a fair and decisive leader, his under-lords and knights honored him with their respect and fealty. Reasonable taxes and tribute were paid on time, for no one wanted to face his rage, which, as I detected, could be severe.

I learned that Lady Catherine, who took pride in the meal's portrayal, had arranged this fine French cuisine—the most elaborate in my life. After tasting the chicken casserole en crot, I commented, "Your ladyship this is a wonderful meal, one of the best I have ever tasted."

She said, "I was fortunate to induce a fine French chef and pastry chef from the Parisian court to come with me to Bunkillarny. And, I arranged this special meal for the semi-annual meeting of Lord Edward's council that will hold forth tomorrow."

———

Lord Edward opened the topic of reading, asking me to repeat what I had said earlier. I soon realized that this was a controversial topic, one he wanted his advisors to explore. "Rand here mentioned that if more of our subjects read, Michael would be able to sell more books in Ireland."

The Bishop immediately chimed in, "The first book Gutenberg printed was the bible. With its lower price, now anyone who knew Latin would be able to read the bible themselves. Without the clergy to properly interpret and guide them, they might come to all manner of erroneous conclusions."

The Lord of Ballybrook said, "What use would my peasants laboring in the fields have for a readin'. Any time they spent idling away readin' o' books would just distract them from their farming and reduce me revenues."

Being bad at remembering names, another heavy-set lord whose name I could not recall replied, "If they lernt ta read it might give em ideas and they might think they should get more out of us," to which they all said, "Here, here!" As the table of powerful men turned against my idea, I started sweating and wished I had never mentioned it.

Michael spoke up in my defense, "We have taught several dozen denizens of Bunkillarny ta read and cipher. Most are shopkeepers, craftsmen, and their children who will take after them. The readin' helps improve their businesses for they need to know how ta read, write and do basic calculations in order goods, do pricing and keep their books. Since they are more prosperous, Bunkillarny is more prosperous, commerce has increased, as have the taxes and the King's revenue."

Scowling, the heavy-set lord asked King Edward if that be true, to which King Edward replied, "Taxes from the town have indeed doubled over the last five years, which helps fund our army, which protects the shire from invasion and has provided the peace and prosperity we all enjoy."

The Bishop took the floor saying, "There was a time when Rome was a republic and not ruled by a Caesar, and 2,000 years ago Athens had what they called a democracy, in which each person had a vote. We certainly do not want poor peasants to have a vote, do we?"

With that, the discussion stalled, and although I would have liked to just crawl under the table, Lady Catherine and oddly Lady Marie looked pleadingly to me with encouragement. Nervously I spoke up, "Perhaps farmers do not immediately benefit from reading, but surely, similar to Bunkillarny, the tradesmen in your various hamlets would benefit, for it would enable them to trade with each other and establish better trade relations with England, Scotland and even Europe. As they become more successful, through taxes, you too would have more revenue. How often, after an exceptionally bountiful harvest, have you not been able to sell all of your crops or have to sell them at bargain prices? With a broader market you would be able to sell these for more. Besides, those that could read could help you to manage your properties and increase your wealth."

Feeling more comfortable, having delivered presentations as I did in those management and VC meetings, I stood up and using my hands to punctuate points, thereby becoming more animated. "The tradesmen who cannot read rely on others to interpret documents or give them a fair deal, which we know is not always the case. You all depend upon your ministers to aid in the administration of your various realms. Perhaps some of these ministers are incompetent and you are missing out on potential revenues, or you suspect they might be skimming some of the funds off the top, but imagine if you had more educated men to choose from. As more men become more educated, who knows where the next invention of a revolutionary gun, siege weapon, or cannon will come from. Imagine a gun that could consistently hit a target from a hundred yards, rather than yours that might miss from ten. There are gunsmiths in Italy who may be inventing such weapons. Would you want to fight against these weapons or have them for yourselves?"

Seeing that much of the audience had swung my way, I ventured further, "Even the serfs who till your fields could benefit from better farming methods that may originate somewhere else in the world, which will lead to better fertilization, crop rotation, resulting higher yields. Scientifically based breeding practices might increase your herds by half—methods your ministers could learn through reading of European farming techniques."

Seeing them suddenly becoming interested, his lordship nodded approvingly, "I will encourage you lords to acquire teachers to teach a few of your tradesmen, shop owners and craftsmen to read, but not to teach the peasant farmers or herders. But, if you find some peasant to be exceptionally intelligent yet subservient, you should consider providing education to him too, for he could be an asset to the shire and he will be beholding to you."

The bishop, whose face by now had grown red, replied, "But where are these teachers going to come from? I assure you they will not be my parish priests or monks."

"They will be trained at St. Paul's then. I will construct a new building, which I will call Edward's Hall, whose primary purpose will be to instruct teachers. It will educate those not only from the shire, but throughout Ireland and perhaps nearby Scotland too. After all, as you well know **Bishop!,** the monks of

Ireland became the teachers of the nobles throughout Europe during the middle ages. I want to continue that tradition and expand it not only to European nobles, but to provide that opportunity to merchants, and to tradesmen and to guildsmen. I want Bunkillarny to be a center of education."

"But, how will these "teachers" earn a living? The church will not support them."

"The lords throughout Ireland will want to teach their children as will the merchants and tradesmen for it will increase their opportunities in life. Similar to the courts throughout Europe with our teacher-monks, they will surely house, feed and pay them,"

Lady Catherine grabbed my arm beneath the table and squeezed it. Across the table, Marie smiled at me with her eyes.

In designing systems, I had been in numerous meetings with executives of large companies who were generally of high caliber, but the manner in which Lord Bunkillarny led his advisers and made decisions would match theirs. Of course, the executives were not dealing with matters of life and death as he was. If the executives failed, they would receive a golden parachute and move on to the next company likely at a higher salary. Whereas if he failed, thousands of his subjects, his family, and he might be killed, and he would lose his kingdom, not only for himself but for the succeeding generations.

37:   SHOVE GROATS

After a course of berries, nuts, cheese, and some kind of cherry pastry served with a fruity, sweet wine, the men retreated to another room and I grabbed Michael pleading, "Can we leave now!"

"After such a fine performance, it would be an insult ta leave, lad."

Reluctantly walking at the end of the line of men, we entered another large room with numerous trophies of bears, wolves, deer, boar, and elk, not all of which were native to Ireland. A large fearsome looking stuffed bear with one arm extended up to ten feet stood at the side of the entrance, which startled me. Shaking his other huge paw, they affectionately patted him on the back and greeted him as George. In a corner of the room, there was a chess set, which the Bishop and a lord played. Some others sat down to play an unfamiliar game of cards.

Lord Edward invited Michael and I to join him at a thirty-foot-long highly waxed table to play what he called, "Shove Groats."

I said, "I have never played this before."

Michael said, "It is no that difficult."

Lord O'Flannery, Michael's father-in-law, who had sat at the other end of the table next to Edward, and had not taken a position in the reading debate joined us and teamed up with Michael. I would play with his lordship, which earlier would have been disconcerting to me, but after witnessing his leadership, I now looked forward to it. A servant walked by carrying a tray filled with tankards of ale, whilst another carried glasses of brandy. I took a tankard of ale because it seemed like the kind of sport you drank a beer with.

Michael and I were at one end of the board, whereas King Edward and Lord O'Flannery took the other. Michael told me, "The object is to shove the groat (a metal disk) as close as possible to the end without going over the edge. We each have three groats. For each groat that lands closer than the opponent's to the edge, we score a point. The game ends at 20 points." It was nearly the same as one of my favorite games— shuffle table. I guess this is where that game originated some 500-years earlier.

According to Lord O' Flannery "The bet would be 10 shillings," which embarrassingly I did not have. Michael said, "I will cover you me lad."

Frustratingly, for the first several rounds I could not get the speed right, during which time Michael scored 8 points, Sir O'Flannery 7, King Edward 8, and me none. I either had used too much speed and went off the edge or was pitifully short of the edge and was easily beaten. Therefore, the score stood at 15 to 8, and Edward looked very frustrated with my performance. Then my competitive juices began flowing, and I acquired the delicate feel of the groat skidding down the long, waxed table with a precise spin, scoring one, then two, then three points a turn. Edward was pleased when we won by a score of 20 to 19 and gregariously congratulated me.

I drained my ale and tried the brandy, which was tastier than others I had in my time. The room was filled with the sounds of men having fun, discussing politics, enjoying each other's company. Some crowded around the table to see the main event and cheer their king on. For the first time all day, I felt comfortable, as we won the next two games 20 to 17 and 20 to 13. Edward shook my hand and gave me all of the winnings, far more than I had earned in all the time I had been in Bunkillarny, what would amount to a fortune for some. Since Michael would have funded me, I gave his half back.

Then Lord Edward, seeing my height and sizing me up asked, "What armaments do ye prefer, Rand?"

"To the best of my faulty memory, I do not know how to use any arms, your highness."

"Do you know how to wield a halberd, a mace, a broad sword, a lance?" To each I responded, no.

"I have shot a bow and arrow though."

Then I remembered that I had thrown the javelin in college. Although I never threw a record distance, I was very accurate and sometimes won the contest against other colleges. Therefore, I told Lord Edward, "I had thrown the spear."

"Excellent."

I hoped I had not identified myself as a possible soldier in some future brutal war.

38:   ENCHANTED

Lady Catherine called a servant, who guided us with a candle through the castle's darkened, cool halls to our rooms for the night. The large oaken room had a roaring fireplace, fine, thick, drawn violet curtains that blocked out all semblance of light and a four-poster feather bed the size of a double bed, significantly larger than the twin-sized one with a straw mattress my feet hung out of at the print shop. The room was totally dark.

After an immensely restful, deep, welcome sleep, feeling refreshed, Michael and I went down the massive, oaken staircase. I assumed we would finally leave, but he insisted we stay for breakfast. Still full from the sumptuous meal the night before, and feeling I had narrowly escaped embarrassment multiple times, I reluctantly agreed on the condition we leave immediately afterwards.

We went back to the dining room occupied by a group of about half of our previous night's dining companions, and some formidable-looking men I did not recognize. Michael introduced the knights one by one.

Just back from a victorious battle to the south, serving on behalf of King Henry, the knights, who King Edward had evidently hired out, seemed confident and boisterous as they enthusiastically shook my hand. I am not good with names but one knight stood out, Sir Reginald Van Clieve III, evidently a senior knight and their leader. With long blond hair, a firm cleft chin, Nordic good looks, a strong build and regal manner, he appeared intimidating. When he shook my hand, he used a vice-like grip, which not being prepared for, I could not respond to. Instead, my fingers crumbled within his grasp. Smiling and congenial, he said, "You are rather large one for a printer, hast thou er wielded a sword."

"Never touched one," I replied, to which he pulls out his sword and introduces it as Megan, telling me to hold her. As I did, with a wry smile he says, "Megan is a bonny lass who has kissed many a suitor's neck and captured many suitors' hearts," the thought of which sends chills through my spine. "

Since they were leaving, Lord O'Flannery and his wife graciously greeted us and offered us their seats. Lord O'Flannery smiled and patted me on the back saying, "parful show last night me lad."

The servants cleared the plates and brought us hard-boiled eggs, sausages, bread and various meats. I missed my coffee and consequently spent the first moments of my mornings in a fog, until Lady Marie appeared radiantly in a powder blue gown with golden sash tied around her 22" waist below her ample, low-cut braided bodice. All the men rose, the knights standing at attention, faces shining, looking adoringly at her, all obviously taken by her. Reginald commanded the knight sitting next to him to move down to make room for her next to him, but she floated towards us standing next to the open chair next to me. After Michael elbowed me, I rose and pulled her chair out.

Still affected, I greeted her, "Bonjour Mademoiselle."

In a beautiful, flirtatious voice accented with a gorgeous smile, she responded, "Bonjour Monsieur."

Then proceeding in English in her captivating noble French accent, she complimented me on my previous night's discourse regarding reading for the middle classes, saying proudly, "I have trained moi maids to read."

We discussed various books she had read in Latin. I told her of one we had just published and promise to bring her a copy, which seemed to greatly please her. As the discussion proceeded, I found it difficult to concentrate, instead I found myself staring into her brown eyes, at her up turned nose, perfect smile and narrow heart shaped full red lips, captivated by her alluring, accented voice, enchanted by her French perfume. During a pause in the conversation, I noticed Reginald's eyes shooting daggers at me, and feared I might have enticed the deathly Megan.

In a lilting, vivacious voice, she asked, "Will you be competing in the games monsieur Randalle?" To which I awkwardly replied, "I do not know about the games, me lady."

"Why the biannual Bunkillarny games of course. They came from across the Firth of Clyde in Scotland. As someone so strong and courageous surely you must compete."

"I would, but I am not a warrior, rather a humble printer, a man of words not of weapons."

"But there are so many events; surely there is one for you."

Feeling trapped, wanting to impress her, I said something I immediately regretted, "If you wish it me lady, I shall do so."

After barely touching her food, she says she would be going to the "jardin" to read. I pulled out her chair, bow and not knowing if it was appropriate, kiss her elegant, sensuous hand with long shapely fingers. With a smile and a glance over her shoulder, she floats away, all male eyes measuring her every step.

Afraid of what I had gotten myself into, I looked to Michael who mockingly responds, "Surely vou-oo-oo must compete monsieur Randalle."

Then he tells me about the games, which consist of war-based events such as archery, dueling, jousting, and other lesser feats such as running, putting of the stone and tossing of a log.

"Are there any events such as throwing a spear," I asked.

"There are two, one for distance and one for accuracy."

"I could do that, but surely it's too late to register"

"There is no registration, you just show up at the start of an event."

"But don't you need me to work at the print shop."

"No, tomorrow is a holiday and most of the town will be at the games, as will half of the shire. I suggest you practice at the open field behind the castle where the games will be held, I will be at the council meeting all day and stay here the night. You can take the cart back to town and come back tomorrow morning with Gwendolyn and the rest of the shop."

———

I went through the courtyard where the knights and soldiers were practicing, clanging, crashing, clomping, slashing and slishing away. Then, across the moat over the drawbridge I found a tan hardened dirt road with a patch of grass in the middle, where the cart's wheels did not tread. The road to the back went to the left, but I had seen the gardens to the right, when I first came to the crest of the hill, and hoping I might bump into Marie I decided I would see these first.

The gardens were expansive with a long pool surrounded by trimmed topiaries. One corner containing vegetables, another flowers, and a third held grape vines.

There was a corner obscured by high trimmed topiaries with a path, decorative trees and an arbor sporting trellises. I entered this section that instantly felt ten degrees cooler than the sun baked, dirt covered area I had just departed, following the curvaceous path to where I heard a fountain rushing and splattering. The sound led me to a contemplative open circular, white graveled area, shaded by old growth trees around the perimeter with statues of famous men, including King Edward, with a delightful, multi-tiered fountain in the middle that cooled and moistened the entire area. On such a hot sunny day, it felt cool and inviting.

There, I found Lady Marie sitting on a classically sculpted bench wrapped in a book. I thought I should not disturb her and turned to depart, when I heard a sweet, "Randalle, come sit wi moi."

We talked about what she was reading then she told me how much she loved coming to Bunkillarny, because uncle

Edward had such an extensive library. I asked her what she liked to read and she said," Everything—Greek plays and philosophy, tragedies, comedies, science, math, Dante's Inferno, Julius Caesar, the Canterbury Tales, French literature, everything."

I asked her, "What language do you typically read in?"

"Oh, but I do not read in just one language, but in Latin, Greek, Français of course, Anglais a little, German and Italian."

I was quite impressed. "Have you been to Italy, I hear it is very exiting there now especially in the arts."

"Oui, it is amazin, I have seen so many glorious artworks, some of which I have brought back to my chateau in Burgundy and the palace in Paree. I particularly enjoyed soom works by a young artist named Da Vinci, his portrayal of the human body is magnifique, so real. I brought his scene of a Tyrolean countryside with me to give to Aunt Catherine. But it is not just the painting. The architecture is exciting too and there is a spirit of adventure of the mind there. Oh, and then the books there are magnifique—so many book sellers, so many books from old Rome and Greece and Constantinople too." "Have vou bin?"

"No."

"Oh, monsieur Randalle especially with your interest in literature, vou must go!"

"I would like to someday. Do you play any instruments mademoiselle? I am sorry, should I call you your ladyship or baroness or something? I do not want to offend you."

"Mademoiselle is fine. When we are together you may call me Marie, but not in public. Then you must call me Lady Marie. It tis silly protocol. As to instruments as vou asked, I play the harp and the harpsichord and flute. I would like to play for vou sometime.

"Why yes. I would like that very much." Are vou married or is there someone special in your life?"

"No there is no one. Is there someone special for vou?"

"No, No one."

"But Tu es très jolie and all the men are in love with you. I have seen the way they look at you. Surely, you must know that. That you could have any man in the kingdom."

"Oui, but I have not found 'im yet. Perhaps he is you—but I make the joke, vou cannot take moi seriously."

"My father wanted me to marry the Prince of Austria, because it would be a good alliance for France. My grandfather was Louis XI and my uncle is King Charles VIII. I like my father so much and feel a duty to him, but the prince was so old and cruel. My father said that you can learn to love, but he did not want me to spend the rest of moi life with someone I loathed. That is why I came here to be with my aunt—to forget about et. She is très, très understanding."

Then she changed the subject and asked, "What is your favorite book mon cher."

"Since I lost my memory, I am not sure. But one book comes to mind. It's a about a captivatingly beautiful princess named Scarlet with dark hair and blue eyes, who is pursued by many men in the kingdom, but is in love with her best friend's husband, Ashley. A roguish hero named Rhett pursues her, but she repeatedly rejects him. In an epic war to free their slaves, in which hundreds of thousands of men die, the noble Ashley is killed, the kingdom is set afire and the country is lost. Starving, standing on the ashes of her destroyed chateau, she says 'As God is my witness, I swear I'll never be hungry again!' and she promises to rebuild what she has lost."

"Ou la, la I like this book. Who wrote it?"

"Margaret Mitchell"

"A Woman?"

"Oui"

"May I have thes book s'il vous plaît?"

"I am sorry mademoiselle, with my lack of memory, I do not know where it is, or where I got it from."

"I would like to write a book, but I am a mere woman."

"You could write it under an alias and I could publish it."

"Oh mon cher what a wonderful idea. Maybe I do thes."

"With all of your knowledge, if you wrote a book, I am sure it would acquire an audience. I could help you with it. We are in the midst of a revolution with hundreds of printers throughout Europe producing millions of books every year. Every year more people will learn to read and eventually millions of people will read. Ultimately, we will have universal education, in which even the peasants will have the opportunity to read. So, there should be a market for your book."

"You said revolution. Do you mean that someone will overthrow the king."

"Oh no! But printing will be a transformational event for Europe and the rest of the world, vastly advancing the spread of knowledge, education and communication. It will lead to amazing scientific innovations and transform science itself. When someone develops an invention in say Italy, someone in London will be able to read about it. It will lead to more world trade, more wealth, and more commerce. It will harken back to the time of the Roman and Grecian empires when great authors wrote great books and plays that were performed in theaters across Europe and the Middle East. Eventually, in maybe three-hundred years, it may lead to revolutions, as have occurred in Rome and Egypt and China in the past, but that is a long way off."

Looking fawningly up at me with her big, beautiful brown eyes, but a little stunned by my fervent statement she responded, "Oh mon ami, how do you know all of thes? Did your amnesia give you the sight? Are vou a prophet? Are vou or a seer?"

I realized that I had gone too far. I did not want to talk too much about the future, because I did not want to cause harm in the current time. But she inspired me, she disarmed me.

"Oui madam, perhaps it is the bump on my head speaking."

A gardener entered the fountain area, and she looked uncomfortable. Before she left, she said, "If vou enter a contest,

I shall root for vou, moi champion." Then she kissed me on the cheek and I was in love, for the first time.

39:   THE GAMES

A bit heady from the encounter, I followed the road that wound around the castle to the backside where I saw a large open green field, at least the size of three football fields. They were just finishing mowing the grass with long, curvaceous sickles, the fresh-cut smell of it wafting in a gentle breeze. Other men were noisily hammering wooden stands together and pounding in stakes to mark off the various events—the warm air echoing the sounds off the hill. Towards the end of the field and in the surrounding hills, people were setting up tents, where the rest of the shire would stay. Below them, vendors and farmers were setting up stands to sell food and crafted items to the gathering crowd. Evidently, this was a big event that attracts a large crowd. The busy, cacophonous scene elicited a sense of building anticipation.

Similar to the day before, I had an uneasy feeling in my stomach. What had I gotten myself into? I sat down on the lush, newly-cut, green grass and tried to collect my thoughts, calm myself and meditate, but all I could think about was Marie, her beautiful face, her captivating French accent, her magnificent figure, her enticing French perfume. She assaulted all my senses. But it appeared that every man in the court, whether married or not, adored her, and she knew it. Much had happened over the last day.

There were a few guys throwing spears in the distance. I walked over the fragrant grass and asked them if I could try one. They directed me to a pile of spears hidden under a blanket at the corner of the field. There I found several metal tipped, wooden spears. These were slightly heavier than the aluminum javelins I threw in college and were about 7 feet long vs. my 8-

foot javelin. I stretched and began rotating my arm to warm up, then began throwing the projectile ten to twenty feet. Thinking that was as far as I could throw, laughing, the others chided me.

I said, "I will throw after I warmed up." They evidently insulted me in Gaelic, but having no idea what it meant, found the insults easy to ignore.

I knew from previous experience that if I threw the javelin too hard on the day before a meet, I would throw my arm out and it would be like rubber the day of the competition therefore, I threw it no more than 100 feet, which was enough to impress my scornful companions, who were throwing it as hard as they could to impress each other. This was the first time I had thrown the javelin in over a decade, but seeing it fly through the air like a bird then slowly peak and dive ever faster back to earth, until it stuck in the ground, its tail pointing upwards elicited that familiar joy.

———

Thinking about lovely Marie, I could not get to sleep until the middle of the night and then dreamt about a fearsome sword fight with Reginald wielding a massive, seven-foot Megan.

Gwendolyn woke me from the restless dream saying that I needed to hurry. I put on my robes and then began putting on my shoes, the ones Michael had provided from the cobbler that costs a full month's wages, which I later paid back. Because I knew they would be easier to run in, I took off the boots, grabbed my hiking boots from under the bed, and put these on. I hastily grabbed the Latin book for Marie, grabbed a hunk of bread then ran to the cart where Gwendolyn had taken the reins. Outside, the cool damp air enveloped us in a dense fog off the bay. We could see no more than 50-feet as we set off for the castle obscured in the clouds.

Daisey and the three apprentices sat in the back of the cart with John, his three sons, two younger daughters, and wife walking behind us. We joined a long procession of freshly scrubbed Bunkillarnians walking up the hill dressed in their best Sunday attire. The fog had begun to lift and by the time we were halfway up the hill, it was sunny with a brilliant blue sky above. I could see the long stream of people in front and behind us buzzing like bees heading to the hive in a festive mood.

We wound around the castle to the field in the back, filled with tents and people milling around, the hills above crowded with tents to the skyline. Michael came to us, hugged Gwendolyn and fervently shook John and all the boys' hands. Then his two daughters joined us with their husbands and young, excited children. This was evidently a real family affair.

Michael took me aside and said, "The lord took up my reading proposal with the counsel, and although some resisted, it passed. One, who most fervently resisted had been Sir Reginald, who treats his peasants poorly and over taxes them to fund his exorbitant expenses. He very angrily said, 'My peasants will ner lern ta read. God put them on this earth to till my fields and serve me, not to spend their time idling away reading. Who knows what kind of notions they'd get in their heads, if they cud read."

A while later, trumpets blared from the top of the castle's ramparts, followed by a procession of the shire's nobility in their finest robes walking down the road above us. They settled into the stands as King Edward, Queen Catherine, and their three children, ranging from six to perhaps fifteen, accompanied by Lady Marie appeared to another flourish of trumpets.

In a booming voice, Lord O'Flannery introduced the ruler, "Our august, courageous, noble, King Edward, Harold, Charles, Robert, Earl of Essex, Knight of the realm, Lord Bunkillarny," to which everyone on the field, in the stands, and up into the hills stood, applauded and cheered wildly for at least two minutes. I did not realize how truly popular a king could be and what an honor it had been to play with him last night.

After smiling and raising his hands to unsuccessfully end their fervent cheers, King Edward welcomed everyone to the games saying in a booming, commanding voice, "Let courage, honor, Christ and Mary, his mother, guide the spirit of these cherished games. Let the Bunkillarny games begin!" which was followed by another flourish of trumpets, and the report of booming cannons from the ramparts echoing off the mountain above and throughout the field. Reflecting their childlike anticipation, the crowd again cheered wildly.

Michael told me that the lord used the games as a way to recruit the best men for his army, and to keep his men sharp. "Perhaps I should not try as hard then," I replied.

"Our work at the print shop is too important to the lord to worry about that. We know ye han't had time to prepare like the others, many of 'em who throw the spear are in the army, but we will not expect much o ye lad. Just do yer best Rand, we be all rootin' fer yeu." Then he adds, "You had better go to the back of the field with haste because the spear throwing contest will be the first event."

———

Gwendolyn grabs my arm and wishes me, "God be with you Rand."

As I jog to the competition, with all this unexpected hoopla, my nerves are starting to become tense, and I have a hollow feeling in my stomach and chest, my heart is racing, and my knees are bit wobbly. When I arrive, I see two lines of about forty men each facing each other as if they were preparing for a battle. I join the nearer line, where, judging by their stilted expressions and stiff stands, they are nervous too. People surround the field, and the hills rising above holds thousands of spectators making it seem like an Olympic event.

A man in a red stocking hat with a long tail and white bob at the end tells us all to back up twenty steps, until we are about sixty yards apart to where the crowd stands. Then he tells the facing line to throw and forty spears come streaming towards us, the sound of projectiles whizzing through the air, then multiple thumps as they pierce the earth twenty yards in front of us, sticking out at various angles to thunderous cheers from the crowd, witnessing what to them resembles a battle. Another red-hatted official walks along the line, picks up the ten longest spears, after which the men who threw these walk forward. The others are eliminated and walk to the side cursing.

Meanwhile, I have been stretching, running in place, rotating and extending my arm to warm up, something that must seem strange, because no one else did so. Those that did not already have a spear run forward and grab the best ones first. Being late, the first one I pick up seems wobbly, but the second seems little better. By then, all the best ones are taken. This did not resemble my college track meets at all. For a dual meet, you had six throws, but in a multi-team event with as many participants as this one, you had three tosses to qualify and if you qualified, another three tosses.

When the official gives us the signal, the others throw. None of the men run up to the line, but rather they just stand there, reach back, and throw the spear with a grunt. I did not back up my accustomed twenty steps but rather took ten steps back, which must have looked odd to the other participants and the crowd. Since I stand alone, I stand out and am embarrassed.

When the official gave us the signal, the others throw and being the last to throw, I begin running, gain speed and initiate the crossover of my legs, lean back, slip in a hole and barely get my spear off. The general commotion of the crowd, grows to a deafening roar as the projectiles rise and fall to the ground. Before getting up, I glance over to Gwendolyn standing on the sideline, who upon seeing me slip grabs Michael's arm.

Disappointedly, I thought I was eliminated, but luckily, I was the last one selected by the red-capped ref. Gwendolyn and Michael along with the gang cheer when the ref at last picks up my spear.

For the next round, I make sure my path to the line is clear of ruts, and wish I had my track spikes. Still my hiking boots had rubber protrusions that granted me much better traction than the boots would have.

The facing line throws and this time they select the furthest five javelins. The others had more of a sidearm motion versus my football throwing style, where I brought the spear past my ear. My college javelin had a rope wrapped around the middle I used to rest my second finger on and obtain that last bit of acceleration, whereas this spear does not. I bring my trusty multi-purpose knife out and crouching down to hide the modern tool, with the razor-sharp 2-inch blade quickly carve a little notch in the spear near its balance point to rest my middle finger on and thereby facilitate that last, all-important motion.

Again, the official gives the signal, the others throw, and I run up to the imaginary line, turn, cross my right leg over the left, bend backwards nearly touching the spear's tail to the ground, then in turn fire my leg, back, shoulder, arm, wrist and finger muscles, flicking it by the notch at the end to cause the javelin to rotate and better slice through the air. I think I will finish first, but one of the knights beats me by several feet. I go over to him, shake his hand and congratulate him, as he does me with a broad inviting smile, introducing himself as Thomas Brogan.

For the final toss, the referee gathers us all together and informs us that the ten of us would each throw individually. Thomas and I are last in the line. My last toss was less than 150 feet and I knew I could do better, but I would only have one more chance to do so. Being over a decade since I threw a javelin regularly, I knew I could not expect my old results, but working the Devil's Tail, had built my throwing arm up, which was finally warmed up and supple, and running had helped build up my legs., which are as important as the arms.

Some of the men in the line, who were likely spear throwers for the army, adopt my style, run a few steps and get off better tosses. I was afraid my style was illegal, but evidently it is not—there are no rules. Thomas got an even better toss— the furthest of the day by far, at least ten- feet beyond the others.

This time I run up, cross-over and spin the spear with my fingers. As it releases, it feels effortless. The thin projectile flies high into the pristine, blue sky, finally cresting, then begins its arched descent back to earth. I hear the ahhs! from the crowd assembled on the hill, while the group at the end of the field beats a hasty retreat as the spear approaches them, landing with a slish, sticking out of the ground, accented by a reverberating twang. It has flown twenty feet beyond Thomas's. The crowd and my hometown fans cheer wildly. I turn towards them, smile and shake my fist in the air. Gwendolyn hugs her father and sisters.

The official gathers the top three finishers together, pours a couple of shots of whiskey into tiny tin cups and toasts us to the cheers of the crowd surrounding the field and up into the hills, we raising our cups to them. The whiskey tastes like un-aged Scotch, which given how close we were to Scotland is probably where it came from.

I later learned from Michael that up until that time, the whiskey had been primarily distilled by Monks for medicinal purposes, but after the Irish and Scottish royalty adopted it, it was starting to gain a following among the populous.

Thomas pats me on the back several times and says, "That was bonnie Rand. In all the years of throwin' the spear, since I were a wee lad, I ner seen a toss like that un." Then he pats me several more times and seems more excited about it than I am. What a nice, handsome, gracious young man, I think.

I ask him, "Are you related to Jimmy Brogan who does our Latin translations."

He says, "Why yes indeed I am, He be me uncle, me da's brother. He was going ta be a priest, he was, till he discovered the girls. Now he has a pack of bearn– me cousins. Do you work at the McCarron's print shop?"

"I do"

"Tis a fine place, a place o' lernin, where I lernt how ta read meself before I be at the college and before I became a knight."

Even though he was one of the knights I met at breakfast, Thomas did not seem as full of himself as the others, and I had noticed that he was the only one who did not fawn over Marie. Tall and handsome with dark black hair, blue eyes and square face, dimpled cheeks and forthright cleft chin he seemed genuine and honest—someone I instantly liked and felt to be trustworthy.

———

In the accuracy competition, simulating a real battle, we throw spears from 120 feet at a five-foot, ugly, fearsome-looking dummy that looks something like a scarecrow. Thomas is the only one to actually hits the dummy, thereby finishing first. I land about three-feet away, finishing third and have another dram of whiskey.

I meet our group, who toast me with beer, and we eat a tasty lunch of bread, cheese and slices of pork that Daisy had packed. She says, "In all me years, I ha ner enjoyed the games more than this-un and I'm so proud o' yeu. Thought that wonderous object wud ner come back to earth. It flew like a bird, it did."

As I look up the grass laden hill and the large field, I see large family groups similar to ours gathered together, talking, joking and eating in a festive mood. Kids running, playing tag and throwing sticks as if they were javelins. It reminded me of

Blossom Music Center, where people brought picnic baskets on the fourth of July and lay on the green lawn feasting on the large hill overlooking the amphitheater, waiting for the world-famous Cleveland Orchestra to play Tchaikovsky's 1812 overture, accompanied by booming cannons and spectacular fireworks that captivated the kids and lit their faces in awe.

Extremely loose now (perhaps from the whiskey and ale), I decide to enter the race in the afternoon. About fifty of us line up each taking off their shirts, but leaving their pants or kilts on, or in the case of some of the nobles, their tights, and in many cases, their hats too. The motley gathering is nothing like those at a track meet, where everyone is in a uniform. I wish I could have worn shorts or one of those kilts, for it was sweltering. But since the others are shirtless I take mine off and toss it to the side. I am one of the older participants, who according to another red-capped official, will run twice around the field that had been marked off with wooden pegs—a distance that looks to be about three quarters of a mile.

Expecting to hear, "Runners to your mark, get set, go, the official merely fires a matchlock pistol and then they begin running with me just standing there. The others start sprinting, whereas being towards the back of the pack, I pace myself. I wish I had my track shoes, but the rest run either in their bare feet or in their boots, both of which do not provide much traction on the matted grass, some sliding and falling around the square turns. Glad to be towards the back, I avoid the pushing and shoving ahead of me—evidently there was no such thing as a foul.

After the first lap, I move up to the middle of the pack and have to fend off one guy who shoves me and another, who as he attempts to trip me, I jump over his leg, nearly falling but stumble forward. Michael, Gwendolyn and the gang cheer me on, those in the viewing stand paying little attention yet, except Marie who seems to smile at me in a lascivious way. I go into fourth gear passing one after another of the exhausted runners as they run out of gas. As expected, they started too soon and had not run regularly, as I had been doing.

Prior to the last turn, there are five runners in front of me. I sprint ahead passing one, then another, then a third, who spent, begin to stumble and walk. With my heart pounding, my lungs burning, my legs like rubber, shins splinting from the ill-suited shoes, I push myself to pass a fourth runner, then with but a few yards left, give it all I have, but fail to pass the last runner, and fall to the ground sucking in air.

Finishing second, I earn another round of whiskey. I raise my glass to the crowd, take a sip, and give the rest to Michael. Gwendolyn kisses me on the cheek, which is a more welcome reward.

Now, thoroughly enthralled with the games, I join the stone toss, which is really a cannon ball that resembles the shot-put I tossed in college, except that it was a little lighter than the 16 pounds. No one that joins the line for this event is my height, but several are much broader and look much stronger. I knew, though, that it was not just about arm strength but leg strength and technique too.

They rely on their arms and backs—some throwing it like a baseball and injure their arms. Using the 21st-century technique that no one emulates, I stand about eight feet back of the chalk foul-line, cock the stone under my chin, kick my leg back, twirl, bend low and using all the muscles from my toes to my fingers propel the ball forward in an explosion. The other contestants and those in the stands have mouths half-open, as if they were thinking that is the craziest thing they ever saw. I toss the stone about sixty-feet finishing first, garnering another dram of whiskey, none of which I consume.

Encouraged by this result, comparable to a college track meet, totally enmeshed in the competitions that are so easy to join, I enter the line for the log toss, because I always enjoyed tossing logs around in the woods or breaking 'em between the forks of a tree for firewood. This is a very congenial group, who joke, jeer and tease each other, which I join in. I see many from the stone-throw, who serve in the army and congratulate me on my performance accepting me as one of their beefy own. For this event, you grab an eight-foot by ten-inch log in the middle and toss it. It is great fun, but I finish maybe in the middle of the hefty contestants at best, afterwards shaking the hands of the top three and patting them on the back, glad I did not have to drink any more whiskey.

Afterwards, I go over to where our group had assembled. They are all smiling broadly and patting me on the back, except for Daisy and Gwendolyn who have left. Michael shakes my hand vigorously saying, "Ye haft done a marvelous job. You must attend the ball tonight to accept yer reward."

Thinking the reward was more whiskey, I say, "Do I have too?"

"It wud be an insult to the King if you di no go. Besides the prizes be quite a bit of shillings."

Not wanting to insult the King and having little money to buy prized books, I say, "I will be honored to attend."

40:   THE BALL

Thomas appears and says we should wash up, then leads me into the back of the castle, down the stairs into a lower section where there is a large stone pool with about three and a half feet of water. Servants carry buckets of hot water to pour into the pool, whilst the overflow spills into a drain. With the smell of stone, mildew, and boiling water the pool area is steamy. We strip off all of our clothes and enter the water where there is a large group of knights and nobles—a jovial group, similar to those I had seen in numerous other locker rooms, talking enthusiastically about the events they had just participated in.

Thomas says, "The idea for the pool originated with the Romans, when they occupied France and England. They thought of this as important in building camaraderie. King Edward's father learned about it while touring Roman ruins in Paris and had it added to the castle."

I greatly appreciate this hot-tub-like experience, for other than washing myself with a cold bucket of water from the river, I had not had a real bath in weeks.

After they cleaned up, the men went in to an ante-room where they had their clothes hung on hooks. As I begin to put my dirty clothes and boots on, because all the others are adorning themselves in regal looking vestments, I soon realize these will not be appropriate for the ball. Dejectedly, feeling I would not be able to attend the ball, I put on my pants, shirt, and boots back on and am walking out when Michael appears with a bag of garments he tells me to don.

After the race, realizing I would be invited to the ball, Michael tells me Gwendolyn and Daisy had hurried home. They hastily sewed an old outfit of his that he had outgrown, so that it would fit me. The outfit consists of a green tunic that went below my hips with something that, although I could not believe it, looked like a white miniskirt that covered about half of my thighs. In the bag, I also find green tights and put these on, then adorn myself with a Kelly-green cape that contrasted with rest of my outlandish outfit.

I follow some of the last men up several flights of stairs to the main floor. I feel embarrassed, but since my vestments are similar to those the other men wear, I have to accept it. I guess during this time, the men were the peacocks and I wonder when that changed. I comfort myself thinking that I was attending a Renaissance themed, costume ball, except this is a real Renaissance ball and these are not costumes, but what they actually wear back then or now, which still is shocking!

With a lump in my throat, I feel that same sense of excitement and dread you feel when you walk into an unfamiliar formal affair by yourself, wondering if you will fit in, or somehow embarrass yourself. Everyone is adorned in a fascinating array of colors and styles. Michael and Gwendolyn greet me with a welcome mug of ale. Similar to a girl at her prom, in her white and blue form-fitting gown, she looks stunning. Tall and statuesque with perfect poised posture, a braided blue belt hangs down in the middle of her thin waist, and with her long reddish-blond hair tied up, she is already attracting the attention of the assembled young nobles, who cluster in various circles, stealing glances at her while talking to each other.

After a while, the trumpets blare and we all turn to bow to King Edward and Queen Catherine as they enter the room. After they sit down, we sit at long tables filled with lamb, beef, pork, goose, loaves of bread, carrots and pitchers of ale. Other than the carrots, there are no other vegetables. I think potatoes would be a good accompaniment—after all this is Ireland. Then I realize that potatoes came from the Americas, which Columbus will soon discover. There would be no yams, tomatoes or corn yet either, for these too hail from the Americas.

Gwendolyn's sisters are not invited to the ball—only Michael, Gwendolyn, John and his wife, but we have a grand time toasting each other with ale, as did the rest of our table composed of the prominent Bunkillarny merchants.

McNab, the pub owner, toasts, "Hars ta tha man tha brought pride ta us in Bunkillarny." They all join in chiming, "Hars ta Rand, 'hars ta Rand." As the feast proceeds, the toasts became more slurred and more maudlin, but they make me feel as if I had just won the Olympics.

Flannery, the baker next door toasts –
"My friends are the best friends
Loyal, willing and able.
Now let's get to drinkin!
All glasses offn the table!"

O'Neal, the pub owner –
"There are good ships,
and there are wood ships,
The ships tha sail the seas.
But the best ships, are friendships,
And may they always be."

They toast my feats so many times, I become embarrassed. The trumpets blare and we all leave the tables as servants and soldiers come in and take them out. Then a stage appears that a band soon occupies and after warming up, starts playing music. Many of the instruments look familiar—cornets, bagpipe, viols, lutes, flutes, something that looks like a clarinet and a drum. The nobles in the room pair up and proceed to perform a choreographed procession that involves various positions and handholds that seem too intricate for me to attempt.

Michael tells me that, "The tables were set up in the field below the castle, where oxen had been roasting for hours and Lord Edward had sent kegs of beer. The king will appear from a backside gate and will proceed to the viewing stand. After we hear the distant trumpets blare and the cheers die down Michael adds, "He will welcome everyone to the bi-annual feast, then introduce the bishop to bless them and thank God for a parful harvest, the meal and prosperity of the shire."

The cheers and applause accompany the lord as he returns to the hall, glowing from the merriment. The music stops and he takes the stage along with Queen Catherine, Marie and Reginald. In the latest French courtier, Marie looks stunning and I cannot pry my eyes away from her off-white gown that hugs her shapely figure, trimmed below in an intriguing gold and blue Grecian pattern. As she walks, the long gown pulls slightly accenting her perfect figure, with each step. In the front of the gown, a three-feet surge of light blue silk rises up to a point at her tiny waist. Her low-cut, powder-blue, tightly fitting, ample bodice is trimmed with a black satin collar that caresses her breasts then rises to hug her bare shoulders. On top of her flowing, blond-highlighted, brown hair stands a two-foot blue and gold pointed hat that has lace cascading below to her waist. She resembles a Disney princess—Cinderella or perhaps Aurora, except that she is real, not animated. Mine are not the only eyes fixated on her. All the men, as are many of the ladies, look at her as the symbol of the latest Parisian fashion.

Reginald announces the winners from each event from third to first. When he calls my name, Michael tells me to go to the stage, where I am joined by Thomas and Lorcam Mc Pherson, who finished third. The Lord gives Lorcam a crown and Thomas two crowns, then me a pound. Reginald shakes each of our hands.

Lady Catherine smiles and kisses me on both cheeks. Lady Marie bestows a red satin sash around Lorcam's shoulder and neck and a blue one around Thomas's shoulder. When I follow them and stand in front of her, she looks longingly into my eyes, kisses me fervently on both cheeks, whispers "Mon chéri, vou are moi champion," and places a golden satin sash around my neck, punctuated with a subtle tug of the sash towards her. Before we exit the stage, there is a flourish of trumpets as I shake Lorcam's hand. Thomas gives me a manly hug, saying once again how much he enjoyed witnessing my feat and that my record would never be broken.

I still did not thoroughly understand the English money system but had learned that

1 pound (L) = 20 shillings (s) or 4 crowns
1 crown = 5 shillings
1 shilling = 12 pence
1 penny = 4 farthings

When I return to the table, McNab says "That there pound could purchase 100 gallons of ale," and getting the hint, I promise to buy a couple of rounds at the pub.

Flannery says, "Ye could buy two cows or rent a craftsman's house for a year wi' it." (something that would cost me $40,000 to rent in San Francisco).

Now, I realize why so many men participated in each event, and why the competition had been so fierce, glad that I had not known this earlier, for instead of being relaxed, I would have been nervous and probably not have performed as well.

Then Reginald calls my name again for placing third in the spear targeting contest, which Thomas won and I won a crown for. As the awards proceed, I won another two crowns for the run and another pound for the stone throw. Lady Catherine, who had left the competition early, seems particularly pleased to see me again, her smile warmer and more enduring each time. With each award, Marie, who did not witness the stone throw, kisses me on the cheek more fervently. Reginald's announcement of my name seem more disappointing, his congratulatory smile falser, and his handshake more punishing. Being prepared, I now meet his vice-like grip with my own, eliciting a grimace from him.

The main event of the day had been the broadsword and saber competitions held in the castle courtyard, both of which Reginald won, with Thomas finishing second in the saber. At the end of the ceremonies, Reginald announces that the wrestling tournament, and "The main event of the games, the joust, will be held tomorrow."

Each time I return to the table, the rowdy group congratulates me, pats me on the back and toasts me.

O'Leary, the butcher –
"I drink to your health when I'm wi you,
I drink to your health when I' be alone,
I drink to your health so often,
I'm startin to worry bout me own!"

Never handling praise well, I feel more embarrassed each time, but at the same time, I enjoy it and enjoy standing out with four red, blue and gold sashes draped around my neck that distinguish me from the other men at the ball. As I walk around the hall, they greet me as if I am a celebrity. Its ironic how this feeling hasn't changed from high school. In the back of my mind, I always wanted to be the hero of the game. But when I achieved that distinction, and was rewarded with the adulation of my fellow students, teachers and coaches, I felt embarrassed and deflected their praise. I wanted to stand out, but, didn't.

The band reassumes the stage and begins playing more festive tunes, including some Gaelic ones. Gwendolyn grabs me for a circle dance, in which we hold hands to a tune played with a bagpipe and a harp. By this time, even though my moves are awkward, I am totally into it and having a lot of fun. I notice that Marie and Reginald are dancing next to each other. As the large circle rotates, she occasionally glances at me. Earlier she had danced with several young knights, each vying for her hand, she performing each dance gracefully and flawlessly, flirting with each, each in turn, fawning over her. I think I am foolish for ever thinking she might be interested in me, and I am jealous of Regie.

As we head back to our group, Marie grabs me by the arm saying, "I must have a dance with such a charming champion, mon cheri."

I tell her that sadly, I did not know any of the dances, but she insists. Even though I am a good dancer in my time and shamelessly improved by copying other's moves, I had never seen dances this intricate before. In this one, what she calls the "Hey," the female dancers wind enchantingly around their partners.

Thomas immediately sweeps Gwendolyn up. The dancing has helped to reverse the effects of all the toasts, which had dulled my reflexes. Becoming more coordinated, I enjoy the rhythms of the medieval beat. I quickly learn the relatively easy male part as Marie sensuously swings and sways around me, with a constant beguiling smile and enticing look, me becoming more enchanted with each rotation, trying mightily not to fall for someone all the gents worship, but I can't take my eyes off her. For me, there is no one other than her in the room. When the dance ends, she whispers in my ear to meet her in the throne room after the next dance, which surprises and thrills me.

41:   IN LOVE

With palpable anticipation, I move towards the far exit of the hall. After the following dance, I quietly exit the ballroom and with expectancy walk down the dimly lit hall to the throne room, where there are no guards. The door pried partially open, I slide into the cool, completely darkened room, where I can see nothing. As my eyes adjust to the all-enveloping blackness, I hear a "shush" and make my way to Marie with my arms extended, feeling my way, careful not to fall over some unseen obstacle, and attract the attention of the guards. Then, I feel her hug me tightly from behind and whisper into my ear in a sultry voice, "Oooh, mon cheri vou es sooo viral" "Vou venez avec moi."

Holding her hand, I follow her out the back of the room, through a dimly lit hallway, to the right and down another hallway to a doorway. We pass through the doorway, leading to a circular staircase, she starts climbing with me closely behind her. Being somewhat inebriated, she stumbles, and I catch her, nearly kissing her, but teasingly she pulls away and entices me to follow. After so many toasts and ales, I too am a little intoxicated, but more tipsy by her presence and enticing perfume.

At the top of the stairs, we open another door onto the top of a round tower. As I hold her soft, sensual hand, we walk to the edge, where we can see the blackened sea in the distance, the moon glistening off rolling white waves and the darkened, shadowy town—the edges of the blackened buildings highlighted in moonglow—a spellbindingly, romantic scene.

Caressing my arm, she leads me to the other side of the turret, where we see hundreds of the shire's subjects frolicking below—groups playing music, dancing, drinking, cavorting, kissing. Lanterns emitting glowing, radiate light like flickering fireflies dotting the field, extending up into the hills. In a sexy low voice, she whispers, "I wish I was a shopkeeper, who did not have all the responsibilities, all the scrutiny of a royal. Then with abandon, I would dance the night away with vou, mon cher, till the sun rose in the sky."

She massages my shoulder and my arm saying in a low guttural voice, "Oh mon cheri you are sooo virile. When you ran, I could not take moi eyes from vou. I know vou would be victorious! My champione." Then she caresses my chest, "Ooo, I liked vou without your shirt too!"

Holding her tiny waist tight against me, she leans in and I kiss her. Having been so busy and focused on work back home, it had been a long time since I had kissed a girl. Her shapely full lips responded to mine felling like a powerful hallucinogenic drug that erases all sense of time and place. Then I began French kissing her, to which she responds with increased fury, with her surprisingly strong and toned body, she pulls me to her, our bodies swaying in a primordial rhythm.

After what seems a heavenly eternity, we finally gasp for air. She says, "Ooo la la! Mon cheri vou es magnifique! No one has ever kissed me like this! I want more of vou!" I began kissing her ear, then her neck, then her chest, when she hears someone laughing on the stairs and immediately withdraws.

By the time they reach the top, she scurries to the opposite side of the tower looking out at the sea, looking as if she did not know I was there. The group of six jolly, drunken, playful, gaily dressed young nobles sweep her up into their party, as I, hugging the turret, dejectedly, stealthily retreat down the circular staircase.

By the time I reach the ball, the band has stopped playing, and most of the attendees have left, leaving only the heartiest souls, some of whom are passed out, sleeping against the walls as the weary servants clean up. I glance down at my watch fastened above my wrist to avoid suspicion that tells me it is

4:00 A.M. Where had the time gone? Michael and Gwendolyn had left with the cart, so I begin walking down the long road to town that I had climbed up nearly a day ago—what a day. I had performed well in the contests and had won the equivalent of a year's wages. And I got to kiss an exotic, enticing, drop-dead-gorgeous princess. The long walk in the cool damp air provides an opportunity to sober up and think about all that happened. Fortunately, a full moon under a star-filled sky lights the way, otherwise I might stumble and roll all the way down to town.

———

As I walk down the hill, my thinking somewhat muddled, it still feels as if I am in a dream. How can I be in 15th-century Ireland? How can I be dressed like this in green tights and what seems like a mini-skirt. Talk about gender confusion. Well I guess the male birds are the bright ones, maybe that's where they got the idea—from the birds—*I laugh to myself*.

How could I have played all those games? Maybe being a jock finally paid off. Participating on four teams in high school, I was such a jock—all I really cared about. I was good enough to be on the first string but not really the star. Even now, or even then, or in the future I guess, before the app I participated in multiple sports, which I guess helped me to perform well in the games, and for the first time, I won more than a ribbon, more than a letter or a trophy—I won a substantial amount of money. Those were a lot of fun, the kind of thing I loved to do, which made me feel at home, as if I was at a typical 21st-century picnic.

How could I have kissed such an enchanting princess? That really seemed like a dream. She was way out of my league. I could not think of an equivalent woman in the 21st century—well maybe an heiress of an old family fortune that lived at a fabulous, family estate, someone that I would never meet, or if I did meet at say a charity event, would never pay much attention to me.

No doubt, I am just a passing fancy for her. Every young noble in the kingdom is in love with her. I'm just a printer's assistant. Sure, I'm really a computer guy, but they won't exist for another 400-years and that's not a regal profession anyway. What chance do I have?   And then there's Reginald, who obviously thinks he has a claim to her. He's a formidable, battle-tested knight, who has killed many a man with that foreboding Megan. Someone I would not want to cross.

When I settled into my tiny bed in the attic, I cannot stop thinking about Marie. I know it made no sense, but I am totally smitten.

42:   THE JOUST

Too few hours later Tommy wakes me. My aching head feels like mush, and I find myself still in that absurd costume. My muscles are stiff as a heavily starched shirt from the competitions, and it takes me a while to change into my other clothes, feeling fortunate that I had others, because people these days don't have many changes of clothes. I make my way down to the kitchen, where Daisy reheats some mush and sausages for me.

Seeing my hazy state, she smiles, and then the dear girl gives me an unexpected and much appreciated peck on the cheek, saying, "You ad such a day and by the looks o you, such a nigh. I'm sooo prod o yeouu! You don us all proud, ya did. Folks from the town or any of the hamlets rarely wins any o' the games. Mostly, it's just the soldiers and knights who wins 'em. It's a victory for us, us common folk, it tis."

My head throbbing, swearing to never drink again, I ask where everyone is? "They went ta see the jousting, they did. Should be a startin soon."

"Why didn't you go?"

"I don like sein all those knights crashing inta each ore. Me da was kilt by a lance in the great battle. Besides, I got ta see what you did yesterday. That was a plenty fer me. Nuff ta last the year. I'm soo proud a what ya don. Maybe you was a knight fore ya lost yer memry."

More than anything, I desperately need coffee or even tea, but they do not have either yet. During my recovery when I first made it to the kitchen, I had asked Daisy for some tea, but she did not even know what tea meant, other than it was a letter. No doubt tea had been brewed in China for over a thousand years but had not made it to Europe yet. Coffee probably existed somewhere in Africa or Arabia, but I would not be able to go there—certainly not like going down the block to the nearest Starbucks, of which there were three within three blocks back home. I so, so missed my San Francisco.

I had left my clothes in the bag in the room next to the pool back at the castle, and thought I had better retrieve these before someone threw 'em out. It was my only other change of clothes, my going to church garments. So, I gather myself together and head back up the long hill, slowly at first but as my muscles loosen, the trek becomes easier, the fresh air and movement restoring my body, spirit and clearing my clouded mind. When I reach the castle, the sun is at its peak and it's unusually hot.

As I sneak into the castle, it's cool air feels refreshing. I can hear muted cheers from the field behind the castle and other than a couple servants and guards, see no one—they all wanted to attend the main event. My clothes are fortunately still there. I change out of my ink-stained work clothes into these more presentable ones. Then, at the bottom of the bag, I notice the book I had meant to give Marie. I had to give it to her—it would be a good excuse to see her.

Despite the logic against it and her ignoring me, I desperately yearn to see her, to be near her, to be in her presence. She was, no doubt, at the viewing stand presiding over the jousting tournament, each combatant vying to win each contest to catch her attention and win her favor.

Knowing, since this is the major attraction of the games, I will not be able to get close to the competition or viewing stand, I find my way back to the throne room, where a soldier stands guard. Searching for an excuse, I say that I had been drunk and thought I left my sword on top of the tower.

He says, "You can na go through here." But he directs me to a series of halls that lead to the tower—what a maze this place is. I thought I was getting the hang of it but am constantly lost.

On top, I can look down upon the tournament and see the fair Marie in the stands waving her kerchief at a heavy-set knight, who after striking his lighter competitor off his horse, canters over to the stand and bows to the King, Queen Catherine and to Marie. The field is packed with people jostling to see the joust, and I can see there is no viable path to get close to her. Several others have gathered on the tower too, which is a grand place to witness the sport below—similar to nosebleed seats at Progressive Field or from the Goodyear blimp, but at least you can see all the action. An announcer says the next one up will be Sir Reginald, who wears a red plume on his helmet. The announcer states that this is the first of the two last matches before the finals and this winner would face the winner of the next joust.

Sir Reginald has a massive 18-hand, black warhorse outfitted in black breastplates and faceplates to protect the monster from the lance's mighty blows. As they go to the reviewing stand to salute the king, you can see how much larger the black warhorse is than the other knight's—at least two hands higher. They gallop to opposite sides of the field where a long curtained, four-foot-high wall separates them, the pensive horse snorting, looking forward to what was about to happen. On the Kings signal, they rush towards each other in a mighty gallop. The smaller knight's lance splinters into a thousand pieces as Reginald's lance skillfully connects in the middle of the knight's chest armor easily knocking him off his steed, the knight slamming into the ground twenty-feet away in his 100-pounds of armor, the multiple interconnected, polished steel plates crashing to the ground, sounding as if it were a car crash. The crowd and my companions on the tower cheer voraciously.

Reginald parades around the arena stopping in front of the reviewing stands saluting the King with his lance and a bow of his head. Then he turns towards Marie, takes off his helmet and bows to her, she flirtatiously stands and curtsies back. I feel a sudden pang of jealousy, then realize I had kissed her where I stood earlier that morning—unbelievable—the thought soothing my fragile ego.

Two knights set up for the final match of the semifinals. When I ask another well-dressed, friendly spectator on the tower who was competing, I learn that the knight with the blue plume is Sir Thomas, which draws my interest. I notice that all the other twenty people on the tower are much better dressed than I and ascertain that they are probably nobles. It seems I have entered into a restricted party, as if I had entered a loge surreptitiously, but given the excitement below, they do not seem to mind my transgression.

On the first charge, neither knight is able to knock the other off. Then, Thomas scores. He salutes the king, then takes his helmet off and bows to Gwendolyn, presenting his lance to her, where upon she places her lace kerchief on the tip of the lance. He brings the lance back, rests the lance on the horse's withers, reaches for the kerchief, smells it, and never taking his eyes off her, bows to her with a love-sick smile.

I am greatly surprised that I had not even noticed her and Michael in the stands. They were sitting with Lord O'Flannery, and I suddenly remembered that she was the lord's granddaughter—a noblewoman herself. I felt like a proud big brother pleased to see my beautiful sister pursued by a man I greatly admire. I vow to talk to her about him, and let her know how highly I regard him.

After an intermission, while the squires tend to the horses and their knights, the final competition begins with a flurry of trumpets and deafening cheers from the crowd on the field and up into the hills. Thomas and Reginald square off against each other, Thomas on a smaller, but still mighty, well-trained, fearless, chestnut steed.

On the first charge, clumps of dirt flying off the horses' hoofs create a dusty, gray cloud behind them, the pounding sound of those hoofs resonating throughout the arena. When they converge, their lances bounce off each other's shields producing a clanging sound. On this second charge, Thomas's lance is about to score when at the last second Reginald, by crossing his lance, fends it off. The standoff continues for four more rounds with four more broken lances. The crowd is totally engrossed in each round, releasing a unified sigh as each one ends. With each round, the tension and excitement builds, and I find myself totally engrossed in the stunning event, connected to the crowd, my heart racing, feeling as they do, more drained each time, desperately rooting for Thomas. The knights, gasping for air, are exhausted and their horses are sweating profusely. Each time, it takes longer for them to recover and line up. Their squires tend to them and their horses, as if they were prize-fighters in a ring returning to their corners. When they assume their positions opposite each other, both knights look bedraggled, and must be sweltering in their oven-like armor under the hot midday sun. It appears as if they cannot muster the effort, then suddenly, like a bolt of lightning, they gallop towards each other at a blistering speed.

A hush comes over the crowd and digging deeply, they charge once again. Thomas's lance hitting squarely, bows and shatters. Reginald's lance catches Thomas under the chin and he is knocked off his horse. At first, the crowd cheers and when they see that Thomas isn't moving—a hush envelops the stadium. His head askew, it looks as if he has broken his neck but as they carry him off, he lifts his armor-clad fist to the cheers of the crowd. Gwendolyn looks sick—as if she will soon faint.

Since this is the last match, I run down the stairs and hurry down the hall to the back entrance. With the book in hand, I hope to give it to Marie, but I can't get near her. The crowd presses ever closer trying to get a glimpse of the champion, who bows to the king and to the queen, then presents his lance to Marie, who, according to custom, places her kerchief on its tip. The crowd cheers wildly.

Reginald walks up the steps to the stands where King Edward vigorously shakes his hand in his two hands and smiling broadly, pats him on the back repeatedly. The games are over and I see no way to get close to Marie. There are two lines of soldiers creating an aisle to the castle that the royal party will soon be ferreted through, and I am at least twenty souls back. Since I am tall, all I can hope for is to catch a glimpse of her.

Then King Edward does something astounding. He sees me standing above those around me and calls me to the viewing stand. The crowd parts until I reach the aisle of soldiers, where I have a clear path. When I reach the stands, I just stand there, somewhat nervously, wondering what will happen.

Edward says, "This has been one of the best games ever, and before I declare the game's over, I want to recognize some outstanding participants. First, I want to recognize our noble knight, Sir Thomas Brogan, who placed in four events including placing second in the joust, for which he will be awarded an extra pound. I surely hope he is all right. He is one of our bravest knights and accomplished warriors."

Then he calls me to him and says, "Next, I congratulate our tall printer here, Rand Roberts, for winning the spear throw and stone toss and placing in two more events," for which he rewarded me with two pounds, after which the crowd of thousands cheers excitedly.

Finally, he brings Reginald to the center of the stands saying, "Our noble Lord Reginald Van Cleave has exceeded all others winning three events including placing first in the prestigious joust." He awards him five pounds. After a flurry of trumpets, Edward declares the game's over.

Marie, Edward, Michael, Gwendolyn and Lord O' Flannery come over to congratulate me. Marie says she is so proud of her champion and she kisses me deeply on both cheeks and I hand her the book. Then Gwendolyn kisses me on both cheeks and King Edward and Lord O'Flannery vigorously shake my hand. Reginald, glances angrily at me and as he sweeps Marie up and leads her out toward the castle. Once the royals pass, the aisle closes, soon obscured by the throng of enthusiastic, milling subjects. I look towards her just as she looks back yearningly and smiles her intriguing, captivating smile.

There is nothing I can do, so we start back to get the cart left at the overflowing stables to head back to town. I can see Gwendolyn is crying, so I ask her if she wants to see Thomas and she says, "Oh yes, please!"

We go back to the back of the castle, to the back gate, where guards block our passage. Michael says that he wants to check on Sir Thomas's injury, because Thomas had presented his lance to his daughter and she wanted to see him. The guard says he cannot let us in. Then Michael says that he is a member of the royal council. Still, the guard will not let us pass, until he sees that I was one of the contestants honored by the King, saying, "Oh you be Rand the printer, the one who won so many contests, I will let you all pass then." That was the first time I felt my winning was anything other than frivolous fun.

The doctors' rooms are up one flight of stairs and down two, cool, dark, stone corridors. There we find a long line of people, most of whom had the kind of the injuries that seemed to sprout from any large gathering. Thomas is not there but had been taken to a room down the hall. There he is surrounded by his parents, sisters and brothers, including his uncle, my associate Jimmy Brogan, who nods and smiles sadly at us. Thomas's father and Jimmy's brother, Lord Brogan, is the lord of a large, populous village.

Thomas is obviously in a lot of pain. Seeing Gwendolyn and realizing that Thomas admired her, the large family moves back to allow her space to be with him. She holds his hand and gazes lovingly into his eyes, which seems to bring relief to his face.

The doctor tells Lord Brogan that Thomas sustained a serious spinal injury, and that he is paralyzed below his chest. Lord Brogan goes into a rage saying that Reginald had purposely aimed for his head—an act that violated the code of honor, and that he should be disqualified and severely punished.

43:   THE HERO

While Gwendolyn comforts Thomas and his family, concerned about my new friend, but not able to offer any aid, I desperately want to see Marie. I quietly sneak out the back of the room to search for her. The castle is so large it is not easy to find my way around. I wind up a stairway, down one hall then another, where I see a guard who prevents a well-dressed lord in front of me from passing, "The games ar oer sir. No on is permitted beyond this 'ere."

Not knowing where to go, I approach the large guard, saying, "The king said that he wanted to see me." He hesitates and I thought I would be sent back when he replies, "Oh its you sir Rand. I sawr you throws the spear and the stone.

"Yer a strong man like meself and ye barely beat me in the throwin o' the stone, I a takin second and a crown. You may pass."

"Sorry Padrick, I did no recognize ye in your uniform. You wud o beaten me if you used your legs more lad." I was starting to sound more Bunkillarnian. Dipping down and spinning, I show him my form, which he, in turn, emulates.

Pleasantly surprised, figuring that the king's rooms must be near to Marie's, I ask Padrick directions. After several more turns and staircases, I see Marie's dainty maid, Emily, in the hallway, and attempting to compliment her say, "Marie told me you are an excellent reader, a rare and valuable skill."

In the modern busy world, always feeling the pressure of evaporating time, I had been very brusque in my daily interactions with others, but had learned that here I had to engage with them on a personal level before getting to the point. As I had learned, if I did not do so, they would be offended and reluctant to help.

"Thank you me lord. I feel very fortunate that me lady cares for moi, and I enjoy reading her books so much "

"I would like to speak with her. Do you know where she might be?"

"Me lady is in her room now sir. I will let her know vou are here, moi lord."

As she walks down the hall, I hear a scream. I rush down to where it emanates. There, a guard looks confused and has not taken any action, so I readily push him aside, throw open the door, and see Reginald with one hand up Marie's skirt, revealing her leg and another over her mouth. Incensed, before he notices me, from behind I grab him by his collar and the top of his tights, lift him over my head and toss him like a log 8-feet in the air. He lands in the corner, turns and growls, swearing French epithets. Then in an instant, he bounces up to his feet, and with a menacing face, draws his sword and takes two steps towards me saying, "I will kill you, you inky bastard."

I hastily look for something to defend myself with and with my adrenalin flowing, afraid for my life, pull on one of the thick bedposts, breaking it off in a single motion. He faces me, assumes the on-guard position, swishes his sword back and forth in the air, then playing with me as a cat plays with a mouse, he strikes a couple of blows that I meet with my club, realizing that once this mass-killer became serious, I will not stand a chance.

Marie, coming to my aid says, "Reginald you cannot kill a 'ero of le games. The king would have your head."

Reginald hesitates, turns, goes to the door and tells the soldier he had posted to give him his sword, which upon turning back into the room, he throws to me saying, "Prepare to defend yourself printerrrr."

Having never touched a sword in my life, I had no idea what to do with it. When he approaches, he begins toying with me, just slashing at me, our swords touching. He unleashes a torrent of slashes and stabs me in the shoulder, me struggling to block each one, he balanced and poised, me looking like a fool. I felt as if I was playing tennis against Nadal or Djokovic, totally outmatched, lucky to get my racquet on the ball—lucky to block his thrusts.

Next, he begins stabbing me, piercing my feeble defense, poking me as if I were a pin cushion, just enough to draw blood in my arm, the left side of my chest, then the right side, then each of my thighs, all while taunting me with a broad, menacing grin, daring me to stop his skillful patterned incursions. I feel totally out matched and helpless. He slices my arm, creating a deep gash, swings a blow from the right, which I barely block, then with a flick of his wrist in a twisting motion causes my sword to fly out of my hand. I go to reach for the bedpost club, when he trips me from behind, and I fall against the wall with a thud. As I sit up, he instantly brings the tip of his sword to my neck, drawing blood saying, "Now Megan will kiss yet another feeble suitor's neck."

There is nothing I can do. If I move a muscle, he will push Megan through my windpipe, and I will gasp to draw breath. Similar to a predator relishing a kill, he hesitates for a fraction of a second, smiles at Marie, pulls back for the deadly thrust, when suddenly I hear, "Reginald what are you doing? Stop this immediately!"

It is Lady Catherine. She saves my life. Frustrated, Reginald turns to me saying, "This is not over." Then he bows to Lady Catherine, bows to Marie and defiantly leaves the room in a huff.

"I am sorry Monsieur Rand that should never have 'apened."

Still breathing heavily, feeling totally defeated and embarrassed, having given up my life, trying to make sense of what transpired, I go to kiss her hand saying, "Your majesty, you saved my life. Merci Bouquet, Merci Bouquet!"

Marie comes over to my side, puts her hand around me, kisses me gently on the cheek and says, "Vou, Sir Rand saved mi 'onore. I am forever indebted to vou." Then she grabs a long yellow silk scarf from her dresser and begins tending my wounds.

I say to her, "Marie that is silk and must be very valuable. Perhaps you can use something else."

"We, it comes from Lyon, but it is of no importance compared to vou."

The gash on my arm is large and though she tries, Marie cannot staunch the bleeding. Lady Catherine, examining the wound tells Emily, who just entered, "Run to my room and fetch moi sewing case on top of the cabinet and the brandy that is inside. Vite Emily, vite!"

She takes the yellow scarf and wraps it around my arm to stem the bleeding. When Emily returns, Catherine splashes brandy on the wound, dabs it, and hands the bottle to me saying, "Drink monsieur Rand, drink as much as you wish."

With needle and thread, she begins stitching me up. Without a local anesthetic, the pain is intense, but the brandy seems to help, so I take another big gulp—so much for my vow to never drink again. I am not as manly as I would like to appear to Marie and with each stitch, I grimace, moan and gnash my teeth. I feel like I am in a dentist's chair being operated on without Novocain.

To take my mind off of it, as she sews, Catherine says, "When we were young, I used to accompany moi husband on his campaigns. He had many wounds that I tended to. I did not trust the doctors to take care of 'im and I had done this in France for moi father and brothers. My 'usband is a brave man, but he carries many scars from his battles. They are his souvenirs—something he is très proud of. Sometimes he shows these to his knights to inspire them, and to let them know that he too has been in battle. Now, you, Rand, will have something to be proud of—to display to your comrades—a scar that recalls when you fought for the honor of a princess." What she said eased my anxiety and along with the brandy makes it easier to absorb the pain.

After she applies ten perfect-looking stiches, I take another sip of brandy and knowing how prevalent infection can be in this time, splash some more on my wound.

Queen Catherine looking confused asks Gwendolyn, "What happened 'ere?"

"Reginald came into my room uninvited," Marie revealed. "He had lust in his eyes and I was very afraid Aunt Catherine. I commanded him to leave. He said that he knew I wanted 'im, that all women want 'im, and that it would be my privilege to finally have 'im. He came towards me, and as I tried to escape, he grabbed me, pulled me towards him and began kissing me and pawing moi breasts. I slapped him and he slapped me back harder. He lifted up my skirt and was about to have his way with moi, when I screamed and out of nowhere Rand came to rescue me. He was amazing Aunt Catherine. He grabbed Reginald, lifted him over his head and threw him across the room like a sack of grain."

"Oh my dear, I am so sorry you had to endure this. How did the sword fight start?"

"I thought moi ordeal was over, but Reginald was enraged, his face red, his eyes red like a raging bull's. He went to the hall where he had posted a guard to protect his despicable acts, retrieved his sword, threw it to Rand and intended to slay him, saying it was a 'fair' fight now."

"Oh my dear. Rand we owe you a debt of gratitude for coming to my niece's rescue."

"I want him arrested and hanged," Marie demanded.

"That may be difficult my dear. I understand that what he did was disgusting, but he is the King's most senior knight, who is in charge of much of his forces. Did you encourage him at all?"

"For a second I kissed him back, but then I slapped him and tried to wriggle away from 'im, which only excited 'im more"

"My dear, many subjects have seen you flirting with Reginald and with others. Sadly, it is a man's world, especially for the warriors. Reginald has, no doubt, done this to many conquered women. As men of war, they feel they are entitled to such spoils. We demand chivalry from our knights, but he is not chivalrous. I will tell the King what happened. He will likely do no more than warn Reginald not to do something like this again. It will be a black mark and count against him. Unfortunately, we are women and even as noblewomen, our power and influence are limited. At least, thanks to Rand, he did not succeed in spoiling you. Then he would have hung."

Marie began to cry on her aunt's shoulder. I was shocked. Even though I found it difficult to believe that such travesties still existed in the 21^s-century and women were still struggling for justice, this was so different from my time. This time was much worse. Ironically, if I hadn't intervened, Reginald would have been hung. So, I saved his life. But more importantly, I saved Marie from what would have been an even more traumatic tragedy.

Catherine hugged her as she sobbed, saying, "Please leave us Rand, you are a parful man. Nous are very reconnaissante to vou."

Before I leave, Marie comes to me, pulls me close and gives me a sensuous kiss that Catherine is surprised to see, but considering the circumstances accepts. As I retrace my steps out of the castle, nearly walking into the walls, I am still dizzy from that kiss, which seemed worth risking my life for, and had oddly erased the intense fear that had gripped me but a few moments earlier. I may be a little dizzy from the brandy too.

———

Michael had retrieved the cart and was waiting for me at the back entrance with Gwendolyn. While with Thomas, she had held back her tears but cried a torrent now. We are in a somber mood on our way back to town. The taste of Marie's sweet kiss still fresh on my lips, the smell of her French perfume still lingering. But the blood seeping from my neck, running down to my chest brought back the horror of having a sword's point sticking in the indentation of my neck, wielded by a fierce warrior, about to kill me. I had so much to think about and too much to digest. Up until now this had all seemed like a delightful, fantasy dream-world inhabited by a beautiful princess in a castle; suddenly, it had become very real and very dangerous. I longed for San Francisco and my safe life, for a life of merely coding—a life I had thought to be so tough, but was nothing compared to this.

When I had been flushed down the rapids, I felt I would die and had reluctantly accepted that. Once I was transported into the 15th century, I felt as if I had died. Reginald had toyed with me, bullied me, mastered me, and embarrassed me. By the time Megan pierced my windpipe, I had given myself up. I had never felt like that before. Sure, I had lost games, but I never gave up.

———

The next day Michael tells what transpired after that afternoon, "With a vengeful Marie present, Queen Catherine told King Edward what Reginald had perpetrated. Kindly, Edward asked Marie to leave them and sent four of his personal guards to apprehend Reginald.

When Reginald appeared, seeing the dour expression on Queen Catherine's face, he knew he was in trouble. As if steam poured off the top of his head, he was furious.

The King said, 'Reginald, Lady Marie has leveled serious charges against you. She said that you came into her room, accosted her and were in the process of raping her when Rand Roberts came to her rescue.'

He bowed and trying mightily to contain his anger replied, 'My lord, after the games ended, thrilled by my glorious victory, Marie enticed me into her room. Then she kissed me, and I could tell she wanted me. We were making love when that bastard Rand interrupted us.'

Catherine interrupted saying, 'You know that is not true. Uninvited, you charged into her quarters and forced her to submit to your will. You even posted one of your men to prevent others from coming to her rescue.'

'No me lady, after the games she seductively whispered in my ear to come to her room. You and many others have seen how she has thrown herself at me.'

'If this were true, why did she scream? Reginald, there are witnesses, including her maid and others. Why would Rand have entered the guarded room, unless he had heard the scream?'

The King said, 'Reginald, I am very disappointed in you. You have behaved very badly and are not living up to the guidelines of chivalry I demand from my knights. Do you realize that Lady Marie is a member of the royal court of France and if word of this got to King Charles, our little kingdom would be in serious jeopardy, and they could well hang you. And King Henry would also find your actions despicable.'

'Still no damage was done. I will suspend you for a month and banish you from the castle. We will not speak of this to the troops, but they will suspect you did something shameful.' Then he commanded Reginald to return the five pounds, saying, 'You do not deserve such an honorarium.'

Reginald reluctantly reached into his pouch and returned the prize. Trying mightily not to continue arguing his case, biting his tongue, he reluctantly apologized to Lady Catherine, saying, 'It will never happen again.'

Glaring hauntingly at him down her equine nose, she said, 'It had better not!'

As he left the room, he vowed revenge against you. Perhaps he will try ambush you and make it look as if those robbers had finally gotten you."

"From one of the knights I heard that he also thought about how he might get even with the King and Queen Catherine –

'How dare they? He was the hero of the games. The hero of many battles. The king should have willingly offered his niece to him. Commanded her to marry him. He vowed to have his revenge."

44: DESPERATELY SEEKING MARIE

Michael asked me to work with Gwendolyn to improve their bookkeeping methods before I sailed for London. The next day I sat down and taught her how to do double entry bookkeeping, how to produce a balance sheet and an income statement. Despite being depressed over Thomas's condition, she proved to be a remarkably intelligent student, someone who instantly absorbed everything I taught her.

She was highly motivated because she could see how these methods would better help her to manage the print shop's business and produce reports for the king. Her innovative father, a highly accomplished writer, editor and publisher, did not have much of an aptitude for numbers, therefore, Gwendolyn complemented him well, often preventing him from overextending the business. Sitting close to her, working intimately with her, I felt an even deeper bond.

I was finally able to understand the monetary system and realized how profitable printing could be. We were able to sell one to three books for a pound. Compared to earlier days when a monk may take a year to produce a single book, we could produce thousands—our competitive advantage. Printing resembled the early days of the Web, when immense wealth was generated from a world-shattering form of mass communications. After all, each of the trillion-dollar, 21st-century companies specialized in enhanced forms of communications – Facebook with its friends, Netflix with its streaming movies, Google with its search engine, Microsoft with its Internet Explorer, and Apple with its iPhone. Amazon, itself, specialized in buying goods over the Internet along with an ever-evolving array of communications services, such as Amazon Web

Services. Printing was the Internet of the 15th century—a lucrative business for those who dared to advance it.

That afternoon I desperately wanted to see Marie, to comfort her and to be with her, so I grabbed a favorite book I know she'd enjoy and headed for the castle. On the road to the castle, I walked past the bakery. Flannery came out and reminded me that I had promised to buy a round at the pub. I tried to say that I would do so tomorrow, but he insisted. After buying a couple rounds for all of our friends, McNab said that there was a schooner leaving for London soon. Michael said he would check with the captain and that I needed to hurry to pack, so I would be able to make the trip, because it might be weeks before another such opportunity presented itself.

Wanting to say goodbye to Marie, I grabbed a horse and rode off to the castle where I discovered that she and the royal family had left for a hunting lodge earlier that day. I decided to leave the book with a message for her, so I asked the guard where I might find a quill and paper. He directed me to the scribe, a Lord Boston, who handled the kingdom's accounting.

I found Boston inhabiting a dimly lit room under the main staircase with piles of paper hiding his balding, bespectacled head. Not knowing who might read my inscription and instinctively not trusting this guy, who resembled a weasel, I realized I could not write a love note. Consequently, I wrote:

Dear Lady Marie,

I hope you enjoy this enchanting book for it radiates beauty and elegance in its loveliness. I hope this finds you well and in good health. I hope to be with you once more on my return from London.

Your obedient servant,
Rand the printer

I knew she would realize that I was not talking about the book, but rather about her.

I asked the scribe who I could leave the book with. Smiling through his thin pale lips, he uttered, "I will surely give it to her... Ray-and."

I had not introduced myself, so I inquired, "How do you know my name? Were you at the games?"

"No, I do not care for such trivial pursuits."

"Well pleased to meet you, Rand Roberts."

As I reached out my hand to shake his, in a haughty tone he exclaimed, "I am Lord Boston, keeper of the royal books." When I shook his small, bony, lily-white hand, as if it belonged to a corpse, it had a clammy, sweaty, limp feel—a moment that reminded me of when Jimmy Stewart shook Potter, the banker's, hand in *It's A Wonderful Life*. I instantly sensed that this was not someone I could trust with my disguised love note for surely he would read it, peruse the book and see that the two did not agree.

"Sir Boston, I would not want to bother someone who has so much responsibility with such a trivial matter. I will find her maid, Emily."

"Oh, It's no bother Ray-ndd, I will have one of my minions take care of it. I heard you had a run in with Lord Reginald. I don't know of anyone else who has faced him in a sword fight and escaped with his life. You must be a skilled swordsman."

I was tempted to respond to his query, but sensed I should not continue this discussion "Thank you, I will take care of delivering the book." And before he could say more, I retreated.

I found Emily who was so happy to see me, saying, "You are truly a 'ero Sir Rand. I heard of everything vou did for moi lady. I too am grateful to vou." I entrusted her with the book, knowing that she would ensure it was given to Marie without anyone else seeing it.

Before I could leave, she said, "Lady Marie gave me something to give to vou. I will fetch it. Please wait 'ere."

In the meantime, Lady Catherine appeared and took me aside saying, "What you did yesterday was magnifique. You seem to be innocent in the ways of the court. An unmarried lady's honour and reputation is her most valuable possession, without it she has nothing. Vou saved my niece's honour, for which we are eternally grateful.

She reached into a pocket hidden in her royal gown and pulled out a wooden object that she handed to me saying, "This is a small token of my appreciation for vou. Edward also wanted to show his appreciation, which Michael will disclose to vou later."

When I opened the elegantly decorated, polished, maple box, it revealed a golden quill holder, a golden inkwell and a notebook. She added, "With these you can record your journey."

A quill would be inserted through the quill holder, which provided a more secure and predictable writing instrument. Since I was still getting used to writing with the medieval instrument, this was a gift I greatly appreciated.

"Merci, your majesty. This is a marvelous gift. One I will surely use and treasure."

Emily came back and gave me a sealed letter from Marie, saying, "Please monsieur, thies is for your eyes only. Do not let anyone else see thies."

I took the letter to the garden, where I had first engaged Marie and with the restorative sound of the fountain in the background, the smell of flowers in a light, warm breeze, I broke the red seal and opened it.

Mon Amour,

As I write this to vou, I can recall the taste of your lips on mine. No one has ever kissed me that way or made me feel so much. During the games vou were so virile. Such a champion. I could not take my eyes from vou.

I am sorry that I left you on the ramparts, but for someone such as myself, my honour is all, and seeing me with another would have caused such a scandal in the court. But when you came to rescue me, you saved my honour from that dastardly Reginald. Even though you did not know how to wield a sword, vou were such a hero, even more than if vou did know the sword. I can never thank you enough for rescuing me. Vou will always be in my heart.

When I feared all was lost, suddenly vou threw him off of me. I was very angry that uncle Edward did little to punish Reginald, who I hate so much for what he intended to do to me. Rather than staying in the castle, where the despicable act happened, Aunt Catherine persuaded me to leave with the hunting party.

Just before we were to depart, I learned that vou would be traveling to London and that I would not be able to see you once more. I do not know how I will be able to bear being without vou.

Aller avec Dieu. I look forward to seeing vou when you return and being with vou alone once again.

Votre amour,

Marie, Joan, Catherine Beauchamp

My heart was so full, I practically flew back to town.

——

I did not sleep much that night and the next day was a blur. Michael brought me into the office, saying, "I have paid for your passage to London. Here are a couple of pounds for your initial expenses. The widow of our departed agent, Colleen, will have significant funds to give to you from the sales of our books. Her mother, Elaine, was my dearest cousin. After Elaine's death, she became like another daughter to me.

I have discussed this with Edward. What you have done for our shop in terms of your innovations has greatly increased our profits. I doubt that there are many print shops in all of Europe that can produce more pages with fewer people. If all goes well in London, and you're able to find a suitable agent, we plan to promote you to a junior partner."

"Oh Michael", I said with a deep sense of pride, "I appreciate this so much. Even more than the partnership, your and Edward's confidence in me means so much."

John gave me a pair of matchlock pistols to take along with some round lead balls and powder in a carved-out bull's horn then showed me how to load and fire it. The ancient weapon, state-of-the-art for the time, had a match or what amounted to a wick that had to be kept lit to work. Fortunately, I had my BIC from my old cargo shorts that I took along to light the wick, otherwise I would have to walk around with a lit pistol or hunt for a flame, which if I was in danger, would be useless. I was sure to pack my Swiss Army knife and watch. I also packed my iPhone, not sure of how I would use it, but thinking it might somehow come in handy. Daisy sowed a secret pocket into the top of my trousers to hide the money and I wrapped the coins in cloth to prevent them from jingling.

45:   SAILING AWAY

The light of day began to pierce the usual morning fog as we set off for the pier. Michael brought along a wooden crate filled with books the deceased agent had ordered and provided me with the location of the agent's house in London. I shook his hand and those of the apprentices then went to say goodbye to Gwendolyn. With tears in her eyes, she looked into mine then gave me a hug and fervently kissed me on the lips, after which I felt a little weak in the knees and a bit dizzy. I walked up the gangplank onto the caravel, where I met the captain—Captain Black, a short, stocky, swarthy commanding guy with a thick black beard, black hair and a salt-worn ruddy, red complexion, who I hoped was not a pirate, for he certainly looked the part.

Soon the ship cast off and I waved goodbye to my friends, who shouted good wishes. Still affected by her sweet kiss, I could not keep my eyes off of stunning Gwendolyn, her golden hair radiantly glowing in the early morning light, standing there, thin, perfect-postured, beautiful looking up towards me—a vision I would recall on my nascent adventure.

The captain had a cabin boy show me where I would sleep, which consisted of a tiny cabin with two, too-small, built-in bunk beds. As I was used to relatively large hotel rooms, at first it felt claustrophobic, until I saw that the crew slept on hammocks stacked four on top of each other. I soon discovered that I would share the room with a merchant from London who snored like a hibernating bear.

———

I didn't spend much time in my crowded, dark cabin but rather enjoyed being up on the deck looking out over the Irish sea, breathing in the fresh sea air, watching the crew man the fluffy, white sails. At times the sea was choppy and the day cool, so I wore my thick woolen sweater Daisy had knitted for me. On a clear day with a bright sun beating down on the wooden deck, it became toasty—the smell of sea water and baking wood stirred by a gentle breeze, the ship slowly pitching up, then gradually down, the shifting wind causing the sails to flap crisply, and the nearby ship's brass bell to tingle. During the long voyage, I had plenty of time to think, and gain perspective on all I encountered. I still did not know how it happened, but somehow, I ended up here in the 15th century, a fact I had finally, reluctantly, came to accept. When I arrived, due to the traumatic experience, my body feeling like scrambled eggs, I was dying. If it were not for Gwendolyn finding me and nursing me back to health, I surely would have perished.

During my convalescence, I heard the amazing story of Michael's life, his adventures traveling around the world, and how he became the first printer in Ireland, the second printer in all the British Isles. Through him, I beheld, then read the first priceless books ever printed in English. If I could find my way back to my own time, I would take these with me and be able to sell them for a fortune. I did not want to do this just to be wealthy—what good does that do—but wanted the world to be able to see and experience what magnificent works of art these unblemished documents represented. It was not just the words but the artistry of the fonts, the graphics and fine leather bindings, carried over from the previous period of laborious transcription, but still during a time when books were treasured works of art to be passed on from generation to generation.

In a karmic sense, this somehow made up for our app being stolen. With the funds from the book sales, I would get my team back together, give them stock and build the next app we had planned without the VCs and Steve—an innovation far beyond what they stole from us, something highly valuable that the world would adore.

I also learned to operate the Gutenberg press—the most transformational invention in over half-a-millennium—not just how to manage the machine but all the steps leading up to the printing process of these magnificent bound books, constructed to last for centuries—steps that were remarkably similar to my work designing webpages. My webpages dwelled in a virtual world, whereas these magnificent books had substance and were tangible—part of the physical world.

I also came to know the citizens of Bunkillarny, a delightful, colorful group of characters, who although they shunned me at first, became my dear friends. I would miss them and long to see them again.

My previous burned-out life had been dominated by screens—up to 16 hours a day, 7 days a week. I had wanted to divorce myself from these and become human again, for although they give you much, in return, they seem to take away a portion of your humanity. In the sense of being careful what you ask for, I obtained my wish, which I regretted for a time, but now had adjusted to. Considering the lack of modern conveniences, it is difficult to surmise, but my life now seemed fuller. I still have my iPhone loaded with Wikipedia that allows me to see into the future—a power I must be careful how I apply, for I do not want to alter the course of history, and, anyway, I don't have much battery left.

I had a lot of fun competing in the games and I think I had won the heart of an elusive, beautiful princess, but had gained a formidable enemy, who nearly slaughtered me like a feeble pig. I cannot stop thinking about her—when we kissed on the ramparts, wow what a kiss, and after I saved her honor. But as a royal, I am afraid she will reject me, for I am but a lowly printer. Perhaps, if I become a partner of the king, my prospects will improve. After all Michael's wife was a noble.

I am headed for London, carrying a letter of introduction from Michael to William Caxton, the first printer in the British Isles. I cannot wait to meet such a famous personage and hope to acquire those first famous English texts, such as the *Canterbury Tales* and have him sign them. If I can hire a new agent there and get our business back on track, Michael and King Edward have promised to make me a junior partner. I do not know if I believe in fate, but somehow, I feel that this is where I am supposed to be, during this remarkable time at the center of the transformation of humankind from a Medieval, meager, feudal existence to a more intellectual, free-thinking, expansive realm, when the Renaissance blooms and the enlightenment commences. I do not know what adventures lie ahead of me, but I am psyched, confident, and look forward to them.

46:   REGINALD SEIZES CONTROL

Unbeknownst to Rand after he departed Bunkillarny and sailed to London, the political landscape of Bunkillarny dramatically changed.

Because their lands bordered those of the Brogans, where Gwendolyn visited Thomas every day, she went to live at her grandfather, O' Flannery's castle. Holding Thomas's hand, she encouraged him and read to him continuously from her father's Gutenberg Bible. At one point, it seemed he might recover. With her urging, he was able to move his big toe and then his feet providing merciful hope to the large Brogan clan that he might soon fully recover. In his weakened state, during the coldest week of fall, he caught a flu that deteriorated into pneumonia, and a week later he perished.

Lord Brogan blamed the death of his young, strong, warrior son on Reginald and at the funeral tried to strangle him, until Reginald's knights, Thomas's conflicted comrades, reluctantly pried Brogan's hands from his throat. Gwendolyn became severely depressed, despondent and dressed in black. She returned to the print shop, assisting her father, but went about her daily tasks as if she were a dazed zombie. The life had gone out of her normally effervescent spirit, which negatively affected the other employees in the shop too. The normally happy shop became subdued. Although he would not show it, the only one who took Thomas's death positively was Seamus, for he thought it cleared the way for him to marry Gwendolyn, especially since Rand was out of the picture too.

In Rand's absence, Michael promoted Seamus to the status of Journeyman. With his business booming, and in anticipation of renewed business from Rand's success in England, he ordered a second press from Germany. If Rand succeeded, he planned to make him a junior partner. He probably should have waited for Rand's return, but he was impulsive, something Gwendolyn would have prevented if she were herself.

———

Reginald still bore a grudge against Lord and Lady Bunkillarny and vowed to obtain revenge. After his disgraceful behavior towards Lady Marie and brief suspension, he bided his time. After all, it was a man's world, and as he told all who would listen, she was a flirt—someone who flashed her enchanting smile and tossed her beautiful locks, but once captured, scorned you.

Before the suspension was over, wanting him to be away from Lady Catherine and Marie who abhorred Reginald, Lord Edward soon returned him to regular duty as a mercenary assisting Henry the VIIth in England. In a crucial battle, he and his men excelled turning the tide of the campaign and winning praise from King Henry, who awarded Reginald a silver cross. It is said he single-handedly killed a dozen men, proclaiming, "Megan had stolen many hearts and kissed many a man's neck with her ruby red lips that day." Upon his triumphant return, against Catherine's counsel, the lord made Reginald the general of his forces.

Primed by the glory of war, feeling invincible, feeling she should be part of his prize, after a raucous celebration in the great hall, Reginald followed and again approached Marie in a darkened hallway. In a drunken slur he asked her to marry him, "Me lady now that I am a hero and a general, I need to procure me a wife. I know that I could ha' any woman in the kingdom, single or married, but I have chosen you to have the honor. We would make a fine pair and there is no limit to what we can conquer. There is no one I would want beside me or in me bed, more than you. Despite that dastardly Rand's interruption, I know you want me. Admit it! Admit it to yourself! Don't deny yourself your passion!"

Looking down the hall, desperately hoping someone would come her way and interrupt her assailant, thoroughly disgusted by the smell of whiskey and ale on his breath and his misogynistic, controlling behavior, but fearing what he might do, and wanting to be tactful, she replied, "Reginald I compliment you on your victory and thank you for your generous proposal, but I think we are ill-suited."

He growled, slapped her sending her sprawling to the floor, "You wench. Who do you think you are? I have had younger, fairer maidens than you in my bed every night this week."

Sprawled on the floor, her face turning red and crying, she knew that he wanted her prized lands in Burgundy to help build his own kingdom, saying, "I would not have you if you were the only man in England, or Ireland, or France. You disgust me! You are a cur!"

He raised his hand to strike her again then stormed off raging. That night he got even more drunk, banged and bellowed excessively at her door. Later he started a fight and killed a man, saying, "It was a fair fight" — was it not." Marie hid in Aunt Catherine's chamber, cried all night on her shoulder, and fled to London the next morning.

———

In early December to gather meat for the upcoming winter, the nobles of the castle, as they did every year, journeyed to the hunting lodge in the southwestern portion of Bunkillarny. Hunting on a foggy, cool, dew laden morning with freshly fallen leaves carpeting the forest floor, crunching and sliding under their horses' hoofs, the colorful forest had that unmistakable earthy, fall smell. King Edward soon shot a five-point buck with his crossbow and as the wounded deer vaulted off, galloped after him, followed in turn by his dutiful general, Reginald.

The deer ran up the side of a steep mountain, with snow covering the fallen leaves, melting under a light drizzle beneath a grey, muddled sky. At the top, Edward had the pitiful, snorting, wounded, winded animal cornered. Cranking his crossbow, inserting the shaft, he shot the climatic arrow, the recoil of which caused his horse to rear up and slip on the wet leaves. With both hands on the bow, Edward lost his balance falling off his horse onto some shale loosened by the icy snow that slid away over the edge of a 200-foot cliff taking Edward with it. He quickly grasped the trunk of a sturdy pine and began climbing up, when Reginald appeared offering his hand.

The king smiled, "Do you believe Rex balked just as I got my shot off. Did I hit the buck?"

"Yes your highness, hit him squarely in the shoulder. He has perished."

As the king released the sturdy trunk to grasp Reginald's extended hand, Reginald let go and the king fell down the slope grasping onto a protruding rock six-feet below.

Holding onto the tree, Reginald eased down the slope saying, "This is for suspending me and undermining my authority with my men. I told myself someday I would get even. This is that day. Your kingdom shall be mine." Then he pushed on the lose rock until it rolled off the cliff. Edward grabbed some shale which likewise slid off the cliff face, he falling into the gorge far below, yelling, the words echoing throughout the fog-shrouded valley below – "**Reginald**!... **Reg**inald!... Reginald!"

Reginald looked around to see if anyone else had witnessed his treachery and spied, slimy Lord Boston hiding behind a tree, who he approached saying, "The king's horse bolted, and he tragically fell to his death. What did you see?"

"Is that what happened, is it?" Lord Boston replied with a snaky smile.

With a threatening grimace, his hand on Megan's hilt, Reginald queried, "What do you think you saw? You know with the king departed, there will likely be an opening for the minister position, which, if all goes as planned, I think you would be the most qualified to occupy."

Boston, who had longed schemed to advance himself and resented the king keeping him in what he thought was a lowly position replied, "It will be as you say, provided that position be mine."

By then, the rest of the hunting party arrived. Mimicking shattered faces, Reginald and Boston told the tragic story of the king's death. All were in shock. With few exceptions, they all loved King Edward.

Lord O' Flannery, Edward's best friend broke the news to Lady Catherine, who upon hearing the love of her life had perished, in shock, collapsed into his arms. She wanted to cry and lock herself in her chamber for weeks but had to be strong for her young children. She forced herself to participate in the funeral arrangements, for which she would spare no expense— she wanted it to be a testament to her husband's magnificent reign. She only wished that her favorite niece, Marie, were there to comfort her. There were plenty of ladies of the court who tended to her, but she did not feel close to or fully trust them.

47:   FUNERAL

Edward was to be buried at the newly dedicated Bunkillarny Cathedral. After a ceremony at the castle, a grand procession wound down the hill into town. Traveling from the furthest corners of the shire, thousands of loyal subjects lined the road. Other nobles from throughout Ireland, including the "King" of Ireland from Dublin and nobles from Scotland and western England came too. King Henry VII would send an emissary, but given the amount of time for the news to arrive in London, and for the emissary to sail back, he would not arrive until after the funeral.

Just before the ceremony was to commence, Marie appeared at Catherine's door.

Desperately hugging her niece as a torrent of tears, held back like a dam, finally released, Catherine said, "Marie, I am so pleased you came. You have no idea how much it means to have you here, but how did you get here so quickly?"

"On the ship on the way back to London, I met Lord McIntosh and his lovely wife Matilda, who insisted I stay with them in Glasgow for a fortnight. When word of Edward's death reached there, I hired a sloop and immediately sailed."

Reginald rode at the front of the procession leading a guard of twenty splendidly dressed knights on horses and forty dragoons with halberds. As the casket pulled by twelve horses draped in black passed, all of the peasants and merchants bowed deeply, many of the women crying uncontrollably, while the men fought back their tears. They all loved King Edward deeply, respected him immensely as their august leader, and appreciated how well the shire had faired under his long reign and the peace and prosperity Edward had brought to them. Everyone in the shire was closely bound together that morning.

After the hearse, the people saw their lovely queen, and her three beautiful blond headed children, and Marie. The King's second son of his first wife, John, also rode in the open carriage. The people all felt sorry for them. Then came the lords from throughout the land with their families in various conveyances followed by Edward's counsel, which included Michael, Lord O'Flannery, and Lord Brogan all on horseback.

At the funeral ceremony, so many lords lined up to speak about Edward, the funeral went on for three hours, but no one cared. Hundreds who had not been invited into the cathedral stood outside on that cold, crisp, blue-sky day for the duration with their hearts broken—a testament to their king. Lord O'Flannery spoke of Edwards' exemplary moral life of service to his land and his people, commenting on how much they loved to hunt and play groats together. "When we were younger, we had fought side by side in many a battle. Skilled with the sword, spear, and crossbow, there was no better warrior than Edward. When he first sponsored the games, insisting that no one give him quarter, he participated and often won the contests."

Other lords spoke of the prosperity Edward's reign ushered in when their economy grew by leaps and bounds. They spoke about what a wonderful administrator he was, and how despite low taxes the kingdom's coffers were always full. They spoke of how fair, just and yet merciful a ruler he was. They spoke of how much he loved books, music, dancing, his children, and how much he looked forward to the bi-annual games, immersing himself in every details to be sure each would be the best yet.

In the back of everyone's mind was the succession. Edward's oldest son had died a year earlier in the typhus epidemic. His second son, John, who married into the O'Neal Clan would be the presumed heir. John and his wife rode with Catherine and as their stepbrother, loved his younger siblings. John, whose first wife had died in childbirth, did not have any children yet. If anything happened to John, Catherine's eldest son Patrick would assume the throne. Catherine felt that John would treat her children and herself well. She had a close, motherly, loving relationship with John's younger wife, Sarah, who would become the new queen.

———

Reginald spoke at the funeral in a self-serving speech. Immediately afterwards, he and anemic Boston hatched a plot to undermine John's ascension to the throne and take over Bunkillarny. Reginald sailed to the O'Donnell's lands to the west on a speedy sloop. There he told King Rory O'Donnell that John would soon assume the throne, which would create an alliance between Bunkillarny and the O'Neals, one that would drastically shift the balance of power away from them towards the O'Neals.

He continued, "As the General of the Bunkillarny's forces, if you support me, I can be of assistance to you. Because of John's allegiance to the O'Neal's, you will naturally want to depose his ascension to the throne. I will say that we would not want the O'Neals ruling Bunkillarny, and that we should instead support Prince Patrick's ascension.

Since Prince Patrick is only fifteen, I will be his regent and effectively rule the kingdom."

"But what happens when Patrick is old enough to rule?," Rory quired.

"By that time, I will be in control of the kingdom with all the ministers and army beholding to me. I will spread the rumor that Patrick is incompetent or such and assume the throne myself."

"But the O'Neals and most of Bunkillarny's lords will not stand by while all of this happens."

Reginald brought out the iron cross he received from Henry the VIIth saying, "I am sure you recognize this as one of the highest honors for valiantly serving the King of England."

Obviously impressed, Rory said, "Yes, that is truly an admiral testament to your skill and courage."

"I did not acquire this as some mere bureaucrat. I have trained myself to be the ultimate man of war – there is none better. With your and my armies banded together, the O'Neals would not dare oppose us. We will force John to sign documents renouncing his thrown. If the O'Neals are foolish enough to oppose us, we will annihilate them. With the army under my thumb, the lords will not oppose me. Those who do, I will crush."

Seeing Reginald's plan as a way to finally overpower the O'Neal's or at least neutralize them, even though he did not care for the devious, duplicitous man before him, King Rory agreed to Reginald's diabolical plan.

———

Rory sent an emissary along with a letter to King Albert O'Neal:

> *Dear King Albert,*
>
> *We signed a peace agreement, which has lasted for three years now. We are concerned that if John of Bunkillarny, your son in-law, assumes the thrown of Bunkillarny this will violate our agreement. Therefore, we sincerely demand that he does not assume such throne.*
>
> *We would however support the coronation of Prince Patrick.*
>
> *Yours in Christ,*
>
> *King Rory, Michael, Louis, O'Donnell*

Duke of Cornwall
Lord of Donegal

Meanwhile, Lord Boston commenced an undermining campaign within the King's council and court to oppose John by spreading salacious rumors about him, saying he had several mistresses including a Devil's sorceress and had fathered numerous bastard children, which would cloud the succession line—none of which was true. John was actually a devout Christian and husband.

Reginald needed to gain the support of the Queen. He had been on his best behavior after he had committed the regicide, helping to oversee the funeral arrangements, providing a 24-hour honor guard and taking care of the family's needs. He had spent much time with Patrick comforting him, playing groats with him, teaching him how to wield a sword and bow, thereby eliciting his friendship.

The Queen appreciated his efforts but did not fully trust his motives. After an appropriate time following the funeral, he approached her saying, "Your majesty, I have heard that the O'Donnell's have strongly objected to John's coronation. Since John is married to the King's daughter, they fear an alliance between the O'Neals and Bunkillarny will upset the balance of power and will disturb the peace between us all."

"On numerous occasions, Edward told me not to become involved with the constant battles between those two. It was something he was most proud of—keeping Bunkillarny out of their border wars, which as you know has provided long-term peace and prosperity for Bunkillarny. I do not think you would want to see that peace disturbed, would you?"

"No, but I propose that for the peace of Northern Ireland that Patrick ascend to the throne of Bunkillarny."

"But he is only fifteen."

"He is a bright lad with a parful character. With your and my guidance, in a few years I am sure he will be as a fine King as his father."

"Like his father! John is a parful man and would make a fine king **now**! You will see."

"I have heard that John has perversions and has consorted with an evil, temptress and sorceress."

"Those are just vicious lies. He is my stepson and I know his character, which is of the highest caliber. He is a fervent Christian. You will see this to be true."

With a smirk, unable to hide behind a false veneer of respectability any longer, talking between gritted teeth, he said, "Think it over me lady. Events beyond your control may already be in motion."

Afterwards, feeling a chill up her spine, she became suspicious of Reginald's true motives. She realized why he had been so solicitous to her, her children and especially to Patrick. It could only be that he wanted to gain some advantage, and although she could not prove it, suspected he might have had something to do with Edward's untimely death. After all, he and Boston were the only ones there and she never trusted duplicitous Boston. She knew Edward thought he was skimming funds and had planned to expel him from the council before the next meeting.

48:   NEW KING

A month after the King died, two weeks after the funeral, the King's council met to elect a new ruler. It seemed that these matters should be straight forward, but never were, leading to innumerable wars across Europe, as heirs battled to rule and to consume power. But in this case, the succession was obvious, wasn't it?

By that time, not wanting to have anything to do with the ever-present Reginald, who made her feel noxious, Marie had left. She wanted to stay longer to comfort her aunt, but felt at least she had helped her over the initial blow.

Many members of the council including Lord O'Flannery, Lord Brogan and Michael McCarron thought the meeting would be straight forward and be over in no time, but they were blindsided. Despicable Boston had stirred up many of the nobles by repeatedly labeling John as "John the philanderer," and, as if repeating it numerous times made it true, some of the lords had bought into the lie.

During the heated discussions, Michael and Lord O'Flannery argued vehemently against the assertions but faced a stiff and unwavering assault from Boston and his converts. Finally, Michael said, "I have known John since he were a child, teachin him how ta read. He is one of the finest men I know and I be sure he would follow in his noble father's footsteps. For those of you who are uncertain of his character, I propose that we have him come and speak to us and face these spurious allegations, so ye can judge for yerself."

Reginald who presided over the meeting, letting Boston do all the dirty work, posing as an unbiased leader, spoke up, "We have gone too long without a King. I propose that we take a vote now."

The vote was 8 to 6 with John's supporters barely carrying the day. One more vote and it would have been tied with Reginald able to make the final decision against John. Michael could not believe that Boston was able to sway that many of the men he considered his wisest friends— *Where were their heads at? Could no they see through Boston's lies. It seemed the more persistently he told the lie, the more it swayed them, as if repetition made it true. But, by the grace of God, the matter was settled and John would be king. They would soon see what a fine man and king John would be.* The coronation was scheduled for three weeks.

———

After the meeting, Lords O'Flannery, Brogan and Michael conferred with each other at McNab's pub at a secluded table off in the corner and agreed to send a message immediately to Prince John so he could assuage the rumors that had been brought against him. They did not trust Boston and were suspicious of Reginald's motives, especially since he now controlled the army.

With the exception of his red hair, which he inherited from his Irish mother, John had his father's good locks, his square dimpled jaw, piercing blue eyes, sturdy brow and high cheekbones. Unlike his father and brother, who had a certain forcefulness to their faces, his countenance seemed at peace. He had been a frail, sickly child until his mother died in a runaway carriage accident. After their mother's death, he and his older brother became very close. Edward III, named after his father and grandfather, would inherit the throne, something John had no desire for and was glad would not be his.

They were very competitive though. Edward was naturally athletic—good at everything he tried, whereas John had to work hard for any success he achieved. He sought to build himself up through riding, swordsmanship, archery, spear throwing, and wrestling. No matter how hard he tried, though, his three-year-older brother always beat him, seemingly without trying.

Of their castle playmates, John was the thinnest, and smallest and weakest of all. One day one of their playmates, Reginald Van Clieve III, bullied John incessantly, calling him a dirty Gaelic name. Edward interceded, boxing the larger foe, until pinned against the ground, Reginald relented, and reluctantly promised to never bully John again. Their father, King Edward favored his oldest son, but greatly appreciated how much his younger son tried, something he never told John before he died.

As the castle's librarian, Michael's duties included tutoring the young princes. Favoring more active pursuits, Edward was a reluctant student, whereas John easily absorbed the lessons and constantly delved further into his father's extensive library. As a result, Michael and John became close friends.

In his mid-teens, John grew a foot in height, filled out and became stronger. With an eagle eye, he was finally able to beat his older brother at something—archery. Indeed, during the games, he finished first in the archery competition and third in the sword. He attended Saint Paul's College and became very religious, thinking he would become a priest.

Queen Catherine took the place of his departed mother and they developed a close relationship—he adored her. When he talked to her about entering the priesthood, she encouraged him to pursue the vocation, telling him that with the family's connections, he might one day rise to become the bishop of Bunkillarny. Knowing that Michael had also considered the priesthood, he consulted with him too. After graduation, faced with the imminent, gnawing decision, he prayed for guidance and resolved that this was not to be his calling.

His father arranged a marriage with Princess Emily O'Neal, who once he met her, he immediately fell in love with. During the war with the O'Donnells, John distinguish himself as a mighty warrior, especially with the bow, while charging fearlessly on his mighty steed. King Albert awarded him additional lands, which along with his dowry, now amounted to over two-thousand acres. Following his father's example, he was an able and admired lord and master. Under his stewardship, instituting new scientific methods he discovered while touring Europe, his crops grew in abundance and his herds multiplied.

Emily died during childbirth. He was a broken man. Following a fraught year of mourning, seeing how despondent his son-in-law had become, King Patrick persuaded him to marry his younger daughter Sarah, a delightful, spirited 17-year old at the time. Not having any sense of direction, he agreed to the marriage, merely going through the motions. Eventually through her persistent, magnetic personality and faith, she won him over.

49:   TOMMY

Reginald sent his knights to each of the lords to have them round up their men and bring them to the castle for the pending war. Other knights travelled into town and throughout the nearby lands surrounding the castle gathering up men for the battle.

One Knight, Hugh of Aberdeen, in his quest to recruit men, came to the print shop, where Seamus asked, "Do you know Sir Reginald?"

"Yes lad, I'm his second in command."

"I'll join you then."

"Fine. Report to the castle's field tomorrow at dawn."

Tommy was only fifteen but wanted to join too. Similar to a NFL football star, Reginald was Seamus and Tommy's hero, someone they often spoke of and looked forward to seeing perform at the games. "I'll be there too," Tommy added.

Looking over Tommy, assessing his abilities, Hugh said, "You look to be but a wee chiseler. How old are you lad?"

"I'm sixteen and strong as an ox from a pulllin' the Devil's tail."

Needing all the men he could muster, but having doubts about this one, he relented saying, "All right, we'll see you there too."

Gwendolyn and Michael had been out of the shop gathering supplies and were surprised when they heard the chiseler had signed up for the fight. Michael felt that he couldn't do anything about Seamus because he was over eighteen but thought that Tommy at fifteen was too young and too wee, therefore he forbade him to join.

"But I'm in my 16th year and you ain't me father."

"In the absence of your parents and as your master I am responsible for you. I think that it is honorable that you would want to help defend Prince John. I have been in battles before and believe me it's not all glory. Besides, Bunkillarny is not being directly threatened, and this is not a mandatory call to arms. You canna go."

Tommy's parents had both perished. When he was four, his mother died in childbirth. He was her favorite child because he was sensitive like her. His father, Lorcam, who worked diligently, until his wife's death, morphed into a drunken brute, who after his binges, regularly beat his children. Without his mother's protection, because of his sensitive nature, Tommy became the object of his father's bitterness, who thought he needed to toughen the chiseler up so he could deal with the cruelties of the world.

After consuming too much whiskey at McNab's one dark, drizzling night, Lorcam galloped recklessly along the homeward path swaying from side to side, the horse struggling to interpret his confusing commands. While trying to navigate a sudden left turn at excessive speed, the horse had its hoofs slip on the muddy surface, causing it to stumble. The horse regained its balance, but inebriated Lorcam summersaulted over the horse's head, landing on his head and breaking his neck.

Tommy's older brother, Lorcam Jr., took over the farm and as the child of abuse was nearly as abusive to Tommy. Tommy's only refuge was his classes with Michael. Printing technology fascinated him and he stayed after school helping wherever they would let him. An excellent student, at twelve he joined the shop as an apprentice. Tommy's older sister, Colleen, who resembled his loving mother's in appearance and character, wanting to escape her harsh, abusive father, who treated her as his wife and wanted to bed her, migrated to London, where she married John Jones, Michael's agent. She had been Tommy's only refuge in the family and after she left, Tommy was desperate for escape, which he found at the print shop with his cousins Michael and Gwendolyn.

Before dawn, Tommy snuck off and joined the army.

50:   PRINCE JOHN

Prince John had mixed feelings about becoming the King of Bunkillarny. It was certainly a great honor and came with a large amount of power however, it also came with a huge amount of unwanted responsibility, especially if he tried to live up to the example of his illustrious father. His old teacher, Michael, had sent him a letter informing him of how the shire was divided, and that there had been salacious rumors regarding his reputation that he needed to counter before he assumed the throne.

He enjoyed his position in Nealland as a warrior and successful landlord, both of which he excelled at. He did not relish all the politics and backstabbing accompanying the role of a king. Still, he felt it his duty to follow in his father's footsteps. If only his brother were still alive. At least his new wife, a princess in her own right, is up to the challenge, something she, unlike him, looked forward to. Sarah would be a grand asset, someone Bunkillarny would fall in love with. She is familiar with the court, has boundless energy, and a good heart, plus his stepmother adores her and will help her to assume her new role. With her dark hair, blue eyes, regal bearing and fair skin speckled with just a dash of freckles, she even resembles her mother-in-law.

As they set off for Bunkillarny and the reluctant coronation, with reluctant enthusiasm and mixed emotions, he looks forward to their new life. Not long after they depart, a squire gallops up to their carriage and tells John that the O'Donnell's are massing on their southern border, that there is going to be a battle and that he needs to return immediately to command his troops.

Reginald brought his army to a hill overlooking the newly grassy plain ostensibly to defend John. To the north lie the

O'Neals, to the south the O'Donnells, each with lines of calvary and foot soldiers facing each other on the grassy plain, brandishing their weapons, yelling, and ramping up their courage for the inevitable rumble, each man alone with his thoughts, each interconnected to his brothers.

After horns blare, with the cavalry out in front, the two sides charge each other and clash in battle, a battle that rages for two hours with a multitude of men on both sides either dead or wounded. John kills or wounds many a man with his precise bowmanship. King Albert and John finally gain the advantage but look up to the hill, and wonder why the Bunkillarny forces had not yet joined the fray in support of their future king—something that would have ended the bloodshed immediately and saved many lives on both sides.

Finally, Reginald on his massive black warhorse, Magnus, with Megan raised high, yelling to his knights and soldiers to inspire them to action, charges down the hill into the bloody knoll below. King Albert is shocked, when instead of charging into Rory's forces, Reginald's troops begin killing his men on the left flank, where John holds the line.

Reginald had ordered three of his most trusted knights, including Hugh, to search for and kill John, for if they could slay the heir apparent, Reginald would gain control of Bunkillarny. Knowing that John wore silver armor with a purple feathered plume, the three track him down and charge him simultaneously from three directions. At the last second, John realizes they are bearing down on him and just in the nick of time, gallops forward narrowly escaping, then turning to face them, repeatedly holding off their relentless blows, his sword and armor dented from their persistent strikes, his deadly arrows not able to pierce their armor.

Skillfully guiding his horse to and fro, ducking, weaving and spinning, he tries mightily to escape their persistent attack until he and his horse tires. Similar to a cornered, exhausted elk, pursued by wolves sensing pending victory, the chase approaches it inevitable, deadly conclusion. Pinning John between them, Hugh moves in for the final merciless blow. Just then, King Albert appears with three other knights and beats the foes back.

With his face contorted like a devil's, bloodthirst in his eyes, mouth drooling, Reginald with Megan kills man after man, slicing the foot soldiers heads off in one blow. More than anything he loves killing and revels in war. Before long, he makes it to King Albert, who being betrayed, sensing defeat, and not wanting to lose any more of his young men's lives, yields.

Instead of being chivalrous and honoring the surrender, still enflamed with the taste of blood, adrenaline raging, Reginald raises Megan and is about to let her kiss her first king's neck, when King Rory gallops up from behind and commands him to, "**Stop**!"

Dejectedly, Reginald quickly gallops off searching for John, whose head he wants more than all the others. When King Albert had sensed impending defeat, he insisted that John ride away. John refused to follow his father-in-law's advice until he was ordered to so. Albert tells him, "Go without hesitation to the port and sail the royal sloop to Scotland and then to London where ye can plead our betrayal to King Henry."

One of Reginald's knights says that he had just seen John ride off. Reginald quickly gathers Hugh and three other knights and rides after him.

John rides at a sustained pace until on the top of a hill covered in fallow farm fields he looks back to the top of the past hill, and sees Reginald with four knights charging towards him. He knows it is Reginald because his massive warhorse, Magnus, is unmistakable. He turns and commands his horse to gallop forward.

Exhausted by the long battle, his mighty white steed choking and wheezing from the desperate ride, John reaches the docks, but there is no crew to man the ship. At the base of the gangplank he yells, "Is there anyone onboard this ship?" After which, the cabin boy, who looks to be about twelve appears.

"Where is the captain?   Where is the crew?   Don't you know we're at war?"

Recognizing the prince, he responds, "Sir John, the captain ordered the crew to stay nigh. I thinks they be at the Salty Wench. If you wants, I'll fetch 'em."

"Go immediately with haste lad. It's a matter of life and death."

Realizing the importance of the situation, the chiseler begins running down the dock, when John sees Reginald and his men appear on the beach to the right of the dock. Concerned that the crew will not arrive in time, that he could not stay out in the open, where he would be an easy target, and that if he hid in the sloop, like a rat they would flush him out, John calls the boy back.

I'm going to take this rowboat out into the bay. Tell the captain to pick me up there. Can you ride a horse?"

"Yes sire, I grew up on a farm."

Hastily, throwing the chiseler like a bag of potatoes onto the saddle, he says, "Take my horse and go immediately to fetch the captain." He quickly rides off, the resonant sound of hoofs clomping along the sea-worn boards.

Reginald, spying John at the docks rides after him, his knights in pursuit. With John in a rowboat, but twenty yards away, he grabs a spear from a knight and tosses it towards him. Pleased to see his projectile heading for John's chest, Reginald thinks he will spear his target, but John, who rows facing Reginald, sees its flight, and as it approaches, drops one oar and skillfully bats it away with the other, taunting Reginald as the spear innocently slices through the water. Meanwhile, two of the knights had loaded their muskets and fire at him. John ducks as one bullet whizzes over his head, the other striking the boat just below the water line on the right side. John rows fiercely getting out of range before for they can load another round.

Reginald sees a second boat on the other side of the dock and commands the knights to it. As if it were a *Three Stooges* comedy routine, with their clunky armor they have difficulty boarding and manning the oars without clanking into each other. By that time John has shed his top pieces, plugged the hole as best as he can with his under shirt, used his helmet to pour out the rising water, and rows shirtless out into the bay. He purposely shifts his weight to the left side, so the hole on the right will stay above the waterline as much as possible.

Still in their armor, the two rowing knights make little progress towards John. Reginald orders the other two to shed their armor, and when they take over rowing, they begin rapidly catching up. By then, John has transited from where the waves are mild into the choppy sea where he now faces three to four-foot whitecaps. As an experienced sailor who spent his summers at the King's summer estate on Craggy Point, John knew he had to keep rowing into the waves, otherwise if he went sideways, he would capsize.

Too soon Reginald's fresh crew is in range and begins firing their matchlocks. To make matters worse, John's temporary patch pops out and the boat is quickly filling with water, thereby slowing his progress. In addition, his arms are burning with pain, but he fights with every ounce of waning energy to command his legs, back, and shoulders to lean into the oars and up the pace heading into the waves—up one side, balancing briefly on top, down the other.

Their first shots are far off the mark, but after each reloading as they draw closer, the lead balls begin tearing at the boat. Their next rounds will be at point blank range, John will be defenseless and all will be lost. Another regicide close at hand, glaring at John, Reginald can taste blood and victory.

Meanwhile, the crew of the royal sloop had hastily gathered, cast off the lines, set sail, and headed into the bay. Seeing John being fired upon and losing ground to Reginald, they sail directly towards the assailants. Just as Reginald's men are about to fire the fatal rounds, focusing on their quarry, unaware of the approaching ship, one of the knights slams Reginald on the shoulder with his fist. So close to his goal Reginald refuses to be bothered, but hearing the sloops sail flutter, suddenly realizes they are about to be rammed, capsized and tossed into the raging sea. He orders the rowers to quickly turn and sprint ahead just as the ship's bow kisses the starboard corner causing the little boat to rock and spin uncontrollably, throwing one of the knights into the frothy waters. Pulled down by his heavy mail, the knight can barely keep his head above the tall waves, until one of his mates gives him a hand and begins pulling him out. Then a wave crashes into the side of the teetering boat, sending the rescuing knight into the drink. The first knight climbs onboard, but the second knight, who is now separated from the boat, trying mightily to stay above the churning waves is dragged down by his mail before they can turn the boat and rescue him.

Reginald realizes too late he should have taken control of the ship when he had the chance. As the sloop plucks John out of the water, Reginald stands up, shakes his fist and cries out, "I will get you yet John and your kingdom shall be mine."

After John struggles up the last rung of the rope ladder, he extends one weary, limp arm towards the captain thanking him for his quick action and saving his life. The captain orders the cabin boy to bring up a bottle of Scotch and they all toast the remarkable rescue, the warming scotch settling John's frazzled nerves.

The captain then asks, "Where's to sire?"

"To Scotland, to Glasgow, as quickly as you can, captain."

Reginald does not pursue John and the uneventful voyage to Scotland, under friendly skies with a mild constant, warm breeze powers their journey. Despite the captain's protestations, paying close attention to the charts, John insists that he help man the sails and the wheel. He had sailed a sleek picard by himself, but had never sailed a ship this large and revels in its size.

The scenic, placid voyage grants him time to assess his situation. The fact that Reginald had led the attack against the O'Neals and had so vehemently pursued him, indicates that he opposed John's accession to the throne. In the letter from Michael, he learned that Reginald and Boston supported Patrick's coronation and had spread salacious rumors regarding him. John and his younger stepbrother were very close, riding in the woods and hunting together. Indeed, he was the one who taught Patrick how to hunt. They would spend hours in each other's rooms talking about things that interested them, neither one coveting the throne, happy that their older, able brother would eventually assume it. He could not oppose Patrick, but he did not trust Reginald and worried about his beloved stepmother, Catherine. He felt a fierce loyalty to the O'Neals and loved Bunkillarny worrying about its fate. He also worried about his dear wife Sarah, hoping and praying that she was safe.

51:   TOMMY'S STORY

A couple of days following the battle, the apprentices, Seamus and Tommy along with John's son Ryan appeared at the print shop. Other than being scuffed up, dirty and exhausted from their ordeal, Seamus and Ryan were fine, but Tommy had bandages over his right arm. Hiding his arm behind his back, Gwendolyn had thought that he had a minor injury, but as she came closer to comfort him, she realized that he had lost half of his arm. She went to console him and began crying, which elicited a torrent of repressed tears from Tommy too.

Finally reaching home, seeing their family and friends, relieved after their ordeal, Seamus and Ryan were greeted warmly by Michael and John, who were aghast at Tommy's loss. Michael, feeling deeply sorry for the youth he knew so well, inquired as to what had happened.

He told them the story of what transpired saying, "That night I keeps a flippin and a floppin in my head, not able to sleeps: back and forth whether I should go ar not. Finally, I gets up in the middle of the night, hid along the road and waited for Seamus. When he comes, we makes our way up to the field behind the castle, where they had the games at. There all the men from the town were told ta gather under Sir Hugh who had us march all the morning long. Ryan gives me one of the swords he brought from the shop and we be practicing all afternoon. That were good cause I ner 'andled a sword before.

The next day we marched along the road farther than I had ere been before in me life, us boys from the town keeping together talkin' excitedly along the way, bout how we wud all be 'eros. The next day we did the same, until we be out o' the shire, and then we did notin' but sit around for another day until we was bored as stumps, a wantin' to get on with it."

Tommy shifts into another gear, varying his cadence, pitch and tone, becoming faster, higher, more animated and focused on his story, "The next day we was up on a hill where it all started. I could no see a thing, cause there was two lines o' men in front o' me. I could hear all the noise below though—men a roaring, men a yellin', and a screamin' for thar lives, horses a whinnyin,'. sounds of guns exploding and swords a clashing, smoke rising above. It were a fearful thing, it were. Even though we was up on the hill, when the wind blew our way, I could smells the burnt powder, the sweat, the blood and the death, I could. I wish we would ha charged right away 'cause as the time went by, I be getting' more scart and ta wishin' it was ore, and I was back in the shop a pullin' the Devil's tail.

Then I hears Sir Reginald in the distance yell out fer us ta be ready. Then Hugh yells at us to charge and we was off a running down the hill yelling like banshees, me not able to see anything other than the ars of the man front o' me.

Then we are into 'em, swingin' away at 'em, them a swingin' at us. It be hard ta make out whose who cause they looks just like us other than Hugh gives us red tears o' cloth ta wear round ar necks. We was holdin' ar own and be beatin' 'em back. I had no ones to fight, so feeling bad, I looks for someone ta clash swords wi'.

Then ta ar right I hears the sound of thunderin' hoofs. Thon knights lit inta us something fierce. I see this knight on this massive brown warhorse a slashing at us. He swings once at Oisin Mc Nab and cuts his head clean off. I cud see the horrified look on his face as his head spun in the air, his bloody body slumpin inta the mud without his head.

Then he comes fer me. I squares off ta face him then swing at his knee but me sword just bounces off his steel. I can't do nothin to him nor his horse, cause its got armor too. He swings at me with the broad sword and I ducks. Then the horse raises up and snorts like a mighty dragon. It was a fearsome devil of a beast it were. He swings at me agin, and I blocks it with me sword. But the force o' it makes me stumble in the slippery, bloody mud. It all goin' so slow, he rides towards me, cocks his arm back and swings, and as I's a rasin' ta block it, he slashes me arm and cuts it clean off. I falls ta the ground and I's lookin' at me bloody stump, blood a gushin' out o it, I fainted.

Next thing I knows Ryan has wrapped me arm wi a piece o his shirt and ties another piece round me arm to stop the bleadin', he did. Then, it's all ore. Did na last long—I guess, cause Ryan says I was not out fer long. He takes me ta ole Doc McDougall and he fixes me up. Even though they gives some whiskey it hurts real bad. Never felt so much pain in me entire life afore."

Gwendolyn seeing how traumatic this was for Tommy, goes over and hugs him to her breast, which causes him to break down and cry.

John whispers to Michael, "This will be a traumatic event fir the lad for the rest of his life. Causing him nightmares like it did for us after we fought that war down south with King Edward."

"Yes, I too still have the nightmares," Michael replies.

Ryan adds, "It wasn't till we were heading back pushin' Tommy in a handcart that we's heard from Freddy that we fought the O'Neal's and not the O'Donnell's. Can you believe that?"

That night Daisy cooked up a large meal for all in the shop and John's family to celebrate the returning heroes. They all toasted Seamus, Ryan and Tommy with their steins of beer and sang some sea shanties. The merriment and being home with his adopted family helped Tommy feel better.

Later, John fashioned a device that would attach to the remains of his forearm, which would allow him to work on the press. Not something many employers would do, Michael kept him on, telling him," You will always have a place here, Tommy."

52:   EPILOGUE

Despite their differences and constant battles, King Rory had great respect for King Albert and the O'Neals, as did Albert of Rory. He did not imprison Albert and the terms consisted of them forfeiting their arms and paying a large, but not unbearable tribute, and seeding the long-disputed border lands to the O'Donnell's. The balance of power had shifted to the O'Donnell's, but the O'Neals would still be able to manage their own affairs.

For his role in the betrayal, Reginald was given a third of the tribute and captured arms, which instantly made him the richest man in Bunkillarny, and vastly increased his armaments and power. He rewarded his trusted knights, such as Hugh, with a portion of the spoils—the only ones who knew of the betrayal beforehand. Although some of them wondered what was going on, the soldiers and lower level officers in the confusion of battle, thought they were attacking the O'Donnell's and were surprised when they heard the outcome.

Life in Bunkillarny settled back to normal. But it was a new normal. The brief war had ended and people went about their daily lives as they had before. The seasons and days of the year gradually passed by as they had before. Farmers tended their fields, shepherds tended their flocks, and the merchants tended to their stores. The fishermen went out every day searching for their catch. The brewer brewed his beer, the tanner tanned his hides, and the baker baked his bread. Everyone went to church on Sundays and looked forward to Christmas and the annual holidays. But, there was a subtle uneasiness that permeated the land, for despite ignoring the signs, their lives were about to change in unknown and unfamiliar ways.

Reginald and Boston hatched a plan to explain away the betrayal and seize control of Bunkillarny. In Glasgow, John planned his next steps of petitioning King Henry and returning to Bunkillarny. Even though he had not wanted the throne, given Reginald's treachery, and how much he loved his homeland, and his father's legacy, John had to save the kingdom.

Meanwhile, Rand had traveled over the sea to London to find a new agent. He remained unaware of the chaos that had transpired in Bunkillarny, Gwendolyn seeking his return, desperately hoping he might somehow save the shire.

THE END